International acclaim for

BODY COUNT

Also by

P.D. MARTIN

THE MURDERERS' CLUB

P.D. MARTIN

BODY COUNT

MIRA

MIRA®

ISBN-13: 978-0-7783-2521-5
ISBN-10: 0-7783-2521-0

BODY COUNT

Copyright © 2005 by Phillipa Deanne Martin.

www.MIRABooks.com

Printed in U.S.A.

ACKNOWLEDGMENTS

Lots of people to thank... First, I'd like to thank my agent Elaine Koster and everyone at MIRA Books, especially Margaret Marbury and Selina McLemore. I'd also like to thank Pan Macmillan Australia for giving me my first "break."

Thanks to my test readers (friends!) who reviewed *Body Count* at various stages—Marlo Garnsworthy, Adele Whish-Wilson, Nicole Hayes (a big thank-you to Nicole for her editing skills and support), Martina McKeon, Verity Stewart, Kirsty Badcock and Rhian Richards. Thanks also to Alison Goodman, who provided an in-depth manuscript assessment of a very early draft.

Body Count also needed extensive research before and during the writing process. I'd like to thank the many people in law enforcement who write such detailed nonfiction books, providing great case studies and theoretical knowledge for us fiction writers. I'd also like to thank the FBI; ex-FBI agent and profiler Candice DeLong for answering my questions on profiling; Associate Professor David Ranson of the Victorian Institute of Forensic Medicine for his autopsy knowledge; Sifu Gilbert Broadway for the Tiger and Crane Kung Fu training; and Jay Johnson for some last-minute DC facts.

Thanks also go to Guy Franklin and Gillian Ramsay of Momentum Technologies Group for designing www.pdmartin.com.au.

Lastly, I'd like to thank all the people who have believed in me throughout the very long aspiring-author stage. Particular thanks go to my family and to Marlo Garnsworthy—for their never-ending faith in me.

BODY COUNT

BODY
COUNT

Twenty-five years ago

The house is quiet. It's 3:00 a.m.

The sleeping figure of a young girl takes up a small section of a single bed. She's on her side, curled in a ball, with Paddington Bear standing watch from the corner of her bed. A desk lamp lights the room, and light also emanates from the hallway to guide her way to the bathroom during her usual nightly excursion.

She tosses, ending up on her back. A small whimper escapes her lips. She's having one of her nightmares.

"No. Please no."

She moans. Her breathing quickens. She whimpers again. Her heart is racing. She thrashes her legs and the covers become untucked from the sides of the bed.

The boy in her dream is running, but someone's behind him. The man is gaining on the boy. "Watch out," she says, barely audible. She must save the boy.

Her breathing becomes labored. She gasps for air.

She sits bolt upright and screams. But not even the sound of her own screams can wake her. The nightmare is too intense, too real.

Down the corridor, her mother wakes up. Immediately she realizes her daughter is screaming. Another nightmare. She grabs her robe and drapes it across herself as she runs down the hall.

She throws her arms around her still-screaming child and rocks her back and forth. The screaming stops and the girl wakes up.

"Mom? John. Where's John?"

"It's all right, sweetie. It's just a dream."

"Where's John?" she shouts.

"Okay, okay, honey." The woman picks up her daughter and walks into the corridor, then into John's room. They stand at his doorway.

"What's up?" John says, more asleep than awake.

"See, sweetie, he's in bed. He's fine."

"Oh, another nightmare," John says, turning on his side and burrowing into his bed.

The woman puts her daughter back into bed. She glances at the bedside table, noticing an Agatha Christie book. "Sweetie, I've told you about reading those books. You're too young. No wonder you've had so many nightmares this week."

Two nights later

The little girl takes one almighty gasp of air and wakes up. She breathes in and out, in and out, trying to get air back into her lungs.

"John's in trouble," she says out aloud even though no one's there.

She looks into the hallway. It's dark. Why is it dark? Her mom always leaves the light on for her. She gets out of bed and stands there, trembling. She's cold and frightened. She grabs Paddington Bear and steps into the dark hallway, holding him tucked under her arm. She inches her way down the hallway, back against the wall. Another few steps and she'll be at the light switch. There. She switches it on and takes a deep breath in. It's better now. It's not dark. She walks past John's room, frightened to go in. But she must. She holds Paddington tighter and switches on the light in her brother's room. The window's open and John is gone.

Then images hit her hard and fast. She looks down at John—she's suddenly taller than he is. Her hand reaches out, but it's a big hand. A man's hand. She's someone else. John's crying and she feels the pleasure the man feels at John's pain. Her big hands encircle John's neck and push, harder and harder. John splutters, gasping for air. She feels the killer's feelings. She feels happiness and a surge of adrenaline as John goes limp.

She collapses on the floor.

Present Day

My breath is shallow and fast and the sound of my beating heart resonates in my ears. This is the first field assignment I've had for a while and I'm a little rusty. I steady my breath. We'll be moving soon.

I study the area, waiting for my cue. I've parked on the right-hand side and have a good view of the street and the apartment building that's our target. The street is quiet. Eerily quiet, as if everyone's hiding in their homes, somehow aware of what's about to go down and waiting for the storm to pass. Then again, it is 2:00 p.m. on a Wednesday. The only sign of movement is a mother pushing her stroller about thirty feet in front of me on the footpath, and a few people waiting at a bus stop sixty feet down the road. I take in my surroundings, counting the people, entering information about them into my memory—I may need it later. For the moment, nothing looks suspicious and Boxley, our target, entered the building about half an hour ago. I take another deep breath. Soon. It will be soon.

I love this feeling; love knowing that finally the hunter has become the hunted. I bet he feels like this when he's stalking a victim, knowing that any minute she'll be his. But he's in the wrong, and we're in the right.

He's probably already selected his next victim. I imagine him closing in on her, just as though she was my sister, best friend or even me. My teeth clench and my hand goes instinctively to the gun in my ankle holster. My fingers tighten around the bulge…it's guys like the creep inside who drew me to law enforcement.

"This is Mad Dog, are you in position…one?" Detective Flynn's voice crackles softly through my earpiece. It's a joint task force—D.C. police and FBI—with Flynn from D.C. Homicide taking the lead.

"Check," says the leader of the first unit.

"Two?" Flynn says.

"Check."

I listen to the units sound off, ending with the one headed by Agent Josh Marco. We've worked together closely on this case and have become friends. Maybe more than friends.

"Okay, Goldilocks, we're ready to roll," Flynn says.

Flynn is with two other officers to the left of the apartment, covering the fire escape. He looks up and nods at me. From this distance I just make out a smile.

I get out of the car we organized for the operation, a

red Ford, and grab the briefcase of samples and my black coat from the passenger seat. I ease one arm into the coat, eager for its warmth, and then slip in the other arm. For the job I've chosen black pants that flare slightly at the ankles but hug my hips, and a tight-fitting red V-neck to show off as much cleavage as I can bring to the party (with some major help from a push-up bra). I am a little vulnerable without my bulletproof vest, but guns don't seem to be this perp's style. Besides, we can't risk arousing his suspicion with added bulk on my upper body. Over the outfit I wear a black scarf and a black coat. The look is completed with black leather gloves.

Here I go. I've been living and breathing this case for the past five months and it feels good to almost have the bastard in our grasp.

The perp lives in a fifteen-story building that's in pretty good condition despite its obvious sixties look. The pathway is concrete, lined with a waist-high box hedge. The sides of the long path are framed by lawn, and a few flowering shrubs add color to the grayness.

I go over the routine one more time…my name is Lauren. Lauren Armstrong. I work for Clean-a-way Living and I'm here to sell our perp…I mean, my client…our effective and environmentally friendly range of cleaning products.

Flashes of the victims lying in pools of their own blood intrude on my thoughts. I push the images away. Focus.

I scan the apartment buzzers on the inside wall. *Robert Boxley* is written next to apartment 104. I ring the buzzer. A couple of minutes drag by like ten, and finally I hear the hiss of the intercom system.

"Who is it?" a husky male voice asks.

"Hi, it's Lauren from Clean-a-way." I use a richer, throatier version of my natural voice and play on my Australian accent, broadening it slightly.

"Lauren. Yes. Come up."

The buzzer sounds and I walk in through the security door. My stomach does a flip and my "spider sense" tingles. I've got a bad feeling about this. I push it aside and flick the ring on my little finger with my thumbnail. It's just nerves because this is my first field assignment for a while.

"I'm in." Confirmation for Flynn and the rest of the task force.

The small inside foyer is decorated with brown speckled tiles and the walls are painted a dull green. A faded safety certificate hangs on the left wall next to a rusty fire extinguisher—probably both from the sixties. Opposite the entrance is a small elevator. I look above it and notice that number eleven is dimly lit. The elevator isn't moving. Our suspect's only one floor up, so I head for the stairs on the right. I grasp the wrought-iron banister, which rattles in my hand. With each step my heart seems to pound even faster, sending vibrations through my body with every beat. It's so loud the guys can probably hear it through my mouthpiece. That's not good. I want to make a strong impression on my first bust.

I knock on apartment 104's door. I hear two locks rattling in the door frame, and then I'm greeted by Robert Boxley. He looks a little different than the picture we got from his employer, but I recognize him nonetheless. Five-ten and stocky, with a paunch. He's clean-shaven and his skin is smooth and translucent, though a few beads of sweat hang above his top lip. Nervousness? His black hair is cut tightly. He wears blue jeans, a loose white T-shirt and sneakers. If I didn't know what a monster he was, I'd think he was good-looking.

"Hi, Robert." I immerse myself in my character, shoving my revulsion way down into the pit of my stomach.

"Hi, Lauren," he says, eyeballing me with intense dark green eyes. "Come in." He steps away from the door and motions me inside.

I walk past him, momentarily turning my back on him. I'm not keen on the physical advantage he has over me for these few seconds, but it can't be helped. Besides, I'm safe. Not only because of the size and skill of my backup, but also because it's unlikely he'll nab me. I'm his type, but he likes to stalk his victims for a couple of weeks. He might mentally enter me into his victim pool for another time, but he's already picked his next girl and he's too orderly to let me jump the queue.

I take in every detail, hyperaware of my surroundings. Even an odor could mean something. But I smell nothing, other than the remnants of last night's curry.

"Your coat?"

I put my case down on the carpet and slowly take off my coat. He watches me carefully, running his eyes across my body. The look penetrates me, but I smile and hand him my coat and scarf. It sickens me to be civil to this man, but it's all part of the job. Soon the tables will be turned.

He hangs my coat and scarf on a peg near the front door.

I look around. His apartment is immaculate.

"Nice place you got here."

He's gone for the minimalist approach that a lot of guys like. Truthfully, I don't know if it's the look they like or the lack of dusting duties. From the door I can clearly see the main living areas. Directly in front is the living room, which contains a large-screen TV, a DVD player, a coffee table with the latest edition of *Premiere* strategically placed, and two two-seater couches. The living room also has an oversize window. A bar separates the living room from a spotless kitchen. I notice a few magnets and one photo on the fridge. It's a woman, but I can't see her face.

Boxley doesn't take his eyes off me. "It's not much, but I call it home."

"It's great. You should see my place. It's a dump." I hand him the position of power that he enjoys.

"I'm sure it's not that bad." He motions me farther inside. I pick up my briefcase and follow him into the living room.

"Have you been in the States long?" he asks.

Polite chitchat.

"Only seven months." I see no reason to lie. I arrived here seven months ago, gave myself a month to settle in and then started working at the FBI.

"Like it?"

"Oh yeah. I love it here." Also true.

As we exchange small talk I look for signs of his other, more sinister occupation. I focus on the fridge once more, and the photo.

"She's pretty. Your girlfriend?" I move in for a closer look. Bingo. It's a picture of one of the victims.

He moves in behind me and I can feel his eyes on the

back of my neck. He's only a couple of steps away, and he's invading my personal space.

He hesitates. "Ex, actually. We came to a—" he pauses, seemingly trying to find the right word "—messy end."

I've seen the photos, it was messy all right. What a sick bastard.

"These things can get messy, can't they," I say, talking about both relationships and murders. "I can tell you're still a bit sweet on her."

He pulls up next to me and leans on the fridge. "No, not really. I must take that photo down."

"What's her name?"

"Kathy."

"Kathy. She's very pretty," I repeat, happy that he used the victim's real name. Flynn and Marco will know who I'm looking at. Kathy's picture is evidence. The bust is looking good.

"Clear your throat if it's our Kathy, Goldilocks," Flynn says through my earpiece.

I clear my throat, then turn it into a slight cough.

"Do you want a glass of water?" Boxley asks.

"No. Thanks, I'm fine." I move back into the living room. "Before I start, do you have a roommate or someone who'd like to see the products too?"

"No, there's just me."

Good. No roomie. We'll be going ahead.

"Well, Mr. Boxley, I can see you take pride in the cleanliness of your home and you're going to love our products," I say, getting into my well-rehearsed sales spiel. I put my case on the coffee table in front of the windows, right where I want to be positioned—near the sharp-shooters in case they need to take a shot at our Mr. Boxley.

I have the suspect's full attention.

I open the black vinyl case. Inside are several compartments that contain cleaning products and a few cloths. The lid of the case has elastic stretched across it horizontally, holding in place two small pieces of laminate. From the main section of the case I select the all-surface cream.

I hold the bottle up with the label facing Boxley. I glide one hand in front of the bottle, hovering over the label like the girls do in the game shows. I've always wanted to do that.

I start. "This gentle cleansing cream is our top seller because you can use it on just about everything. Stove tops, washrooms, toilets, kitchen counters and so on."

I take a piece of predirtied laminated board from my bag. "This has got a couple of red-wine stains on it here, and this is a curry stain." I point to a reddish-brown mark. "Always a tough stain."

I'm rushing it. I need to slow it down.

I take out a cloth. "Now, you don't need much of this little baby." I purr the words, in character again. I squeeze the bottle so the white foamy substance oozes onto the cloth. I lean forward and reveal just enough cleavage to get his mind, or more likely his body, going.

Boxley responds, shifting ever so slightly to get a better view. Creep.

"Then it's just a gentle wipe." I speak slowly, softly and let the "p" sound pop on my lips.

"Goldilocks, you're getting me going." It's Marco's voice. I don't react. I'll get him for that later.

"Very impressive." Boxley is clearly talking more about me than the cleaning products.

I smile, let my eyes linger on his, then cast my gaze quickly down his body, averting my eyes at his groin as though suddenly aware of, and embarrassed by, my own actions. I follow it with a small yet forceful push of air through my nose that verges on a giggle. While he's absorbing this development, I cast my eyes around the room once more, looking for any sign of a weapon.

"See." I show him the clean piece of laminated board. "Spotless."

He smiles.

It's time.

I take the appropriate bottle out of my sales bag.

"Our next product is the window cleaner."

I turn around and walk toward the window, exaggerating the swing of my hips. I spray the window and before I start the wiping action I look around at Boxley with my head down slightly, eyes up, and I smile.

"You're going to love this one." My voice has a more serious, tougher tone and I'm out of character for a split second, knowing that soon he'll be mine. I wipe the product away, giving our guys the signal. The bust is a go.

"Mad Dog, this is seven, we have the signal. Repeat, we are a go," a voice says in my earpiece.

"Move in, people," Flynn says.

I turn around and notice a strange look on Boxley's face. He's looking at my feet. No, my ankle. Oh God, my ankle holster. Have my pants edged their way upward as my arm completed the wiping motion, high above my head? How could I be so stupid? My cockiness might cost me dearly.

"Anything wrong?" I keep my voice casual, steady.

Boxley looks at me, silent. I know that look. He's about to take action.

He lunges, arms outstretched. I dart to the side, just in time to escape his lethal hands, then immediately take a step forward with my left leg and send a swift, hard right kick his way. I aim for his back, targeting his kidneys, and the top of my foot meets its mark. He stumbles forward from the force of my kick and winds up on his knees in front of the window. He turns around to make another run at me. I grab my gun from the ankle holster and draw it, taking the safety off.

"FBI!" It's the first time I've announced myself as FBI and I like it. The adrenaline is well and truly pumping now.

Boxley pauses.

"I *will* fire, Robert, so don't even think about it." I look at him and all I can think about are his victims. I lower my gun from his heart to his crotch. It has the desired effect.

"There are twenty police officers and agents on their way up here right now and we've got sharpshooters on the surrounding buildings." He's standing right in their line of fire. "Try anything and you're dead."

"You bitch."

"Flynn, I have the suspect."

"Okay, Goldilocks, we're a minute away."

I walk backward and unlock the front door, keeping my eyes and gun trained on Boxley. "Roger that, Flynn, door is open."

"You bitches are all the same," Boxley says.

CHAPTER 02

I sip my peppermint tea, trying to elicit a soothing feeling from it. Instead, I wish I'd gone for coffee number five. I put the mug back down on my desk, lining it up with a day-old coffee ring. I could do with a dash of Clean-a-way myself.

My office is quite small, like most of the offices in the unit, about ten feet by ten feet. But hey, it beats open plan. The decor is stark—white walls, gray furniture and fairly new blue-gray carpet. I've just finished an office tidy-up and my large wall-mounted whiteboard is sparkling clean. My four-drawer filing cabinet has only three files on top of it and my desk has more than a few patches of laminate visible underneath the papers. I've even placed the two visitor chairs neatly in front of my desk. To finish off, I water my corner plant, the office's only homely feel, and contemplate wiping my desk.

Even from my office I can see that the building is

quiet and partially dark. I look at my watch. It's seven o'clock and I should join the others. When they left half an hour ago my boss, Andy Rivers, was pretty insistent.

"What are you doing, Anderson? File it tomorrow. It's time to celebrate. God knows, you deserve it."

"I'll come over soon," I promised. But instead of going to the bar, I started filing the case notes.

I place the last of my handwritten notes, case files and photos into the file and box it up, ready to go to the D.A. for prosecution. I'll definitely be called to the stand for Boxley. Eventually my boxed notes will end up in the archives room, where all the solved ones go. Never to be seen again, just like Boxley; he'll never see the outside of a prison again.

I like filing the notes as soon as the case is closed. It's symbolic. I try to erase the case from my memory, at least until the trial.

I bend over my desk with my back to the door.

"So—"

I jolt with fear until I process the familiar voice. Agent Josh Marco.

"—you did it, hey, Anderson?"

"Marco, how *do* you do that?" He can enter a room without making the slightest sound.

"It's my job. What's your excuse?"

"Finishing up the paperwork and closing the file."

"Well, though I can see that's more important than joining us for a drink, I actually meant how do you get so damn close with your profiles."

"Oh, that." I act coy. "It's my job. Besides, you get close too."

"True, but you…" He pauses. "Let's say I'm impressed with your skills. In fact, you may just be the best profiler I've ever worked with."

I blush. I love my job and I like the thought of being the best, but I'm not there yet. "Nah." I fidget with the files on my desk. I'm the rookie in this department and the compliment makes me feel uncomfortable. "We all get the profiles right," I say.

"That's what they pay us for." He smiles. "I'm going over now, you coming?"

"Soon."

"Come on."

I look at my relatively tidy desk. I guess I can send the files to the D.A. tomorrow.

"All right, already," I say, putting on my best American accent.

"You still ain't got it."

"Getting there?"

"Yeah, another year and you might be able to pull it off."

"Well I'd like to see you try. Americans are shit at the Australian accent."

"I reckon I come pretty close," he says in a perfect Australian accent.

"I'm impressed. You've been hiding this talent from me for six months?"

"I had to go undercover as an Australian once, but if I tell you any more, I'll have to kill you." He leans on the doorway and gives me a wink.

"That line might work on the girls in the bars, but it won't fly with me." I give him a smirk and an exaggerated flutter of the eyelashes.

"Guess not, Goldilocks."

"Am I getting you going again?"

"Always, Goldilocks, always." He smiles.

Over the past six months I've discovered bits and pieces of the Josh Marco jigsaw, but it still doesn't amount to much. I know he started off as a cop, was in the air force and did some time as an FBI field agent before coming to the unit. I also know he's a good agent.

"Come on. Let me drag you away before Rivers gets pissed," Marco says.

Rivers...I've got even fewer pieces of *that* jigsaw.

"You said he's single, right?" I ask.

"Yeah. Heard he was married once, though."

"Divorced?"

"Guess so. It's the way things go in this unit." He folds his arms across his chest. "No one knows squat about Rivers anyway. You know what he's like."

"Yeah, I guess." But the psychologist in me wants to know more.

Marco straightens up and motions his head toward the door. "Let's go."

I turn off my computer and put the boxed files under my desk. Case closed. And hopefully my mind too, closed against the nightmares.

"I've just got to lock up," Marco says.

I follow him through the rabbit warren of corridors toward his office. The FBI offices at Quantico take up a small part of the large complex that is the FBI Academy, the national training center for the Bureau. The FBI has three hundred and eighty-five acres at its disposal, and the whole training complex includes three dormitories, a dining room, a library, an auditorium, a chapel, a gym, a large running track, a defensive-driving track, several firing ranges and the famous Hogan's Alley—a simulated town that agents train in. There are also some centralized departments operating from Quantico rather than the D.C. head office. Our unit, the Behavioral Analysis Unit, is one of those departments, as is the Forensic Science Research and Training Center.

The BAU takes up the basement of the building and consists of narrow corridors and small offices with not a window in sight. It took me a long time to get used to this place.

Eventually we take about our tenth left and come to Marco's office. His room is still set up for the Henley case, the one we've just busted, and the decor spoils my sense of closure. The whiteboards are covered with writing, including my messy script, and photos line the room. Lots of dead girls photographed from every angle, a photo of a knife, and photos of the locations where the bodies were found. Christine Henley was the first girl murdered. That was two years ago. But things really hotted up five months ago, a month after I'd become the newest addition to the unit. The killer murdered the mayor's daughter, and the heat was on. Strings were pulled, and our involvement changed from the FBI's usual consulting role to Marco and I working the case full-time and in the field. Sometimes it takes a kick in the teeth up high to get the resources together. Particularly these days when the FBI's number-one priority is terrorism. Serial killers are small stuff after September 11.

We got Boxley three murders after the mayor's daughter. It's the last victim in a case that always gets to me. I think about her a lot. Could we have got him before her? *Should* we have got him before her?

I scan the room, reliving the murders, the chase. Marco watches me.

"I'm not as organized as you," he says.

I smile and consider telling him that my filing isn't really about a neat, orderly personality. But he can figure it out for himself. Or maybe he already has. He comes toward his door and I take a step back into the hall. He flicks the light switch, closes his door and locks it. I notice the closeness of our bodies, and the slight butterflies that I often get around Marco rise in my stomach.

He turns around. "I'll file it tomorrow. Let's go."

We walk out of the building and I'm immediately hit by the late-fall wind. I draw my arms in closer to my body and put my head down.

"You sure you're ready for your first American winter?" Marco says.

I rub my gloved hands together. "It's bloody cold all right."

"It's not even winter yet, you know."

"I think this is colder than Melbourne ever gets."

"Australia doesn't really have a winter, does it?"

"We do." I'm amazed at Marco's ignorance.

"What temperature does it get down to?"

"In Fahrenheit…" I pause, doing the mental calculation. "It'd be about thirty-five as the low and fifty-five as the high."

"Like I said, no winter."

I push my body into his and he feigns being knocked off balance.

"Come on." I pick up the pace, keen to get into my car and put the heater on.

Marco walks me to my car first. I get in and start the engine.

"See you there?"

"Of course," he says.

I close the door and give him a wave. Once I'm out of the parking lot, it takes me nearly two full minutes of driving to get to the perimeter. I pass the security gates and drive to downtown Quantico, if you could call it that. Quantico itself is a small town that was built mainly to service the massive marine corps base. The township's main strip consists of a grocery store, a bakery, a real-estate business, an Internet café, two café restaurants, a few bars and four barbers—Quantico is crew cuts galore.

From the bars on offer, the Bureau has picked Club Victor as its local. Most nights it's wall-to-wall agents and marine officers, with a smattering of husbands, wives, girlfriends and boyfriends thrown in for good measure. There are usually quite a few from forensics too—the fingerprint guys and lab techs. The only difference between Club Victor and the usual special-forces haunt is that police officers are replaced by the corps.

The FBI agents often nurse soft drinks, or "soda" as they call it here, looking on the marines with some envy. I'm still getting used to the Bureau's mandate about alcohol. We have to be "fit for duty" at all times, which means only a couple of drinks. I'm sure that rule's broken by many of us in the privacy of our own homes, but in public the armed forces slam them back like there's no tomorrow, while we get labeled sissies.

Tonight, Club Victor will be full of agents who want to help us celebrate the case's end, plus the usual crowd from the marine base. Then of course there'll be our boss, Rivers, and maybe even the unit head, Jonathan Pike. Flynn and some of the other police officers who live on this side of D.C. may make the trip too.

I pull in around the corner from the bar and break into a light jog to the main street. The flashing neon light gets closer and I walk down the few steps to the bar's sunken entrance. A horn honks and I look up. Marco's pulling in to a parking spot right out front. I give him a wave and then walk into the bar. The contrast in temperature is dramatic and within a couple of seconds a hot flush runs through me and settles in my face. I peel off my coat, and take off my gloves and scarf. The heat generated by forty-plus bodies crammed into the small bar, coupled with the building's heating system, is stifling.

The room is long and thin, with ten booths along the left-hand wall and the counter and bar stools on the right. It's dimly lit and fitted out with lots of wood. Tonight the place is crowded. I search the faces for a familiar one in the mostly male clientele. I see our group toward the back.

The door opens and Marco enters.

"Drink?" he says, sidling up next to me.

"Yeah, I'll have a—"

"Becks."

I smile. "That's the one."

I stand near the bar and have a closer look at who's here. There's a group from the lab, including Marty, Marco's roommate. He's one of the Bureau's top forensics guys, a team leader who specializes in fingerprints and blood spatter. He smiles at me and beckons me over uncertainly. He's pretty shy. I smile back but then spot Sam Wright, the person I really want to see, standing on the other side of the little huddle that Marty is part of.

As usual, Sam's surrounded by males who are captivated by her every movement, her every word. I don't know exactly what it is, but that girl's got something. Her wavy brown hair hangs halfway down her back and is cut in long layers, and every now and again she runs her fingers through one side. Her face is sculpted by high cheekbones and a strong jaw. Intense green eyes capture most people's attention; however, by far her most distinguishing trait is her wide natural smile, in the style of Julia Roberts.

I fight my way through a group of ogling marines. Rivers makes a beeline for me. He pulls me in next to him just as I reach the edge of the group.

"Here she is," he says, raising his full glass of beer skyward and nodding at me in a slightly paternal manner. "The Aussie wonder."

I was the one who saw Boxley's pattern. It broke the case for us.

Everyone raises their glasses. The blood rushes to my face. Sam gives me an amused wink and I grimace in response. I hate being in the spotlight. Most profiling work is behind the scenes, although the press try to make it more public. They love talking to the profiler on a case. But I avoid the reporters. And when the case breaks, I push the attention onto the local cops, the ones usually breaking down the doors and making the arrests.

Marco arrives with my beer and clunks my bottle heavily. "Cheers," he says.

"Ah, and here's the Rock. Cheers, Marco," Rivers says. I'm still not sure why Marco is called the Rock.

"Cheers," I say, toasting and taking a swig directly from the bottle. It tastes better that way.

With the official toast over, the other agents go back to their conversations. I like seeing Rivers like this, even though it's only for an hour or so. Every time a perp's caught from one of the unit's profiles he transforms, letting himself live a little before his controlled, authoritarian persona returns.

Marco disappears into the sea of agents, leaving me with Rivers.

"So, how did you do it?"

"What?"

"You know what I mean. Your profiles are good. Exceptional in fact. That's why we got you."

"I'm no different from the others."

"Maybe not yet, but I've got a feeling about you. You're a natural." He pauses. "I knew that from the moment I saw you."

"You didn't even notice me," I laugh.

He smiles. "Okay, at first you were a face in a sea of many. But I noticed your questions."

Rivers is referring to his profiling sessions that I sat in on. The Victoria police sent me to the FBI Academy's International Training Program, a six-week course at Quantico. One of the main subjects was profiling, an area my bosses wanted me to refine. I don't think it had ever crossed their minds that I might end up leaving the force because of it. I still feel a little guilty about it too.

Rivers took me aside after the course and asked me a few questions. When he found out I had dual citizenship, he offered me a job on the spot.

"There's something different about you," Rivers says.

A slight chill rises slowly up my spine. The problem is, I vaguely know what he's talking about. I feel it myself sometimes. But I can't explain it.

"It's—" He is interrupted by Sam.

"Let me guess, you filed it?" she says, pulling in close enough to talk.

"Yep. Files are ready to go." I notice, with some amusement, that Sam has several disappointed men looking at her back, but I don't think she would ever mix business with pleasure.

"Were you giving her a pep talk, boss?" Sam says.

"Of sorts." Rivers smiles at me and only slight creases form around his mouth. His dark skin is smooth and looks like a thirty-year-old, yet I'd place him at around forty-five. Like many African-American men, he wears his age well and even the small patches of gray near his temples add distinction rather than age.

"So what dragged you away from your filing?" Sam asks me.

"Marco. He was insistent."

Sam discreetly gives me a conspiring look. She knows me well. In fact, so far she's the only person I'd say was a good friend, besides Marco. That's no mean feat when you move countries. Nothing can replace ten or more years of friendship. Of history. But with Sam we clicked straight-away. History has to start somewhere.

"Well, ladies, I'm off," Rivers says.

"Why don't you stay, sir," I say, even though I've never seen him stay. He has a beer or two and that's it.

"No…" He drags out the "o." "Besides, I have to let any would-be thieves know that the house isn't abandoned."

He does work hard. Long hours.

"Have a good night but don't forget our eight o'clock meeting," he says.

Sam and I look at each other and respond in unison. "We won't."

Rivers comes in close but doesn't lower his voice. "She'll be a bad influence on you, that one." He points his finger at Sam.

"Me?" Sam winks at me.

Rivers raises his hand in a saluting goodbye. "Good night all," he yells over his shoulder and then disappears out the door.

Sam's admirers soon join us and I watch Sam enthrall her captive audience. One night, about a month ago, she insisted we go clubbing. But instead of going out in our normal clothes, she managed to convince me to dress up in cheerleading garb. We pretended we were up from Texas for cheerleading tryouts—Sam's from there anyway—and I even attempted a Texan accent. The guys were all over us, thinking they'd stumbled onto easy marks. I went along with it for about two hours before one of the guys spotted my gun in my handbag. Suddenly we didn't look like "easy lays" and they were gone, moving on to a couple of women at the bar.

The gun scares off lots of men. It probably doesn't help that I carry it with me everywhere. Perhaps I'm paranoid, but you never know when you'll need it. In

Australia I used to carry my gun and badge all the time too. The problem is, I know what, or should I say who, is out there. I see their handiwork every day. At least here I've got an excuse—it's Bureau policy that we're armed at all times.

Sam's telling the guys a story but I'm only half listening. Tonight I don't feel like joining in on the fun. I think about the case and the victims. I find it hard to party with Christine Henley and the others staring at me with wide, frightened eyes. I see so much in a victim's eyes.

Marco brings me back. "Thinking about home?"

"No. Not home..." I pause. "Do you think we should have—"

"We got him, Sophie. That's all that matters now. That's all you can think about."

"Yeah. Yeah, you're right."

Everyone else seems so good at separating the horror from their everyday lives. Everyone except me. Or maybe they're just better at putting on the front. The BAU has one of the highest burnout rates in the FBI. It's easy to get too close, too absorbed in a killer's mind.

A few hours later Marco and I walk out of the smoke-filled bar. I take in a deep breath of fresh air, already regretting the late night.

Marco walks me to my car, not saying much, but it's a comfortable silence. I'm glad of his company. I say good-night to him and bundle into my car. I jump on the I75 to Alexandria, where my apartment is. It's between the unit's base in Quantico and D.C.

I walk into my apartment and dump my bag and keys on the hall table.

"Hi, honey, I'm home."

Silence.

I took this job knowing I was leaving my boyfriend of seven years, Matt, and my friends and family. I couldn't pass up the chance to work at the FBI. The real deal. It had been my dream since…well, as long as I can remember. I guess that's what happens when you grow up on *Charlie's Angels,* James Bond and *The X-Files.* But it's hard coming home to an empty house, knowing the people you love are on the other side of the world. I look at the two clocks on the wall, which I've labeled *Washington* and *Melbourne.* It's just past midnight here, which makes it around 2:00 p.m. in Melbourne. I consider ringing home but then decide I'm too tired to have an intelligent conversation.

Before I go to bed I perform my nightly ritual. You're never really safe, especially not in your own home. Perps wait until your guard's down, and what better place than when you're at home, or fast asleep.

Gun in hand, I check out my apartment, starting with my tiny kitchen, even though it's hard enough to prepare a meal in it, let alone find a hiding spot. But to satisfy my inner demons I check it anyway. I move to the living area. It's a large, open space and I've managed to fit a small dining table with four chairs in one corner and a two-seater couch, coffee table, bookshelf and stereo system across the room. A few potted plants liven up the place and four black-and-white photos give the room a personal touch. All the photos are of Melbourne: a tram, Luna Park, Flinders Street Station, a sculpture on Swanston Street. The space is roomy, despite the furniture. I check this area quickly and then move on to the linen closet in the hallway, one of the few good hiding spots in the apartment.

With the linen closet clear, I move down the hallway toward the bathroom and my bedroom. Bathroom first. Large white tiles cover the floor and halfway up the walls. The sink is a large frosted-glass dish. This one feature transforms an otherwise standard bathroom into something a little different. I check behind the shower curtain and then head to my bedroom, which is at the end of the hall. I've given the room a Japanese flavor, with a dark wood slatted bed, matching bedside tables and a dressing table. A small Buddha sits in the corner, and next to that I've placed a Japanese screen. I check underneath the bed and inside the built-in wardrobe.

Satisfied that I'm alone, I return to the living room, check the locks on the doors and windows, then put on a Sarah Vaughan CD. The last part of my ritual is to close the curtains.

I hit the mattress and my body sinks in appreciation. I'd like to go straight to sleep, but experience has taught me to read first; it seems to help the nightmares. Something light and escapist like fantasy is the best. I become absorbed in the fantasy world, rather than my world of violence and bodies. I used to get the nightmares back in Australia if a case was really getting to me, but since I've been profiling here the nightmares have been worse. I don't know why.

Tonight I read Julia Gray's *The Dark Moon* and give myself over to the world of the floating islands.

I wake with a start at 4:00 a.m., my left calf muscle cramping hard. I reach down and grab my calf, wanting to stop the pain. But I just have to ride it out. As I stretch against the spasm, I have a vague recollection of a nightmare…

A naked girl, lying down. Her eyes are open, her head turned. She looks at me. But she's dead, her body still and cold. A symbol flashes big and bold, then I see the dead girl again. On her leg I see the symbol. It's a tattoo on her upper thigh.

Then a different girl, a redhead, walks to a car. We're in a parking lot and it's deserted. I watch her in my side mirror as she gets closer. But I'm not me. I'm watching her through someone else's eyes. I feel the desire to kill bubbling through this person.

Then I run. I'm running for my life.

I like to get to know my girls. It's important. That's the problem with the world these days. Everyone's in a hurry. But there's no need. Life takes...well, a lifetime, so why rush through a day and speed the process up? Especially when it may be the last day of your life.

People don't like to wait—for anything, including sex. But they should. People jump into intimacy way too fast. Not me. She has to be special, and it takes time to know if she's worthy. I like to breathe in her scent. Her flesh. I know what perfume she wears, what shampoo and brand of makeup she uses. I absorb it all.

Sometimes I even talk to her. But usually I watch her from afar first, until it's time. What sort of person is she? Hurried and annoyed, or courteous and kind? Does she smile? Is she worthy of my special love? Not many of them are in the end, but I try. And I'll keep trying until I find the one. Someone who truly appreciates me.

But regardless of who she is, when I see her I smile charmingly, smug in the knowledge that soon she'll be mine. Mine to touch, mine to hold. Mine to love.

CHAPTER 03

At 6:00 a.m. my alarm goes off. I fight the tiredness and swing my legs over the side of the bed, forcing myself into an upright position. I remember waking up at 4:00 a.m., and I remember some sort of nightmare. But the additional two hours of sleep has pulled a thick veil over the memory. Someone was killed, but that's what most of my nightmares are about—murder.

I chop up two carrots, peel two oranges and cut them into quarters. My noisy juicer screens out the sounds of next door's television and within a couple of minutes a nice thick, bright orange mixture is in my glass. I dish out some fruit salad from a large Tupperware bowl in the fridge and sit down at the table to read the *Washington Post*. I flick through the news section while I eat.

Fifteen minutes later I pull the couch across to one side of the room and roll out my Pilates mat. My thirty-minute DVD routine consists mainly of abdominal work, with some leg and butt work. I notice with triumph that my flexibility seems to be improving. I was always pretty flexible from kung fu, but through Pilates the stretches are becoming easier. By the end of the routine I'm sweaty but happy with my healthy start to the day. Perhaps the good start, with the help of one or ten coffees, will make up for my late night.

I stumble into headquarters right at 7:59 a.m., coffee in hand. I open my office, dump my bag and grab my notebook and a pile of files from the top of my in-tray. I've tagged ten in all as higher-priority cases out of the forty waiting for my attention. We have to prioritize, but every file that is pushed back in line could mean another life. It's overwhelming. That's partly why the unit has such a high burnout rate…and a high divorce rate.

Some of the files have been sitting on my desk for weeks. We're not supposed to take them home—it's Bureau policy that no files leave the building—but we do. You have to when so much is at stake.

My slight heels make a clip-clop sound as I hurriedly move through the Bureau corridors to meeting room 2 in the center of the building. I rush in and take a seat next to Sam. I'm not the last, not quite, but Rivers is just about to start. He glances at me, a look I can't decipher. He removes his glasses and starts.

"Since our meeting last week, two cases have been closed. Congratulations to Agents Anderson and Marco for their work on the Henley case." He pauses. "Also, the Night Fever case Agent Hammerston profiled a couple of months ago has been closed. The LAPD caught their guy on the weekend and got the confession too."

He looks to his left, at me. "Anderson, you go first." He waits, pen poised and glasses back on.

I start my rundown. "I've picked out ten cases for the next two weeks. Two of the cases look like they're a perp's first kill, but both of them will kill again. We need to get the perps now."

Heads nod around the room in acknowledgment. First-time murderers often make mistakes and it's good to get them early before they become better at hiding their tracks.

"The other eight I've selected are longer-term cases, but some of them are particularly nasty. Like the Whistler case in Canada. The perp's escalating big-time."

Rivers scribbles something in his notepad and keeps his head down as he talks. "The media love that case, even though it's in Canada."

"Yeah. It's a hot one all right." I glance around the room, conscious of keeping the pace moving. "I've also got to do a few follow-ups for the profiles I did before the Henley case."

Rivers stops scrawling, looks up and nods.

We continue around the room, with each profiler running through their caseload in turn. I sip my double-shot coffee hoping the caffeine will kick in soon. But concentration seems impossible…how nice it would be to be lying on a beach somewhere. I close my eyes, imagining hot sand on my skin. But this relaxing image is suddenly replaced by a naked dead girl. My dream comes flooding into my conscious mind. I open my eyes with a start and the girl fades.

I tune in to the meeting again and am shocked to hear Sam finishing off the run-through of her workload. Had we gotten around everyone?

"Okay, people. Sounds like you're all busy, but that's nothing new," Rivers says. "And I'm afraid we're going to have to shuffle some cases around, but I'll let Pike explain." Rivers is unable to hide the hint of gruffness. "He'll be here in a moment. Now, I've also got three new cases. We've got a child killer in Texas. A strangler on the loose in Boston—"

A ripple of grim laughter fills the room.

"I kid you not," Rivers says, acknowledging the absurdity of another Boston Strangler. "And we've got a request from the French police for a profile of a band of bank robbers." Rivers looks down at his notepad again, "James—"

Peter James stops flicking his pen against his notebook and looks up.

"—you can have the strangler. Tuldoon, you've got the Texas case—"

Jim Tuldoon, always a stickler for paperwork, writes furiously in his notebook. What could he be writing at this stage other than "killer in Texas"?

"—and Wright, you've got the bank heists."

Sam looks up, winks and clicks her mouth at Rivers. Only Sam could get away with it.

I think a smile plays on Rivers's lips before he moves on. "No surprises there. So—"

Rivers is interrupted by the entrance of the director

of the unit, Jonathan Pike. Pike wears his standard well-tailored dark gray suit, which provides a contrasting surface for his dandruff. He hovers at the door.

"Sorry, Andy. Do you want to finish up?"

"No, no. I was done anyways." Rivers says the right words, but his tone implies something altogether different. I've never noticed any animosity between the two before.

Pike takes the podium. "Okay. Well, first off I'd like to congratulate Agents Marco and Anderson for their work on the Henley case." Pike motions his right hand toward us in a stiff manner. "As you know, it became a high-priority case for us and I'm glad to say we delivered for the politicians, yet again. So thanks to you both for the long hours." He pauses, withdrawing his right hand, and for a minute it looks like he's going to give us a round of applause. Instead, his arm returns to his side. "Now, I'm afraid I've got some other news that won't thrill you."

Everyone groans. I knew it. No wonder Rivers is pissed.

"Yes, I'm afraid so. It's Hunter this time. He's been reassigned to the Counterterrorism Unit. I know things are getting tough for us over here, and I'm doing everything I can to keep as many resources as possible. But we can't afford another 9/11. Director Mueller has to answer to the American public." He looks at his unconvinced audience. "Rest assured he *does* value what we do here. I'm sorry, people, I know you're already busy, but there's not much I, or we, can do about it. Andy?" And with that Pike hands it back to Rivers and leaves the meeting.

The unit had twenty people in it before September 11 and now there are only twelve of us. Eleven after Hunter leaves.

"Any cases in Hunter's load that appeal?" Rivers says, eyeing the rest of us.

"I'd like those religious murders down in Arkansas," James says, furiously tapping his pen against his notebook again. The man drinks too much coffee. Not that I can talk.

"And I'll take the kidnapping in Rhode Island," Hammerston says.

I missed Hunter's case rundown. I should have paid attention. As the other agents call out their preferences, I try to remember at least one of his top-priority cases. My mind is sluggish and refuses to respond.

"I'll take the D.C. one," I finally say. I can't remember the case, but Hunter had one on the go in the city. A serial killer, just my style, and only two known murders to date…I think. At least, that's what I remember from last week's meeting.

Everyone turns their heads and looks at me. The room falls silent. I've said or done something foolish.

"What?"

Sam breaks the silence with a lighthearted laugh, taking the impatient eyes away from me. "I just asked for that one, honey."

"Oh." I feel suitably dense.

"Do you want it?" Sam says.

"No, no, I'll take—" and there I stop, because for the life of me I can't remember any of Hunter's other cases.

"Why don't you take that Australian one, give you a taste of home," Sam comes to my rescue again.

How could I forget that Hunter was doing a profile for the West Australian police? "Sounds good."

"So what have we got left?" Rivers says, checking his notes. "There's the rapist in Miami. Marco, why don't you take that one. And the global credit-card scam." Rivers looks over his glasses and sweeps his eyes around the room. "Actually, you can finish the profile for that one this week, Hunter, and then pass it over to Wright for follow-up. And we've got those hate crimes in Pennsylvania... Silvers, you take that one. Hunter, I want a list of your other cases and recommendations for reassignment by the end of the day."

"No problem, sir."

"Well, that's it, folks. Let's get back to work. I'll come and see you all individually about Hunter's cases."

Sam and I are already standing, ready to go, when Rivers speaks again.

"Oh, and we'll have a send-off for Hunter on Friday night."

Sam and I are first out the door. "What time did you get home?" she whispers. We keep walking, moving away from the other agents.

"I left about thirty minutes after you."

"You look wrecked, girl."

"Thanks."

"You know what I mean."

"I didn't get much sleep." I think about the dream again, and the elements replay themselves more vividly. The dead girl with a tattoo, some sort of a Celtic symbol perhaps, and a woman walking by herself in a parking lot. Then I was running.

I dismiss the dream; after all, I often dream of death and stalking. An occupational hazard, I guess.

Sam brings me back to the world of the living.

"No sleep? Any particular reason?" She has a cheeky look on her face.

"No." I know what she's hinting at and head her off at the pass. "It's strictly professional between me and Marco," I say, making sure no one's in earshot.

"Maybe for the moment, honey. But he knows how to work the ladies."

"Well, that's a good reason to stay away, isn't it."

"He just hasn't met the right woman yet. Someone like you?"

"But what about Matt?"

"*Matt?* What about him?"

"It doesn't feel right yet."

"Honey, you told me it was over with him."

"Yeah, it is. We agreed we wouldn't try the long-distance thing. So it's over."

"Well, start acting like it. You left Matt back in Australia seven months ago. At this rate, you're heading for the nunnery."

I have to admit, celibacy is getting a bit hard to handle.

Sam doesn't let up. "You're single, gorgeous and successful. You can have anyone."

But it's not that simple. Sam could have anyone. And I mean anyone. But me? Besides, how do you let go of seven years of your life?

I smile and change the subject. "So, will Hunter be happy? Pissed?"

"We're all half expecting it at the moment. Who knows who'll be next."

"Surely they can't reassign anyone else." I can't take any more cases.

"Let's hope not. Things are going to get pretty hectic here."

"They already are."

"It'll get worse."

I bite my lip, guilty. Rivers has put me on a pedestal and I don't think I deserve to be there. I might get one or two things the other profilers don't but it takes me a lot longer.

We arrive at my office and I open the door.

Sam keeps walking down the corridor and then stops and turns around. "I might actually get your opinion on that D.C. case. Maybe tonight after work?"

"Sure." I find it hard to say no, despite my caseload. Besides, it's Sam. I'd do anything for Sam. She waves and disappears round the corner.

In my office I flick through the files on my desk, looking for the girl that's haunting me. I must have seen her somewhere, but where? Fifteen minutes later I give up. I've been through every file and my recently tidied desk is a mess again. I put Hunter's West Australian case at the top of my pile. Even though I've never been to W.A., it still makes me think about home. The past seven months have gone quickly, but I still miss Australia.

A few hours and a quick lunch break later I hit send on an e-mail to Detective Peter O'Leary, the homicide cop in charge of the W.A. case. One down, forty to go. I move the W.A. file from my "to do" tray to my "follow up" tray. I'll give O'Leary four weeks before I contact him to see if there've been any more murders or any breaks. I print out a copy of the profile and place it in the file. The profile should give O'Leary something.

I've got an hour and a half before I'm due to meet Sam in the gym. I take my phone off divert and check my messages. Nothing that can't wait until tomorrow. It's a good time to do some follow-ups. I look through some of the crimes I profiled before I went on the Henley case, and spend the next hour and a half talking to cops about any developments. After each call I add updates to the files. Two cases have been solved, so I request more documentation from the cops so I can close off the files.

It's just past six-thirty when I hurry down to the gym and into the locker room. I tie up my sneakers and Sam walks in. She looks stressed.

"Hard day at the office?"

"You bet, honey," she says, rolling her eyes.

"What's up?"

"The D.C. case. There's something not quite right about it."

"That's our dinner-date conversation, remember? Let's concentrate on exhausting ourselves first."

"Deal. I'll see you out there."

The gym's busy, with about twenty guys and only two other women there. One of the women is Dr. Amanda Rosen, the departmental psychologist. She, Sam and I often work out together, and occasionally Amanda joins us if we catch a movie or a bite to eat after the gym. I'm sure she'd socialize with us more if it weren't for the fact that she has to do our six-monthly psych evaluations. I don't think she wants to get too friendly.

I recognize the other woman from forensics, but I haven't worked with her yet and don't even know her name. I make a mental note to get Marty to introduce me.

Amanda sees me and smiles. I smile back then begin stretching. I jump on the treadmill. The rhythmic motion and sound of my feet hitting the tread sweep over me, and I let the day's thoughts wash away.

I used to go for the wrong sort of girl. I'd pick the dumb ones because I thought they'd be easier. Which they are, of course. But I've refined my art and skills and moved up in the world over the years. Now I like the smart ones. The harder ones. Sometimes I even consider going for the fancy ones…the women who live in the lap of luxury with their designer clothes, six-figure incomes and think they're untouchable. But that's the nice thing about my calling—no one is untouchable. I can have anyone I want. And sometimes I enjoy just that, picking the hardest prey and watching the cops chasing their tails. Idiots! That's partly why I moved here. For the challenge. I'm right under *their* noses. I wonder what they'll make of me?

I'm sick of being the nameless, faceless person who never gets any recognition. If only they knew how smart I was, what I'm truly capable of…maybe then they'd see me.

I've picked the next special girl. To her I'm just one of the millions living in this city. But soon she'll know me. Soon, they'll all know me.

04

I pull the cork out of a bottle of Australian shiraz from my small collection and Sam opens the pizza box. We've gone for marinara on a thin crust with extra cheese. She pulls a piece upward, stretching the mozzarella until the piece finally detaches from the rest of the pizza.

She takes a hearty bite and says through her mouthful, "Damn, your pizza shop's good."

"Thank God we got our workout in," I say, taking a bite and pouring wine at the same time.

I place Sam's glass in front of her and hold mine up. "Cheers."

"What are we toasting to?" she asks, picking up her glass.

"Who knows...good health?"

"As good a toast as any."

We clink glasses and both take a sip.

"Good wine, girl."

"It's an Australian shiraz. What do you expect?"

"Not biased, are we?"

"Well, maybe a bit.

We finish our first slice of pizza in silence, concentrating on filling the holes in our stomachs. We both take another piece.

"So, Sam…"

She looks up at me, midbite.

"Marco's had lots of women?"

"Finally!"

"What?"

"You've been feigning lack of interest for months and finally you've realized you're into him…and boy is he into you."

"I don't know about that…"

"'Course you do."

I smile. Maybe I do. I've never told Sam about the night Marco and I nearly kissed. "So, the question?"

"Not that I know the man's every move, but I've worked with him for the past year and he's dated a few women. That I know of."

"Yeah, and for every one you know of there's probably another one or two you don't."

"Possibly. He's a good-looking man."

I smile, picturing Marco. Even the standard FBI dark suit can't hide his physique, which, I must say, is pretty close to my idea of perfect. Marco is six feet tall, with broad shoulders and well-defined muscles. His upper body is complemented by a muscular torso and long, strong legs. His ass looks pretty good too. His hair is dark brown and short, the standard Bureau cut, and his facial features are broad, with a well-pronounced jawline. It gives him the classic, masculine chiseled look. You can see his Italian heritage in his coloring, especially his slightly tanned skin and rich, intense brown eyes. His one imperfection, a scar that runs across one eyebrow, only adds to his sex appeal. He's good-looking all right. I don't usually go for them that good-looking.

"Have you ever?" I say.

"Me? Marco? No. He's a good guy, but not my type." Sam takes her third slice of pizza. "Dig in, girl, before I eat it all." She takes a mouthful and follows it with a large sip of wine. "Marco's too serious for me. But he's right for you."

"I didn't know matchmaking was one of your talents." I hold my wineglass to my lips and give her a cheeky smile before taking a sip.

"I'll have you know, I've introduced two married couples to one another."

"Really?" I'm genuinely impressed.

"Sure. And my money's on you and Marco."

I laugh. "Are you taking bets?"

"I can if you want. We could run a pool in the unit. Take bets on when your first kiss will be."

"That'd be terrific," I say and roll my eyes.

"Just say the word." She takes another mouthful. "Look, as far as I know, they were just dates. It doesn't mean he sleeps around or is only after one thing."

"They're all after that."

"Well, yes. But some of them realize that a good woman isn't about conquest."

It's true. At least I have to hope so.

"But we work together," I continue. "I don't know if it's such a good idea."

"It's not ideal. But if the spark is there, it's there."

Sam's right.

"And you wouldn't be breaking any rules, or anything," she adds.

"No?"

"The official line is that it's okay for agents to date one another."

"That's good to know."

"But you would get flack from other agents. In fact, the Bureau's even coined a term just for FBI couples."

"Really?"

"Uh-huh. If you and Marco get together, you'll both be called double agents." She pauses. "You'd make a good double." She laughs.

"Gee, thanks."

I take the last piece of pizza.

Sam gets rid of the box. "Shit, it's nine o'clock. We better get started."

She spreads the contents of the D.C. file over my dining-room table while I move the plates and bottle onto the counter. I refill our wineglasses and hand Sam hers. As soon as I see the photos I freeze.

"What's up?" she says.

"I...I've seen this girl before." I hurriedly put down my wineglass and pick up the photo of the first D.C. murder victim. It's the girl whose face I saw in my dream. But I don't mention this to Sam. Instead, I rationalize to her, and to myself. "I must have seen this file before."

"From Hunter?"

"I guess so." I need time alone to think about this. Images of a case I'm not even working on?

Sam studies my face. "Are you all right, Soph?"

"I'm fine. I was just surprised to see the girl. Like I said, I must have seen the file before, that's all."

But I haven't seen the damn file.

Sam is less than convinced, but I turn away and move toward the window. A cold shiver runs down my spine as I go to close the curtains. For an instant I think I see someone standing across the road looking up at my window. But when I look again, no one's there. I close the curtains and return to Sam.

"So, let's look at this case," I say, forcing the unease I feel to the back of my mind.

We both stand over the table to get a better view of the photos. I take in all the details. The wounds, the body placement, everything, already starting to form an opinion. There have only been two victims so far. I pick up all the photos of the girl I recognize and look for the marking on her thigh. But it's not there. She has knife wounds surrounding the area, but no tattoo. I sink into a chair. I don't know whether it's a good or bad thing that the tatt's not there.

"What's wrong, honey?" Sam puts her hand on my shoulder, worried.

"Mmm? Oh, nothing. I was just thinking about another case," I lie.

Sam looks at me oddly.

I push the confusion away, focusing on the case. "You've got my undivided attention. Are Flynn and Jones on the case?"

"Yeah, they took it over as soon as the Henley case closed."

"They're good cops. Good guys."

Sam starts taking me through the case. She's reading from her own notepad, and the original files lie on one end of the table. It's the usual assortment—the coroner's report, police reports covering the crime scene and detailed information about the victims. Profiling is a four-step process—analyzing the profiling inputs, reviewing decision models, an assessment of the crime and then drafting the profile itself.

We start with five major profiling inputs—the crime scene, the victimology, forensic information, the preliminary police report and the all-important photos.

At the crime scene we study the physical evidence, including weapons, body positioning, and any other patterns that may be visible. Next we look at the victimology to get an insight into the victim. By getting to know the victim, we can understand the perpetrator. We consider a victim's age, occupation, background, habits, when she was last seen and so on. The forensic information includes time and cause of death, wounds, sexual acts (pre- and postmortem), the autopsy report and lab reports on blood splatter, fibers and so on. These four things combine with the prelim police report—which gives us information about who reported the crime, anything the cops on the scene noticed, and also covers background on the neighborhood—to give us a better understanding of the crime.

Next we look at a variety of decision-process models, including homicide type and style, primary intent (for example, was the primary intent robbery or murder?), victim risk (high, moderate or low, for example, prostitutes are in the high-risk category because they're accessible and vulnerable by the nature of their work), offender risk (did the offender take risks during the crime?), time required for the crime, and information about the location. We also look for signs of escalation—does it look like our criminal will become more violent, repeat the offense or intensify his activities from, say, kidnapping to murder?

The third step is crime assessment. During this stage we reconstruct the crime to determine how things happened and how people behaved, focusing on the interaction between the victim and perp. We classify the type of crime and look at any staging elements that may be present, like a staged robbery, and we also look at possible motivations and the crime-scene dynamics, such as cause of death, location of wounds and crime-scene location.

From here we generate the criminal profile itself. In reality, though, the first three steps are often blended together rather than looked at in isolation.

"Okay, so this was the first one." Sam picks up a photo of my girl. In this photo she's alive and well, smiling for the camera. "Jean Davis. She was killed five months ago. Twenty-eight years old, worked as a producer's assistant at WX40TV. A real career gal, by all accounts. Very friendly and outgoing."

I pore over the other photos of Jean. The crime-scene ones. Her body is in the back seat of a car—where I can't tell, although the area looks quite remote. She lies slightly turned, with her knees resting to one side and both arms raised to about forty-five degrees on either side of her body. Her head is turned, eyes open. Just like she was in my dream. The body positioning reminds me of a back exercise, except her head faces the same way as her knees instead of vice versa. Her body is messy, with multiple knife wounds. Most wounds are quite long, indicating the killer pulled the knife across her body rather than stabbing inward. Unusual. There are several large cuts across her abdomen and breasts, ranging between four and ten inches in length. Most of the cuts had formed scabs before her death, except one smaller cut just above her belly button and two deeper cuts on her left breast. Her throat also contains several older, shallower cuts. Similar cuts are on her upper arms and upper legs, with a heavy concentration on her thighs, in line with her crotch. There are five or six cuts that are obviously newer, quite fresh at the time of death. There must have been a lot of blood during the time he had her.

"He likes blood," I say, verbalizing my last thought.

"Blood, penetration, or both."

I nod—knives often represent the sexual act for killers. Although more through deep, stabbing cuts than this style of knife wound.

"Coroner reported fifty cuts in all." Sam points out the gashes covering Jean's body.

"But it wasn't a blitz attack."

"No. It was controlled, metered. And over a long period of time."

That's one item on the profile decided. Criminals can be broken into two broad groups, organized offenders or disorganized offenders. Organized offenders plan their crimes, often meticulously, whereas disorganized offenders act in the heat of the moment. The cuts show control and planning, two traits of an organized criminal.

"Did she die of these wounds?" I ask, standing up.

"Yeah, eventually. Our guy bled her to death, but real slow. Many of the cuts were superficial, but these two here—" she points to one of the cuts on her thigh and one on her breast "—were deeper and near arteries. Coroner says that without the intervention she would have died in about ten hours."

"Intervention?" I lean over the table to get a closer look at the photo.

"You'll love this one, honey. The guy bandaged her up tight around the wounds. He wanted to keep her around. Coroner estimates she was kept alive for an extra ten hours with pressure bandages."

I tighten my grip on the top of the dining-room chair I'm leaning on. "Bastard." I loosen my grip. This could turn out to be to our advantage. "Medical training."

"Sure is a possibility. Strong one, I'd say," Sam agrees.

"How long did he have her?"

"Last sighting was five days before time of death."

"He have her all that time?"

"We think so. A neighbor was the last to see her. She took the trash out at 10:00 p.m. on June 23, but never showed for work the next day. Her best friend at the station dropped by her apartment that night and called the police when there was no answer. So our guy either grabbed her the night of the twenty-third or the next morning, four or five days before death."

"So he likes to play."

"Don't they all?"

"Pretty much," I say with disgust. "He's a high-risk offender, given the amount of time he spends with them. Presumably he's got somewhere private he takes them."

"Yeah. He ties them at the hands and feet. We're thinking spread-eagle," she says, searching for another photo. She picks out two close-ups, one of Jean's left leg and one of her left arm. Sam points to the ligature marks on Jean's wrist and ankle. "Probably to a table, bed or some other flat object. The ligature marks indicate a separate binding for each limb and the marks are deep."

I examine the indentations in Jean's skin. "He tied her up tight."

"Real tight." Sam throws the two photos back on the table and grabs one crime-scene photo of Jean's body and one of the autopsy photos. She holds up the crime-scene photo first. "She didn't die in this position." She brings the autopsy photo up next to it, for comparison. "Lividity indicates she died flat on her back and on a flat surface."

I nod. The autopsy photograph Sam has chosen is one of Jean lying on her stomach. The photo clearly shows Jean's back and upper legs.

Lividity refers to the way the blood settles after death. Once your heart stops, blood stops pumping around your body. Gravity takes over and blood settles. Jean's back shows pink-red discoloration evenly across her buttocks and upper back. That means she died lying on a flat surface and the blood settled evenly when it stopped flowing. If she'd died in the position her body was found, the discoloration would be concentrated and darker around her right buttocks and hip.

"Anything else from lividity?" I ask. Sometimes if the body is transported soon after death discoloration can appear in definite patterns. The body can even show you an imprint of a car jack if the body was in someone's trunk.

"Nothing."

"That's something in itself, I guess."

Sam looks at me, puzzled.

"Jean was lying on a smooth surface."

Sam looks at the autopsy photo again. "Very smooth."

We pause for a moment.

"He likes to get to know them," says a voice… It's my voice.

"You don't think it's just the power? To prolong the experience and have them at his mercy?"

I think about it, unsure where my revelation came from. "Not just that, this time. He's taken a lot of care. He's had her for the whole five days. He spends time with them. To get to know them. There was rape, I presume?"

"Yeah. But not as violent as we often see. No bruises around her thighs or hips. No tearing. The fucker was gentle," Sam says, her nose wrinkled with disgust.

"He thinks of them as his girlfriends." A shiver runs up my spine. "He's not rough with them. He's tender. They're special to him in some way."

"Charming," Sam says, staring distantly at one of the photos of Jean's body.

"So, would Jean have played along?" I ask.

"Everyone who knew her said she was smart. Real smart. So she may have if she thought it was going to save

her life. The full victimology is around here somewhere."
Sam shoves the photos to one side and shuffles through
the papers. The photo of Jean alive falls off the table and
I pick it up. This is our only reminder of her as a living
person. It's precious.

"Here it is." Sam hands me a typed report.

I take the document but rest it on the table. I've got
more questions first. "Let's get back to this later. No
semen, I take it?"

"Nope. Safe sex for our guy, in every sense of the word."

I nod, picking up Sam's double meaning—no risk of
sexual disease and no risk of DNA. "Any other trace
evidence? Hairs, fibers, prints?"

"Nothing. He's clean."

"Let's face it, a lot of perps know how to clean up after
themselves these days, especially with all the press on
DNA. Anything on the knife?"

Sam flips through the coroner's report and paraphrases
it. "Could be any sharp kitchen knife. Based on the
incision length and angles, our guy's left-handed and the
knife is between seven to ten inches."

I do the mental conversion to centimeters. Between
seventeen and twenty-five centimeters. "The left-hander
narrows things down."

"You bet. Once we have some suspects, that is." Sam
pulls out a chair and sinks into it. She looks defeated,
which is unusual for Sam. Even her bright green eyes
aren't as dazzling as usual. Her hair falls from behind her
ear across her face.

"What about positioning when the cutting was
done?" I ask.

"Angles indicate the vics were lying down and he was standing over them."

"Supports the flat surface from the lividity."

"Yep."

"Nothing else?"

"Our guy's a real pro. No fingerprints or footprints that haven't been accounted for."

"What about tire treads? Where'd he park when he nabbed Jean?"

"No treads, but we're assuming he parked on the street out front or back. No one saw anything."

"Victim's fingernails?" I ask in a last-ditch attempt to find something, anything.

Sam shakes her head. "Scrubbed clean and clipped back. Like I said, a real pro."

"But this is his first on record?"

"Officially, yes. It may be the first we know about, but it certainly ain't the first time he's killed." She stands up again and starts pacing, glass of wine in hand.

It is too perfect, too rehearsed for a first-time kill, unless the guy had done his research and planned for months, or perhaps if he's a cop who has decided to try murder for himself. But it's more likely he's killed before. One of the two thousand-plus serial killers doing their rounds in the good old U.S. of A.

"What about VICAP?" I ask.

VICAP is the Violent Criminal Apprehension Program, a nationwide database that contains details of murder cases and other violent crimes around the States to analyze patterns and track criminals that may cross law-enforcement boundaries. Pretty effective too. Cops enter in the details and the database comes back with any similar crimes. Of course, it relies on all law-enforcement officers entering their cases into the database in the first place, something that doesn't always happen. Some cops think VICAP is just more red tape and paperwork.

"Flynn and Jones entered in both D.C. murders and got two matches in Chicago. They followed up with Chicago Homicide. It looks like it was our perp, but there weren't any significant leads or suspects in Chicago, so it was a dead end. I talked to the VICAP guys myself and they're going to get someone onto it. Do a fresh, more detailed computer search and then get one of their best analysts to look at the cases manually. Should have the results in a couple of days, but the guys are swamped down there. Our perp could have been active in states that don't use VICAP, so he could have been getting away with murder for years."

"True." I move back to the table and pick up my glass of wine. I take another sip.

Sam also takes a contemplative sip. "I think the perp has moved here recently. God knows how many he's done in other states. I'll bring it up at tomorrow's meeting and see if anyone recognizes the MO."

"Good idea. I don't think he's transient, though. I think he's set up shop here."

"Well, I'm not complaining about that. Those wandering bastards are hard to pin down." She takes another sip. "How about a work transfer? Or maybe the cops were getting too close for him and he decided to move on?"

"Possibly."

"Pretty stupid to move to D.C. near all the profilers."

And then it hits me. "Maybe that's the point. Maybe he wants to see if he can get away with it under the Bureau's nose. Under our noses."

"A thrill killer? Living on the dangerous side?"

"This might be his idea of fun. And the evidence does point to a high-risk offender."

"Soph, this could be disastrous."

I nod. "He'll hit hard and fast to show us up."

"But he's only done two in five months."

"He may know it takes a little while before the Bureau steps in."

"Waiting until he has our attention?"

"Could be."

"We need to get this guy sooner rather than later."

I'd like to get them all sooner rather than later, but Sam is right. If he has come to D.C. for the thrill of killing under the Bureau's nose, he'll step things up once he knows we're involved.

"We need to get to know Jean a little better," I say.

An hour later we've reread the victimologies for both girls, analyzed every crime-scene photo and double-checked the coroner's reports and all the police reports. We both sit at the table.

"So what do you think?" Sam plays with her empty wineglass.

"He hasn't left us much."

"Time to pull a rabbit out of a hat." Sam laughs.

"This is a science," I say, playing along. Since its inception nearly twenty years ago, the unit has been struggling with the notion that profiling is all subjective mumbo jumbo. It's really a sensible combination of psychology and the profiler's ability to walk in the killers' and victims' shoes. To give your mind over to them—their lives, their habits, their actions and responses.

"Okay. So the second victim, Teresa Somers," Sam says. "She was abducted in the parking lot of her apartment building. Her car keys were found on the ground and we're assuming she struggled."

My mind replays my dream of a girl walking to her car, but the girl in my dream was a redhead and Teresa's a brunette—not the same girl. I push the image aside.

Sam puts the photo of Teresa, alive, on the top of the pile. "She was strong and fit. She put up a good fight."

"Besides the keys, anything else to indicate a struggle?"

"She was already decomposing when we found her, but the coroner noted a cracked rib."

"From the struggle?"

Sam looks at the photos of Teresa's body. "Possibly. The perp may have got more than he bargained for."

"This guy likes a challenge. For the moment, let's assume he's chosen D.C. for a reason. For us. He's pushing his 'skills' to the limit." I stand up and start pacing, on a roll. "He doesn't go for the easy targets. He chooses a woman, a professional woman, and stalks her, waiting for his opportunity. He gets to know her routine. So I think he knew Teresa worked out every day. That she'd done self-defense classes. That she was a strong woman." I stop in front of Sam and lean closer to her. "I mean, for God's sake, she was a high-level manager at CIBC Bank. And that's what turned him on. She was smart, educated, self-sufficient. Yet he could still get her."

"That would fit in with Jean, too. Professional. Hardworking. Only difference is that she was at the start of her career rather than the pinnacle."

"Well, she was five years younger."

"Did you notice they look the same age, though. Teresa was thirty-five, but she looked about thirty, thirty-one," Sam says, selecting the two photos of our victims when they were alive.

I look at the photos again. "Yeah. I think our guy's in his late twenties or early thirties."

"And he's been killing for a while. If he's like most serial killers, he probably started between the ages of eighteen and twenty-five, so he's probably been killing for quite a few years."

"So, how would Teresa have reacted?" I say out aloud, verbally going through the process I usually go through in my head.

"She would have fought. All the way. She was hard. Tough. In business and pleasure, by all accounts."

"Yes, but she would also have tried to negotiate. She was a businesswoman. It's one of the things she did best," I say, sitting back down.

"So she was tied up to a table or something, being sliced, yet she was still trying to bring the dynamic around." Sam keeps pacing. "The fucker would have thought it was amusing. He wouldn't have been threatened."

I nod. "He's experienced. He's worked his way up to women like Teresa. He would have loved it. Got off on it even. Ultimately he knew he had all the power. He knew that, deep down, she must have been scared shitless, despite the business front." I finger two photos of

Teresa—one from the crime scene and one from when she was alive. It's hard to recognize her features in death.

"So he played with her. Maybe even made her think he was coming around. That he was going to release her," Sam says.

"Yep. He would have beaten her down. He wanted her to go from believing she still had some sort of control over the situation to admitting defeat."

"At his mercy."

"Then as soon as she broke, he killed her. He'd won and the challenge was gone."

In Teresa's case he'd inflicted multiple cuts, like Jean, but the cause of death had been one massive knife wound across her throat.

I look at the photos, then at Sam. "How long did he have her?"

"The body wasn't found for a while, but the coroner's time of death puts us at eight to twenty days after abduction."

"The lower end sounds more likely, given the pattern with Jean."

"I agree," Sam says.

"That whole time was a war between their minds. After eight days or so, she finally begged him for pity. For mercy."

"And he gave it to her, in a form. The son of a bitch killed her."

We both pause for a moment.

Sam sits down on the sofa. "It looks like he raped her several times. Again, the coroner says it's hard to say because of the length of time and the lack of bruising and other signs of sexual violence."

"How do you think she would have responded to the rape?"

"Maybe used it in her negotiations. Made him think sex was something she could offer him. A bargaining tool."

"She was tough, all right. She lasted through eight days of torture. I think we can assume that after the first struggle, she may have stopped struggling. She would have been planning her escape. Looking for a way out. Maybe even trying to convince him to undo her hands and legs under the pretense of being able to sexually satisfy him."

"But her tied up at his mercy was what aroused him."

"Yeah. Still, I reckon she tried damn hard to get out," I say.

"Concentrating on getting out alive. Negotiating or escaping."

"She would have distanced herself emotionally from what was going on, so she probably didn't struggle too much with the rapes. This would have fed his fantasy of her as the girlfriend."

I'm drawn back to Jean by a photo of her. I pick it up and look into her eyes. They are open in death, and the killer has chosen not to close them. It's the same with Teresa. Jean stares back at me and I can imagine her tied down, wondering if she is going to live or die and praying for release. Just as she looked at the killer and begged for mercy, now she looks at me and begs for justice.

I answer her call. "Let's go back to Jean."

I will have to think about the case properly later, when Sam isn't here. Usually about now, once I have all the facts, I close my eyes and imagine the killer. I see the killer.

I become the killer, stepping into his world. Somehow my subconscious takes over, and I find myself so fully immersed in the process that I don't usually come to for hours. I don't know whether it's like that for the others or not. I probably shouldn't get so involved in the cases.

Sam stands over the dining table. "Jean was ambitious. In fact, this baby wanted to work in front of the cameras. She was working her way up, trying to get noticed within WX40. She wanted to be an anchor someday and had a pretty good reel together." Sam picks up her notepad. "Everyone who knew her described her as…" She reads from her notes, "'Outgoing,' 'fun,' 'gregarious,' 'funny,' 'entertaining.'" Apparently she liked everyone and everything, and always saw the positive in any situation."

"I wonder if she managed to do that on the table."

Sam continues. "She was also very charming and quite a flirt. She had a boyfriend she saw a couple of times a week, but he says it was casual. Says Jean liked to play the field. Her female friends corroborate this."

"So, did she flirt with our guy? Did she know him before he abducted her?" I say, not expecting any answers.

"They think he nabbed her from her apartment. Inside."

"Forced entry?"

"Didn't look like it."

"So we're thinking he knew her, or there was some other reason why she let him in."

"Must be."

"Any sign of a struggle?"

"No. But the guys found a bottle of wine, which was almost empty, and one glass with her lipstick." Sam shuffles through the photos and finds the one of Jean's kitchen.

"There was enough saliva for a DNA test. It was positive for Jean. The glass on the sink—" she points to a wineglass that's upturned on the draining board, "—was clean—no prints, no saliva, no DNA. We don't know whether it was from the night before or if she was drinking with the killer and he had the good sense to wash the glass after him."

"Could be either. What about the boyfriend? When did he last see her?"

"Two days before. His prints were at the apartment and we found a couple of hairs that have been confirmed through DNA as his. But he's got an alibi for the night she went missing."

"Good one?"

"Solid."

Sam glances at her watch. "It's getting late."

I look at the clock. It's 11:30 p.m. "He's taking shape."

"Yeah, I'm starting to get a real good picture."

"Let's sleep on it. We can talk again in the morning."

"Okay, Soph. Listen, thanks for your help. I know you've got a heavy load at the moment."

"No problem. As the saying goes, two heads are better than one."

She grins, a tired smile. "Can't argue with that. I'm going to work on the profile tomorrow, then you can have a look at it."

"I'll see if I've got anything to add. God, we didn't even get to the dump sites. Where were the bodies found?"

"Jean was found dumped in a stolen car on Roosevelt Island, under the Keys Bridge."

I know that area. The island is quite isolated and not many people visit it.

Sam gathers up the photos and documents and puts them back in the file. "Coroner estimates she died about four days earlier."

"So the killer couldn't have been too worried about physical evidence."

"No."

"What about the stolen car? Whose was it?"

"The car belonged to some old lady in Garfield Heights. Looks like the car was dumped well before the body."

"What about Teresa? Where'd they find her?"

"She was a bit different. She was found about four weeks after her death and farther out, in Cedarville State Forest."

"That's strange. Nothing else turned up at Cedarville?"

"No bodies, if that's what you mean." Sam yawns, puts the file in her briefcase and grabs her handbag. At the door she gives me a kiss on the cheek. "Good night, honey."

She bobs her head back around the corner just before I close the door. "And Marco—go for it."

I laugh. "Get out of here, you."

"Sweet dreams."

I don't respond. I wish I could dream about Marco instead of murder.

I close the door.

The apartment feels so empty now. I quickly do my pre-bed security check, even though Sam has been here, before collapsing on my bed. As soon as my head hits the pillow I see the redhead from my dream. But this time she's screaming.

The scream floods my ears. I slit her throat, silencing the bitch.

I only kept this one for three days. She wasn't worth any more than that. She seemed smart, strong, genuine and happy. But I was wrong. How could I have been so wrong? In the end she was a pain-in-the-ass, stuck-up bitch who wasn't even worth getting to know.

I can't believe I had sex with her. The thought repulses me. I'm guilty of what I often complain about—rushing into things without getting to know the person.

But I couldn't have kept her. This way the timing is perfect. Fate has worked in my favor and I have to make an impact. I want to see fear creep into their lives as they start looking over their shoulders. No one's untouchable.

It's time to get personal.

05

The next morning I sit in the meeting room waiting for the last of the team to file in. Rivers closes the door and I notice Sam is absent. Sick?

Rivers gets straight down to business, as usual. "Right, folks. Let's get an update. We'll make this a snappy one. We've all got work to do. Oh, and Wright won't be joining us. There's been another murder with the trademarks of the D.C. killer. The boys in blue called it in and she's checking the murder scene firsthand." He glances around the room. "Let's start with James."

Half an hour later I'm in my office when the phone rings.

"Agent Anderson speaking."

"Soph, it's me. Sam. I think you better get up here."

"Why? What's up?"

"He was watching me last night."

"Who?" I ask, but even as I say the words I know.

"The killer. He left me a note at this crime scene."

"It's definitely the same perp?"

"Looks that way. Unless we've got us a copycat. Multiple knife wounds in the slice-and-dice style, and the same body positioning with head turned, eyes open."

I look at my watch—nine-thirty. Hopefully the I-95 and 395 won't be too busy. The trip to D.C. can take anywhere from half an hour to two hours or more, depending on traffic.

"I'm on my way." I scribble down directions before gathering my stuff together.

When I pass Marco's office he's standing at his desk, putting things into his briefcase. I hesitate.

"Anything wrong?" He comes into the corridor.

"The D.C. killer left Sam a note at his latest crime scene. It seems he's been spying on her."

"Does Rivers know?"

"No, we'll brief him when we get back."

"He'll go ballistic." He pauses. "I'm going to the D.C. Field Office in about ten minutes. Want a ride?"

I look at my watch, hesitant. Sam sounded unsettled. Marco walks back to his desk. "Give me two minutes." I smile. "Okay, you're on."

Marco rifles through his desk, quickly gathering a few more files and putting them into his briefcase. Next he hovers over his computer and types a hurried e-mail.

"Done," he says, grabbing his briefcase and coat.

We jump into his car and forty minutes later we're pulling off Independence Avenue into East Potomac, a huge parkland area just south of D.C. West and East Potomac Parks, separated by D.C.'s Tidal Basin, and taking up seven hundred and twenty acres of riverside land. I've been told on several occasions about the park's famous spring cherry blossoms. But will I be able to come back, after what I'm about to see?

I direct Marco toward the midwest point of the park, like Sam told me. Soon enough we're greeted by flashing lights and several cars. The coroner's black SUV is parked partly on the sidewalk and tilts to the side. There are two regular D.C. police squad cars and Flynn and Jones's unmarked car, a white Buick. Off to the corner I see Sam's Bureau-issue, and Marty's car is parked behind Sam's. Marco pulls up to the curb, behind the coroner. Except for the flashing lights the area is quiet.

"Thanks, Marco."

"Anytime."

I glance in the side mirror. Two TV vans pull up behind us…the peace will be short-lived.

"TV's here." I open my door.

"Be careful, Soph."

I get out of the car quickly and race the press, eager to get out of their view before they set up. I follow the meandering pathway near the cars. The route is lined with skeletal cherry blossom trees and I imagine what they'd look like in bloom. I keep walking. From this viewpoint the park looks peaceful. But over that ridge there's a dead body, with all the trimmings—police, forensics, morbid onlookers and, soon, the press. I come to the second park bench and take a right, up the hill, following Sam's instructions. My first step off the path is accompanied by the crisp sound of fall leaves crackling under my shoes. For a moment I let myself enjoy the sensation, knowing that soon my senses will be assaulted with very different sights, sounds and smells.

It's a steep walk, and as soon as I reach the crest I can see down into the crime scene. The police have cordoned off a large area, and around the tape a few curious onlookers gather. The main activity is off to the left slightly, in a scrublike area with dense foliage and bright flowers. The foliage hampers my view, but I can see movement and camera bulbs flashing. For the moment it's just the crime-scene photographers, but soon it will be the media, trying to get a glimpse of a body.

I make my way toward the cop who's obviously the point guy. He's young, fresh out of the Academy by the looks of him.

"I'm sorry, ma'am," he says, holding out his hand, "this is official police business." The words have a practiced ring.

I smile. I was that green once. I grab my ID from my handbag and hold it up. "I'm with the FBI. I've been called in to look at the crime scene."

He blushes slightly but looks closely at my ID— perhaps a little thrown by my accent.

"Sorry, ma'am."

"No need to apologize, you're just doing your job." The poor kid's probably already had some egomaniac detective chew him out this morning.

He points to the activity. "She's just in there."

The protective tone in his voice makes me wonder if it's his first dead body. He said "she" and not "the victim." He *is* green, but I like it.

"Thanks, Officer." I make my way toward the activity.

Again I flash my ID as I get closer, and then I spot Detective Flynn from homicide standing with Sam and the coroner. Flynn is in his late thirties and has a full head of black, slightly wavy hair. He's about the same height as Marco, but he hasn't got Marco's six-pack. He's tall with a sizable potbelly that is further accentuated by his otherwise thin frame. He usually sports a five o'clock shadow, no matter what time of day, and I'm sure today will be no exception.

The coroner and Flynn are engaged in intense discussion. From here I can see that they are hovering next to the body, which is resting in a flower bed in the middle of the foliage. The rest of the crime-scene area is taken up by forensics, including some FBI employees. Marty is working the scene, probably coordinating the forensics effort. At the moment he's crouching down on his knees about five feet away from the body. Maybe this time the perp's left us a shoe print. God knows we need something.

I hunch over and clamber into the undergrowth.

Flynn turns. "Agent Anderson. It doesn't let up, does it?"

"It's certainly been a busy six months. What have we got?"

I peer through a gap between Sam and Flynn and see the dead woman. It's her! Her face looks just as it did last night, when I saw her throat being slashed. My legs go weak. What the hell's going on?

"Her name's Susan Young. Twenty-nine years old, ran her own training firm," Sam tells me, though I am barely listening.

I force myself back to the scene. "Who found the body?"

"We got a tip-off early this morning," Flynn says.

I take my eyes away from the victim. "The perp call it in?" Killers like to get involved in the case, and sometimes they report the crime itself.

"Probably. The caller said he was a jogger, but it would be pretty hard, if not impossible, for a jogger to see into here from the path," Flynn says.

"So why'd he want us to find this one so quickly?" I say, looking at Susan. A couple of strands of her long red hair lie across her face.

Flynn shrugs. "The note, I guess."

Sam holds up an evidence bag with a pink envelope in it. "They found this in the victim's pocket."

On the front is cursive writing addressed to:

Sam Wright
Behavioral Analysis Unit
FBI

"Handwriting. Maybe he's not as smart as we thought."
"He is."

I look at Sam questioningly.

"The note is handwritten, but he's printed and used caps."

I nod. Printing and capital letters are harder for handwriting experts to analyze, or even to compare samples. It's not impossible, but it makes the going tough.

"What does it say?" I ask.

Sam and Flynn both flip open their notepads.

"You go," Sam says.

"DEAR MS WRIGHT, I WAS DELITED TO HEAR MY CASE HAS BEEN ASSIGNED TO YOU. I'VE FOLLOWED

YOUR WORK CLOSELY AND AM IMPRESSED. I PAR-
TICULARLY LIKED THE WAY YOU HANDLED THE
MINNESOTA CASE IN 2002. YOU SHUT HIM UP
GOOD, DIDN'T YOU?"

I wince. The Minnesota case was Sam's last in the
field before coming to the BAU. It was a drug bust but
the police hadn't told her they had someone on the
inside. During an exchange of fire he pointed his gun
at Sam. She shot him, naturally, but his gun had blanks.
It caused lots of problems—official and emotional.

Sam gives me a tight smile.

"This is the really worrying bit." Flynn doesn't notice
the exchange and continues reading out the letter. "I
LOOK FORWARD TO WORKING WITH YOU. WITH
LOVE, ME. PS I HOPE YOU ENJOYED THE WINE
LAST NIGHT."

He flips the pad shut. "This is not good."

A rush of images hits me. I'm standing at my window,
pulling the curtains closed and there's a shadow on the
street. Then I am that shadow, watching my living room.
I see myself pull the living-room curtains closed and the
shadow's angry. Angry that I've shut him out. The images
bring with them a burning pain across my eyes and I
stumble forward.

Flynn catches my elbow and steadies me. "Are you all
right, Sophie?" He's never used my first name before.

"Yeah. Sorry. I think I've got a migraine coming on."

This is getting creepy. Real creepy. The girl I saw in
my dreams is lying in a flower bed only two feet away
from me. Are they dreams, or could I be having premonitions? I immediately want to reject the notion.

Sam's voice breaks my train of thought. "Do you want to look around?"

I look up at her, still a little dazed.

"You sure you're all right?" she says.

I pull myself together. "Yeah, just a headache."

"I'll send you both my report once I've done the autopsy," the coroner says, addressing Flynn and Sam.

"Time of death around midnight last night?" I have to ask, to be sure, but I know that at precisely five after midnight, I somehow witnessed this woman's murder.

"Somewhere in that vicinity, yes. I'll pinpoint it back at the lab. How'd you know?"

I have to think fast. "Well, the perp had to have dumped her here sometime between two and five this morning, the quiet time, so he probably killed her just before. Between eleven and maybe three."

The coroner is happy with my response.

"Let's check in with Marty before we go," Sam says.

I'd rather get out of here and try to process everything that's happened, but I can't tell Sam that.

We join Marty, who's now examining some broken branches a few feet to our right. Two other people stand next to him, watching his every move.

"Anything?" Sam says.

Marty turns around. "Hi." He smiles widely. Marty's tall with dark brown hair that he keeps short. His square jaw, freckles and deep brown eyes are highlights of his attractive face, although his eyes are often hidden by thick glasses. He keeps fit, even though he's not in the field.

I got to know Marty quite well when I was on the Henley case. Marco and I often worked nights at their place.

Marty pushes his gelled hair back with his hand.

"Not yet, but we're hopeful." He motions to the man and woman next to him. "This is Jane Crompton and Bill Rust, they're studying at the Academy."

The FBI Academy launched its Forensics Training Division at Quantico in 2003. They've got the best collection of experts and machinery in the country, and run a comprehensive training program. They cover basic forensics and also have a program for professionals who want to improve their skills.

"Learning with the master," Sam says.

Marty smiles sheepishly, embarrassed by the compliment, but Jane and Bill seem happy with the notion that they're studying with the best.

"Did you get a footprint?" I ask Marty.

Marty puts his head down. "No, I'm afraid not. I thought it looked good for a partial, but it's not even a footprint."

I try to hide my disappointment.

"I'm sorry, Sophie. We will get something on this guy," Marty tries to reassure me. "If not today, then next time."

The thought of next time turns my stomach. I want this woman, Susan, to be the asshole's last victim.

"The guy came through this way—" Marty points to a broken branch "—but he raked his footprints on the way out."

"He brought a rake?"

"He did. Clever, isn't he?"

"Guess so." I know the perp's smart, but I'm in no mood to flatter his handiwork.

Sam shakes her head. "Anything on the branches?"

Perhaps the perp snagged his jacket coming through and left us a fiber.

"Not so far."

"Thanks, Marty." Sam's disappointed but still polite. "Let me know if you find anything."

"Will do."

The forensics team will be here for at least another hour.

"Let's go," Sam says.

We walk back the way we came, passing Susan's body. I peer into the undergrowth and look at her one more time, but then tear my eyes away from her. Could I really have dreamt about Susan's murder?

Sam and I walk toward the street. Over the ridge come two TV crews, each with a reporter and a camera operator.

We instinctively put our heads down, hoping to go unnoticed. But our ploy doesn't work. One of the reporters knows Sam.

"Agent Wright, is this the work of the Slasher?"

The press has christened our killer the D.C. Slasher. Descriptive, I guess.

A microphone is shoved in Sam's face.

"No comment."

We keep walking. The other reporter also thrusts her microphone in front of Sam, hoping for more.

"What's the FBI's involvement in this case?"

"You know the answer to that question." Sam quickens her pace and I follow suit.

"What's the killer like? What does your profile tell us?"

Sam ignores the questions and keeps walking. The reporters stay with us for a few steps, then move on, hurrying down the hill to the crime scene. They know they have a better chance of getting a statement from D.C. police than FBI.

Once out of earshot, Sam says, "Damn vultures."

I'm inclined to agree, but I also know they're only doing their job. Even though I avoid them, I'm probably a bit more sympathetic to reporters than Sam. I have to be, one of my school friends from Melbourne is a reporter with Channel 10. She covers crime and often has to hassle cops and witnesses for statements.

I decide to change the topic. "Are you freaked out by the note?"

"A little," she says without the usual melodic ring to her voice.

"So, who knows you're working this case?"

"Well, the whole world now." She glances back at the TV crew, who have parked themselves right on top of the crime-scene tape.

"But who knew yesterday?"

"That's the million-dollar question. I rang Flynn and he told his partner and boss, as you'd expect. Then there are our guys."

"And that information's supposed to be kept quiet."

"Well, someone's talked. The perp knew I was on the case."

"Who would know? Where are the records kept?"

"Well, it's no secret internally. Assistants, Pike, forensics, VICAP, they'd all know. Then admin too, for the files. And on top of that you're talking partners. Say Hunter tells his wife about his cases, and she asks who got what case, she tells her sister, who tells a friend. Especially with the D.C. case, because of all the press it's getting."

"True."

"Or we could have had an internal leak to the press. For all I know, it could have been in last night's edition of the *Post*."

"Yeah, you're right." It would be an impossible lead to track down.

"What do you think of the note?" Sam asks as we reach the ridge.

"He's definitely challenging you. Baiting you. He follows the newspapers and your cases closely."

"And he's been watching me."

"Mmm. And that can't be a good thing." I try to lighten the moment.

Sam looks over her shoulder, down to the crime scene. "Think he's watching us now?"

"Could be. He's probably in that lot." I motion toward the crowd of onlookers. We stop on the ridge.

Sam nods and forces a smile. We both know it's common for killers to watch the discovery of their crime. It allows them to relive the thrill of the kill and the control they felt over the victim. But you can't detain every passerby who stares at a police scene. Crime sites are made for onlookers—flashing lights, lots of police officers and other officials—everyone stops to look. It's human nature, albeit one of our darker traits.

Sam turns back and starts walking again. "Well, we've got his picture then."

I'm soon in step with her again. "Yep."

It's standard practice to photograph all crime-scene voyeurs, just in case. There have been cases that have broken that way—the same face turning up at two or more crime scenes. Cops get suspicious, start to investigate. And then that face turns out to be the perp.

We step off the grass and onto the pathway.

"I'm going to work up the profile as soon as we get back. After I've seen Rivers, that is," Sam says.

"I wonder what he'll make of this. He won't be happy about the killer's contact with the unit."

"No. Hey, why don't you come with me to see him? I'll tell him that you've been helping me out."

"Sure, if you want."

"Well, it won't hurt bringing the teacher's pet along." The normal Sam surfaces again.

"Ha, ha," I say. "Has it ever happened before? A killer contacting the profiler?"

"I think there have been a couple of cases, but not since I've been with the unit."

"No doubt Rivers has got procedures. Marco reckons he'll be pissed."

"You're off the case!" Rivers says to Sam.

"What?"

I bite my tongue. Neither of us is prepared for the intensity of his response.

"You heard me. That's the procedure. If a killer gets personal with a profiler, we reassign. We can't play into his hands and give the killer a relationship with one of our people."

"But surely we can't just submit and give him the power," Sam says. "It'll make him think we're afraid."

"It's not fear, it's good sense." Rivers stands and moves away from his desk. "This is the best approach."

"But why?" Sam's standing now. "I've done most of the work and it will only take a few hours to come up with a complete profile. Hunter has refined the cops' victimologies, except for the girl today, and I've already started the profile."

"I don't care. It's procedure. End of story." He sits down and stares at his desk. "Tuldoon can take the case." He doesn't look up.

Sam gives me a look, raises her eyebrows and mouths the word *you* at me.

I smile. "I could take it, sir."

Rivers stares at me. "Why are you even here, Anderson? Haven't you got enough work?"

I take it like a punch in the stomach.

He flicks his eyes away and I can tell he feels guilty. It's out of character for him to lose his temper.

Sam steps in. "It will take Tuldoon at least a day or two to get up to speed—"

"For God's sake, Wright, sit down."

Sam sits. "And all Sophie would need is...?" She looks at me.

"A few hours, five tops," I say. "Then I can go back to my other cases."

Rivers doesn't say anything. I take this as encouragement.

"Why don't I draft the profile, then hand it over to Tuldoon? He can do the last victimology and check the profile against it." A compromise.

Rivers drums his fingers on his desk. He can't afford to lose two days of Tuldoon's time when it would only take five hours of mine.

"Anderson, why have you already spent time on this anyway? It was assigned to Wright."

"Sam and I did some work on the case last night, sir. Strictly after hours. Two heads are better than one."

"And what about your little outing this morning. You call that after hours?"

Now he's got me cornered.

"I asked her to come, sir," Sam says. "To be honest, I was a little unnerved by the letter."

"Exactly. Because the perp got personal with you."

"Yes, sir," Sam says. But I can tell she wants to fight him on it.

"And what if he was there?" Rivers says. "Maybe he thinks he's got two FBI profilers working his case." He shakes his head. "I don't like it. It feeds his ego."

"I'm happy to hand the case over," Sam says convincingly. "But it makes sense to give it to Sophie. By the time I brief Tuldoon on it…" She leaves the last sentence hanging for effect.

I jump in. "I can have the profile ready tomorrow. I'll do most of it at home tonight."

The fingers drum again. "And then you're off it. You hand it over to Tuldoon."

"Yes, sir."

"And Wright, you're off this now. I don't want you to have anything more to do with this case. I want you off it. Do you hear me?"

"I'm off."

"And Wright, watch yourself. In fact, I'm going to arrange for the cops to swing by your place a few times when they're patrolling."

"But—"

"No buts. You're getting drive-bys. We need to make sure his spying activities were a one-off and not the start of a stalking routine."

Sam takes a breath in but then thinks the better of arguing.

Rivers looks back down at his desk and starts scrawling on his notepad. Our dismissal is obvious.

"That was intense," I say to Sam in the corridor.

"I've never seen him like that. Did you see the vein on this head?"

"That sucker was pumping."

"He's not usually such a stickler for procedures either," Sam says.

She's been working with him for a couple of years, so she'd know.

"I guess the pressure's getting to him. His team is dwindling."

Sam nods then says, "So we'll work on it together?"

"I knew you wouldn't hand it over."

"And I knew you knew that." She waves her finger at me and smiles. "Thanks for playing along in there. And don't worry, I know how you hate breaking the rules. It will be our little secret. Deal?" She holds out her hand.

"Deal," I say and we shake on it.

"Maybe we should have spit on our hands. Or blood perhaps?"

I laugh.

We get to Sam's office first. "So, do you want to see the profile tonight? After the gym?" she says.

"Shit, I'm training." I remember the sparring session I'd set up with Marco a few days ago. "Marco."

"Really? Just you and Marco?"

"Do you want to come?"

"You know what they say, honey. Three's a crowd," she says with a wink.

"Come on, train with us."

"I don't take my hand-to-hand combat quite as seriously as you two. Besides, I know you like the extra workout the guys give you."

She's right. I've been taking kung fu lessons for eight years and Marco has been training for ten. I do get a better workout and test of my skills with him than with Sam. She's better with a gun than her arms and legs.

"Why don't I drop by your place later?" After Rivers's reaction, I really don't want Sam to be working on this case alone.

"Don't worry. I'll drop the profile off at your apartment on my way home. Besides, you might be busy tonight, girl." She smiles, spins and walks into her office.

Incorrigible. I love her.

When Sophie was at the park too, I couldn't have been happier. To have them both there to view my masterpiece was beyond my wildest dreams. Now I have their attention.

Sophie's shoulder-length blond hair had been whisked across her face by the wind, yet every hair was perfect. The cold made her cheeks glow pink against the translucence of her pale, smooth skin and when she looked up I could see, even from where I was standing, the intensity of her blue eyes. She was wearing my favorite suit too. The knee-length, charcoal skirt that shows off her slim legs and hips without hugging too hard to the contours of her body, accompanied by the short, tailored jacket that displays the womanly indent of her waist. So gorgeous, so sexy, yet so seemingly unaware of her power over men. Awkward almost.

Sam, on the other hand, broadcasts her beauty with every step, every movement. I don't know which I prefer.

I relive the pleasure of seeing them. The anticipation. Even cutting short my time with the redhead was worth it.

But the pleasure was the greatest when my darling Samantha looked over her shoulder. She knows I'm watching. She's looking for me. She's trying to figure out who I am right now! She can't see me, but I can see her.

I look at my latest photo of her, fresh from my darkroom. Her face is gentle yet sculptured. Her long curls of dark brown hair are tied up, but a few strands give away the wild nature of her hair. I imagine it flowing down her back. Her chiseled jawline supports her beautifully large mouth, full lips and white, straight teeth. I study her face and imagine it contorting in pleasure. I get more pleasure from Sophie and Sam than I do from *my* girls. They're so close to me.

Bliss rushes through my body and settles in my groin. I relieve myself with thoughts of Samantha Wright and Sophie Anderson.

CHAPTER 06

I slam my leg into the punching bag Marco holds, and smile as he's thrown off balance by the impact. I get a lot more power from my legs than my arms. It's probably true for most women.

Marco moves the bag up and down his body, mirroring a moving target, and I aim for the center with each strike and kick. Then he moves it from side to side, gaining speed. I react and deliver a series of kicks: right front kick off the back leg; two swift side kicks with my left then right leg; a 180-degree side kick; and finally a high roundhouse kick, aimed at his head.

"Nice," he says. Then responds by mixing it up more, moving forward and backward. I adjust accordingly and add punches. After about ten minutes, I'm dripping with sweat and the power in my kicks and punches is waning.

"Come on, Sophie."

I rise to the challenge and deliver another series of kicks, culminating in a 360-degree side kick that harnesses all my remaining strength. It has the desired effect and Marco staggers to the side.

"Not bad." He grins. "For a girl."

But I'm not biting. I know my muscles aren't as powerful as a man's. It means I have to be better and faster. I have to train harder. I guzzle three-quarters of my water and rest my hands on my thighs with my head down to get my breath back.

Marco moves closer and takes a few sips of his water. He stands close, real close. I look up at his face. He's barely got a bead of sweat on him.

I pick up my towel and wipe the sweat from my face.

"Your turn." I reach for the bag that's resting on Marco's leg. He picks it up and hands it to me. Our hands brush gently. I look at Marco. He's noticed the contact too.

I smile and remember the heat of his body next to mine the night we nearly kissed. There was that awkward silence that often seems to occur before a first kiss and I could feel our bodies getting closer. Our faces getting closer. And then, just as our lips were about to touch, I pulled away. It wasn't Matt that stopped me. Matt and I would have ended even if I hadn't moved to the States. It's not a man in Australia holding me back, it's me. There's just something about Marco that I can't quite put my finger on. My fear that he's a womanizer? But Sam's right. I do like him and maybe I *am* ready.

I crouch in a low horse position, with the bag up, covering the side of my body, ready to take the strikes. I brace myself heavily, knowing how hard it is to keep on my feet when Marco gets going. He's strong and fast. I use my speed instead, and keep on the move. It's heavy work for me and I'm exhausted by the time we've finished the bag work. Marco is finally dripping with sweat.

I refill my water bottle and wipe my face again, ready for some one-on-one sparring. We suit up with a mouth-guard, protector pads, gloves and helmets. Standard martial arts safety gear. The gym has almost cleared out and the section we're in is empty.

I glance at my watch. "Seven-thirty. No wonder I'm hungry."

"Me too. How about we finish up in fifteen?"

"Sounds good. You attack first."

We stand side by side and move into low horse stances, arms in guard position. I take a deep breath, readying myself for the incoming strikes and kicks.

Marco starts with a hook punch that's coming directly to my head. I block it with my left, outside arm and look to the right, ready for his second punch. This is aimed at my stomach and I use a lower block to divert it. I take a step back, swapping legs, and Marco sends a round-house kick my way. A cross-block stops it dead. I love being able to match Marco. It also makes me feel safe— I could defend an attack.

I sense his hands coming down from above me and I immediately form an upper cross-block with my hands above my head, catching his double punch. I dodge and deflect a straight punch, followed by a side kick. Our dance continues for five minutes before we take a two-minute breather and swap positions. Now I attack and he defends. I think quickly, coming up with a fast series of punches and kicks, but only one meets its mark. I keep them coming, as hard and fast as I can, but my energy is waning. The intensity is broken when I throw a sloppy crescent kick, which Marco catches instead of blocking. A quick, sudden backward movement from him sends me up in the air, only to return to the mats on my back. I hit the mats hard, but only my pride is hurt. Marco's grinning face comes into my field of vision and I can't help but laugh.

He offers me his hand, but instead of taking it I hook my left foot around his right ankle and position my right foot just above his knee. If this was a real-life situation I'd go for a direct hit on his knee, but it's too risky for training because I could damage a ligament. I bend my left leg quickly, folding it inward so my ankle comes toward my butt. At the same time I push Marco's thigh with my right leg. I complete the whole move within a split second, not long enough for Marco to prepare himself for the conflicting forces on his leg. He tumbles backward onto the mat. I rock back on my hands in a somersault position and push off, legs going skyward. I arch my back and land on my feet. It's a move I learned not in kung fu but from a Gene Kelly movie when I was twelve. Now I stand over Marco, grinning.

"Not bad, Anderson," he says.

I smile again, give him a flirtatious wink and make an overdramatic turn and take one step away.

"That's it," he says, grabbing my ankle. Holding on to my ankle, he rolls away from me. I don't have time to steady myself or break free, so within a couple of seconds I'm down on the mat too. We lie next to each other, laughing. I casually drop my arm onto his stomach. And we both stop laughing. I withdraw my hand and we lie there silently for a few seconds, getting our breath back.

Marco gets up and offers me his hand again. "No tricks this time."

"Never."

I take his hand and he easily pulls me to a standing position in tight to his body. We're close again. Too close for work colleagues and too close for friends. I become extremely aware of the fact that he's still holding my hand. I gently pull away.

"Let's hit the showers," I say, then realize the line's come out all wrong, like an invitation for him to join me in a shower. My cheeks flush. "I mean, I'm going to have a shower."

Marco smiles. He lets go of my hand but speaks before the contact is totally lost. "How about dinner, Sophie?"

"I don't think that's a good idea."

"And why not?"

I'm silent, thinking of a response.

"So it's settled. I'll see you out front in twenty minutes." He grabs his towel and then he's gone, leaving me a little shell-shocked.

I walk to the change room. So that's it. My first date with Josh Marco…and I've only got twenty minutes to cool down and make myself look respectable. I decide on a lukewarm shower, hoping this will calm down the redness in my face. I lather myself quickly but thoroughly. I want to smell just right.

My mind is cluttered with thoughts about the date. Already I'm making assumptions and trying to make decisions. Will we kiss each other? Should I sleep with him? Should I simply excuse myself to avoid the whole situation? Why are relationships so complicated? And that's before I even start seeing someone.

I towel-dry myself and catch a glimpse of my reflection. Despite the coolish shower, big red blotches still cover my face and my hair is clumped together in sweaty strands. I should have washed it but it takes so long to dry. I have some magic to work to make myself look decent, let alone attractive.

Once I'm dry, I turn on the cold-water tap and hold my wrists underneath the icy stream for a couple of minutes. Cooling down is my first priority. Then I dry my hands and open my locker. What have I got to work with? I'm relieved to find some fresh underwear, though it's a basic light blue cotton set. Nothing fancy. I pull on the panties and fasten the bra, jiggling my breasts into the cups. I put on some deodorant before grabbing the skirt of my suit and stepping into it. Next I pull on a black, three-quarter-sleeve cross-top. The stockings stay in my locker, I'm way too hot for stockings. I slip into my heels.

Makeup. I check the time. It's been fifteen minutes already. My skin is still blotchy, but it's gradually calming down. I spray a fine mist of toning solution on my face, hoping it will cool down my face. A thin layer of tinted moisturizer follows, spread evenly over my pale skin. A dusting of powder finishes the base and hides most of the redness. I smear pale pink lipstick on my lips and cover it with gloss. My face is done. I don't bother with mascara as I get my eyelashes and eyebrows tinted every six weeks. One of the necessities for blondes.

Hair. The problem child. I pull it out of the elastic that tied it back during my workout and shower, and shake my head from side to side to see what I've got to work with. Better than I was expecting. Most of the sweaty parts are now on the underneath and it's only around the front hairline area that it needs work. I rummage through my locker until I find my hair dryer and plug it in. I gently blow-dry the front area, with the dryer on low. My body temperature rises again, but it can't be helped. It doesn't take long to dry the front roots and soon I'm brushing my hair and fastening it with a barrette. I stuff my workout clothes back into my gym bag and push it into my locker. I'll take them home for a wash tomorrow.

Time for the final verdict. I stand in front of the mirror and look myself up and down with the critical eye of a woman. Not bad. The heel and skirt show off my shapely legs, a trait that all the women in my family share, and the fitted skirt and V-neck top outline my slight curves. I pull my neckline down slightly to reveal a little bit of cleavage and move closer to the mirror to do a final check. My hair hangs almost perfectly straight, with just a small upturn at the bottom. My naturally strawberry-blond hair has added color with a few blonder highlights and some thin, orange-toned highlights. Parted on the side, the clip holds back the heavier side and I push the other side behind my ear. My facial features are compact—my fine nose and thin lips are traits that I dislike, but my light blue eyes and high cheekbones make up for them. My skin tone looks quite smooth, with only a little redness left in my cheeks. A healthy glow?

I walk out the front door. Marco is standing outside, hands in pockets, looking just the right combination of businessman and athlete. The sight of him leaves me wondering if the only decision I'll be making tonight is "your place or mine?"

I've actually done incredibly well to resist him for six months. Especially when his personality, so far, seems just as good as his physical appearance. Of course, in my experience most guys in the law-enforcement business aren't as straightforward as they appear. Plus, they tend to be pretty macho, which is a real turnoff. It's hard to find the right balance between masculine strength and macho bravado. So far Marco seems to be treading that fine line right down the center. He is a little secretive though, which plays on my natural curiosity.

We choose an Italian place in Dumfries and within fifteen minutes we've both parked. Five minutes later we've ordered. The waiter returns with two glasses of Chianti. The ambience is romantic, a little too romantic for my liking. Dangerous.

I guess Marco senses it too, and we're both silent. I can almost hear us both trying to think of a topic of conversation. Stupid, really, we've never had difficulty before. It's just that I can't seem to think straight.

"So what did you think of your first look at East Potomac Park?" Marco tries.

"Pretty." I pause. "Except for the dead body."

"That'll always spoil a first impression."

We both laugh a little.

"Are your folks still coming out in the spring?" he asks.

"Looks that way. I've put in for my leave, just waiting for Rivers to approve it. I can only get a week though."

"Well, you haven't done your time yet, not like the rest of us Bureau boys…and girls."

"No." I smile at his last-minute addition. Women are moving their way up the ranks of the FBI, but we're still outnumbered by almost six to one. It can be pretty boysy. But law enforcement's like that all over the world.

A beat of silence again.

"So, where are you going to take your folks?"

"I'll show them around D.C. a bit, then I think we'll go to New York and Boston for a couple of days. They're flying in via Hawaii." I roll my eyes. "Then L.A. to visit Dad's family."

"Does he miss the States?"

"Not anymore. He said he did at first, but that once we were born his family was in Australia anyway."

"We?"

I take a sip of wine and compose myself. "I meant me. Once I was born."

Marco pauses and looks as though he's going to pursue the matter. No one here knows about my brother. About what happened to him all those years ago. It's in my file obviously, but I don't volunteer the information. Even at home not many people know about it. I never even told Matt. Even with him I didn't drop my final layer of defenses. Sometimes I wonder if I'm even capable of it.

Time for a topic change.

"No doubt they'll give me a hard time about my new job."

"At least they're consistent," Marco says with a smile.

During the Henley case I told Marco about my parents' distaste for my chosen career. They thought I was heading along such a sensible path when I studied psychology, but I never lost sight of my ultimate ambition—to save people.

"My parents hated it when I was on the force in Melbourne and they hate it even more now that I'm thousands of miles away."

"And hunting serial killers."

"Yeah, that too." I smile.

"You can never please parents." Marco shrugs.

"Yours too?"

"Oh, yeah." He drags the words out. "My dad's devastated I'm not following in his footsteps. But who'd want to be a politician?"

"I'd have to agree with you. Is he retired?"

"Not yet. He keeps promising Mom 'next year,' but next year never comes."

"Is your mom patient?"

"She has to be to put up with him."

I smile. "And you never thought about politics?"

"Not really. I've seen what my folks have been through."

"He's governor somewhere, right?"

"Uh-huh. Governor of Massachusetts at the moment, but he had high hopes."

"Top office?"

"You got it. And when it was obvious he wasn't going to make it, I was his second chance." Marco takes a sip of wine. "Like I said, no pleasing parents."

"There's time for you yet."

"You and my folks could be a team."

I laugh. "No, I think I'd have to take your side on this one."

Marco changes the topic. "Hawaii's nice."

"You've been there?"

"Yeah."

"For work or pleasure?"

"Work."

"Bureau? Air force?"

"Air force. I was stationed at Hickam Air Force Base for a few months."

"Which island is it on?"

"Oahu. Right next door to the Honolulu Airport."

"Nice."

"It's not a bad work location." He smiles.

I imagine kissing Marco. Kissing Josh Marco. But the spell is broken when the waiter puts down our meals.

The first few mouthfuls are eaten in silence, and hurriedly. We're both starving after the workout. But it's more than that.

I keep eating, keep my head down, afraid to look up. Afraid of Josh. Why am I so nervous? I'm being ridiculous.

I look up. "How's your risotto?"

Josh maintains eye contact and smiles. "Good. Do you want some?" He pushes his plate slightly toward me and I take a forkful.

I return the gesture. "Gnocchi?"

"Sure."

He pierces one piece of gnocchi with his fork, pops it into his mouth and follows it with some wine, all the while holding my gaze.

"So, what did you do in Honolulu?" I say, trying to hide my nervousness.

"Nothing much. Training missions mostly. And some real missions too." He pauses.

"Oh, right. This is the 'if I tell you any more I'll have to kill you' moment."

He takes a sip of wine. "Something like that."

I narrow my eyes, unable to tell whether Josh is dramatizing or if perhaps he really was involved in some top-secret missions when he was in the air force.

"Nothing more to say on the subject?" I pursue it.

"Not much more to tell." He takes some more risotto, grinning in between chewing.

Bastard is enjoying the secrecy. I won't give him the satisfaction of asking him about it again. My stubborn streak takes over.

He breaks the silence. "So, run me through the D.C. case."

I'm reluctant to fill our first date with shoptalk, but I'm too nervous to think of a better topic. We spend the rest of the meal talking about the D.C. murders and trying to come up with something new. But there's nothing new to be found. Not yet. We're still waiting on forensics from the park, of course. Maybe Marty will find something.

We're drinking coffee when another moment of awkwardness interrupts our conversation. Looking at Marco, silent, I'm suddenly acutely aware of the fact that it's been over seven months since I've had sex and every inch of me is tingling in anticipation of what might happen tonight. My resistance is falling by the wayside. My feelings for Josh are undeniably powerful. And Sam's right—I've always felt this way about him.

We pay the bill, with only scattered conversation. No plans are verbalized and out in the cold air my defensive wall starts to rebuild itself. But Josh is too quick, and he grabs my hand, holding it gently. The wall crumbles.

"Josh?" But instead of voicing my concerns, silence falls and once again our bodies move closer. I smell the familiar scent of Josh's aftershave, Acqua de Gio, and I like it. He presses his hand into the small of my back and leans down until our lips meet. It's gentle, hesitant at first. I move myself closer into him and put my arms around his neck as we kiss again, this time parting our mouths. Again, it's gentle, tentative, hesitant on both our parts. Then the third kiss is more intense and overtly sexual. Our bodies are pushed close against one another as we kiss again.

"Wow," Josh says.

I nod, happy that we're both feeling the same thing. I'd forgotten how wonderful first kisses are—I was with Matt for seven years, after all.

"Want a ride home?" Josh says.

But we both know that isn't the real question. My car's around the corner, just like his.

I hesitate, my head fighting my heart and sex drive. "Sure, why not."

The car ride is filled with silence and sexual tension. The first kiss has whetted my appetite and I want more. But will it only be a one-night stand with awkward moments at work, and our professional relationship, not to mention our friendship, ruined? Maybe that's what

Josh is into. But I don't want that. Not from Josh. I'd go outside of work if all I wanted was sex.

We get to my place and I hesitate again. Josh doesn't push the matter.

I press my lips together, unsure. "You want to come up?"

Josh answers quickly. "Okay." He puts the car in Park.

We walk briskly up the stairs, eager to be in each other's arms. I fumble with the lock and pick up the large envelope that's underneath my door.

"Sam," I say, placing the envelope on the dining table as we move inside. "It's her D.C. profile."

Josh comes in, and we both look at each other, uncertain.

"Josh, I don't want things to be awkward. At work, I mean." I finally manage to voice my biggest concern.

"They needn't be."

I pull away and move into the kitchen. "Do you want a drink?" My eyes dart around the room, anywhere but at Josh.

"If you're having one I will."

I don't really want anything else…except Josh. I walk back to him and wrap my arms around him. We kiss. A deep, lustful kiss. We don't stop as we fumble our way to the bedroom, losing items of clothing on the way. By the time we reach the bed, Josh's shirt and belt are off and both my jacket and top are off too. I'm surprised to see and feel a hairless chest, especially given his Italian heritage. I run my fingers over his smooth skin and squeeze my hands down his biceps.

He slows things down, running his hands up my spine and then down and across to my stomach. He kisses my neck. Gentle wet kisses intermingled with the heat of his breath. I breathe heavily in response, kick my shoes off and undo his pants. He runs one hand through my hair and unzips my skirt. I step out of it as Josh steps out of his trousers. We're both down to our underwear. I push him onto the bed.

"It's going to be like that, is it?" he says, half joking but obviously excited.

With seven months of celibacy and sexual tension… you bet it is.

CHAPTER 07

I peel my eyes open and am greeted by Josh's face. He's propped up on his arm, watching me.

He kisses me gently on the shoulder. "Good morning."

"Morning."

"You were having a bad dream."

"Was I?" I ask a little too quickly. "What was I doing?"

"You were tossing and turning and talking, but I couldn't make out the words."

"Mmm." I don't remember it. Not last night's.

"You often have nightmares?"

"Yeah," I say, hesitant to reveal this fact to Josh.

"The cases?"

"I think so. I usually can't remember the dreams. You sleep okay?"

"I got a bit of shut-eye in there somewhere."

I smile. We both woke up a couple of times for repeat

performances, not being able to get enough of each other. I roll onto my back and splay my arms out. "I'm exhausted."

"Me too." Josh's free hand runs over my stomach. Perhaps I haven't tired him out enough. But the touch turns into a cuddle and he draws my body close to his and gently kisses my neck.

"What time is it?" I ask.

"A quarter after seven."

I sit up. "Shit, I was supposed to go over that profile for Sam. I told Rivers it would be on his desk this morning."

"Do it at the office."

"I'm supposed to be doing it after hours. In fact, Rivers pulled Sam off the case and he thinks I'm doing the whole thing."

"Really? I didn't pick you for a rebel."

"I'm just helping out a friend."

"Why don't I drive us in, you can go over the profile in the car."

"That still won't be enough time."

"At least you can have a quick look at it."

It's my only option. Besides, my car's still in Dumfries.

The car ride is filled with silence as I read then reread the profile, making notes in my diary. There's more. More to the killer.

My first stop at Quantico is Sam's office. I've got a lot to talk to her about, personal and professional. I'm going to tell her I dreamt of Jean and Susan, and what happened to them. I wonder what she will make of it.

I wind my way through the corridors. The building is still quiet and my heels clip the linoleum floor loudly.

About half the offices I pass are dark and unopened, while the other half show signs of people just settling in. Sam's office is dark and locked.

I was counting on her being here so I could spill my guts. She must be running late. A huge pressure is building inside me and I need to release it. Where the hell is she?

Once in my office, I ring and leave a message for Sam and send her an e-mail.

I try desperately to refocus my mind on my cases. I try not to think of Josh, to replay the events over and over in my mind. Him touching me…me touching him… The only way to get my mind off last night is to absorb myself in a profile. I pick up my files and choose my next case. The Whistler case in Canada.

I've only just read the coroner's report when Sam drops by.

"You rang, honey?"

I smile, beckoning her into my office.

"That's a big smile," she says, obviously already guessing or hoping something's happened between Josh and I.

I nod and smile again, confirming her suspicions. Sam closes my office door.

"So, what happened?" she asks with glee.

"We trained. We had dinner. And we wound up back at my place."

"It's about time. How was it?"

"Great. Really great."

"So Marco showed you a good time?" she says with a wink.

"Yes," I say and feel myself blush.

If Sam was Australian, within a couple of minutes she'd have me giving her a blow-by-blow reconstruction of the whole evening's events. An Australian woman wouldn't be satisfied with yes as a response.

"You can't wipe that grin off your face, can you?"

I laugh.

"And you're an official double agent now."

"I guess so. But I presume I'll only be hearing that term from you. I certainly won't be telling anyone else about this yet."

"When's your next date?"

"I don't know." I furrow my brow. "We didn't talk about that."

"Don't worry! He's sweet on you."

"I hope so. The last thing I want is a one-night stand with a fellow agent."

"Stop being so serious. Besides, it ain't gonna go that way."

"God, could I do with a dose of your confidence."

She laughs, her loud, raucous laugh. "You certainly don't have any reason not to be confident. Especially with men. You're smart, tall, blond, gorgeous and thin, not to mention good-hearted. Too good-hearted."

"Stop, you're embarrassing me. Besides, you're forgetting stubborn, untrusting, shy and defensive."

"You? Stubborn?"

"Very funny." I pause, seeing a way to introduce the other topic I desperately need to speak to Sam about—another one of my "traits," these dreams and nightmares. Hopefully Sam can come up with a rational explanation. But I stop myself. It'll sound too crazy.

"The bad news is I didn't get much of a chance to look over your profile," I say instead.

"You mean *your* profile."

"Yeah, right. My profile. I had a quick read, that's all."

"Any thoughts?"

"There's something missing. There's more to him."

"I agree. But what?"

"I'm not sure yet. We can hand it to Rivers now, or we can work on it some more tonight."

"Well, you're going to have to deal with Rivers because I'm officially off this case."

I'm worried about missing my deadline, but the profile's not right yet. "Let's hold off for a day. I want to get this perfect."

"Up to you, honey."

"I'm going to take the wimp's way out though. I'm sending him an e-mail." I type a quick message. "Done." I click the send button.

I was so excited about telling Sam about Josh, I've totally forgotten about the killer and his note. Sam was unnerved yesterday.

"Any sign of him. The killer?" I ask.

"No." She speaks softly. "All's quiet."

"You are being careful?"

"Of course. I checked the apartment as soon as I got home last night. Then checked all my locks before I went to bed. I've also been wary about being followed."

"Good. And the boys in blue?"

"Cops did two drive-bys that I saw and probably a few more in the middle of the night."

"Good," I repeat. "So how are you feeling about the note?"

She pauses. "To be honest, I'm still a little bothered by it, but I'm off the case now...kind of."

"But does the killer know that?"

She shrugs. "I'll be extra careful for the next week or so."

I raise my eyebrows.

"Okay, until we nail the guy."

"That's better."

"I don't think I'm a target. He'd be stupid to take an FBI agent."

"True."

"Anyways, you'll be there to protect me tonight." She smiles.

"Together, we're indestructible." We both laugh.

It's eight at night and Sam is serving up bean burritos at her place. She lives in Key Towers, a sixteen-story apartment block in Alexandria, which is less than ten miles from the heart of D.C. It's a really nice apartment complex and we've even talked about moving into a larger apartment in the complex together when our leases run out. Sam would be a great roommate. Her apartment is modern, with cream carpet, thin Venetian blinds and the safety of white decor in the bathroom and kitchen. She has livened the place up with splashes of color, including two bright red sofas.

Sam plonks down my plate and a bottle of beer in front of me.

"It's like having a husband," she says.

"I thought it was only Australian men who liked to have beer served to them."

"A universal male thing, I'd say."

I laugh.

Sam dishes up her own burrito and keeps talking. "I had a case once when I was working homicide…a poisoning case," she says, slopping some guacamole and sour cream on top of the bean mix. "A woman poisoned her husband. I interviewed her and she looked me in the eye and said she just got sick of cooking his dinner and serving him beer every night." Sam rolls her burrito, sits down and takes a swig of beer. "So one day she's cooking their evening meal and decides, 'Hell, I don't want to do this tomorrow, or ever again.' So she gets some rat poison from the shed and mixes it in with his meal."

"Nice."

"It gets better. She wanted to go for justifiable homicide."

I laugh. "That would open up a floodgate."

"The law didn't see it as justifiable, but I bet there'd be a lot of women who would argue for it."

"You think you'll ever get married?" I ask.

"Me? I don't think I'm cut out to be a wife. Besides, I've got other plans for my life."

"Such as?"

"I want to be the first female director of the FBI."

"You *have* got plans," I say, not sure how serious she is.

"Well, I don't know about director, but I do want to get somewhere with my career in the Bureau. And I want to travel. What about you? Do you think you'll ever get hitched?"

"Maybe…one of these days."

"Marco could be your man," she says with a wink.

"It's a bit too early for that sort of talk."

I play with my meal and take another sip of beer.

"Anything wrong, honey?" Sam says. "Worried I'm poisoning you?"

I laugh. "No. If you wanted to kill someone, I reckon you'd be a gun kind of girl."

"Do you now?"

"Just a shot in the dark."

"Ha, ha. And what about you?" She studies me through narrowed eyes, moving her head from side to side slowly in an exaggerated gesture. "You'd like to do hand-to-hand combat. You'd want to do it the hard way."

"Only if I knew I was going to win."

Sam's eyes are on me, watching my fork circle a mound of refried beans.

"Oh, come on, Sophie."

I quickly shovel a big forkful of food into my mouth. But it doesn't stop her.

"I know something's up. Is it Marco?"

I finish chewing. "No. Everything's fine. In fact, he paid me a visit and booked our next date."

"Really?"

"He's going to cook for me. At his place."

"Really?" repeats Sam. "So things are going well."

"Yeah. I think so. Like I said, it's early days." I smile. "But he seems to have a lot of attractive features."

"I'll say."

"I'm not just talking about that."

"No, I know. He's a nice guy. Even if he is a ladies' man."

I draw a quick intake of breath and open my eyes wider.

"I'm joking. I'm joking," she says. "Jeez, you *are* sweet on him."

"Yep." The truth is, I've been pushing Josh away for so long, and now I've done an about-face. I'm falling for him all right, and hard. I barely want to admit it to myself, let alone Sam.

We finish our first burrito and Sam dishes us both another one. We're halfway through when she broaches the topic again.

"If it isn't Marco, then what's up?" she asks, taking a mouthful.

I take a deep breath, preparing myself. Sam leans in.

"I don't know how to say this without sounding crazy. Totally crazy."

"Just spit it out, girl. You're amongst friends. Well, friend."

I still hesitate. Do I really want to do this? Once I tell Sam, there's no going back. But I need to get someone else's opinion, and Sam is the only candidate. I don't think I have a choice. I take the plunge.

"I've been seeing things. About cases."

"What do you mean?"

I don't respond. How do I say this?

Sam gives me a long hard look.

I stand up, move away from the table and stare into the distance. "It sounds crazy." I turn around and take a breath. "You know Jean, from your D.C. case file?"

"Yes." Sam puts her fork down and turns in her seat to face me.

"Remember I recognized her and told you I must have seen the file."

Sam nods.

"I've never seen that case file before. Hunter never showed it to me, but I've seen her. Twice in fact."

"What do you mean?"

"I had a dream. A nightmare. And in it I saw Jean, dead, positioned just like she was at the crime scene."

Sam doesn't respond.

"And then there's the latest victim—Susan," I say.

"What about her?"

"In the dream I saw her walking to her car."

Sam's face wrinkles in confusion. "Susan was abducted in a parking lot, just like Teresa." She stands up.

"Yes, I know. I saw her from the killer's perspective."

"Okay. Okay. Let's think about this logically." Sam sits on the sofa and rests her chin on her hand.

"There's one other thing."

"What?"

"The night Susan was killed, I witnessed her murder."

"In a dream?" Sam seems unconvinced.

"Not quite. I was dropping off to sleep when it happened. It was after you left my place, at exactly five past midnight. I saw Susan being killed."

"What do you mean *saw*?"

"It's like seeing a series of still photos or watching a poor-quality video. Images of her flashed into my mind." A tightness comes across my chest and I fight back the tears and panic.

Sam tries to absorb it all.

"Has this ever happened before? In Australia?"

"I often have bad dreams, but I usually don't remember them." But as I say it I'm taken back twenty-five years, to John. It *had* happened before. The week

John disappeared I had several nightmares, but the worst one was on the night he was taken. It was so vivid, and when I woke up John was gone. The police decided he was a runaway, but I knew what had really happened to him. He was kidnapped and murdered. I'd seen his murder with my own eyes. I'd felt his killer's emotions. I tried to tell the police, I tried to tell Mom and Dad, but no one believed me. After a few days, I doubted myself—why would I think and say something so horrible? It was just a nightmare. But then weeks passed. Months passed. And still no word from John. By then it was too late. Just over a year after he was taken, John's body was found in the bush, sixty miles from Shepparton, where I grew up. Maybe if I'd made them believe me, I could have stopped it.

"Sophie?"

I wipe the tears from my cheek and turn around. "I used to get hunches, but everyone gets hunches." I'm not ready to tell Sam about my brother. Not yet.

"Lots of police work is based on hunches," Sam says. "But that's not what we're talking about?"

"Not this time."

"Getting too involved?" She's grasping at straws now.

"I wish it was that simple. But no matter how involved I get, how could I see these things? I thought it was my imagination until I saw Susan lying there in that flower bed."

Sam nods, obviously bewildered by it all.

"Have you ever worked with a psychic?" I stumble over the forbidden word.

"Yes, a couple of times. They were helpful. Once, the

woman actually saved a young girl who had been abducted."

"Sam, I've been fighting this for days now, and it's the only explanation."

"Okay, so let's assume you're having premonitions."

Another taboo word.

"It's crazy, isn't it?"

Sam thinks before she speaks. "I don't know much about this stuff, Soph, but I know you. I trust you."

I smile, relieved.

"Have you had any more premonitions about the D.C. killer?" she asks.

"No, not since the other night, when Susan was murdered."

Silence.

"I think we'd better keep these visions of yours between the two of us for the moment," Sam says eventually. "Unless you want to tell Marco."

"Are you crazy? That'd scare him off for sure!"

She laughs. "Possibly. What about Dr. Rosen?"

"I thought about her. But I don't want this on my record. Especially when I don't really know what's going on yet."

As the Bureau psychologist, Amanda would feel compelled to tell Rivers or Pike. She'd probably think I was crazy and pull me off active duty. Another burnout in the BAU.

"Okay, so we've agreed. We'll keep it between the two of us."

"I know it must sound weird."

"Well, it's certainly a little out there, but it does happen. So, you haven't had any other visions?" She breaks the tension with a little too much emphasis on the word *visions*.

"No."

I'm relieved to have a confidante, except that talking about it makes it sound even crazier than when I think about it in the confined space of my mind.

She stands up. "Come on. I've slaved over the stove and you're going to let it go to waste."

I laugh and we sit back down and finish our dinner. After we've cleared up she empties her briefcase onto the kitchen table and we spread out the D.C. photos.

"So Jean is the girl you saw dead?"

"Yes, but she had a strange marking on her thigh. Just below her hip and on the outside. A tattoo, I think. It looked Celtic."

Sam picks up a photo of Jean, dead, and examines it closely. "I can't see anything, but I'll ask Flynn and Jones for a blowup. Her thighs are cut up pretty bad. It might be tough to see a tattoo."

"He's really gone overboard with the stabbing," I say.

"Yes, but like we talked about at your place, it's still controlled, rehearsed, rather than an overkill pattern." Sam shuffles her profile to the top of the pile. "I've officially classified him as an organized offender."

I nod. Organized offender rings true with other elements of the crime too. They tend to plan their attacks in detail, use restraints, personalize the victim, demand submission and transport the victim or body. Our guy did all these things. Perhaps the time of death was a moment of disorganized MO, but the killer was definitely in control of the abductions and murders. Unfortunately for us, organized types are also harder to catch—they tend to have high IQs.

"Any trophies?" I ask.

Serial killers usually take trophies of their kills so they can relive the murder over and over again. Just looking at the trophy gives them pleasure, in their sick way.

"Jean usually wore a bracelet, but it was never found, and Teresa used to wear a ring on her little finger."

"It'll all be evidence," I say. The serial killer's habitual trophy-taking usually forms part of the physical evidence against them. That's partly how they got Milat's conviction for the backpacker murders in Australia. The police found water bottles, backpacks, scarves and even a tent belonging to the victims in Milat's attic. Pretty good evidence in a court of law. "When was Susan abducted?" I ask.

"Looks like three days before she was killed."

"Susan for three days, Jean for five days and Teresa for eight days."

Sam nods and picks up a photo of Jean.

"So…um…do you want to touch the photo? To hold it?"

I look at Sam quizzically, not understanding. Then it hits me—psychics like to touch things. It can trigger their visions.

"Oh. Yeah. Right," I say awkwardly.

I take the photo and close my eyes, waiting for something, but I'm not sure what. I feel ridiculous. A smile plays around my lips.

Sam picks up on it and next thing I know she's chanting. "Ommmmmm. Ommmmm."

We both burst out laughing.

"This is ridiculous!" I snort in between laughs. I take a mouthful of beer and then almost send it across the room as another peal of laughter escapes from me. I put the photo down.

My near miss with the beer sets Sam off and she collapses onto the chair, laughing hard.

But the moment of release disappears quickly. I look into the eyes of Jean once again and a searing pain races through my eyes. I fall forward. Sam rushes to me and for a moment I see the shadowy figure of a man play across my field of vision. It's the killer. But before I can make out any of his features the vision fades.

"God, honey, are you okay?"

"I think I saw him."

"The killer?" She supports the underneath of my arm.

"Yes." The pain in my head and eyes eases slightly.

"Could you make him out?"

"No. It was dark. Like it was nighttime or he was in a darkened room. I could only see a shadow. A lurking presence. But I know it was him."

"You're as white as a sheet. Do you feel all right?"

"I've got a headache. A bad one."

"I'll get you some Tylenol. Hold on." Sam sits me down on her couch.

She returns a few moments later, pills and glass of water in hand. I gobble the pills. The pit of my stomach is filled with hatred, dread and fear. The hatred is his, the killer's, but the dread and fear are mine. I can't shake the feeling that something bad is going to happen. I think again of John and the nightmares I had all those years ago.

"Psychics often get very physical reactions when they see things," Sam says.

I hope my physical and emotional symptoms are just part of the insight and that they'll fade soon.

"Could you see where he was?"

"No. I was looking at the photo of Jean when it happened, so perhaps it was when he grabbed her."

"In her apartment?"

I shrug. "I don't know."

"Could you tell if it was inside or outside?"

"No. I couldn't make out anything except for his shape."

"Well, that's something. What was his shape like?"

"You think it was in proportion? To me?"

"Let's assume so."

"Okay." I run with the idea. Height and weight are something at least. I stand up. "I'd say he was about three inches taller than me." I hold my flat palm above my head. "I'm five-ten, so that makes him about six-one."

"Okay. Was he skinny? Fat?" Sam scribbles on her notepad.

"He had a muscular build. Not fat, but broad." I pause. "That's it."

Sam nods. "It's something."

"You reckon?"

"Well, if Flynn and Jones start interviewing a short, fat guy, we can steer them away."

I laugh. "You should try stand-up."

"I don't like big audiences," Sam says, but I can't imagine it's true.

"Do the cops have any suspects?"

"Not yet. They won't even have anyone to run the profile against."

"What about the note? Anything on that?"

"Nothing interesting yet. Marty's got the guys in Questioned Documents on it, but the perp used a standard blue Bic ballpoint, the type you can pick up just about anywhere."

"Paper?" I ask. But if the guy knew to use a run-of-the-mill pen, he probably did the same with the paper.

"Spirax notebook paper. And who knows how many of them have been sold in the U.S. in the past year."

"Great. No prints, I take it?"

"Nothing. The note's going to a handwriting expert for analysis tomorrow and they've got a forensic linguist looking at it too."

"Maybe that'll give us something."

"They're usually pretty good at pinpointing where the writer was raised, based on the dialect. And the handwriting expert will be able to tell us if he was trying to disguise his writing," Sam says.

"Where he grew up could help narrow things down."

"Especially if we cross-reference that with the VICAP info when it comes through."

"Surely we'll have to get some hits. Listen, I'm sorry I didn't look over the profile last night."

"Don't worry. You had other things on your mind."

The thought of Josh eases my headache a little more. "Back to business?"

"You don't look up to it, girl. I doubt you'd even be much good with Marco tonight."

"Very funny. My headache's going. Let's sit for a couple of minutes and see how I feel."

"Okay, but you're still very pale."

I rest my head on the top of the couch. I close my eyes for what feels like a minute, but when I open them Sam is nowhere in sight.

"Sam?" I get up from the couch and look at my watch. It's 9:30 p.m., which means I've been asleep for nearly an hour.

"Ah, you're awake," Sam says, walking into the living room. She carries a half-full glass of water. "I was just watching TV in my room."

"Sorry, I can't believe I fell asleep."

"Don't worry. How's the head?"

"Yeah, it seems to be better. Do you want to get back to it?"

"Do you? I don't want you feeling sick again, honey."

"This is all so weird. I don't know what to do."

"Why don't we go through the profile, and you can leave the photos for another time. Besides, maybe Flynn and Jones will have enough with the profile."

"Sounds good. I don't know if these visions are going to be productive anyway. So far all they've given me is tiny pieces of a much larger jigsaw."

"I'd still keep them between you and me until you know exactly what you're dealing with."

"I don't think I'll add it to my résumé quite yet!"

"Sophie Anderson, Profiler and Psychic. I can see your business cards now."

"Yeah, real good look." I smile. "Okay, let's go through this profile."

Sam puts the printout on the table and we stand over it, ready to go through each element together.

Sex:	Male
Age:	28-35

Race:	Caucasian
Type of offender	Organized—lack of evidence indicates well-planned murders and/or knowledge of crime scenes. High risk—keeps victims for long period of time (more chance of getting caught).
Occupation/ employment:	Possibly medical/scientific background—cuts indicate knowledge of how deep to cut before mortally wounding victim plus evidence that pressure bandages were correctly applied to prolong life after fatal wound inflicted. Maybe in law enforcement or related field (perhaps rejected from FBI and/or police force).
Marital status:	Single but sexually active
Dependants:	No
Childhood:	Probably an only child or has much older sibling(s) Good at school Kept to himself at school Awkward with women during his teens His victims represent women he wants Absent father or father abusive to mother

Personality:	Charming, but still slightly introverted Well-spoken
Disabilities:	None
Interaction with victims:	Stalks beforehand. Chooses women and thinks of them as his girlfriends. Chooses low-risk victims—career women, etc. Loves the women, but also punishes them (abusive father?).
Remorse:	No—victims not hidden and eyes open
Home life:	Lives alone or shares with one other. Lives in house (murders committed in basement or garage) or has somewhere to take the victims.
Car:	Van
Intelligence:	High IQ
Education level:	University educated
Outward appearance:	Well-presented and groomed

Criminal background:	Long history of murder—probably in other states—committing murders and refining MO for last 5–10 years, but probably no record. No other criminal background.
Modus operandi (MO):	Abducts in deserted areas, possibly posing as law enforcement.
Signature:	Body positioning Trophies—jewelry
Media tactics:	Will be following the media—could use media input to draw out the killer. Perhaps stage a murder and attribute to the killer—he'll then contact media, police or FBI to set the record straight.

Sam starts. "We've covered the age before. Caucasian."

I nod. Killers tend to hunt within their own racial group. All three of our vics are Caucasian, so it's a safe bet.

"And we've also talked about him being an organized offender. So the next item is occupation. Like we said the other night, a medical or scientific background, perhaps even nursing, is likely. All the nonfatal wounds were very carefully placed without being too deep. For instance, with this wound here—" she points to Jean's upper arm "—we've got a vertical cut that missed her arteries by only a fraction of an inch. Any more to the left and that would have been a fatal wound. And this one here—" she points to a cut on

Teresa's hip "—another fraction of an inch deeper and he would have hit an artery and she would have bled out."

"Sounds pretty precise," I say.

"Exactly. If our guy hasn't studied anatomy formally, he's taken it upon himself to study it outside of his usual occupation."

"Med student?"

"Potentially," Sam says. "Might be something for Flynn and Jones to look into."

I read from the next section of the profile. "Single, but sexually active." It makes sense. "I think our guy has had girlfriends in the past, but the fact that he thinks of his victims as girlfriends indicates he's single at the moment."

Sam takes a swig of beer. "We can't rule out the possibility that he's picking these women up at bars or nightclubs then nabbing them later, after the first meeting, perhaps even after sexual contact."

"He may have even been in Jean's apartment. Invited up for a glass of wine."

"But then someone would have seen him, surely."

"Were the victims at the bars alone? Did their friends see them dancing with some guy before they disappeared?" I ask.

"Flynn and Jones haven't turned up anything like that. No common males in their lives. Jean was a party girl, though."

"Jean was his first in D.C. Maybe when he was stalking her she noticed him. Thought he was an interested guy. A suitor."

"The boyfriend said she liked to play the field," Sam says.

I run my hands across the photos. The victims. "The killer must have a face. Someone must have seen him."

"Let's say he's a cop, he could get into a girl's apartment that way, and probably get them in a car, spinning some story about a relative or friend in need. Jean may have been different. But perhaps she never met the guy before either. The glass could have been hers from the night before."

"Yep, the evidence is vague for Jean. I like the cop angle. Maybe he's met them before, maybe not. But he either is a cop or poses as one. That gets him the trust he needs to abduct them in the first place."

We move to the next section of the profile.

"No kids," Sam says.

"Agreed. Goes back to the girlfriend angle. So, his childhood."

Sam continues. "He's confident, overly confident, which is often a trait of an only child. He also keeps to himself, and that correlates with a single child or perhaps a child with much older siblings."

"The menopause pregnancy?" I've heard of it happening. The woman thinks she's starting menopause but then finds out she's pregnant.

"Exactly. He may have felt unwanted, or in the shadow of much older, successful siblings. So he's trying to prove himself. Show them what he's capable of." Sam moves on. "Given his knowledge of anatomy I'd say he's smart, and this would have showed through in his grades at school."

"Whether he got into med school or not, he studies hard." I read the next point out aloud. "Kept to himself at school, just a few good friends."

"I think at least in his youth he was socially awkward. That's why he keeps the girls for so long, because he thinks he doesn't make a good first impression."

"Confident in killing, but not confident with women," I say.

Sam nods hesitantly. "What do you think?"

I pause. "I like it. In some ways contradictory, but not really. Lots of intelligent guys are overconfident about their intellect and underconfident with women."

"It ties in with the next two points here too." She indicates the childhood section. "Awkward with women during his teens and the victims he goes for now reflect his taste in women."

"What's your line on the father?"

Sam takes a sip of water from her glass. "Two things. The way he controls the women, it's about power, almost a discipline. Perhaps he grew up as the man in the house and took on a disciplinarian role and he likes to inflict that on others. Also, he treats these women as his girlfriends, yet he cuts them up. Like he's punishing them. That could be about the discipline or it could be he saw that sort of relationship growing up."

"The husband who beats his wife and then tells her how much he loves her."

Sam nods. "Personality," she says, moving on. "He must be well spoken and well groomed to fit into the places he went when stalking his victims, especially Teresa. She was a high flyer and he knew her routines. He was able to fit in, in her surroundings."

"He's one of the charming ones," I say.

"The men women think are too good to be true."

"And they are."

"What about Marco, is he too good to be true?" Sam's ready to take on my cynicism.

"Josh? At the moment he's pretty good, but we're in our 'good behavior' period."

"They're always so accommodating when they've only just got into your pants."

I laugh.

"So, back to our guy," Sam says. "No disabilities. He stalks his victims, and we've covered the relationship he has with his victims. Next is remorse, an emotion our guy doesn't feel."

A lot of serial killers don't feel remorse and that's a major indicator of a psychopath. But the way the bodies were found also *shows* us his lack of remorse. Generally, a killer who feels guilty about his crime will cover the body with something and close the eyes so the victim's not staring at him. Psychologically, open eyes correspond with judgment to a guilty mind, so he closes her eyes. Our guy left all three girls in open areas with nothing covering their bodies. Their nakedness was on display and their eyes open. He wasn't worried about them judging him because he felt no remorse, no guilt over their deaths.

"Agreed," I say.

"Home life."

"I think he's got a roomie," I say. "He's shy, but not a complete loner. Not anymore at least. And he probably functions normally in social settings. His behavior also indicates he's a thrill killer. Having a roommate on the scene would heighten the thrill for him because it's more dangerous."

"But he's keeping these girls somewhere personal, like his home. Surely he couldn't get away with that if he had a roommate." Sam plays devil's advocate. "Any feelings on this one?"

"You mean hunches or psychic feelings?"

"Anything will do."

I shrug. "Maybe our guy rents out a basement? It's got a bit more privacy."

"Sounds risky."

"All part of the challenge. He comes to D.C. Rapes and murders under our noses and under a roommate's nose."

Sam nods. "It would certainly raise the stakes."

"Or if he takes them somewhere else, it might be somewhere that feels homey to him. Like an abandoned building in a suburb where he grew up."

She moves on to the next area. "Van. Obviously he's got a van or a similar-type vehicle if he's transporting these girls from parking lots or their apartments to his place or some other location."

"Yep, that's a sure bet."

"Intelligence and education level are largely based on the fact that he's an organized offender and leaves no clues on the bodies for us."

"They're a given." I read off the profile. "And the outward appearance we covered in personality. The guy's blending in, so he looks pretty good."

Sam sits down. "What do you think about his criminal history?"

"I think he's been murdering for a while. Although it's possible he's just been rehearsing it. Playing it over in his mind. Maybe even seeing crime scenes in his day job, and now replicating the cleanest ones."

"Yeah, I bet we could commit a pretty good crime," Sam says, giving a half-laugh.

"We could throw the cops and profilers off, no worries."

"The perfect crime."

"But we're forgetting DNA, and DNA doesn't lie," I add.

"We ain't got any DNA on this guy yet."

"He knows his stuff, all right."

Sam stands up and looks at the last few items on the profile. "MO and signature we know. And the media stuff… pretty standard." She pauses. "So, have you got anything you'd like to add to the profile? The missing something?"

I lean back in my chair. "I can't put my finger on it."

"Me neither," Sam says.

"I'm sure that tattoo I saw on Jean's leg is important. Important to us and important to the killer."

"But we don't know how."

"No. Besides, we couldn't put it in the profile. It's based on my visions."

We're silent for about five minutes.

"Crap," I say.

Sam stands up and walks to the window. Her eyes follow something on the road. "Patrol car."

"I'm glad they're keeping an eye on you."

"Sensible, I guess." She shivers. "I think we have to leave the profile as is. We don't have time to go any further."

"No, not with Rivers breathing down our necks."

"Your neck, honey. Your neck."

"Gee, thanks for reminding me."

I'm frustrated we haven't gotten any further, but I don't think there's anything more to get…not yet. "We can add to it on the sly later. Tuldoon can take the credit."

"He won't mind that a bit."

"Maybe it's the last victim who holds the secret. Hopefully Susan will tell us something that Jean and Teresa couldn't."

I watch her body move as she walks toward me. Each step brings her swaying hips closer to me, within my grasp. I imagine having her. Devouring her. Watching her body squirm as she lies on my table. But I must wait. I bring my newspaper to my face and read about my latest exploits. I love reading about my accomplishments. They're calling me the D.C. Slasher. Not very inventive, but it's catchy. And finally I'm getting the attention I deserve.

My mind is full with images of Susan. Her annoying habits recede into the darkness as I remember my hands in her red hair as we made love.

I leave my next prey and hurry to the nearest bathroom instead. I cannot wait to be home to relive the sensation of pleasure. Of power. I am in control. I control my girlfriends, I control the police and I control the FBI.

CHAPTER 08

At 5:30 a.m. I give up on sleep. I've had another restless, nightmare-ridden night, but I can't remember any of the dreams.

By 7:00 a.m. I'm at work, exhausted. The thought of seeing Josh tonight for our second date manages to wake me up a little. In bed with Josh…that's a welcome distraction.

I pick the top file from my in-tray and get sucked straight into it. This one's a kidnapping profile that's come from the Chicago Field Office. All profiles in the field have to be checked by us before being forwarded to the cops in the area. I haven't seen a profile from the Chicago office before, though I've been told Matt Johnson, the profiler there, is excellent. I make my way through the coroner's reports, crime-scene photos and police reports, jotting down notes as I go. An image of the kidnapper forms in my mind. Not as detailed as if I was doing the profile from scratch myself, but enough to have a pretty good picture. Then I compare my notes and impressions with Johnson's profile, reading through each element. I agree with all points of his profile and whip up a covering memo for Rivers.

At 8:45 a.m. I walk the file, memo and the D.C. Slasher profile to Rivers's office, passing Sam's office on the way. Just like yesterday the door is locked and the lights off. She's having a bad week.

"Here's the Chicago file for Rivers, and the D.C. Slasher profile," I say to Janet, Rivers's assistant, handing her the documents.

"Thanks, Sophie."

"No worries," I say.

She gives me a smirk and a nod. She loves it when I use Australian expressions.

I return to my office and as I pick up the phone, Marco's frame fills the doorway.

"Hi," he says, leaning against the doorjamb.

"Hi." A slight blush rises in my cheeks.

He smiles. "We still on for dinner tonight? My house at seven?"

"It's a date. But can we make it quarter to eight? I want to get a workout in."

"Sounds fine."

Marco turns around and I watch his rear end disappear. I smile, imagining it naked. I let the thought sit with me for a couple of minutes before I force myself back to work.

My computer chimes as a new e-mail arrives. It's the daily staff list. Who's sick, who's on annual leave, who's working from another office, etc. I quickly scan the e-mail and am surprised to see Sam's name under the Sick heading. I dial her cell phone, but get voice mail. I leave a message.

"Hey, you. I hear you're sick? For real? Give me a call and let me know how you're doing."

I hang up and look at the pile of files in my in-tray. I take a deep breath and plan to work solidly until I go to the gym. I need at least two profiles off my list today. The first file is a child abduction and murder. Two sisters were taken from their home in Miami.

The time flies and before I know it it's 6:00 p.m. I'm very happy with my day's work and I finally feel as though I'm making some progress with my cases. I call it a day and head to the gym. I only do a light workout, just fifty minutes. My body's too tired to take any more than that. But even with the short session, somehow I manage to run late and end up rushing around at my place to get ready on time.

I get to Josh's place at 8:00 p.m. He lives in a three-bedroom terrace house in Georgetown, a ritzy part of D.C. Josh comes from money and I presume his parents must have kicked in for him to be able to afford this place. His street is tree-lined and Josh's is one of the smaller houses on the block. The entranceway consists of a red brick fence and a wrought-iron gate. I walk down the pathway to the front door. The garden is immaculately kept—roses, daffodils and a few small trees. A black wooden door is complemented by leadlight of geometrical shapes. Frosted-glass panels line either side of the door. I ring the doorbell and within a few seconds I hear footsteps coming down the hallway.

Josh opens the door. "Hi. Come in."

"Hi."

He scoops me up in a kiss and we continue walking awkwardly down the hall, kissing one another. We get roughly to the dining room when I hear a very purposeful throat-clearing.

Both Josh and I turn around.

"Sorry, Marty," Josh says, laughing.

Josh doesn't seem too fazed, but I'm embarrassed. Firstly because we all work together, and secondly because I prefer private displays of affection, particularly sexual affection.

"The hot new item," Marty says, smiling.

Again, I'm embarrassed and this time Josh seems a bit awkward too. I wonder if he prepped Marty on the latest development.

"Marty is going to join us for dinner," Josh says.

"After that performance maybe I should excuse myself. They say three's a crowd."

"Don't be silly," I say. "Stay." I still feel embarrassed but am eager to keep the mood friendly.

Marty pauses. "I've got work to do tonight anyway, but I have to eat, right? Besides, Josh's cooking is too good to pass up."

"That settles it. I cooked for three anyway, and it'll be ready in a few minutes. Marty, you can be the host while I make the finishing touches."

Marty clicks his heels together and does a slight bow. "A drink, madam?"

Josh laughs and moves down the hallway into the kitchen. Marty and I take a left into the dining room.

The house is laid out with a long hall down the middle. There are two bedrooms at the front of the house, one either side of the hallway, and the third bedroom, Marty's, is the second right off the hall. Josh's bedroom has an en suite and the main bathroom is next to the back bedroom. To the left of the hallway is a large open dining-living room and at the end of the hall is a modern kitchen, full of stainless-steel appliances offset by polished wood countertops and polished floorboards.

"I'll have a glass of wine," I say.

"White or red?"

"Either." I'd prefer red, but I'm trying to be a good guest.

Marty exits the living room and I take a seat on the sofa. The living area is large, with two long couches, two armchairs and a frosted-glass coffee table, all focused around the room's centerpiece, a widescreen TV system with surround sound. Every man's dream. To the side is a bookshelf that doubles as a cabinet, with rounded squares containing photos, a vase and some books. The room is carpeted in a rich mushroom pile that I know would feel great on bare feet. The couches and armchairs are royal blue with modern square cuts, and the windows are covered by timber Venetians. Josh has got taste.

Tonight the table up the other end of the large room is set for three, with two long white candles in the center. Already on the table sit cutlery, salt and pepper, and some butter.

Marty comes in the far door, carrying two glasses of wine. Red.

"Pinot."

"Thanks," I say, taking the glass.

Marty sits down in the armchair to my left.

"The chef is dishing up. It looks good."

I've only experienced Josh's cooking one other time, when we were working the Henley case. Most of the time if we worked late we'd get takeout because it was easier, but one night he whipped up an Asian stir-fry with scallops and egg noodles. It was delicious.

"So, what's he got in store for us tonight?"

"He's doing the French thing." Marty pauses. "Perhaps in your honor?"

I shift uncomfortably in my chair and take a sip of wine. "The Pinot's good."

"Josh said you're a bit of a wine connoisseur. He was gone for about an hour choosing this one."

Really? He is trying. "I like wine, but I'm no expert."

I've actually done a wine course in Australia and both my parents are wine lovers. I can usually pinpoint grape variety, but I'm not like some people who can pick the region or year with a couple of sips.

"Any breaks in the Slasher case?" I ask, not being able to keep off the subject for long.

Marty shakes his head. "You're a workaholic."

"I'm not that bad," I say.

Josh comes in, laden with plates.

I jump up and put my wineglass down on the coffee table. "Need a hand?"

"I'm fine. We're ready to eat."

Marty stands up too and we both move to the dining table, glasses in hand. Josh puts two plates on the table, and Marty and I sit down. Josh is back a few seconds later, juggling another full load. In his left hand he holds his plate, and tucked under his elbow is a basket of sliced French bread. His right hand holds both his glass and the bottle. He's slipped the glass in between his ring and little fingers and holds the bottle by its neck with just his index and middle fingers. It looks precarious, but he has no trouble unloading.

"Beef bourguignon," he announces.

The three wide but shallow white bowls are full of a hearty mixture of beef, vegetables and a rich sauce. Steam rises and my nostrils are immediately filled with the delicious aroma. A perfect meal for a cold fall night.

"Yum," I say, now absolutely starving. I pick up my fork, eager to dig in, even though the food looks way too hot.

Marty picks up his fork too. "Anyway, Sophie, I'm afraid the answer to your question is no."

I blow on a small mouthful. "I was hoping you wouldn't say that."

"Fill me in," Josh says, taking a piece of bread.

"Miss Workaholic here—" Marty motions my way with the fork "—wanted to know if we'd turned up anything on the D.C. Slasher case."

Josh butters the bread. "What are you still processing?"

"Most of the stuff from the third murder. We found some blood at the scene. DNA on it should be in tomorrow."

"Victim's?" Josh asks.

"We're not sure. She was moved postmortem, so we wouldn't expect blood flow from her. Which leaves us with the perp."

"Sounds promising," I say.

"Hopefully."

"Anything else?" Josh takes his first mouthful of beef.

"Not so far. Coroner did the usual swabs and tests. Nothing unusual. Fingernails were clean and cut back, and we couldn't find a single hair or fiber on her. Bloods came back all clear. Just a slight trace of alcohol, .01, but no other drugs or anything strange."

"The letter?"

"Still with Mark in Questioned Documents. He's got a bit of a backlog but he's going to let us jump the line a bit."

Silence.

"You want this one bad, don't you?" Marty says before eating some stew.

Josh smiles. "She wants every one bad."

It's true. I've always been like that. Psychologically speaking, I know it's because of my brother. I still need justice for him—his killer was never found.

I keep quiet and decide to enjoy the meal.

I take a few more mouthfuls. "This is really, really good."

Josh beams. "Thanks."

"Definitely worth hanging around for," Marty says.

We eat the rest of the meal steering well clear of the case. Maybe I *am* a workaholic.

Just before nine, Marty excuses himself.

"You sure you don't want dessert?" Josh asks him.

"No, I'm fine. I'm just going to finish off a few reports and then do a bit of surfing before hitting the sack."

We both nod.

"I'll leave you two to it." Marty smiles and we say our good-nights. He disappears into his room.

"What's for dessert?"

"Lemon tart."

"I love lemon tart."

"Not homemade, I'm afraid."

"You mean you didn't get a chance to whip it up after work?"

He laughs. "No, not tonight. But I did get it from an excellent French bakery." Josh stands up. "Back soon."

I get up to stretch my legs and wander around the living room, finishing what's left of my second, and last, glass of wine. I make my way to the bookshelf to look at the photos. Most of them are of Josh and his family—his parents, his sister and her family. There's a fairly recent one of Marty and Josh, taken in the courtyard out the back, obviously in summer. They both have beers in front of them and I can make out a few other people from the unit, including Sam, Peter James and Rivers. I study the photos until Josh comes back in.

"Let's sit down here for dessert," he says. He puts both plates on the coffee table and brings over two spoons from the dining room. I take a seat on one of the couches and Josh sits next to me.

He picks up his plate and has his first bite of lemon tart.

I follow suit. The tart melts in my mouth and leaves a tingling sensation from the slight bitterness. "It's good."

"Best lemon tart in D.C."

I lean forward and cut off another piece with my spoon. My hair falls across my face and Josh runs his hand through it and draws it back behind my ear for me.

He plays with the lemon tart on his plate.

Silence. Something's up.

Finally he breaks. "Sophie?"

"Yes."

"Look, I'm worried about this D.C. case."

"Why?" I say, putting my plate down on the coffee table.

"What if the killer knows you've been assigned to the case and is watching you now?"

"I handed in the profile today. Tuldoon's got the case. End of story."

Josh doesn't seem satisfied.

I sway like a pendulum between two reactions: one, being flattered that he's moved so quickly into protective mode, and two, annoyed that because we slept together he suddenly doesn't think I can handle myself.

Before I come down on one side or the other, I test the waters. "You having a macho moment?"

"I know…I know…it sounds bad. I'm really trying not to do the macho thing, I'm just worried is all."

"Josh, I've been in worse situations."

"I'm sure you have."

"It's just a profile."

He takes the hint and lets it go. "So, how did the profile come out?"

A wise topic change.

"Good, but there's something we're missing. I'm not sure what yet."

Josh still seems a bit uneasy. I put my hand on top of his.

"Look, the D.C. Slasher has just killed again. We've got at least a couple of weeks before we have to worry about who he's stalking. And by then, he will have forgotten all about the profile," I say, perhaps with more conviction than I feel. Being the prey for a serial killer is one of my biggest fears. I know how hard it can be to escape, even if you're strong and trained in psychology and martial arts. Often they knock you out and next thing, you wake up tied to a bed or table. Is there any way to win in that situation?

I push the thought away and pick up my plate. I wait until the last bite of tart is eaten before giving Josh the final verdict. "That was a delicious meal."

"So you'll come over for dinner again?"

I smile. "Definitely."

Josh puts his arm around me and we lean back into the couch.

"You told anyone?" I ask.

"Just Marty. I didn't want to sit down to dinner and pretend nothing was up. You?"

"I mentioned it to Sam."

He nods. "Sam'll keep it to herself." Then he smiles. "We can go public in a few months."

I'm thrilled and relieved to hear Josh confirm we're starting something real. I agree we should wait a bit, but I already hate the secrecy part of the relationship. Then again, the whole damn FBI's like that.

I clear the plates and stack them straight into the dishwasher. Josh follows me into the kitchen and as I close the dishwasher he puts his arms around me from behind and kisses the back of my neck.

A slight moan escapes my lips and the volume increases as he moves onto my ear. It sends a tingle through my body. He's already found one of my hot spots. He pulls my skirt up and I push myself against him, reaching my hands back and around his buttocks. He keeps kissing the back of my neck and my ear and I run my hands up and down his backside.

My lust for Josh is taking over, but my rational mind is still functioning.

"Condom?" I say.

"Bedroom." He breathes heavily into my ear and then onto my neck.

I talk in half sentences, distracted by Josh. "We should… go bedroom…anyway…Marty might…come out…for a break." But I'm enjoying the spontaneity of the kitchen.

Josh releases my earlobe from between his teeth and moves backward. I pull my skirt back down over my hips. We hold hands and tiptoe up the hallway, past Marty's room and into Josh's bedroom.

I always love sex the first couple of times with a new partner. It's so exciting and full of the unknown. Our second time is no exception.

Afterwards we lie on the bed, sweat still glistening on us. I rest my head on Josh's chest. He strokes my back.

"Sophie."

"Yeah."

"I'm worried about you."

"Not the D.C. case again."

He nods.

I push myself up and rest on my elbow. "I told you, it's not even my case anymore. And it's just a profile, it's not like the Henley case where I was in the field."

"That was different. I could look out for you on the Henley case." He pauses, realizing he's dug a very large hole for himself.

He's treating me like a child. "Look out for me?" I pull myself into a sitting position. "You think I need looking out for?" I don't let him answer. "I don't need looking after, Josh. Not only am I a grown woman, I'm also an accomplished police officer—" I move in and lower my voice "—and an FBI agent. You think I would have got here, to the FBI, if I didn't deserve it. If I couldn't look after myself?" I pause for a breath.

Josh fills the short pause. "I care about you is all."

I want Josh to care for me. I *want* him to be falling for me. But I'm not going to be controlled by him.

"You of all people should be able to accept what I do for a living. That's important to me." I throw the sheets off and start fumbling for my clothes, which are scattered around the bedroom.

"What are you doing?" Josh asks.

"Going home."

"Don't be ridiculous. Stay."

But I'm too angry to stay. Right now Josh reminds me of my parents, who are constantly trying to get me out of law enforcement. Telling me it's too dangerous for a woman. But they're wrong. I pull on the last of my clothes. "I'll see myself out."

Josh gets out of bed and pulls his boxer shorts on, but there's no stopping me.

I take the long way home, feeling the need to drive and go over things in my mind. I think of the empty flat and bed waiting for me and start wondering if maybe I overreacted. If it wasn't for my parents' attitude it wouldn't have bothered me as much, and I shouldn't take that out on Josh. But he does need to realize that I can look after myself.

By the time I arrive at my apartment, my mind is full of conflicting thoughts. But the confusion evaporates the instant I walk into my apartment. I'm uneasy. I hesitate, halfway through the door, and look around. A breeze gently caresses strands of my hair and I notice the kitchen window is open. Open? I jolt into action and draw my

Smith & Wesson. I take the safety off and throw my handbag down, not taking my eyes off the open space in front of me. Besides the window, nothing looks suspicious. I move toward the kitchen to check behind the counter.

I take a deep breath and inch along until the kitchen floor comes into sight. It's clear.

Adrenaline pumps. I do a full sweep of the living room, then on to the linen closet. I'm ready to fire. Nothing. That brings me to the door between my living space and the bathroom. I count to three then throw the door open, hard. It bounces off the wall, nearly flying back into my face. I double-check through the crack and go into the bathroom. The shower curtain is drawn and my heart pumps harder as I jerk back the curtain, gun trained on the shower. Nothing.

I see movement in the corner of my eye and swing around quickly. My finger starts to depress the trigger then I release the tension. I'm staring at my own reflection. Goddamn, I nearly fired at a mirror. That would have been a hard one to explain at the office—I have to report all shots fired.

My shoulders release some of the tension. Only one room left to check. I come out of the bathroom and hold my gun up, pointing toward the bedroom. The door's ajar and I check behind the door through the crack, before edging into the room. It looks undisturbed but I check the whole room, including the wardrobe and under the bed. Again, I find nothing and no one. Satisfied and relieved, I reholster my weapon.

Back in the kitchen I cross to the window, closing and locking it.

I opened it when I got home to let some fresh air in, but did I leave it open? I thought I closed all the windows, but then again I was running late for Josh so I can't be sure.

I inspect the window. The lock's holding and there's no sign of forced entry. I must have forgotten to close it. Suddenly I see a woman lying naked on a narrow surface. She's spread-eagle and ropes tie her to four stakes positioned at the corners. A man leans over her with a knife. He cuts her arm and she screams. I open my eyes and take in a quick gasp of air. The image could have told me much—the victim's identity and the killer's—but it was faded and out of focus. The only thing I can say with certainty is that both the woman on the table and the killer had brown hair...along with more than half the population. Great. Another useless vision.

I take off my clothes, put my gun in my bedside drawer and get into bed, still uneasy. I wish I'd stayed at Josh's house. Doubt and fear take over and I check the apartment again from top to bottom, making sure the windows and doors are securely locked. But I still don't feel safe. I go back to bed and read, hoping the fantasy book will win over my morbid imagination and fears.

An hour later I close my eyes, hoping to sleep. I doze and images flash through my mind.

A woman lies on a bed and the room is covered in blood.

I wake up; bolt upright, gasping for air, tears streaming down my face. I try to shake the horror. Who is this woman? Jean? Susan? The D.C. Slasher's next victim? Or is it only a dream this time?

I clear my mind, desperately wanting sleep. My digital clock flashes 4:10 a.m. My thoughts drift to the night my brother disappeared. I experienced his death through the eyes of the killer. I *enjoyed* it as the killer. Nausea hits me. I grab my book and move to the couch, determined not to think of my brother and the role I played in his death. I read for thirty minutes, the story engrossing enough to quiet my fears. I return to my bedroom, leave my bedside light on and gradually fall back to sleep. But immediately I'm back in the dream. The body has been found and I'm there. Then the dream jumps, like a faulty record, and time passes.

I look up to see the shadowy image of the killer coming at me with a raised knife. The knife penetrates into my skin, into my leg, and I wake up.

I gasp and start hyperventilating, panic taking over. I open my eyes and see a dark shape in my doorway. I stifle a scream. There's someone in my room.

I lie paralyzed. My gun is in the drawer. Can I get it and fire before the killer attacks? Then the figure distorts and I stare at the dark space, trying to decipher the shadows, the shapes. What the hell's going on?

I move as fast as I can, fumbling for the gun and the light switch, ready to shoot. But the light only illuminates the empty room.

I can still smell her clothes. Smell her body. I know her so well, perhaps even better than she knows herself. But she's for later.

I will enjoy this one, for now. She is a fine catch. Now I'll get the recognition I deserve. I'll be noticed.

"Do not fight, darling, you cannot escape."

"Please. You don't have to do this."

"No, I don't have to. But I can," I say with a surge of power. I bend down and kiss her gently on her cheek.

"I haven't seen your face, you can let me go."

"No, you haven't. Yet. But you've heard my voice. Do you recognize it?"

"No. I've never heard your voice before."

"No?" I stroke her hair.

"Please, my name is…"

"Shh," I whisper and put my hand over her mouth. "I know who you are. I know everything about you," I say as I reach for the duct tape, silencing her and covering her luscious, rose lips. Her skin is flushed with excitement. But that can wait.

"I have to go now. They're waiting for me." I walk backward to the door, taking in every inch of her beautiful, naked body.

"See you soon, my love."

The image of her is indelibly etched in my mind. But I must go to work. No one must suspect.

CHAPTER 09

It's hard to concentrate on my cases. Another night's restlessness has taken its toll. I know I had another nightmare last night, but once again the foggy, dreamlike veil blocks my memory. My weary body and puffy eyes are a testament to my insomnia. I smile to myself, imagining Sam's response to my obvious lack of sleep. One guess what she'll think kept me up all night! God, Sam. Between work and Josh I never phoned her back to see if she was feeling better.

I pick the handset up, but then sense someone in the doorway. I look up, expecting and hoping to see Josh. I think perhaps I owe him an apology.

Instead it's Rivers.

"Morning, boss," I say, eager to hide my weariness and my disappointment that he isn't Josh. I fiddle with my keyboard, moving it closer to me. Rivers is silent, I look up. I'm immediately concerned by the look on his face. "What's up?"

"It's Sam, Sophie."

"What?" A tiny voice squeaks out of me.

"She's missing. Cops think she's been taken from her apartment."

"What?" I stand up, sending my chair reeling backward. It hits the wall noisily and bounces back.

Josh enters my office with a strange look on his face.

"Have you heard?" I ask him.

"Heard what?"

Rivers intervenes. "Wright's missing and there's evidence of a struggle at her apartment."

"Oh my God," Josh says.

"What happened? When?" I ask, leaning heavily on my desk.

"Her cleaner called it in. She turned up at seven-thirty this morning to find clothes and furniture strewn all over the place. Sam could have been abducted anytime in the last thirty-six hours."

"She phoned in sick yesterday, didn't she?" Josh says.

I'm too shell-shocked to say anything.

"Yes, but it certainly looks suspicious now."

I should have known something was up. Sam's never been sick the whole time I've been here. If I wasn't so distracted by Marco…

"Did she speak to Janet personally?"

"Janet swears it was her voice on the phone. Croaky, but her voice. But we can't be certain. We're getting phone records pulled now."

"What about the drive-bys? Did they see anything?"

"No. Patrol cars have been going by every couple of hours, but nothing so far. We're tracking down the officers on duty in the past thirty-six hours."

I nod, still not able to absorb what's happened.

"I've got to get over there." I start for the door, gathering my bag and searching for my keys on the desk. "Who's heading up the investigation?"

"They've got Sandra Couples on it."

I know Sandra. She's the best in Missing Persons.

I remember the vision I had at Sam's place, an image of the killer. I saw him behind Sam! It wasn't an image from Jean's death, or Teresa's or Susan's—it was a premonition of Sam's abduction!

"Oh my God," I say, stepping backward and sinking into my chair, nearly missing it. "It's the D.C. Slasher. He's got Sam."

"Let's not jump to conclusions," Josh says. "It could be a kidnapping. Someone who figures they'd get a good ransom for an FBI agent."

"We're looking into both possibilities," Rivers says.

"Who's working it our end?" I ask.

"The Washington Field Office. They're the best people to investigate it at the moment."

"I want in."

"Anderson, you and Wright are friends, you can't be objective."

"But I know her. I know her movements. For God's sake, I was with her the night before last." I can't believe Sam's missing. And *he's* got her.

"The night before last?" Rivers says.

I nod.

"If it was a fake phone call yesterday, you might be the last person to have seen her. What did you do?"

"We worked on the Slasher profile at her place."

"What? Wright was supposed to be off that case!" Rivers shouts, taking his glasses off.

"She was helping me out. Handing over the case. I left around ten-thirty. Please, sir, you've got to let me help with this case."

Rivers is silent. I think he knows that I was helping Sam out rather than the other way around, but he doesn't pursue it.

Finally he speaks, putting his glasses back on. "Look, go over and tell Couples what you know. I'm not saying you can work the case, but you can go over to Wright's, have a look around and talk to Couples."

I stand up. "Thank you, sir."

Josh steps farther into the room. "I'd like to be involved too."

"Get real, Marco. I'm not sending you both over. We've got D.C.'s finest, Agents Krip and O'Donnell from the field office, Marty from the lab and now Anderson's going over there too. How would it look?"

Rivers is right. If we send over too many from Quantico, it looks as though we don't trust the local forces or even our own field agents. There'd be political ramifications.

"Besides, we want to keep this quiet for the moment. The last thing I need is the press getting hold of it."

"I'm gone," I say, maneuvering past Rivers and Josh.

They both look at me, and Josh mouths, "You okay?"

I force a smile and a nod before dashing out the door.

I unlock my car and the memory of last night's dream comes back. Murder. Could it have been about Sam? No, it can't be. Not Sam. I remember the blood in my dream and bile rises. He's got Sam. I begin to hyperventilate and I lean on the car. I take in deep, slow breaths. Think of something reassuring...

He keeps them. He keeps his victims for three to eight days. I've still got time to find her. Time to find him.

Sam's apartment is busy with activity when I arrive. I flash my FBI credentials to the local cop at the front of her apartment block and proceed up the stairs. I show my badge again at the door to Sam's apartment. Inside there are about ten officials. Camera flashes go off every couple of seconds, and several forensics people are at work, looking for fingerprints and other evidence. Marty is directing one of the photographers, getting him to zoom in on a piece of pottery that lies shattered in Sam's hallway. A potted plant. Dirt surrounds the pottery. The place is a mess. There was one hell of a struggle.

Marty sees me right away and comes over. At first he doesn't say anything. What can he say?

Then: "I'll let you know the minute we find something."

"How does it look?"

He looks away.

"That good?" I bite my lower lip.

"We have fingerprints, but it'll be a day or two before we see if we've got any unfriendlies."

"You'll need to eliminate mine as well. I was here the night before last."

Marty nods. "Yours are on the FBI database anyway."

Sandra Couples sees me and walks over.

"Agent Anderson," she says formally.

Marty takes this as his exit cue and gives me a forced smile before going back to supervise the forensics team.

Now in normal conversational range and just the two of us, Sandra's tone changes.

"God, Sophie, I'm so sorry. I can't believe this has happened." She pushes her hand through her neat, graying bob. Her skin is weather-beaten, no doubt from the fifteen-odd years she spent down in Florida, and her large, hazel eyes blink every couple of seconds.

"Thanks, Sandra."

"I've got my best guys on it." She looks over her shoulder at the hive of activity.

I get straight down to business. "I was here the night before last."

She nods and flips open her notepad. "What time you leave?"

"About ten-thirty."

"Looks like you may have been the last to see her."

"That's what Rivers said. The call's being checked?"

"Agents Krip and O'Donnell are getting her phone records. So what did you guys do on Wednesday night?"

"We were working on the Slasher case, looking over the profile." I look at the photos and files, still spread across the dining-room table.

Sandra follows my gaze and nods. "We haven't touched anything there yet. Do you want to have a look? See if it's the way you left it?"

We walk across to the table. Why didn't I realize Sam was in danger? Why didn't I realize that the image of the killer was a premonition? I wish the visions had never come back.

Come back? Why had they come back? Why now? First John, then Sam. Someone close to me was in danger when I was a child, and that must have triggered my psychic abilities. I shiver, remembering how I felt as John's killer. And now the premonitions are back because someone else I love is in danger—Sam. But I didn't see it.

I'm overwhelmed by guilt. Old guilt from John, and now new guilt from Sam. It's too much.

I pull myself back. I need to be objective to help Sam. To save Sam. I look around the area and the struggle is obvious. The coffee table is cleared of magazines, glasses and the clock. These items are strewn across the floor.

Sandra sees me eyeing the area.

"This is where the struggle started," she says.

I pull out some surgical gloves from my bag and move straight to the area. I kneel down with my back to Sandra, examining the area. It looks as if Sam was dragged across her carpet, grabbing at the coffee table for leverage and for a weapon.

I look up. Sandra's standing next to me, waiting until I'm finished. I stand up.

"She ran this way—" Sandra points to the only path between the living room and Sam's bedroom "—and into the bedroom."

The bed is ruffled but not slept in, and the bedroom window is open.

"Have you found her gun?"

"Yeah, it's underneath the counter in the kitchen.

Think it may have been kicked there in the struggle." We make our way back into the main room.

I look around. "So, how the hell did he get in?"

"No sign of forced entry, but the bedroom window was open."

I shake my head. "I don't buy it. Sam told me she was checking the locks. Being careful."

Sandra scribbles in her notepad. "We'll keep looking."

"Any idea of the time all this occurred?" I ask.

"Yes, actually." For the first time Sandra smiles and the creases that run between the sides of her nose to the corners of her mouth deepen. "Doesn't get better than this."

She puts on her gloves and carefully picks up the clock that's usually on Sam's coffee table. She turns it around.

"Ten forty-five." The hands have stopped.

"So we're either looking at fifteen minutes after you left, ten forty-five the morning she phoned in sick or ten forty-five last night."

"What about the neighbors?"

"I've got two of my people interviewing everyone they can get their hands on, but most people are at work."

"Someone must have heard something."

"That's what we figure. Downstairs particularly, but no one's home."

The people who live directly under Sam would have been the most likely to hear the scuffle. Glass was broken and the potted plant would have made quite a racket as it toppled over.

"So, do you want to look at this stuff now?" Sandra asks, pointing to the dining-room table and the D.C. files.

"Sure."

I move toward the table, trying desperately to recall how it had looked when I left on Wednesday night. Was anything missing? Was anything new on the table?

"Is that how you left it?"

"I think so." I finger the photos with my gloved hands. "To be honest, it would be hard to pick up one missing photo, or one extra."

"Yeah. I know."

"We'll have to check the files against the inventory. Make sure everything's there."

"My guys have photographed it extensively." She pauses, and then whispers, "Do you think it's the Slasher?"

I look up at her and bite my lip. "Yes."

My visions are proof of that, but I'm not going to tell anyone about them. Sam is still alive and I'm going to save her. If I can just control these visions, maybe they can help me do just that.

"I might call in Flynn and Jones. Get them to check out the place too," Sandra says.

"Good idea. We've got to find him, and fast."

Sandra puts her hand on my arm.

I return my focus to the table and see Sam's completed profile underneath a stack of photos. "Make sure you run this for prints, Sandra."

"We'll try everything."

I think about our guy, our perp. He wears gloves but I can imagine him wanting to touch the paper that words about him were written on. It would make him feel closer to it and give his ego a boost—to hold his own profile in his hands. It would add to the thrill.

"I'll give Flynn and Jones a call now." Sandra flips open her phone.

"Mind if I hang around?" I ask out of professional courtesy.

"Go for it," she says, dialing the number and walking away.

I look at the table and case notes sprawled across it but I still can't see anything out of place. I lift up some of the photos, careful not to upset the orderly mess. Given that there are over sixty photos and dozens of printed pages, I decide the process is futile. We'll have to compare the contents of the files with the inventory list.

I force myself into Sam's bedroom, hopeful to find something. Some clue. I resist the urge to curl into the fetal position and cry. I need to stay rational and focused on the case. That's the way I can help Sam.

I sink down on the edge of her bed, staring glassily into the mirror above her dressing table. I'm going to assume Sam was taken the night I was here and then the perp forced her to phone in sick, to delay the inevitable discovery of her disappearance. I close my eyes and do the math in my head. I've got between thirty-six and a hundred and fifty hours to find Sam, if the guy sticks with his pattern of holding the victims for three to eight days.

I open my eyes and see it.

A small pendant hangs from the side of the mirror. Insignificant enough, except that I've never seen Sam wear it, and the shape it forms is an exact replica of the tattoo I saw on Jean's thigh. This symbol must mean something. The killer's deliberately left this in Sam's bedroom, taunting us, assuming no one would discover the clue, or know what it meant. I use a pen to lift the pendant off the small hook it hangs from and hold it up to the light. A small smile plays on my lips. The killer has slipped up and I'm one step closer to saving Sam. This is the something we were missing.

CHAPTER 10

Pike stands at the head of the table. We sit, waiting. Rivers arrives and hovers near the door.

Pike starts. "We're setting up a task force."

This is a turnaround from Rivers's stance only three hours ago. Did Pike initiate or did Rivers push? Or maybe it's coming from higher than Pike. For an FBI agent to be kidnapped or abducted is bad PR. We're supposed to be invincible.

I'm keen to get the task force moving in the right direction. "It's the D.C. Slasher." Most of us have come to this conclusion anyway.

"Why do you say that, Anderson?" Pike asks.

"It fits the profile. The killer's purposefully moved here to be under the FBI's nose. Under our noses." I force evenness in my voice. "He likes the thrill, the challenge, and what better way to step up the chase than by nabbing an FBI agent—and the one profiling him." I was wrong about this guy before. I didn't think Sam was in serious danger. I certainly didn't think she could be the next victim. Surely she would have noticed someone stalking her. We're trained for that.

"Anything else?" Pike asks.

"The note on the third victim."

Rivers shoots a look my way. Did he tell Pike that Sam was supposed to be off the case?

"Yes, the note," Pike says.

"He wasn't just involving Sam, inviting her into his world, like we thought." I keep my voice even. "It was part of a stalking ritual."

I'm making headway with Pike.

"Plus, in Sam's room there was a pendant that isn't hers. The killer left it there." Of course I can't tell them that it's exactly the same as an image I've seen in a dream—one that I know is related to the D.C. Slasher because I saw it on Jean's thigh. But hopefully its mere existence, a foreign object at a crime scene, is enough.

"You really know every piece of jewelry Sam Wright owns?" Pike says.

I think fast. "Sam and I went out two weeks ago and went through each other's jewelry, looking for items to match the dresses we were wearing." An embarrassing but necessary lie.

"To match your dresses?"

"Yes, accessorizing." With Sam gone, there's only one other woman in the room, Anthea Stall, who leans toward the butch side. She wouldn't be too worried about accessorizing. Anthea raises an eyebrow and the other agents stare at me; even James's constant pen-tapping stops. But I don't care if I look stupid. None of that matters. We have to find Sam.

Pike studies me. "Rivers, you happy to go with the Slasher rather than a kidnap situation?"

Rivers, who still hasn't taken his eyes off me—his form of punishment for going against his orders—finally diverts his gaze.

"Anderson's instincts are usually right. Unless we get a ransom note in the next twenty-four hours, we have to assume it's the Slasher."

James's pen-tapping resumes.

Pike gives Rivers a curt nod. "Okay. It'll be a joint D.C. police/FBI task force."

I clasp my fingers together under the table and press my front teeth into my bottom lip. I want to get on this case. I *need* to get on this case. Please let them assign a full-time profiler. With these circumstances they should assign at least one of us.

Pike continues. "Detectives Flynn and Jones from Homicide, Sandra Couples, and from our end we've got Krip and O'Donnell from the D.C. Field Office. We're also going to assign two of you—"

Thank God. "I'd like to be involved," I say.

My voice is quickly followed by Josh's. "I'd like to be on the team too, sir."

"You two have just come off the Henley case. What about your other cases?" Rivers says.

Marco responds first. "We can do a bit of overtime, sir. Besides, we worked together well on the Henley case."

I take over the baton. "And we know Flynn and Jones. We *all* work well together."

Rivers and Pike exchange looks. A nod from Rivers, then one from Pike.

"You two have got it," Rivers says, leaning against the wall.

Would they give it to us if they knew Josh and I were seeing each other? Possibly not. But it doesn't matter. Josh and I did work well together on the Henley case and hopefully nothing's changed.

"Anything from the officers on duty? The drive-bys?" I ask.

Rivers shakes his head. "I heard back from Couples. None of the patrols saw or heard anything suspicious."

I sink slightly into my seat at the disappointing news.

Pike clears his throat and addresses the whole team. "I've set up appointments for you all to see Dr. Rosen. Given the situation, it's for the best."

I can see from the faces around the table that no one's happy with this development. A few arms cross and sideways glances are thrown. Most agents don't like to talk about their feelings, me included. Besides, I know she'll tell me I'm blocking my emotions and compensating with work. You bet I am. I can't do Sam any good if I let myself think about her, where she might be and what she's going through, for more than a fleeting moment. I have to catch this guy and that's all I can think about. Catching him.

"Janet will send you all your appointment times." Pike unbuttons his gray suit and leans on the desk. "And there'll be no excuses." He looks around the table and makes sure he eyeballs us all. "I mean that. No excuses."

I shift in my chair. We need to get out there. Now.

"O'Donnell will be in charge of the Bureau's efforts," Pike says, addressing Josh and I.

The meeting's finished and we all file out.

Josh walks next to me and we move through the rabbit warren. He walks close, but not so close that the recent development in our relationship would be obvious to an observer.

"You seem to be taking this pretty well, Soph." He doesn't sound convinced.

"We're going to find her." I quicken my already fast steps.

Josh hesitates. "Yes. We will."

"We *have* to find her." My fingers tighten on my notepad.

"Sophie, I don't think the reality of the situation has hit you yet." Josh gently takes my arm and brings me to a stop.

I don't like it. I need to keep moving.

"Don't be ridiculous," I say. But I'm lying. It feels as if it's happening to someone else or I'm watching the events unfold in a movie. To be honest, I prefer it that way.

I start walking again. It's bad enough that the departmental psychologist's going to be poking around inside my head—I don't want Josh in there too. I leave Josh in the corridor and enter my office, but he lingers in the doorway. I look up at him.

"Do you want to ride to D.C. together?" he asks.

I can't think about this now! Why is he asking me this now?

"Um…" My mind labors through the options and one thought remains—I want to be alone. "Let's take two cars."

Josh nods, then pauses. I shuffle papers and keep my head down, hoping he'll get the hint that I don't want to talk.

There's silence for a few moments. "I guess I'll see you there," he says finally. I can tell he's upset that I'm shutting him out, but I just don't want to—no, *can't*—talk about any of it. I need to focus on the facts.

I look up and force a smile. "I'll see you there soon."

He pauses again, and then leaves.

I stop my meaningless paper-shuffling and actually look at what's in my hands. It's the full report on the handwriting from the note to Sam. On the front is a Post-it note from Marty. *Knew you'd want this. I've compiled the three experts' reports into one. Marty.*

I flick through it quickly before heading for D.C.

The hour-long ride on the I-95 is pure hell, both in terms of traffic on the road and internal traffic in my head. When I finally park at the D.C. Field Office and make my way into the building, I'm even more frazzled than when I left, if that's possible.

The field office is a modern building on Fourth Street in the northwest quadrant. I sign in at the desk and catch the elevator to the seventh floor. The project room is large, with floor-to-ceiling windows that look over D.C. In the center of the room is a large rectangular meeting table and ten black high-back chairs. Two whiteboards are mounted on the wall, and the room is equipped with multimedia facilities, including a projector system and video conferencing equipment.

Around the table sit the main members of the task force, including Josh. We'll have access to backup if—

no, when—we find the guy. I take the nearest seat and we all say our brief hellos with tight smiles.

O'Donnell sits directly opposite me. I know O'Donnell. I like O'Donnell. He's a stocky man in his mid forties, with a hairline that's well and truly receded. He shaves what's left of his hair, and the lack of hair accentuates his steel-blue, no-nonsense eyes.

To O'Donnell's left sits Krip. I don't know much about Krip, but what I've seen so far isn't impressive. He's happy to cruise. His external image reflects what I've heard about him. His sandy-blond hair is long for an agent, and this, coupled with his freckled face, reminds me more of an Aussie or Californian surfer than an FBI agent. Krip leans back in his chair, way back. Does he even care that Sam's been taken?

On the other side of O'Donnell is Couples, who sits upright in her chair. The light from the window catches her gray streaks.

Flynn and Jones sit together on my right. I look briefly at Flynn and we make eye contact. Flynn, like O'Donnell, has Irish heritage and amazing blue eyes. The kind of eyes that one moment can look soft and babyish, but the next seem to stab you with intensity. No doubt he uses those eyes on suspects. Today he is wearing a dark brown woolen suit with a cream shirt, no tie. He gives me a brief smile then goes back to his file. He doesn't waste a minute.

Next to him Jones is hunched over his pad, doodling. Jones does some of his best work when he's doodling. He has a more casual look, jeans and a leather jacket. They sit well on his slight frame, but also accentuate his youth. Jones is in his mid twenties, but you wouldn't know it from his work. What he lacks in murder investigation experience, he makes up for in smarts.

"So Sophie, you're sure it's the Slasher," O'Donnell says.

"Absolutely. There's no doubt in my mind." No one challenges me. "Besides, given the high-profile nature, we would have got a ransom note or call by now."

O'Donnell hesitates for only a minute. "Okay, let's work that angle."

"What did you think of Sam's profile?" I ask, getting down to business.

It's Flynn who answers first. "Interesting. The possibility that he's got a law-enforcement background is concerning."

"He might just be posing as an officer. We can't be sure he's a working cop," I say.

"A cop?" Krip smiles. "But Sam's pegged him as smart and well spoken."

Jones comes to the defense of the boys in blue. "I'd put my IQ against yours any day."

We all laugh, even Krip. But the release is followed by a guilty silence.

Finally, it's Couples who speaks. "I still can't believe he's nabbed Wright."

No one knows what to say, so Couples's admission is followed by somber looks and another period of silence.

I glance at my watch and scribble down some calculations, making a mark on my empty page. I've already worked this out in my head, but I do it again anyway.

"If he took Sam the night I was there, then I figure we've got between thirty-three hours to just under six and a half days to find her, assuming he'll hold her for three to eight days, like he did the others."

O'Donnell leans against the table. "I want everyone devoted to this—more than full-time. Clear your schedules."

"No problem," Flynn says.

I smile at him in appreciation. He'll work on two hours' sleep until we find Sam.

"Did Sam lodge anything with VICAP?" Josh says.

Jones stops doodling and writes VICAP on a small blank section of his page. Even though it may not look like it, we've got his full attention.

"Yeah, she did. The VICAP analysts are looking at it now. We'll have the results by four today," I say.

Jones glances at his watch. "Two hours."

O'Donnell looks at Flynn and Jones. "You two already look into VICAP?"

Flynn answers. "Our search turned up two matches in Chicago."

"And?"

"Dead end. They're related, but the perp didn't leave any evidence in Chicago either."

Everyone looks discouraged. I step in. "This search should be a little different. One of our VICAP experts is expanding the search criteria and then analyzing the results manually." You tend to get a better result with individual attention.

"Well, let's see what it turns up," O'Donnell says.

"I also got a copy of the handwriting expert's report before I came over here," I say, handing out copies to everyone.

"You looked at it yet?" O'Donnell asks.

"I had a quick glance."

We all take the time to read the three-page report. Jones jots down a few notes, as do I, but the rest of the team simply reads.

The report brings together several elements, combining the efforts of a document examiner, handwriting examiner and a forensic linguist. In addition to covering the type of ink and paper used, it also includes an analysis of whether the writer is left- or right-handed, whether they're trying to disguise their writing, patterns in speech that may indicate where a person grew up and/or their education level, and their frame of mind when writing the note. In our case, we already know that the perp used a standard blue Bic ballpoint and a page torn from a Spirax notebook, but this information forms the start of the report.

Next comes the general handwriting analysis. The perp's purposefully used printing and all uppercase letters, which makes a handwriting expert's job much harder. But nonetheless, some patterns emerge, and the address details on the envelope are in normal, cursive writing. The slight slant of the writing indicates a left-hander, although the handwriting expert notes that at one point the slant changes momentarily—something that often happens if someone is writing with their non-preferred hand as an attempt to disguise their writing. But the slant change is only for two words and the writing around the words is characterized by more lifts than other sections. A lift is when someone stops writing for a split second, taking their pen off the paper. This can indicate the person is lying, under stress or still hasn't made up their mind about exactly how they're going to phrase the note. Our expert has concluded that the writer is left-handed and that the slant change is due to an interruption of thought.

The forensic linguist has noted that the writer has misspelled the word *delighted* but believes it's inconsistent with the writing in the rest of the letter. The misspelling is a deliberate attempt to disguise his education level. In particular, the linguist notes his near-perfect use of punctuation as good evidence of university-level education. This tracks with our profile. The linguist has also been able to pinpoint a South, Southwest background.

After less than ten minutes, O'Donnell summarizes it. "So we're looking at South, Southwest origin, maybe Arizona, New Mexico or Texas. However, there are some inconsistencies that make the forensic linguist think our guy moved around a bit. He's highly educated and our expert doesn't think the killer rehearsed the note much or at all, and attempts to disguise the handwriting are in the form of the caps and the one misspelling."

"Confident son of a bitch," Krip says, leaning back farther in his chair but still staring out the window.

"Well, at this stage he's got reason to be," I say. "We've got no physical evidence and no real leads."

"What about Wright's place, Couples? Anything there?" O'Donnell asks.

"Not yet. There were prints all over the place. I'm in contact with the FBI lab and they're still running them all against Sam's, Sophie's and the cleaner's."

"How long will it take?"

"Marty Tyrone said they'll be working it around the clock, but it'll be at least another twenty hours or so before they've checked everything, isolated the prints and run them all."

O'Donnell nods and then runs his fingers underneath the frames of his glasses and squeezes the bridge of his nose.

Working to a tight time frame is never easy. These things always take time, and that's the one thing we don't have.

"'Course, we might get an unidentified print in ten minutes' time," Couples says.

"We have to assume there'll be no prints," Josh says, holding his pen up and clicking it twice, rapidly.

"I agree. The guy's never left one before. Why start now?" I say. "Except perhaps on the profile."

"The profile?"

"Yeah. I can imagine our guy wanting to establish a physical connection with the words Sam wrote about him. He may have even taken his gloves off."

"Good thinking. Sandra, organize to have the profile checked out as a priority," O'Donnell says.

"Sure. It's being checked, but I'll get it stepped up in terms of priority."

"I'm interested in the files too. I've been wondering if he took something, evidence of his handiwork, or even if he left an extra photo," I say.

"I've got a list here of exactly what we sent through to your unit," Flynn says, flicking through some pages in his file and digging out a loose page.

Couples nods and flips her cell phone open. "Marty, it's Sandra Couples. Anything?... Get your guys to focus on the files and photos that were on Sam's dining-room table, and especially the printout of the

Slasher profile. Yep... Uh, huh... Good," Sandra says. "I'll fax through the inventory too—get someone to check it, will you." She hangs up. "Done." She takes the sheet of paper from Flynn. "I'll fax this through when we're finished."

"What else have we got?" O'Donnell asks.

I stand up to pace.

Josh double-clicks his pen. "The pendant."

"You entered that in as evidence, didn't you, Anderson?" Flynn says.

"Yeah, it's definitely not Sam's."

"It's already been checked for prints and DNA." Sandra looks around the table and then looks up at me. "Nothing, I'm afraid."

I twist the ring on my little finger.

"What if it belongs to one of the other victims?" Krip says, moving forward in his chair for the first time.

I'm surprised it's Krip who makes this contribution. I stop twisting my ring. "I like it. But I don't think it's one of his D.C. victims."

Jones nods. "Yeah, Sam's profile indicates he's not a first-timer."

"No. Everything's too perfect," I say.

"Well, we know our guy takes trophies," Flynn says. "He took a bracelet from Jean, Teresa's ring, and we just got word from Susan's mom—she thinks a necklace is missing."

Jones looks up at Flynn but keeps doodling. "Not our necklace?"

"No, I described it to Mrs. Young. It's not it."

I take a seat at the table again. "So let's assume it is another victim's necklace."

Josh turns to me. "Or maybe even a girlfriend or relative of the perp."

"We'll have to wait and see what VICAP turns up."

We pause. What haven't we covered?

"Any luck with the neighbors?" Jones pauses his doodling and looks at Couples.

"No one we've spoken to so far heard anything. But I'm hopeful about the apartment directly below Sam. We're chasing down the couple that live there. We should find them in the next hour or so. If not, I've got someone going over there at five to wait for them to get home from work."

"Excellent. It would be good to pinpoint the abduction time," O'Donnell says.

"What about entry points?" I ask Couples. "How'd he get in?"

"Had to be through the bedroom window. There are definitely no signs of forced entry."

I shake my head. I still don't buy it.

"Anything else?" O'Donnell raises both eyebrows and looks around the table.

Silence.

"There must be something," I say.

"Forensics would have found it if there was. You know that," Josh says quietly.

"We're waiting on everything." I flop backward in the seat, my elbows leaning on the armrests.

Josh reaches his hand out to me and then pulls it back, covering the attempt at an intimate gesture by tapping on the table. "Yes." He forces a smile. "But look what we might have by six tonight."

"True." By six we should know if anything's missing

from the Slasher files, if there are any fingerprints on the profile, and when exactly Sam was abducted. It's not a bad start, but I was hoping for more.

"And the call?" Josh says.

Krip, who has resumed his semireclined position, answers. "Made from her cell phone. Doesn't tell us much."

"Krip, go to the cell-phone company and find out what area the call was routed through," O'Donnell says.

Of course. All cell-phone calls are picked up by a tower, usually the nearest one, and we'll be able to get a rough location from it.

Krip nods.

"Sophie, Sam ordered a blowup of Jean's thigh. Any idea why?" Flynn says.

"Yeah, we thought we could see some sort of marking on it." It's not an absolute lie. I'm just not telling him how I saw the marking.

"Here you go." Flynn pushes the photo across the table.

I snatch it up, eagerly examining the top of Jean's thigh. What a mess, there are cuts everywhere. But there's no tattoo. Still, the image must have something to do with the Slasher because not only was the marking in my dream and waking premonition, now there's the pendant too.

"Mind if I keep this?" I ask.

"No problem."

O'Donnell hands us completed case files. "I suggest we use the next few hours to go through the case. Familiarize ourselves with everything."

"I might see if I can add to the profile," I say.

"I'll go back to Quantico and sit on the VICAP guys.

Make sure we get that report," Josh says. He clicks his pen, puts it in his folder and flips the folder closed.

"Let's meet back here at five. Then we'll have the VICAP info and hopefully something from Sam's neighbors. What about the third D.C. victim? Anything more on her?" O'Donnell says.

"Coroner's finished his report." Flynn shakes his head. "Nothing interesting, I'm afraid." He flicks through a pile of papers and brings one to the top. "This one had thirty-two cuts, including the throat wound, which was the cause of death. Time of death has been verified as between 11:00 p.m. and 2:00 a.m. Her fingernails were clean, recently cut back in fact, and there were no foreign fibers, hairs or anything else."

I slump in my chair. "Lividity?"

Flynn focuses his blue eyes, in their soft mode, on me. "Same as the others. She died on a flat surface and must have been transported in something pretty flat too."

"A van."

Jones looks up. "Wouldn't that show ridges, though?"

He's right.

"Maybe something flat in the back of the van?" Josh says.

This guy's good.

"And forensics?" O'Donnell asks.

Josh leans forward. "I spoke to Marty just before I left Quantico. There was blood near the scene but it turned out to be the victim's. Must have got there during transportation. Broken branches showed us his route but no footprints."

"He raked over his tracks," I add.

O'Donnell raises his eyebrows.

Josh continues. "Rake indentations didn't give us anything. A standard model that golf courses use for sand bunkers."

O'Donnell shakes his head.

Flynn adds, "This guy is thorough."

"Very." O'Donnell starts to gather his papers into one pile.

We all follow suit.

"Have you got somewhere quiet I can go, O'Donnell?" I ask.

"Stay in this room if you like."

"Fine." I put the case files back onto the desk. "And your nearest coffee place?"

"There's a Starbucks one block away—turn right as you go out of the building."

I take a few bills out of my wallet as the meeting room empties and then jog to Starbucks. I order a grande caramel macchiato with a double shot of espresso. Caffeine and sugar may be the only things that get me through the next few days.

Sophie seemed upset today. She'll need me soon.

I fill a bucket with warm, soapy water and a sponge. It's time for Sam's sponge bath. She really is beautiful. And she's got me the attention I deserve.

I look at her naked, petite body and gently cleanse away the dirt and grime.

"Does that feel nice?" I ask.

Her response is muffled by the duct tape.

"If I take it off, do you promise to be good?"

She nods.

"Do you promise not to scream?

She nods again.

I pull the tape off her mouth with a quick, sharp movement—I don't want to cause her more pain than necessary.

"Thank you," she says.

"You're welcome." I'm happy for her manners.

We're both silent and I sponge her breasts, her stomach, her legs and finally her groin.

"There. Does that feel better?"

"Yes."

"I don't think Sophie's taking your disappearance very well."

"You son of a bitch, you stay away from her!" she screams, her mood suddenly changing.

For an instant my temper wells up inside me, ready to burst, but then it quickly recedes. Control.

"That's very sweet of you. To be thinking about your friend," I say, moving around the table as I speak. I move in close to her ear and whisper, "But don't forget, you're the one on the table, honey." I emphasize the word *honey.* Sam loves using that word. "Sophie's safe...until I'm finished with you, that is."

She's silent and I presume her smart mind is trying to find a way out of the situation. But I can't see her eyes to be sure of this—I still have them covered.

"My name is Samantha Wright. I was born in a small town in Texas called—"

I interrupt her with a loud laugh. How ridiculous to try that one on me!

"Sam, my darling," I say, "surely you can do better than that. That's first-year criminal psychology, isn't it? Personalize yourself for the perpetrator. Make him feel you're a real person so he'll let you go. You really have no idea who you're dealing with, do you?"

"Tell me. Tell me about you," she says.

"I thought you knew all about me. No?"

She shakes her head.

"You can learn more about me later."

With her body freshly washed I run my fingers along her velvety skin. I murmur endearments in her ear and then we make love.

Coffee in hand, I go through the case notes and photos again. I've only got about two hours to finalize the profile. Much less time than I'd like. Once again Jean and Teresa crystallize in my mind and through them I get a shadowy image of the killer. Next I review the material to date on Susan Young. I pick up a photo of her from the crime scene, naked, eyes open, flowers all around her. I wonder if the killer liked the beauty that was surrounding her.

I go back to Jean, assimilating the facts in my head. I know he likes to watch his victims. I know Jean went out clubbing. Did they meet? How would it have been?

The five W's and the H come to mind: Who? What? When? Where? Why? How? These are the questions we try to answer in a profile. We follow the mantra that journalists follow. Just as they tell a story, we try to find the story and retell it. *Who* were the victims and *who* is the perp? *What* happened—cause of death, anything unusual? *When* did the crime occur and is there anything unusual or significant about that time or date? *Where* did it all go down? *How* was the crime committed—MO, signature, etc.? And finally *why*? In some cases the why, the motive, gives you the who. If it was for money, who would benefit? If it was for revenge, who had a grudge? But in the case of serial killers the why is usually about the ritual and its significance to the killer.

I close my eyes, ready to reenact the scene as it might have taken place. I let my imagination take over, just as I do when coming up with any profile…

Jean's at a nightclub, dancing. He's watching her. He's been watching her for days now. He sidles up to her, moving his hips in time with hers. He smells her skin, her scent, and breathes it in deeply, enjoying the smell that she emanates. Then he moves away, preferring their time together to be private. He shrinks back into the walls, absorbing their dull, plain white features. He is nameless and faceless again. He leaves the nightclub and goes straight to Jean's place.

He runs his fingers through his hair, hard, removing any loose strands. Then he places a hairnet firmly on his head, followed by a hat. Next he pulls his black leather gloves down over his hands. He enters her apartment through the front door, easily. He's been to the apartment before. He walks through the rooms as though they are his—her apartment is his domain. Everything she owns is his, just as *she'll* be his. He rummages around the kitchen and examines the contents of her fridge. There are things past their use-by date, and he throws them in the trash can. His eyes settle on a bottle of red wine on the counter. He pops the cork and pours himself a generous serving. He stands in the stark white of her kitchen and drinks his glass of wine, slowly. Twenty minutes later there is one tiny drop of wine left in his glass. Instead of taking the glass to his lips and letting the wine sink down his throat, he slowly tilts the glass and watches as the dark, rich-red drop hits the white, tiled floor. He smiles broadly, transfixed by the red droplet. He methodically cleans his glass and stoppers the bottle. He takes his place in her hall closet.

An hour later Jean enters the apartment. She notices the bottle of wine on the counter, takes a wineglass down and pours herself half a glass. She doesn't notice the sink. She sits on her couch, watching TV. He can see her now. Later she moves to her bedroom, stripping her clothes off as she goes.

Half an hour later, he emerges from the closet and walks softly down the corridor to her room. He watches the sleeping form of Jean. But he is patient. He creeps back to the corridor before letting himself out.

At 4:00 a.m. he reappears. He buzzes her apartment, and speaks into the intercom. He walks up the stairs and flashes identification at Jean, who is disheveled, still half-asleep. He tells her something and she hurriedly dresses and grabs her purse. He takes her down the stairs, carefully looking around to make sure no one is watching. She gets into his car, not noticing that the streetlight above the car is out, or that the inside car light doesn't illuminate when the doors open.

Suddenly the location has changed. Jean lies spread-eagle, tied to a metal gurney. The killer stands over her with a knife in his hand. He draws the knife along Jean's body and she flails her legs, but they hardly move, restricted by her bonds. Each tug is cut short as the minute amount of slack in the rope tightens in response to her jerky reactions. He smiles, undoes his fly and climbs on top of her. She moves against him but he does not notice.

I open my eyes and try to distance myself from the rape. I down the rest of my coffee. It's not as hot as I'd like, but the caramel sticks to my lips and for an instant I focus on the deliciously sweet sensation and not the killer.

I go back through some of the photos of Jean's apartment and notice the kitchen floor does indeed have a small drop of red on it. It looks like blood, but it's not. Did I see that photo before I pictured the crime scene or has my crime-scene reenactment drawn on my psychic abilities? I'll never know. The photo also reveals some jars, half-full, in the trash can beside her fridge.

I pick up the photo of her dumped body. I imagine Jean on the gurney. A gurney? That would tie in well with the lividity evidence—a totally smooth surface—and it would put the killer at the right angle for the stab wounds too.

I imagine her dead, on a gurney. The killer cleaned up his handiwork. He washed her cuts and scrubbed her down hard, ensuring that any traces of him were removed. He is thorough, so thorough that he even scrubbed at her fingernails and toenails and then cut them back. Sam's notion that he's got medical training comes to mind. Or perhaps it's his law-enforcement training—knowing that a single pubic hair on Jean's body could convict him. I wonder if his DNA is on our files, part of VICAP. Perhaps he's been caught before and wants to avoid a return trip to prison.

I move on to Teresa and, once more, I imagine that I'm in the scene.

The killer watches her, following her daily movements. She has regular routines: gym, work, self-defense classes. The regularity is perfect. And just like with Jean, habitual visits to her apartment are part of his routine. He feels powerful roaming freely in his victim's apartment, just as though he really was her boyfriend. He can do anything. Anything he wants.

She leaves work late, 9:00 p.m., and he's waiting for her in the building parking garage. It's deserted. She walks from the elevator to her Mercedes, her high heels keeping a regular beat on the concrete floor. He watches her in his rearview mirror and when she's close enough he opens the door and gets out of his van. He's parked right next to Teresa. He reaches inside his shirt pocket and brings out his ID.

He spins his story and she becomes upset. He tells her that something has happened to her sister. But then he slips up. She backs away from him and runs to her car. But it's too late. Just as she clicks the automatic locking system and pulls on the door handle of her car, he lunges at her, grappling her in a bear hug. Her briefcase and handbag go flying in different directions. She screams and he moves his hand to her mouth, pinching her nose at the same time. Her scream is stifled before it has time to reach its crescendo. She brings her heel down hard on his foot, elbows him in the stomach, and then goes to hit him in the groin.

It's a standard self-defense move. But Teresa misses her mark. He is too fast for her. He has her up and in the back of his van in less than thirty seconds. He climbs in the back with her and secures her gag and bindings, tying her hands to a railing in the back of the van. She's his.

I pick up the photo of Teresa the way she was found, dumped in Cedarville State Forest. I imagine him taking her there, a silhouette lowering the body carefully to the ground. He positioned her with her knees up and falling to one side, her arms fanned outward to waist height, and then her head turned a notch. This positioning is his signature. Every body was found in the same posture, even Jean who was in the back seat of the stolen car. But what does it mean? They look as though they're sleeping. Perhaps it's related to the notion of the women as his girlfriends. This way, he hasn't killed them, they're just asleep—dormant in his life because he's finished with them and ready to move on to the next girlfriend. Yet he doesn't close their eyes…people don't sleep with their eyes open. I glance at my watch and realize time is passing fast. I must look at Susan's file—perhaps I can find some answers there. I try to imagine her abduction and reenact it in my mind.

Susan is walking to her car, just like Teresa. Again the killer is parked next to her. He comes toward her, flashing his ID. He spins his story again. Something about one of her employees gone missing. Susan accepts the story—after all, he is a cop—and jumps in his car. Just like Jean he drives Susan to *his* location.

Strapped to his table, Susan breaks early. Earlier than the others. She begs for her life, begs for release. She does not hope to negotiate or escape. He has complete control over her and only he has the power to release her. For better or worse, this means she is dead sooner than the others. She only lasts three days. She cries and begs for her life and he gags her to stop her incessant whining. His patience is stripped bare. He's already started staking out his next victim, Sam, so it's easy for him to kill Susan. It takes him one step closer to Sam, just what he wants. He slashes Susan's throat—he's done with her. His special place is silent once more.

I notice from the police reports that many of Susan's friends and colleagues commented on how she came across hard and tough but was really a pussycat. The killer didn't get what he'd bargained for.

I look at my watch—it's 4:30 p.m. and I haven't really got any further, except for confirming he does use a badge. On a scrap piece of paper I write down some additional information.

Either is, or poses as cop or other law-enforcement official
Took Jean and Susan away of their own free will under false pretenses
Teresa was suspicious of his cover story—there was evidence of a struggle

Follow up body positioning
Follow up breaking-and-entering evidence (Was he in their apartments?)
Follow up video footage from parking lot

Then I write underneath in large letters and circle it— What if Sam doesn't break? What will he do???

I close my eyes for a moment. I think about Sam. Where is she? What's he doing to her? To date, my visions have been random, but I need to control them. I've got to at least try to induce an image. I slow my breathing down and clear my mind. I'm rewarded by an onslaught of images.

She's on the killer's gurney, tied up. She has her head turned to the side, as far as it will go. Her eyes are tightly closed and tears run down her cheeks. Her arms are taut, struggling against the ties. Then the image zooms out and I see him, on top of her. He wears a balaclava and his pelvis moves up and down.

I jerk my eyes open and the image disappears.

"Oh God!" I take a deep breath but no air reaches my lungs. I run from the project room to the toilets, just making it in time for the bowl to catch the contents of my stomach. The smell of bile, milk and vomit rises and I lurch again, bringing up the rest of the caramel macchiato and my morning's fruit salad. I haven't been able to eat anything else today. Not since I found out about Sam.

I sink to my knees and a whimper escapes my lips and then turns into silent yet guttural crying. A few quick in-breaths are the only sounds that give away my grief. Tears stream down my face. I let the sobs come, yet they give me no relief, no sense of emotional release.

I try to reassure myself. It might not be a vision, even though I was trying to induce one. It might be me reenacting my worst fears. Then again, it might not be. Bile rises again, but I have nothing left in my stomach.

We have to find him. We have to get this bastard. I grit my teeth, all I can think about is revenge. I want to kill the bastard, or better yet, make him suffer. I shake with rage. I need to get myself together. I have to focus on the case. The clock is ticking. I swallow my tears, grief and anger, pushing them down inside me. Control. It's about control. I've got to get myself together before the team returns.

In the project room ten minutes later I hope I look the model of composure. I study my list and feel slightly discouraged. It's not really any more than what Sam came up with.

I rest my head in my hands and close my eyes. A few minutes later I look up to see Josh hovering over me. Yet again he entered a room without a sound.

"You all right?" he asks.

"Fine. Sorry, I was just thinking. About the profile."

"Did you come up with anything?"

"A few little bits. What about you?"

"The VICAP stuff looks really good. We've definitely got a few matches, including some in Arizona."

My phone rings. "Agent Anderson."

"Hi, Sophie, it's Janet."

"Hi, Janet. What's up?"

"I've got your appointment with Dr. Rosen set up. You're seeing her at ten tomorrow morning."

"Surely this can wait until we find Sam."

"Rivers told me you'd say that. I'm sorry, Sophie, but you have to keep the appointment, no matter what. Rivers and Pike are both insisting that everyone in the unit is assessed because of Sam's disappearance. Even I've got to see Amanda."

"But Janet—"

"I'm sorry, Sophie. They're not accepting any buts."

"Fine… Fine. Bye." I try not to take it out on Janet.

"What's up?" Josh asks.

"I've got my appointment with Amanda tomorrow."

He rolls his eyes. "Me too. I'm up for two in the afternoon. When's yours?"

"Ten tomorrow morning." I shake my head. "Finding Sam is a hell of a lot more important than going to see some shrink," I say. "Even if it is Amanda."

Josh strokes my hair and then puts his arm around me, giving me a squeeze. "How are you holding up?"

"I'm fine," I say, not wanting him, or any man, to touch me. Not when all I can think about is what that bastard is doing to Sam.

CHAPTER 12

The rest of the team files in.

Krip sits next to me and the pungent smell of stale tobacco brings my nausea back.

O'Donnell strides across the room. "Okay, let's get this started. You first, Couples." He sits down. "Anything from Sam's place?"

"Not good news, I'm afraid," Sandra says, smoothing her hair down behind her ear and opening her notepad. "No prints except Sam's and Sophie's on the profile. Same with all the files. And the files match the inventory exactly."

We're all silent. We were hoping for a lead. *I* was hoping for a lead. I slide my ring on and off my finger. How can this be happening?

"Okay. Marco, let's hear about VICAP. Tell me you've

got some good news." O'Donnell rubs the bridge of his nose with his thumb and forefinger, and his glasses move up and down.

"The VICAP guys have sorted through the database matches on the new search and done a first cull. We've got lots of hits." Josh passes out copies of the VICAP report. "That's good news," he says, looking at O'Donnell.

We each end up with what looks like at least fifteen pages.

Josh does a quick double-click of his pen. "The report shows all the computer matches, and the guys have highlighted the ones they think are probably our perp. There are a few that have been logged from Arizona, which would correspond to our writing analysis."

An elimination process.

O'Donnell flips to the first page. "So, let's go through them."

"I had a quick glance before I came over here," Josh says. "I think we've got at least ten definite matches."

Flynn flicks through the pages quickly and then returns to the first one. "Our perp's a busy boy."

Flynn's right. If this is our killer, he's gone from three vics in D.C. to a long, murderous history. The body count is rising.

"Very busy. Across at least three different states over the last eleven years," Josh says. "And these are only the murders that have been logged on the database by the cops." He waves the printout in the air. "We've still got a hell of lot of states and individuals that aren't on the bandwagon."

"Those pesky cops, hey?" Jones says.

"I wonder if he moves for work—his paid work—or for his charming hobby," Krip says.

"That's a question we need to answer," O'Donnell says, pointing his finger at Krip.

I don't think Krip will be trying too hard to answer any questions.

I stand up and walk toward the window, partly to get away from the smell of tobacco, and partly because sitting still is making my skin crawl. I stare at the D.C. skyline. From here I can see the Washington Monument and the top of the Smithsonian.

I turn around and lean on the window. "I definitely think our guy is either in law enforcement or poses as a cop. I had another look at the crime scenes and both Jean and Susan went willingly with their attacker."

Flynn raises his hands behind his head and leans back. "That's more likely than him knowing his victims. We've run down all the girls' acquaintances and there are no matches, no common friends. If they knew him, they would have been seen with him."

"What about security footage from the parking lots?" I ask.

Flynn furrows his brow and his blue eyes fix on me. "No good. Our perp tampered with the cameras. The one in Teresa's lot was reported as malfunctioning two days before, and Susan's the day before she was nabbed."

"So he's cased the scenes. There must be some footage of him from earlier, at least from the days the cameras malfunctioned," I say.

"We've been through that footage several times. Nothing looks suspicious. No vans, either. Maybe once we've got a suspect we can run them against the tape to place them at the crime scene. But with no suspects, we've got squat." Flynn casts his eyes down and leans forward on the table again.

"VICAP," O'Donnell says, refocusing the group's attention on the report.

I sit down. I'll have to put up with the smell of Krip.

We go through the VICAP notes, crossing out murders that are definitely unrelated.

After much discussion—and nearly one and a half hours—we are down to a list of fifteen murders, including the two in Chicago. We've included one the VICAP guys didn't think was relevant and taken out two, but other than that our lists match. I move over to the whiteboard and write it up.

1995–1996: 3 in Arizona
1997–2000: 6 in Michigan
2000: 1 in Florida
2001–2005: 2 in Chicago
2006: 3 in Washington

"Corresponds with the notion of him moving around," Couples says.

Josh scribbles on his pad. "Yeah. I think we can assume he lived in these states during the crime periods."

"Except perhaps Florida," Flynn says. "We've only got one murder down there."

Krip swings his chair from side to side. "A holiday fling perhaps."

"That would make sense. That one's in January. He may have gone down for some sun," I say.

Couples reads down the list. "And the last Michigan one was after the Florida murder. In May."

"So let's assume our guy hasn't lived in Florida, but he's probably lived in the other four states. Agreed?" O'Donnell says. We all nod or verbalize our agreement. "And are we happy that all these murders are definitely the work of our killer?"

"Yeah. We've got the body positioning in all of them," I say.

"But…" Jones flicks through the notes. "His MO's changed."

"Not surprising," Josh says. "He's been refining his art. He also keeps the girls for longer now."

"And he never went for career girls until the past few years," Flynn says.

Couples follows his lead. "His first victim, in Arizona, was a schoolkid. Only sixteen."

I glance through the victim list. We don't have detailed information or photos, but it's obvious from what we do have that the age of the victims has been increasing. He also started off with high-school students, college girls and a few full-time workers, but more transient girls. A pattern. The only one who doesn't fit this trend is the second victim in Arizona. She was twenty-five at the time and worked as a shop assistant. Even had a husband.

"Except for the second murder, the ages have gradually increased, and the targets have changed," I say, my voice quickening with the promise of a lead. "We've got five students, a waitress, one unemployed woman, and this last girl in Michigan worked at a shoe store, but she'd only had the job for three weeks. Then suddenly in Chicago there's a shift in his victim type. He's gone from women who are generally high-risk victims—naive, transient, etc.—to the low-risk victims, women who are more career focused. A receptionist and a personnel officer in Chicago and then here in D.C. he's gone for the real go-getters."

"So why the change?" Couples asks.

There's silence for a moment.

"He went to college in Michigan," Josh says. "Probably a graduate program, given his current age in the profile."

"Of course," I say. "That fits perfectly. He thinks of these women as his girlfriends and as he moves up the social and professional ladder, so do his victims."

"This is getting good," O'Donnell says, taking off his glasses. Even Krip seems interested and leans forward in his chair.

We're interrupted by a phone ringing. It's Sandra's.

"This might be something," she says. "Couples... Uh-huh... Yep... Right... No, of course they didn't report it. Thanks." She hangs up and then addresses us, quickly pushing her hair behind her ears. "Sam's neighbors from below did hear noises on Wednesday night at around ten forty-five. In fact, they even thought they heard a scream."

"Goddamn it," Flynn says, expressing what we all feel. "When will people learn to report this kind of shit?"

People often hear things, bad things, and don't report it. They don't think it's any of their business.

"At least we know when she was taken," Jones says, lifting his pen from the doodles on his pad.

I'm not comforted. If she was taken on the Thursday, it would have given us more time.

After a minute of silence O'Donnell speaks. "So, where were we? That's right, college in Michigan. Getting good."

And with that we go back to the guy's homicidal history.

"So our suspect list is every male who studied in the state of Michigan," Krip says. "Not exactly a small sample to investigate."

Couples drops her pen on top of her notepad. "He's right."

I stay positive. This is a break. "It's a start, at least. A good start."

Josh smiles at me.

I look at him, part of me longing to touch him even in all this mess. And then it hits me. "Hey, didn't you study in Michigan, Marco?" I make sure I use his last name.

"Yeah. I remember the murders well." He flicks his eyes to the window. He seems sad. "In fact, they're one of the reasons I wanted to get into law enforcement."

"What colleges are in Michigan?" O'Donnell asks Josh.

"University of Michigan, Michigan State, Central Michigan University, Oakland University…there're quite a few."

We all jot down the ones that Josh reels off. Even Krip takes down some notes.

O'Donnell stands up. "Okay," he says, "we need a full list of colleges and we need all the enrollment names for 1997 to 2000, just the students who were enrolled for all three years." He walks to the whiteboard and back again. "We also need the full case files—from all the murders—to see if there's anything we can use."

"Particularly the early ones. That's where he may have made the mistakes," Flynn says, looking at me. Flynn's throwing me a bone, knowing how much I need it.

He's right. Those early ones might hold the clue that saves Sam. I want the first murder.

"Anyone got contacts?" O'Donnell asks.

"I'll take Chicago Homicide. Recontact them and get the full files sent over," Flynn says. His blue eyes fix on me.

I take the cue. "I'll do Arizona. I'd like to see how this guy started out."

"You got it, Anderson," O'Donnell says. "And look into this second victim. Why doesn't she fit the victim profile in terms of age and occupation?"

I nod. It's a good question. Maybe she saw something she wasn't supposed to. The first murder was unplanned, but perhaps something went wrong. A witness? So he kills her and once she's dead he can establish his routine. It wouldn't be the first time.

"I'll do Michigan," Josh says. "I worked in the field office for a couple of months in my rookie days."

"Florida?" O'Donnell asks. No one responds. "Krip, you follow that one up."

"Sure."

That lazy bastard better do it.

"Couples, you and I can work on the full list of colleges and students," O'Donnell says.

Sandra nods once, her bob bouncing.

"Anything else?" O'Donnell asks.

"What if it's a cop? Could even be someone who's worked on the cases and moved around," Krip says.

O'Donnell loosens his shirt collar slightly. "I'll look into that." He's new on the case, so he's the best one to investigate, especially if he runs checks on D.C. police and FBI personnel.

There's silence for a moment.

Flynn unfolds a map from his folder. "This shows us the crime-scene locations." He takes the map up to the whiteboards. He sticks it on the left whiteboard, securing it with four magnets.

O'Donnell follows Flynn to the front of the room for a closer look. "With only three murders, any pattern will be hard to see."

We all stand up and gather around the map.

Jones leans in. "We've got Jean Davis in a stolen car at Keys Bridge," he says, pointing to a red cross on the map. "Teresa in Cedarville State Forest." He points to the outskirts of D.C. and another red cross. "And Susan in East Potomac Park." He points to the large park. "It looks pretty random, for the moment at least." He shakes his head.

"Well, let's keep the map up here. We might find a pattern," O'Donnell says. "Anything else?" He turns around to face us.

There must be something else. I think back to my profiling and remember my feeling that he was in Jean's home, going through her things, including the fridge. And I still don't believe Sam would have left her bedroom window open.

"Maybe, hold on a sec," I say. I move back to my spot

on the table and flip through the photos from Jean's, Teresa's and Susan's apartments. I'm looking for their trash cans. I find them in the photo. Teresa's and Susan's are both covered bins but Jean's is open. "Jean was last seen taking out the trash, yet there's stuff in her trashcan." I use the American terms, trash and trashcan, rather than the Australian equivalents. I find myself using more and more U.S. terms—it's easier when you're working with Americans.

Flynn walks back to the table and leans in. "So there is."

"Have we got a contents list for all the girls?"

"We've got everything," Flynn says.

The rest of the team file back to the table, but only Krip sits back down.

"Just a hunch," I say.

Jones starts shuffling paper. "It's in the police report."

We all flip through our reports.

"Here it is. Page five, middle of the page," Jones says.

I read through the section and, sure enough, all women had a few things that could have been past the use-by date. I hold up the photo of Jean's bin.

"Given Jean had just taken the trash out, this bin should have been virtually empty," I say. "And surely if she was going to clean out her fridge, she'd do it before she took out a load of trash."

I'm met with considered silence.

I run with it. "The killer did this. He visits their homes before he abducts them and cleans out their fridges."

"Sounds pretty bizarre," Couples says.

"I bet you anything some of those items are out of date. I reckon he's either a neat freak or a health freak.

He snoops around the houses and can't help himself if there's something out of date in the fridge," I say.

"It'll be easy enough to check," Flynn says.

Josh clicks his pen. "But how did he get in?" He looks at Flynn and Jones. "Any signs of forced entry?"

"No. But I might check the victims' houses again. It's not something we looked for except in Jean's case," Flynn says. "The other two were abducted elsewhere."

"What if he doesn't break in?" I say, remembering my feeling that the killer entered Jean's house through the front door, and thinking about the evidence at Sam's.

"He could pick the lock," O'Donnell says.

"He could be a locksmith." Krip focuses his green eyes on me. "They have lock-picking guns that open most locks in seconds. Gets 'em in anywhere. That's how they can get you in if you lock yourself out."

"That would certainly allow him to move around his victims' homes with ease," I say.

"And anywhere else he damn liked," Josh says. "I've seen these things on the Internet. He wouldn't have to be a locksmith, anyone can buy one. It's a hobby for lots of people."

"Purchasing depends on state legislation," Jones says. "In some states you have to be a registered locksmith to own one of these tools."

"Do the Web sites enforce it?" Josh asks.

O'Donnell takes over. "Jones, follow this up. See if we can track it down somehow. The Web sites must have a database of their customers." He jots down a note in his book, then looks up and over his glasses at Jones.

"I'll look into it," Jones says.

Couples tucks her hair behind her ear. "A master key is another alternative."

Flynn looks at her. "If the perp was a super or friends with the supers?"

Couples nods. "The super or the locksmiths who fitted out the buildings and made the master keys."

"I'll follow that up too," Jones says.

Krip leans forward and gives me a strange look. "We're assuming he gets in."

Krip is questioning my judgment. Part of me is angry that he's challenging my ideas, but logically he's right. It's a lot of time following one direction, one avenue. What if I'm wrong? What if Sam did forget her window that night? Sam's life is on the line here. I bite my lip.

O'Donnell looks at me, deciding. After a couple of seconds: "Let's run it down. See where it leads."

Krip leans back in his seat.

"Couples, have you got photos of Sam's house?" I ask.

"Yeah, I picked them up from the lab on the way over." She rummages in her briefcase. "I'm picking up extra copies for everyone first thing tomorrow morning." She passes them to me.

I flick through the photos, hoping to come to Sam's trash. Then I stop, remembering that she has a pedal bin.

"Sam's got a pedal bin. Get a list of the contents of her fridge and the trash. Get your guys to check the use-by dates."

Sandra nods.

There's silence as we try to think of other leads. But we've exhausted everything for the moment.

"Well, that's all for now," O'Donnell says. He starts a

new page on his notepad and scribbles as he talks. "So, we've got Flynn looking up the Chicago murders, Jones looking into the lock-picking angle, Krip chasing up Florida, Marco is taking Michigan, Anderson Arizona, and I'll get a full list of Michigan colleges. Couples, why don't you stay on Sam's place. See if you get anything new. Who knows, maybe he'll return for that necklace of his." O'Donnell closes his notepad and looks up at us. "Let's try to chase down these case files and we'll meet again first thing tomorrow morning. We'll make it six-thirty," he says, looking at his watch. "With the time difference you should be able to get onto the case files tonight. Catch the cops before they finish up for the day and get them to FedEx the files."

We all nod and check our watches. It's seven o'clock, which makes it six in Michigan, Chicago and Florida; and five in Arizona.

"Also, I've had word from above. Wright's disappearance is hush-hush. Tell your contacts we're investigating the Slasher murders, but don't mention Wright or the fact that the perp's got an FBI agent."

O'Donnell stands up. "Okay. See you back here at six-thirty." At the door he turns back. "I'll get breakfast organized."

It's 9:30 p.m. by the time I get home. I've accomplished quite a lot in the past two hours, managing to contact one of the detectives who worked on the homicides in Arizona. Detective Darren Carter. He's couriered the full files to the D.C. Field Office and I should have them by midday tomorrow. He also faxed through the paperwork to give me a head start on the Slasher's first kills. It's these documents that I'll go through for the rest of the night, until I can't concentrate anymore or until I fall asleep. I've also got the photos from Sam's apartment… maybe I'll find something there.

I sit down at my dining-room table and absorb the police reports, coroner's reports and the original FBI profile from the Arizona murders. The cases manage to distract me from Sam's immediate danger. However, the lack of photos makes the going slow. It's much harder to picture the crimes without any visual stimulus. I concentrate mostly on the first victim, the sixteen-year-old schoolgirl. She's the key to the killer and his identity. In fact, I'd bet my bottom dollar that he knew her. I pore over the reports until I have an insight into how the girl lived and died. It's time to profile, to imagine the crime. I'll have to make some assumptions, but that's par for the course with profiling. I close my eyes, lean back in my chair and visualize what might have happened.

He's kissing her, his excitement building. But he doesn't respect her. She's been with a few guys and he knows she's experienced…he thinks she's too young to be experienced. But that doesn't stop him. He's rough. Too rough and she asks him to stop. He smiles. She slaps his face and it sends him over the edge. He thinks she's a whore, yet she's rejecting *him*.

After years of profiling I can feel the killer's thoughts clearly, almost as if they were my own, and the distorted sensation disturbs me. I feel his anger, his rejection and his superiority. The image crystallizes in my mind.

They're in the middle of nowhere. No one's around.

He has control over the situation. It's his decision, not hers. He puts his hands around her throat, strangles her and forces himself upon her. She tries to close her legs but he pushes them open. He will win. He will have her. Her eyes are wide open. Just as she's about to pass out from lack of oxygen he releases his grip slightly, to prolong her useless life. He avoids her glazed stare and instead fixes his eyes on her throat. He's nervous, angry and excited—each emotion somehow coexisting with the others. Then, as he's about to climax, he squeezes his hands more tightly around her throat. He comes. His sexual release is accompanied by a surge of adrenaline. She's dead.

The adrenaline pumps through my body. And just as heroin users feel pleasure engulf their bodies with their first hit and know they must experience it again, so too does our killer. He knows the power of murder and nothing else can live up to that sensation. His emotions repulse me.

I sit back, letting his energy leave my body. I sit silently for a couple of minutes. Tiredness is winning me over. My eyes are heavy. I look at my watch, it's 11:45 p.m. But I can't go to bed yet. I need to stay awake. For Sam. I move on to the photos from Sam's apartment. I pick up the pictures of her bedroom and study them for a minute or so. Then I close my eyes and will myself to see something. Anything. I want more than profiling, I want a vision.

After fifteen minutes nothing's happened. Physical exhaustion probably doesn't help. I need to sleep…but I'm still not ready to give in for the night. I start up my laptop. Time for some surfing. Perhaps the symbol from the necklace has a specific meaning, something that will help us with the killer's identity. I navigate to a search engine and type in *Celtic symbols*. Over two hundred thousand sites. I click on the first one and it's a good Web site, with pictures of many different symbols. I scan several pages until I find it. It's called a Triquetra or Triqueta and is mostly used as a symbol for the Holy Trinity—the Father, Son and Holy Spirit. Is our guy religious? Interestingly, the symbol dates back even further, and was originally a Wiccan symbol of the triple aspect of the goddess—maid, mother and crone. It's intriguing, but it doesn't give me any leads I can follow.

I force myself to look at the photos of Sam's apartment one more time. I'm looking for a clue, anything that might help me find out who took Sam, and where.

I wake with a start at 5:30 a.m., my arms and head resting on my dining-room table. I raise my upper body and a sharp pain from being slumped over the table travels down my back. I stand up gingerly, and something falls from my back onto the floor. I look down. It's a quilt. The one that my grandma made me. Where did that come from?

I stare at the quilt and back away. I shake my head and slam into the wall. He's been here. He's been in my apartment. In this room.

My training takes over—he might still be here. I unholster my gun and take the safety off. I didn't do my usual sweep last night. Was he in my apartment the whole time? Waiting for me?

I carry out my search the way I always do it, but this time is different. Normally I'm prepared for anything but know that I'm being paranoid and that I won't find anyone. But this time someone's been in my apartment. Touching my things. Touching me. My breathing quickens. If I don't control it soon, I'll hyperventilate. I take a deep breath in, then out, and walk toward the kitchen, my gun stretched out in front of me. I come around the kitchen counter quickly, ready to fire. It's clear. I swing around, aiming my Smith & Wesson down the hall.

I walk slowly down the corridor, pausing at the hall closet. That's where the quilt was. At some stage, the killer was in that closet, and if he's still there, I'll kill him. No, he's the only one who knows where Sam is. I'll shoot, but not to kill. I take two deep, silent breaths and then swing the door open with my left hand. My right hand holds my gun firmly, ready to fire.

The closet's empty. I make my way down the corridor, both hands on my gun again. I check the bathroom, wary as always of the shower curtain. Nothing. Nobody. Part of me wants to find him. I imagine going into my room, looking under the bed and being greeted by his face. Then at least I'd get to Sam. I've got a gun and I'd be able to fire before he could overpower me. But I'll have to aim perfectly—shoot to harm not kill, so I can find Sam.

Finally I'm in the bedroom. I check my wardrobe first, again using my left hand to open the doors and my right to hold my gun. The gun shakes and I'm ashamed of my fear. I'm trained for this. I can take him. The wardrobe's clear.

I come to my bed. I keep my distance, I don't want my leg to be within his reach if he is hiding under there. I sink quickly to my haunches and peer under the bed.

My apartment's empty. I go back into the living room, gun hanging by my side. I hear a noise at the front door…

I'm slumped over the table. What the hell? I look down at my hand. My gun's not there, it's in my holster. I stand up and look for the quilt. It's gone. Still drowsy and confused, I draw my gun. I was dreaming. The noise starts again and I jump. Someone's knocking on my apartment door. I walk toward the door, gun in front of me. My skin is clammy with sweat and my heart still pounds from the dream.

I open the door. A man's frame fills my door. I jolt with fright and my finger exerts pressure on the trigger. I stop myself just in time.

"Josh!"

"What's wrong? What's happening?" He draws his gun too, looks around, and then looks back at me, focusing on my gun. "Is the safety on?"

I lower my weapon and throw my arms around him. "Thank God it's you."

Josh gathers me into his right arm. I like the feeling of being held. I hold him tightly for a few seconds but then push him away gently. You have to be tough in this line of work.

Josh comes inside and closes the door behind him, keeping his arm around me. He's still alert, looking around. I know what a good agent he is and the thought makes me feel safe. I relax a little.

"What's up, Sophie?"

"I…I thought he was here."

"The Slasher?"

"It's all right. It was just a dream."

"You sure?" He looks around the room.

"Yeah. I fell asleep at the table last night and woke up when you knocked."

Josh reholsters his weapon. "Sorry, I didn't mean to frighten you."

"How'd you get in anyway?"

"Someone was coming out and I just grabbed the security door. I should have buzzed."

"No, that's okay." I'm still fighting to bring my mind into reality and out of the dream.

"I think you should come off this case, Sophie."

I can feel the tension in his body.

"I'm not leaving Sam with him. I've got to do something."

"But what if you're a target?"

Has my biggest fear been realized? No, it was just a dream.

"He's got Sam. He won't come after anyone else while Sam's…" I trail off.

Josh pulls back a little and looks into my eyes. His hand comes up to my face and he wipes away a tear that, to my disgust, has squeezed its way out of my eye.

I look down and finish my sentence. "Not while Sam's alive."

Josh looks at his watch. "You better get ready."

I head to the shower and undress. I look at my naked reflection in the mirror. My deathly white skin accentuates dark circles under my eyes. My hair is greasy, making it look brown rather than blond, and strands cling to my scalp and face. I turn the shower on. Josh stands in the doorway, able to see me but not within touching distance.

"Any luck last night with the Michigan force?" I ask.

"They're couriering the files to me."

"Same with Arizona."

I roughly massage shampoo into my scalp, creating a thick lather. I rinse. "I looked up the symbol from the necklace."

"And?"

"It's a Triquetra—the three shapes represent the Father, Son and Holy Spirit."

"So we're looking for a religious nut."

"Could be. Or if the killer did take it from another victim, *she* could have been the religious one."

I rinse the last soap from my body and turn off the taps. I emerge from the shower with water droplets glistening on my naked skin. I grab my towel.

Marco takes in my naked body. "Do you feel better?"

"I'll say."

"Look, Sophie, maybe you should stay with me. Just until this is over." He's being protective again. He moves closer and strokes my arm. "Or I could stay here." His hand moves slowly to my breast.

I look up at Josh and wonder if our timing could have sucked any more. I choose my next words carefully. "Josh, I have to stay focused on this case. On getting Sam back." I pause, hold his hand and take it off my breast. "And spending time with you…"

Josh backs away, offended.

"It's a compliment," I say. "I can't have any distractions, not even one as wonderful as you." I've laid a little more of my emotions on the line than I would have liked.

"We don't have to…what I mean is, we could work on

the case together. I don't want to be a distraction, I want to help. I want to find Sam too, you know."

I withdraw my hand and start towel-drying my hair.

"I'll even sleep on the couch," he says with a cheeky grin.

I look at him, wondering if we'd really be able to keep our hands off each other. I don't want to be by myself, I really don't. And I would feel safer with him in the apartment. But I could never forgive myself if something happened to Sam while Josh and I were fooling around.

"I'll think about it," I say, walking past him and into my bedroom to change. But my mind's already made up. I'm not abandoning Sam. Not now.

CHAPTER 13

"Let's have it," O'Donnell says at exactly 6:30 a.m., turning to his immediate left. Flynn. Sandra Couples walks in and hurriedly takes a seat.

Flynn looks up, addressing all the team members. "I made contact last night with Chicago and we should have the two case files by midday. But like I said, it was a dead end when we looked into it a couple of weeks ago. Detective Hogan who worked the cases said they had no firm suspects and no substantial leads." Flynn counts off on his fingers. "No prints, no DNA, no witnesses to the abduction, no nothing." He places his hands flat on the table. "They saw the similarities between the two murders and were getting ready for a long haul. Waiting for victim number three in Chicago."

"So there were only two murders in Chicago over a four-year period," I say. "Are they sure only the four? It seems very low compared to our perp's activities in other years."

O'Donnell flips the pages of his notepad and on a new page transfers some figures. "He's averaging about two murders a year, except for Chicago."

Flynn leans forward, his blue eyes seeming even brighter than usual. "I mentioned that to Hogan and he said once they connected the second murder they went through past homicides but nothing seemed related."

"So why was he so quiet?" Jones asks, scribbling on his pad and looking at Josh and I.

An unspoken recognition occurs between Josh and I.

"Girlfriend," we say in unison.

Josh elaborates. "The first Chicago murder was May 2001 and the second was in January 2005. Somewhere in the middle there he had a 'normal—'" he makes quotation marks in the air "—relationship."

Krip takes his eyes away from the window but stays reclined in his chair. "Ah, yes. The old, 'I'm not going to kill anyone because I'm getting some at home.'"

"Well, not quite but almost, in terms of the psychology behind it," I say, choosing not to go into detail. I want to get back on track—Sam is waiting for me.

O'Donnell senses my impatience and moves it along. "Jones? Anything on the locksmith angle?"

"I checked it out on the Net last night. There are dozens of sites where you can buy a lock-picking set or one of the lock-picking guns." He hands out a few print-outs of guns and sets. They range from $29 to over $500.

O'Donnell nods. "That doesn't help us much."

"Depends when he got it," I say. "If he got it in Arizona, it may have been before they were available online."

"True," Jones says, scribbling something on top of his doodles.

"Jones, keep checking into it."

Jones nods. "I should also be able to find out which locksmiths did the doors at the apartments today."

"That could end up being our link," I say. Please let it be the link.

"I also went over the files from the D.C. cases and worked on the victimology for Susan Young. I'll have it ready by the end of the day," Jones says.

"Excellent." O'Donnell moves his gaze around the table to Josh.

"I contacted the Michigan Field Office and our guys are sending through the files. I spoke to the original profiler on the case and the agent who worked it. They backed up what we've found here." Josh double-clicks his pen. "The guy's like a ghost. No one's ever seen anything suspicious and he's always very clean in his work. No prints, no DNA."

"Not exactly comforting," Couples says.

"We need to concentrate on the medical, scientific background or law-enforcement angle of Sam's profile," I say.

"I agree. That's what we should cross-reference once we start going through all the student records from the Michigan colleges," O'Donnell says.

"It's going to take some time."

Someone had to say it. Sifting through student names and records will be a nightmare. Sam doesn't have that much time. We have to find another lead, or more things to cross-reference, unless the locksmith angle pans out.

"Let's do this now, while we're on it." O'Donnell gets up and writes *student records* on the whiteboard. "So, we're going to concentrate on med and science students first."

"Who sat their SATs in Arizona," I say and O'Donnell writes it on the board.

"We could use IRS records to narrow it down by tax returns with addresses that correspond to the murder locations," Flynn says.

"Yep, that's a good one. Unless he's not listing his real address," O'Donnell says as he writes *IRS records* on the whiteboard. "Anything else?"

No one responds.

O'Donnell starts a new column. "Let's move on to the law-enforcement angle."

"We could look into FBI and CIA records for recruits and applicants who studied in Michigan," Josh says.

"And maybe the forces in Arizona, Michigan, Chicago and Washington," Couples says.

O'Donnell writes it all up.

Couples smoothes her hair out. "Not looking too bad now."

"Certainly one step up from the needle in the haystack," Krip says.

O'Donnell stops writing. "Anything else?"

No one responds.

"Okay, back to our status." O'Donnell crosses the room and takes a seat once more. "Couples, where are you at with Wright's place?"

"Nothing new from forensics. Still no foreign prints," she says, then looks at me. "I got my guys to check her trash can. There was a half-empty tub of cream past its use-by and a few wilted vegetables."

"Surely that can't be coincidence—all four victims cleaning out their fridges before being abducted?" Flynn says.

Couples shakes her head. "It's so bizarre that he empties their fridges."

"Not really," I say. "He thinks of the victims as his girlfriends and he feels comfortable in their homes. He makes himself at home, completely. In his own sick way, he's looking after them."

"Plus, if he's got a medical background he could be a germ freak. Science guys are often pretty nutty about that sort of stuff," Josh says.

We're silent for a few moments before O'Donnell turns his gaze to Krip.

Krip leans forward. "Well, Florida's more of the same. Clean crime scene. Virtually no real leads or suspects. Full file is on the way." He uses the minimum number of words.

"Okay." O'Donnell stands up and walks to the whiteboard again. He lists the different states and the different leads. He underlines Arizona and turns to me.

"Arizona?"

"I spoke to them last night. The file's on its way too." I force a small smile. "I really think this first victim, Sally-Anne Raymond, is the key. He must have known her. I'd like to fly over there. Find out more about the murder, actually interview her family myself." It would be standard practice for us to reinterview in this sort of case, even if an FBI agent hadn't been nabbed, but I'm also hoping being at the crime scene might somehow trigger a vision. So far the only time I've been able to induce something was yesterday in the project room, when I saw Sam being raped—and I'm sure as hell hoping that was my imagination. If I can't control this psychic ability, I need to at least provide stimuli that might trigger it.

Josh moves uneasily in his seat and again I fluctuate between being annoyed and being flattered by his protectiveness. Should I tell him about my dreams and visions? I will, but not yet. I'd like to have some form of control over them before I drop that bombshell on Josh.

O'Donnell flicks the whiteboard marker against his hand. "Sounds like a good idea. We'll split all the leads up in a moment and work out who's doing what."

"What about the media? Are we going to use them?" Krip says.

The group focuses on Josh and I—it's usually the profiler's call.

"What do you think?" Josh says.

"Could be useful. We could follow the suggestion in Sam's profile and attribute a murder to the D.C. Slasher."

"But with our time frame, I don't know if contact with the killer will help. He's already had Sam for about fifty-six hours," Josh says.

She's been with the bastard for almost sixty hours. I furiously twist the ring on my finger.

"We need to find some suspects and then hope one is right. That way we've got a chance to get to Sam in time," Flynn says. He's trying to reassure me, but his statement has the opposite effect. There are one too many steps in his scenario, and the clock is ticking.

O'Donnell tosses the whiteboard marker back and forth between his hands. "A newspaper story could help us identify him, if it draws him out in some way."

"It's worth a shot. But he may be expecting it," I say. I don't know if it will lead us anywhere, but we have to try everything.

"Let's run a story and see what happens," Josh says.

O'Donnell writes up *Newspaper story* and places a tick next to it. "Agreed."

"I'll give Murray Cavanaugh at the *Post* a call and get him to run something about a fourth Slasher victim," Flynn says. "What dirt are we going to add?"

Jones leans back, pulling himself away from his doodles. "We could release the med-student angle."

"I think we want to run with something we know to be wrong," Josh says.

"I agree. We know he thinks of the victims as his girlfriends and that he's targeting highly educated women. So why don't we say that we're looking for a blue-collar worker and that the fourth victim is a prostitute," I say.

"Or what about a 'lead witness in police custody' angle?" Flynn says.

Josh and I both raise our eyebrows. A good suggestion.

Flynn runs with it. "Someone's got to have seen him. Even though he seems invisible. So we fabricate. Make him think he slipped up."

"Which is more likely to get a response?" I say, thinking out aloud.

Josh looks at me. "The blue-collar worker. He's really improved himself and worked his way up. He's proud of that. Too proud to be thought of as a factory worker or laborer. He's a head man," he says, tapping his finger on his head.

O'Donnell writes the *Post* and *blue collar* on the whiteboard, underneath *Newspaper story.* "Okay, so that brings us to me. I've got the full list of Michigan universities, forty-four in total."

We all moan at this news.

"I know. A few more than we were hoping." He walks back to his place at the table and fumbles through his files. "We'll have to divvy them up. Some we'll be able to cross off altogether if they don't offer a science or medical program." He hands out a photocopied Web page with the full listing.

Once everyone's got the list, O'Donnell goes back to the whiteboard. He works his way across the handwritten leads. "So, this morning. Jones, you're looking into the locksmith thing." He pauses. "Couples, do you need to follow up with your team and forensics?"

"Not really. They'll call me if they find anything. I can work on the college lists."

O'Donnell nods, then pauses, scanning the whiteboard and his notes. "Anderson, you go to Arizona. Find out what you can, but make sure you've got the cops on your side."

"I'll get the next flight out."

"Um. Dr. Rosen," Josh says.

"Shit." Everyone turns my way. "Pike and Rivers have ordered everyone in our unit to see one of the Bureau's psychologists. I'm on at ten, so I'll have to fly out after that."

"If you schedule for the afternoon, the Arizona files should have arrived and you can review them on the plane," Josh says.

"Good idea." I'd momentarily forgotten about the Arizona files. I'll need them.

"I want the rest of us on the colleges. We need a list of suspects," O'Donnell says. He splits up the list of colleges between everyone except Jones and I. "Look at the programs they have first, and if they didn't have science or medical programs while our guy was there we'll rule them out for the moment."

O'Donnell goes through the list and divvies out the colleges. Josh recognizes three names and is able to say with certainty that these colleges have neither a science nor a medical program and never did. It narrows the list down a little.

"And Wright's phone call?" O'Donnell looks at Krip.

"I've got a nine o'clock appointment on that one."

"Good." O'Donnell looks around the room. It's obvious the meeting is closing.

"I'm going to head back to Quantico. I'll work from there until my appointment with Dr. Rosen," I say.

"Okay, Anderson. We'll get you the Arizona files as soon as they arrive. Depending on the time, we'll courier them to either Quantico or the airport. Let us know what flight you'll be on."

"Will do." I walk out of the room, resisting the urge to glance back at Josh. I need to devote my attention to Sam and the killer. Not to Josh.

By 10:00 a.m. I've booked a 1:00 p.m. flight to Tucson, Arizona, via Chicago, spoken to Detective Carter from

Arizona Homicide again, and set up an interview with the parents of the first victim.

I sit in Amanda's office, legs crossed. Her office is very different from the standard Quantico Bureau issue. Most offices are small and cannot hide their seventies origin. Amanda's, on the other hand, is double the size—probably two offices joined together—and it's had a redecorating job this century. The walls are a warm musk color, complemented by several pastels of landscapes. Ironically, one looks like it's of East Potomac Park when the cherry blossoms are in full bloom. The painting makes me think of Susan and the letter. Why didn't we realize Sam was in real danger? Why didn't I see it? Thoughts of my brother also swirl into the storm in my mind—why did I doubt myself then? My rational mind kicks it, but only for an instant: *You were eight years old, for God's sake.*

I take my eyes from the pastel and focus on the room again. The office furniture is also different to the BAU look. Amanda has a large teak desk, which is covered in files and two coffee cups, with her computer squashed up in the corner. In front of the desk are two black leather armchairs, and to the side is a small wooden table. On the table sit two glasses of water and the standard box of tissues—something any good shrink always has at hand. The room is topped off by several potted plants, which help give the room a slight homey feel. No doubt it's all in the name of helping agents open up and feel relaxed. But it has the opposite effect on me.

I sit uncomfortably in the large armchair, with Amanda opposite me. Her dark brown hair curls around her face and is tamed at the sides by two silver bobby pins. Her olive complexion looks smooth, despite her forty-odd years. Amanda's curvaceous figure is highlighted by her clothing. She wears a black V-neck, a purple-plum pencil skirt, black stockings and classy court shoes with a strap around her ankle.

Her full lips turn up in a smile and her dark brown eyes hold my gaze. Empathy.

"Sophie, I'm so sorry. Sorry about Sam and sorry we have to do this."

"Thanks. I know. Besides, you're just doing your job."

She smiles again, this time a tight smile.

"You guys are really close."

"Yes." I gaze down at my clasped hands on my lap. I turn my ring around, three hundred and sixty degrees.

"And you're part of the task force that's trying to find her."

"Yep."

"So how do you feel about that?"

I fight the urge to roll my eyes. It's a textbook open-ended question. Necessary, but it seems so transparent to me.

"Amanda, you do remember that I'm a trained psychologist, right?"

"Yes. But it doesn't change the questions I'm going to ask you." She sits back in her chair and crosses her legs. "It just means we don't have to beat around the bush. I need to assess your feelings and how you're coping, so let's get down to business."

"Okay," I say, but I'd rather be out there finding and chasing down leads.

"How do you feel about what's happened?"

I put my hands by my sides and answer in an even voice. "I'm upset. Sam's a good friend."

"Have you made any other good friends since you've been here?"

"I get along with all the agents."

"But you're closer to Sam?"

"Yes. As you know, Sam and I train together and socialize together."

"Is she your only close friend in the Bureau?"

"Josh Marco." I sigh and glance at the clock behind Amanda's head. "I'm good friends with Josh too." I decide not to tell Amanda about the recent development in that relationship.

"That's good. It must be hard to be so far away from your family and friends."

"It has its moments."

"I bet it does. And Sam helped you fit in here? Feel more at home?"

Tightness takes hold of my throat. "Yes."

"I'd like to explore that a bit with you. Explore your friendship with Sam and how her disappearance has made you feel."

"Pretty damn crappy, obviously," I say.

"We have to do this, Sophie."

"Well, let's get it over with."

"It's not only for Rivers and Pike, you know. It's important that you deal with this. I know how close you were to Sam."

"You mean how close I *am* to Sam." How dare she use past tense.

"Yes. Of course." She presses on. "So, how do you feel about Sam?"

"Sam's great. You know that."

"I know Sam fairly well, but not as well as you do. We're colleagues rather than friends." She takes a sip of water. "So, what makes her great?"

"It's her attitude. She's a glass-is-half-full person. In fact, if Sam were given a half-full glass, she'd say it was just right. Just the amount she wanted." I laugh. "That the glass was too big anyways."

Amanda smiles. "Yeah, I get that impression all right."

"She's the most lively yet down-to-earth person I've ever met. She's a blast, a party girl, but you can always talk to her too. About anything. You know, sometimes you've got friends you go to the gym with, friends you go out partying with, friends you share a pizza and a video with, and maybe friends you go out to dinner with?"

"Sure. You enjoy doing different things with different people."

"But then sometimes you meet someone you click with. Someone you can do all of those things with and it feels right."

"She's a good friend to you."

"Yes. The best." I pause. "I miss her."

"Of course you do."

I edge farther forward in my seat. "We have to find her."

"How's the investigation going?"

I look up at the clock. "It would be a hell of a lot better if I was out there doing something."

She's silent.

That's not the way I'm going to get out of here and

back on the case. "I'm sorry, Amanda. I didn't mean to bite your head off."

"I know this is tough for you."

I nod and rest my hands on my lap again. Tough? What an understatement.

"Your original pysch evaluation indicated that you have a tendency to repress your emotions."

"Those tests aren't always right. We both know that."

"True. But they can also be spot on."

"You need a bit of repression in this job."

She smiles. "Perhaps. A little bit can protect you. But it's a fine line, isn't it, Sophie?"

"I guess so."

"You were with Sam the night she was attacked."

"Yes," I say, the tightness in my throat returning. "We were working on the D.C. Slasher profile at her place."

"I bet you've got a lot of what-ifs happening at the moment."

I narrow my eyes. "I've got a few."

"Why don't you tell me about them."

Again, I look at her, assessing. I can't tell her about my psychic episodes, but maybe I can tell her about some of the other stuff.

"I wish I'd stayed back that night. Stayed over."

"Had you ever stayed the night at Sam's before?"

"No. We don't live that far from one another and there was never the occasion to."

She nods and I know what she's doing—trying to help me release some of my guilt. Of course I'd have stayed with Sam if I'd known what was going to happen. But I didn't know.

But I should have known…I saw it with my own eyes when I was at Sam's place.

I look up and see Amanda's concerned face. A couple of minutes have passed since my last response.

"What else?" she says.

"I wish I'd taken the case from Hunter instead of Sam. I meant to put my hand up for it in the meeting, but I was…daydreaming."

"So you wish you'd been abducted instead of Sam?"

I pause. Of course I don't want that, but in many ways I think I could deal with that better than Sam being taken.

"I wish neither of us was taken."

Silence.

"So do you think you'll find him?"

"Yes," I say quickly. "We've got some good leads. We've got definite matches from the VICAP database and I'm flying to Arizona in a couple of hours to investigate what looks like the perp's first murder. I'll find something. I know I'll find Sam." The pitch of my voice rises with the last sentence.

"I hope you do, Sophie. I really hope you do. But—"

"No! Don't say it. I'm going to find her in time."

"Like you save other victims?"

"Yes. That's right."

"But it's possible you won't be able to save Sam," she says. She looks at me intently.

"I am going to find this bastard," I say through clenched teeth.

Silence.

"Sophie, it's clear to me, and I'm sure to you, that you're not coping very well."

I open my mouth to argue but she raises her hand.

"Which is totally understandable. No one in your unit will be unaffected by this. You're worried about Sam. Worried about what will happen to her. And it brings the one thing you all like to ignore about your jobs into your conscious minds—your own mortality. This work can be dangerous. You're not invincible."

I nod and twirl my ring.

"But what concerns me, Sophie, is the fact that you're involved in the investigation. I'm not convinced it's good for your emotional health."

Her last words sting me. She's going to get me thrown off the task force.

"I can handle this."

Amanda is silent.

"Amanda, please don't. It would be more of a strain on my emotional health if I were doing nothing. I can't just sit at home waiting, and work other cases. I can't do that. Don't make me do that!"

Silence.

"Sophie, this has to be my professional judgment, nothing else."

"I know, Amanda. I do. But professionally, I can handle this."

"Do you think you need to see me?"

"Yes. It will help me get through this if I have someone to talk to."

She shakes her head. "To be honest, Sophie, I don't know if you really believe that or if you're just telling me what I want to hear."

"A bit of both?"

She smiles and pauses. "I guess I can live with that. For the moment at least."

I return the smile, thankful that I'm still on the case.

By the time I leave Dr. Rosen's office I feel a little better. And going over the case has actually helped me crystallize some of the details. For one thing, I'm going to have a much closer look at the photo of the pendant and the blowup of Jean's thigh. I'm convinced the Triquetra means something. It's part of his signature, just like the body positioning.

It must be on Jean, and all the other victims. I just have to find it.

CHAPTER 14

On the plane I sit in the front end of the economy cabin. As soon as the takeoff procedure is complete, I put down my tray table and start looking at photos. The seat next to me is vacant, so I spread photos of the Arizona crime scenes out all around me, using the spare seat and tray table. After about ten minutes the flight attendant comes by.

"Drink?" she says and then her face freezes as she sees what's surrounding me. She turns her head away.

"Sorry. I'm FBI."

She turns back but doesn't look at me or the photos. She looks behind me.

"Drink?" she repeats.

"I'll have a sparkling water, please."

She hands me the small bottle and plastic cup, managing to keep her eyes averted. Sometimes I forget other people don't look at dead bodies all day. Ignorance is bliss? I'm not sure which I'd prefer. At least this way I know what really happens in this world of ours.

The first leg of the flight, to Chicago, takes two hours, but because of the one-hour time difference our official landing is 2:00 p.m. Half an hour later I'm boarding the Tucson flight. Again the flight isn't full and my badge and Aussie charm help ensure I'm one of the lucky ones with two seats to myself. I spend another two hours going over every single detail of the Arizona case files, including the victimologies, coroner's reports and police files. By the time I'm finished I've got a much clearer picture of the murders and the murderer, although the second victim still strikes me as odd. If it wasn't for the signature of the body positioning, I'd think the perp was a different killer.

I spend the most time concentrating on Sally-Anne Raymond. She's our key. Most killers know their first victim. In fact, I'd put pretty good odds on our killer being on the police's original interview list. Another thing that caught my attention was the fact that Sally-Anne Raymond was missing a necklace when she was found. It was never recovered.

The plane touches down in Tucson at 5:00 p.m. local time, 7:00 p.m. Washington time. The airport terminal is warm in temperature but cold in atmosphere, like most airports. I walk quickly, and my overnight bag trails behind me. I pull my phone out of my handbag, switch it on and dial the D.C. office. I'm patched through on speakerphone for the end of the task force's evening meeting.

"So, Anderson, did you look at all the case files?" O'Donnell says.

We ended up getting in files from all the states before I left.

"No, just Arizona." The other files weigh down my briefcase and overnight bag.

"So you haven't seen the Michigan photos?"

"No."

"We've got definite visual links on some of the victims." His excitement is obvious.

"Really? What?"

"That pendant shape was tattooed on the first two victims in Michigan," O'Donnell says.

"Really?" I feign surprise, but I knew the symbol from the pendant and my dreams meant something. I couldn't tell anyone how, but I knew it.

The news also confirms my suspicions—the symbol is part of his signature. But that's not quite right, either. A signature is something a killer is compelled to do. He literally shouldn't be able to leave the crime scene without marking his territory and handiwork in this way.

"But none of the other victims?" I ask.

"No." Josh's voice.

I'm still a little perplexed. "But it *is* signature stuff. Ritual. How could he resist doing it on all the victims?"

"I know, it's strange, isn't it," Josh says.

I sense a hint of fascination in Josh's voice. We could have something new for the textbooks.

Regardless, the Celtic symbol is how we're going to nail him. I know it's important. Really important.

"Any news your end?" O'Donnell says.

"I've only just landed. Detective Carter from Tucson Homicide is picking me up." I stop walking, look up at the signs and turn left. I edge past an old couple and maneuver my way through a family that's trying to deal with a two-year-old's tantrum.

"I want ice cream," she screams, parking her small bottom on the polished floor.

I keep moving. "I'm going to see the first victim's parents tonight. Sally-Anne was missing a necklace. I'm wondering if it's the necklace we found at Sam's."

I can see natural light. Excellent.

"Interesting…we've also narrowed down our college list of twenty-two, based on their programs. For some of them we've already got a list of enrolled students during the time frame."

"And the lock-picking angle?"

"You were right about the time frames. Most of the Web sites started off around 2000, so if he picked up the lock-picking gun during the Arizona or Michigan murders he'd have had to buy it from a registered whole-saler." He clears his throat. He sounds tired. "Arizona law states that owning lock-picking equipment with the intention to use it as a burglary tool is illegal."

"Not very strict."

"No, but the manufacturers are obliged to record buyers and ask for a photo ID. They only have to keep the records for one year, but we might get lucky."

"Right…" It sounds like a long shot.

"Jones is trying to track down a list for Arizona."

"And Michigan?" He may have added it to his MO later.

"Same deal—possession with intention—but the

manufacturers aren't required to keep records. It'll be hit-and-miss there. Some would have kept customer records, others wouldn't."

"He might've had this thing for years," I say. "If so, it's unlikely we'll find records on it. What about the locksmiths for the apartments?"

"All three victims' apartment blocks were done by different locksmiths, but Jones is going to chase down past employees, just in case our perp worked at them all and did get access to master keys that way."

"It's hard to know when he started getting into their apartments."

"We're looking at all the case files for that now. If there's evidence he was in their apartments, we might also be able to work out when he started picking the locks. I suggest you look into that in Arizona," O'Donnell says. "Have I missed anything?" He's talking to the other team members.

"Wright's cell call." It's Krip's voice. "It was routed through the Alexandria cell tower, so it must have been made either from her apartment or within about a five-mile radius. Beyond that distance it would have been routed through another tower."

Silence. I think everyone's disheartened. If the call had been made from the perp's special place, we would have a radius on where Sam was being held. But we don't.

"The media." Flynn breaks the disappointment. "I've spoken to Murray C at the *Post* and he's running a story tomorrow."

I take another left, toward the natural light. "Josh, did you get a look at that?"

"He's sending it through in the next hour. I briefed him pretty thoroughly though. It's important we don't go over the top. We don't want to tip him off that it's a set-up story."

"Good call," I say. Our guy knows his stuff and he could be expecting something like this from us. "Anything else?"

"Nothing this end. Call me when you've met the parents," O'Donnell says. It will be fairly late, especially with the time difference, but we're not nine-to-fivers.

"Oh, and Anderson, be careful out there," O'Donnell adds.

"Will do. Speak to you later." I hang up and stop walking. I need to find Carter. I want to get out to the scene of the first murder before we lose the light.

I search around the arrivals gate, looking for him. After a few minutes I spot someone else looking around. He's about five-eleven, skinny with a very gentle, good-looking baby face. Despite the baby face, I'd say he's in his early thirties. He wears black jeans, a blue shirt and a woolen overcoat.

We hesitantly approach each other.

"Carter?"

"Anderson?"

"Yes," we both say.

We shake hands and I feel an instant electricity. From Carter's face I think he feels it too. I give him an awkward smile and push the feeling away. This is business. Besides, I'm with Josh now. I release Carter's hand.

"Thanks for all your help, Carter. It's great you're still interested in the case."

"Interested? It was my first case in Homicide and it bugs the hell out of me that we never caught the guy."

Perfect. Nothing better than a cop who's bothered by the one that got away. He'll give me loads of time, no matter what his caseload is like.

"Anyways, I've got you hooked up for tonight with Sally-Anne's folks. Thought we might visit the murder site first. Okay?"

"Sounds great." I look at my watch.

"We've got time," he says.

"Oh, it's not that. Remember I said the Slasher had another victim?"

"Uh-huh."

"He's had her for sixty-nine hours now. We've got to catch him soon." It's been nearly three days, the time he had Susan for.

"So you're close to catching the guy?" Carter starts moving and we walk as we talk.

"Yeah. Kind of." But I don't know if it's true. I've been trying to convince myself it is, but in reality, we don't have much. We're on our way, definitely, but these things take time. First we'll have a list of thousands of students from 1997 to 2000, then we'll have to start the cross-referencing process and that is bound to take time, even with computers. Sure, hopefully by the end of it we'll have less than forty names. But how long will it take to get those forty names? I gulp, riding a wave of nausea. I focus on Carter's black shoes. They're real shiny. He wouldn't be happy if I threw up all over them.

"You all right?"

"Sure." I want to explain that I know the guy's current victim. Partly in the hope it'll make Carter put in that extra effort, and partly because I feel the need to explain my obvious attachment to the case. But I can't tell him the killer's got an FBI agent. The brass was pretty straight up about that.

Double glass doors slide open and we walk into the fresh air. It's a lot colder outside than in, but also noticeably warmer than D.C. A line of cabs hugs the curb and we step between two of them and make our way toward a secondary side road.

"This one got to me too," Carter says.

He points his keys at an unmarked car. It's a navy blue Mercury Sable. "This is me." He pops the trunk and throws my bag in. We clamber into the car.

"Your partner coming with us?"

"She just started with Homicide about six months ago. She didn't work this case."

"Who did?"

"Bob Watson. My old partner," Carter says. "He retired last year."

"Can we catch up with him later?"

"Sure. I called and let him know FBI was looking at the Raymond case. He wants to solve it. In fact, he knows Sally-Anne's folks real well. Friend of the family." Carter pauses and stares somewhat vacantly in front of him. He starts the car.

"We worked our asses off on this case. Day and night. And right up to the time Bob retired he still looked at the files on a regular basis. See if he couldn't turn up something new."

"Perhaps I can talk to him tonight, after we've seen Sally-Anne's family."

"I'll call him now." Carter plucks his phone from his

shirt pocket and punches in a number. "Bob, it's Darren… Yeah, she's sitting right beside me… She'd like to talk to you… Yeah… Uh-huh…eight… About an hour… Okay, see you then." Carter hangs up and turns to me. "He's going to meet us in a diner around the corner from the Raymond house. We can eat and talk over the case."

"Thanks. I really need to work this one hard and fast."

Carter nods. "You got any questions about the files?" He starts driving.

"I wouldn't mind finding out more about your suspects. What they're doing now, that sort of stuff. Do you want to wait until tonight with Watson?"

"Yeah. Like I said, he tracked the case after it was officially closed. He might know a lot of that off the top of his head."

About ten minutes later we arrive at a small park, surrounded by a housing estate. Sally-Anne's murder site.

We both get out of the car and survey the area.

"It was just a field at the time of the murder. Part of a farm. But the farmer died and his family sold the land to a housing-development crowd." Carter's eyes drift my way, then he motions toward some houses on either side of the park. "These went up in 2000."

"What about behind?" The park seems to finish on the top of a crest, and then the next crest only has a few houses on it.

"There's a river down there," Carter says, pointing to the space between the two crests. We walk farther into the park. "Apparently at the time, the farmer often used to complain about kids coming down and having sex by the river. Except for the odd occasion when he caught them, they were usually undisturbed. It made it an attractive spot. Marli, Sally-Anne's best friend, said they both used to come down here with guys, on and off."

I nod, remembering that the autopsy showed Sally-Anne had had recent intercourse but there was no semen. A condom had been used.

"He had sex with her, then killed her," Carter says. "Hard to know medically if he raped her, or if the sex was consensual. Given she was killed, we assume she was raped, even though there was no evidence of tearing or bruising." We reach an inviting area of lush grass, daisies and tall trees, with a view of the river. He points to a large oak tree. "She was found right there."

"I can see why the kids came here," I say. "Before the housing, you'd need to be literally within twenty feet to see them in this dip."

"Yep. No one saw them arrive or leave. No one even knew who Sally-Anne was meeting that day. There were several partial tire tracks left on the side of the road, near where Sally-Anne's car was found. But they weren't much good to us."

"What was the problem?"

Carter leans on the oak. "Problems, plural. Firstly it was wet. We only had partial tracks and even then most of them were hard to get a cast off. Plus, the killer could have gotten a lift with Sally-Anne and then walked out after the deed. It's only two miles to the nearest bus stop." He points in a roughly northerly direction.

"I take it no one saw a male walking along the road?"

"No, nothing. But he could have cut across land,

rather than sticking to the road." This time he points directly to the housing estate. "We questioned the bus drivers at the time, but they didn't remember anything unusual. It was quite a busy stop and lots of people got on and off there." He picks a leaf off the ground and examines it, then tosses it.

"Any other problems with the tire tracks?"

"Yeah, there were lots of them and it was hard to isolate the different sets. We did get at least four partial sets. In the end, our experts identified four makes of tires, but they were too common to help us. We could eliminate a few people, but half the city could have parked here."

"I see."

I crouch down and study the grass—I don't know why. Carter follows suit.

"On top of that, when we started our investigations we found that half the city did park here. Well, that's a bit of an exaggeration. What I'm trying to say is the spot wasn't only popular with the kids." He looks down a little awkwardly, then he looks up and keeps his eyes on me.

He's attractive and there's an instant connection between us, but I stay focused.

"Yet still no one saw Sally-Anne or a male down here that day?"

"No. It was midspring. It was sunny that day, but it wasn't into the real popular season yet, plus it had rained heavily the night before. The ground would have been wet."

"But Sally-Anne and her mystery date didn't seem to mind." I say, running my palm over the grass.

"No."

"Mmm." I drop onto my knees, under the tree where things went horribly wrong for Sally-Anne. "Do you mind if I have a minute, Detective?"

"What?"

I seem to have caught him off guard.

"When I'm profiling, a bit of privacy helps. I need to get into the head of the killer and the victim and it's best not to have any distractions." It's true, but I do have an ulterior motive. I'm hoping to get a psychic vision of some sort.

"Sure," he says. He takes another leaf and stands up. He turns his back quickly, as though he's just caught me undressing, and walks slowly away.

I position myself exactly where Sally-Anne was found. I can see her clearly in my mind as I visualize the photographs of the crime scene. I lie back. Carter looks back, glances my way uneasily, then keeps walking. I close my eyes, hoping to see something. I am rewarded with an onslaught of images. Sally-Anne smiling. Sally-Anne laughing. Sally-Anne screaming. Sally-Anne struggling for her life.

I suddenly realize I'm having difficulty breathing. It's as if my psychic reenactment is so strong that I'm suffering the physical effects too. I gasp for breath and open my eyes, hoping this will stop the reenactment.

Blue sky. I'm Sally-Anne. I can't breathe. Now I'm the killer. I feel frenzied excitement as I tighten my grip around Sally-Anne's throat. The first taste—never to be forgotten. Suddenly I'm Sally-Anne again. I see a dark face. I'm blinded by light that comes from behind the face. It's too bright, the sun's in my eyes, and I can't make out the features. I can't breathe! I can't breathe! Then suddenly it's no longer bright and a face is only a few inches from mine.

It's Carter. I take a desperate gasping breath and finally air fills my lungs.

"You okay? What's going on?"

"I'm fine," I say, still a little disorientated. "Sorry, I just…I just dozed off is all." The excuse sounds lame. I know it, and Carter knows it, but he doesn't say anything.

I look around. I think it was the area triggering the psychic episode rather than me actually controlling my insight.

"Come on, we've got to go and see the Raymonds," Carter says.

I glance at my watch. It's 6:30 p.m. Arizona time. He offers me his hand and I take it, feeling a little weak. Carter pulls me up and I'm surprised by the strength of his wiry frame.

I let go of Carter's hand, eager to end the contact.

"This isn't a normal FBI investigation, is it?" he says.

"Sure it is," I say quickly. Too quickly.

He walks back to the car, not looking at me, not talking. I follow him.

We sit in silence and drive. I replay the images of Sally-Anne's murder and try to slow them down, to see things I couldn't make out the first time. Sally-Anne, looking up at the person on top of her. The killer, staring at her throat. Her throat… There's something…something about that image, and I'm left again with thoughts of the necklace.

I'm about to ask Carter if he knows what the missing necklace looks like, when he starts to talk.

"So, it was too bright for you to see his face?"

"What?" How could Carter know what I saw?

"I was hoping you wouldn't lie down, but you did. And then exactly the same thing happened to you. You laughed, a little laugh. You smiled. And then came the scream. It was silenced quickly, and you were gasping for air. Your hands were grasping toward your throat, but he was too strong."

I look at Carter, ready to defend myself. Am I sitting next to the murderer?

He looks at me calmly. "No. I'm not your guy, if that's what you're thinking. The thing is, exactly the same thing happened when we brought someone else to the site eleven years ago. Everything was exactly as it was for you."

"Who did you bring to the site?" I ask slowly.

He pauses, looks at me, ready to read my reaction. "We got a psychic in."

I keep my face impassive. I've got to shut this down. Now.

"I'm asthmatic," I say. God, I'm a crap liar.

"Really? So'm I. And my aunt had the gift. You've got it too."

I look at Detective Darren Carter closely for the first time. His black hair is on the long side and his kind midnight-blue eyes stare openly at me. His face is pale and skinny, like the rest of his body. He has that look of a boy who has grown too quickly and hasn't yet had a chance to fill out. And I've caught a glimpse of dimples at some stage when he smiles. He seems gentle. Especially for a cop. My instincts are telling me to trust this man. In fact, his poise, his gentlemanly manner and those kind, intense eyes…if it wasn't for Josh, I'd be interested in Carter.

"Can't decide whether to deny it or trust me, hey," he says.

I pause. "Sure you don't have some of that gift, Carter?"

He smiles. "Good decision, if I do say so myself."

"So was the psychic your aunt?"

"Yes, she was." His voice is husky.

"Oh no. He didn't…" I had pictured an old aunt.

"His second victim in Arizona. Rose May. Used to be Rose Carter before she married."

"Son of a bitch. She was your aunt?" Now it makes sense.

"Yeah, she was actually a couple of years younger than me."

I'm silent.

"He must have watched. It's the only explanation we came up with. It never got into the press. Was never public knowledge."

"We're profiling this guy as maybe law enforcement. Could he have heard about her through the force?"

"We didn't tell many of our guys. Watson, particularly, insisted we kept it hush-hush. Didn't believe in 'all that shit' as he'd say."

"God, Carter, I'm so sorry." I reach my hand out to him, but withdraw it.

He doesn't seem to notice. "We've all got our reasons to catch this guy."

"While we're doing the confessions, the killer's got a

friend of mine." I decide it's okay to divulge this information. I just won't mention her occupation.

"No wonder you want to get him."

"Yeah." I stare out the window. The area is mostly suburban. Lots of houses and white picket fences.

In my peripheral vision I see Carter reach his hand out to me. But like me, he withdraws it before any contact is made.

"So how long has the FBI been recruiting Australian psychics?" he says and grins.

I laugh. "The psychic thing is new. Really new. The FBI doesn't even know about it."

"This is getting complicated."

"Tell me about it." I smile. "I'm a profiler, like I told you on the phone. That's what the FBI pays me to do. The other is… well, extra."

"How long have you been with the Bureau?"

"Six months."

"Well, I'm sure the psychic ability is a handy talent for a profiler. You must be one of their best."

"They seem to think so, but I'm not so sure. And I'll need more than a few scattered visions to catch this guy in the next forty-eight hours."

"So that's your time frame?"

"I'd say so, based on his pattern in D.C."

"Well, I'll do everything I can to help you. This guy has haunted me and my partner for the past eleven years."

"Thanks, Carter."

"Call me Darren."

"Darren. And I'm Sophie."

He pulls the car into the curb. "Nice to meet you,

Sophie." His eyes linger on me before he grins. "Right. This is the Raymonds'." He uses his thumb to point over his shoulder.

It's a small but well-kept weatherboard, painted white. A veranda reaches along the whole front of the house, and a swing seat hangs in one corner. Next to that is a small table, large enough to hold a couple of drinks and perhaps a book. It looks serene. We get out of the car and walk up the concrete driveway rather than using the gate in the middle of the yellow fence. A red pickup is parked and we move around it to the front door. The garden consists of perfectly trimmed grass, with flower beds around the edges. Each bed has rows of evenly spaced flowering plants. Already I can imagine the kind of people the Raymonds are.

"You got a big team working this?" he asks.

"Seven of us at the moment."

"All FBI?"

We walk up three steps onto the veranda.

"Two from D.C. Homicide, one from D.C. Missing Persons, two FBI field agents and one other profiler."

"Two profilers?"

Darren rings the doorbell.

"Josh, the other profiler, and I have both done lots of fieldwork in our past lives and worked together in the field on a case that closed a week ago."

Darren pauses, about to say something, but then a woman in her mid forties opens the door.

"Hello, Darren. Come in."

Obviously Darren and his partner made regular calls to the Raymonds during the case. Perhaps they continue to do so.

Mrs. Raymond is around five foot one with auburn hair pulled back into a tight, neat bun. She is dressed in black jeans and a loose, light blue denim shirt. Her mouth smiles at me but her eyes don't. Her eyes have the look I've seen way too many times—the look of a mother who has had her child taken away from her by murder. Her eyes will never show happiness again. Just like my mom's won't. She never got over John's murder. Never.

And even if Mrs. Raymond trains other parts of her body, her eyes will always reveal the truth to anyone with a bit of sensitivity. I bet Darren knows this.

"Hi, Janice," Darren says. "This is Agent Anderson of the FBI."

"Hello, Mrs. Raymond," I say.

She looks me up and down with astute eyes. "Hello, dear."

With one ten-second inspection of me I feel as though she knows my inner secrets. Sally-Anne wouldn't have been fooling anyone in this household. Well, at least not her mother.

"Come on in," she says. She looks me up and down again and then glances at Darren. A small smirk plays on her lips and I get the feeling she has us paired off already. Is the physical attraction between Darren and I that obvious?

She leads the way into the house. "Tea? Coffee?"

The front door opens straight onto a homey living room full of trinkets—or "dust collectors" as my dad would say. There are vases, glass figurines and lots and lots of photos. Most photos are of Sally-Anne and a boy, obviously her brother. The photos trace the children's lives, starting with baby pictures. But the photos of Sally-

Anne stop when she's in her teens, and the family pictures go from four people to three. There are no photos of Sally-Anne graduating. No photos of Sally-Anne getting married. This is *his* doing. His fault. And I'm going to get the bastard before he ruins anybody else's life. My jaw stiffens and my teeth grind against one another.

Mrs. Raymond looks at me quizzically. I remember her question—tea or coffee?

"Whatever you're making will be fine," I say, pulling my eyes away from the photos. They are too familiar, reminding me of my own family. Of John.

"Same for me," Darren says.

I get the feeling from Mrs. Raymond's smile that I'll be having whatever Darren normally has. Before she disappears into the kitchen she introduces me to her husband. "John, this is Agent Anderson. The FBI woman," she says on her way through.

Mr. Raymond sits in a large armchair, but it can barely hold his frame. Even though he's sitting down I can tell he's about six-five. His height is matched by a broad, stocky physique that reminds me of a rugby player's. No doubt here he played American football. He definitely would have been one of the guys that clears the way for the ball. Now his middle-age spread also adds to his sizable body. He has a full head of wavy, almost frizzy hair that needs a cut, and his facial features are as large as his body. A freshly folded newspaper lies beside him. He stands up, confirming my guess at his height.

I shake his hand. "Hello, Mr. Raymond."

"So, the FBI's interested in my Sally-Anne again."

I notice the extra emphasis on the word *again*. The

Bureau had drafted a profile of the killer all those years ago, but it didn't lead anywhere. We let him down. I pause for a moment, ignoring his dig. He needs someone to blame. I can understand that.

From the way he says his daughter's name I can tell that Sally-Anne did have one person whose eyes she could pull the wool over.

"We believe Sally-Anne could have been the first of many, many victims, sir. We have a killer in Washington, D.C., at the moment, and we believe he's the same person who killed your daughter," I say, straight up. It's been eleven years, and at this stage they probably appreciate straightforwardness rather than diplomacy. I also speak quite loudly, so Mrs. Raymond can hear me from the kitchen. "We're getting closer."

Mrs. Raymond bustles out of the kitchen and stands on the living room side of the swinging door. "You know who it is?"

"Not yet, no. But we're following several leads, and we've been able to link several murders from different states, including Sally-Anne's and another two murders in Arizona."

"Oh," she says, and disappears back into the kitchen. There have probably been many occasions when she thought the police were close to catching her daughter's killer.

Mr. Raymond clears his throat. "So, what makes you think these murders are related?"

"There are lots of elements that are similar, and in particular the body positioning. It's the killer's signature."

"Lying on her back, the arms slightly raised and her

head turned. She looked peaceful, 'cept her eyes were open," Mr. Raymond says.

"Yes, Mr. Raymond. That's the positioning for them all," I say.

"And our Sally-Anne was the first, you think?"

"Yes, Mr. Raymond. I do."

"What makes you think that?"

"There are elements of her death, her murder, that are different from the others. The killer murdered her in the heat of the moment. But the others, after that, were planned."

"How do you know?"

"Sally-Anne was murdered in the place she was found. The evidence tells us that. She wasn't abducted first, and she wasn't tied up. With his other victims, the killer stalked them, choosing the best time to abduct them. The fact that your daughter's murder was unplanned indicates it was his first. The body positioning tells us it's the same killer, though."

Mrs. Raymond enters, carrying a tray with a plate of sweet biscuits, a pot of tea, four cups and saucers, a jug of milk and a matching sugar bowl. The tea set is white porcelain, with small roses tracing the rim. The cups are dainty and I wonder how Mr. Raymond will be able to hold the handle with his massive hands.

Mrs. Raymond places the tray on the table. "Here we go then," she says with forced breeziness. "Cream? Sugar?" she asks me.

"Cream, no sugar, thanks."

She pours the tea and hands it to me, before pouring out three others.

"We're hoping to identify the killer within the next forty-eight hours. He's just abducted another woman, in D.C., and now that we've linked all these crimes it will be much easier for us to cross-reference locations and other elements to find the killer."

"So, why has it taken eleven years to link these murders?" Mr. Raymond asks.

I take a sip of my tea. "Some of them have been officially linked before, Mr. Raymond. In total there have been three murders here in Arizona, six murders in Michigan, one in Florida, two in Chicago and three in Washington. The ones in D.C. and Chicago had already been linked, so the D.C. force knew whoever they were looking for probably lived in Chicago for a few years. The current task force identified the Arizona, Michigan and the Florida murders as part of the killer's handiwork. This recent link to Arizona is the most important. You see, the killer probably knew Sally-Anne..." I pause, noticing Mrs. Raymond's discomfort. The thought of knowing the killer may be too much for her "—which means we've got the best chance of finding him right here. She's also his youngest victim, at sixteen, which is more evidence that she was his first."

"They've tried to find him for years. What's different now?" Mrs. Raymond asks.

Fair question.

"It's the movement we'll be able to track, Mrs. Raymond. We believe the killer was between eighteen and twenty-five when he killed Sally-Anne. We're pretty sure he went to college in Michigan, likely as a graduate student, and then worked in Chicago and now Washington. How many people who live in Washington would have lived here, studied in Michigan and then worked in Chicago? Then, of those people, who did Sally-Anne know?" I say. We are getting close. "There are other things we know about him too."

Mr. Raymond takes a slurp of his tea. The cup does look ridiculously delicate in his large hands. "It seems you know everything but his name."

Carter takes a biscuit. "That's how profiling works, John. The FBI gives us a profile and we see who matches it. If one of our suspects fits the profile, we know we're on the right track. Then we just have to get the evidence together."

"But didn't you have a profile in 1995?" Mrs. Raymond says.

Carter answers. "We got a profile drafted in 1996, after the third murder. That's when we knew it was a serial."

Police forces can request a profile at any time, but they often follow through other leads first. If they think they can find the guy in a couple of weeks through a witness or fingerprints, why wait for a profile? I'm also guessing that the second murder didn't necessarily indicate a serial killer, given Rose's presence at the first crime scene. It would be safe to assume that Sally-Anne was the primary victim and Rose was simply a clean-up murder.

"I've reviewed that profile, Mrs. Raymond. It was good, but we've got an awful lot more to go on now. We're in a totally different position," I say.

"Anyway, I expect you want to ask us about Sally-Anne," Mrs. Raymond says, obviously not convinced that her daughter's murderer is any closer to being apprehended. No doubt she likes talking about Sally-Anne, even in such morbid circumstances.

"Yes. I do have some questions. But first, I've got a photo of a necklace that was found at the latest victim's residence, Mrs. Raymond."

I've been dying to show them the photo since I walked in the door, but courtesy has been my restraint. I take out the photo.

"Is this your daughter's necklace?"

She reacts immediately. "Yes. Yes. We gave it to her for her fifteenth birthday. It's a Celtic symbol, the Holy Trinity. We thought it would protect her." The eleven-year-old emotions come back for her and Mr. Raymond reaches out and holds her hand.

I hide my excitement. It's inappropriate. "Thank you, Mrs. Raymond. This directly links your daughter's murder to the recent abduction in D.C." I really believe this symbol is going to lead me right to the killer. I think of the Raymonds' need for closure. "If we get him on the D.C. killings, we'll get him for your daughter's murder."

Neither of them seems too hopeful.

"Go on, dear. Your other questions." She has regained her composure and simply looks tired now.

I address both her and her husband. "I'm probably going to ask the same questions Detectives Carter and Watson asked you eleven years ago, but we have to look at Sally-Anne's murder in a new light now, so please bear with me."

They nod.

"When was the last time you saw your daughter?"

Mrs. Raymond responds. "We both saw her on the Saturday she was killed. She got up at about ten in the morning and I made her some breakfast. I wanted to go shopping with her for a dress, but she said she had plans with Marli. That we could go on Sunday instead. She left the house at about eleven-thirty. John was working outside, in the garage."

Mr. Raymond takes over. "She came in to me on her way out. I remember thinking how beautiful and grown-up she looked. She said goodbye and I gave her twenty dollars so she could get a coffee and go to the movies with Marli. She gave me a kiss and said, 'See you tonight, Dad.'" He pauses. "That's the last time I saw her."

"But she didn't meet Marli?"

"No," Mrs. Raymond says, looking down at her lap.

"Did Sally-Anne have a boyfriend at the time?"

My question is answered by a look between the pair.

"She never brought a boy back to the house. Never introduced us to anyone. But I suspected she had someone in her life. And that it probably wasn't her first," Mrs. Raymond says.

Mr. Raymond winces.

"But no idea who it was?"

"I didn't, but Marli told us later that Sally-Anne had just broken up with young Jamie Wheelan. So I guess it was him."

"Do you mind me asking how you knew Sally-Anne was involved with someone, Mrs. Raymond?"

She looks at her husband, apologetic. "I found condoms in her drawer upstairs."

Again, Mr. Raymond's face reacts.

"When did you find these?" I ask.

"About six months before. I had a talk with her. Told

her I thought she was too young. Asked her who she was with. She wouldn't tell me." She takes a sip of her tea and looks at one of the photos of Sally-Anne on the dresser. She daydreams for a few seconds, and I leave her be.

She comes back to the land of the living. "In the end, though, I knew nothing I said would stop her. So I told her to make sure she used the condoms. To protect herself and make sure the boy was, you know, worthy. She huffed and puffed at me, embarrassed and angry I had been in her room. But we never spoke of it again. And I never told John. Not till after. Not till the police became so interested in her actions." She gives her husband another apologetic glance. "I knew then it was going to come out and better he hear it from me than someone down the street." She squeezes his hand. "Sally-Anne was his little angel."

"No father likes to think about it," I say to Mr. Raymond.

He smiles but is still uncomfortable with the topic of conversation.

"So presumably whoever Sally-Anne had organized to meet was her killer," I say.

I've got more questions, but they're questions for Carter and his partner or even Marli. The Raymonds probably don't have anything more to tell me. Obviously their daughter kept her sex life private, like most young girls.

"So neither of you ever saw her with a man?" I say.

They both shake their heads.

"Maybe Agent Anderson would like to see Sally-Anne's room," Carter says, looking to the Raymonds for permission.

"Sure. Sure." Mrs. Raymond springs to her feet. She

leads the way upstairs and we all follow, except for Mr. Raymond, who stays seated. At the top of the stairs Mrs. Raymond turns left and I see her take a key off a necklace that hangs around her neck. She unlocks a door directly in front of her.

Sally-Anne's room hasn't been touched. Like so many parents who lose a child, the room becomes a shrine, capturing the child's personality and youth. The room is clean and dust free, so I assume the only time anyone enters it is when Mrs. Raymond cleans it. It looks like a typical sixteen-year-old's room. There's a TV and stereo on a desk, along with a rather large CD collection, notable for its obvious age. Sally-Anne's dressing table has a jewelry box, makeup, nail polish and a few other knickknacks. On the walls are photos of her with her friends and some with her family. The room also has a few posters. Alanis Morissette, the *Batman Forever* movie poster, and one of George Michael, post-WHAM. It's like a time warp.

I look closely at the photos. "You spoke to everyone in these?" I ask Carter.

"Yeah. That's Marli." He points to the girl who appears in most of the photos with Sally-Anne. "This is Jamie Wheelan. He was our number-one suspect for some time. But he didn't match the profile at all. The original profile said we were looking for a loner, someone who wasn't very socially adept. But Jamie was one of the most popular kids at school." Darren leans in and whispers, "Cocky bastard, too."

Darren crosses back to Mrs. Raymond, who's still standing at the doorway of Sally-Anne's room. "Janice, why don't we go back downstairs and finish our tea. Agent Anderson won't touch anything." He turns to me. "Will you?"

"No, I just want to get a feel for Sally-Anne."

Mrs. Raymond nods and lets Darren lead her downstairs. "I'll come back up and lock the door when you're finished," she says, half to me and half to reassure herself that soon the shrine would be closed up once more. She walks and I mouth the word *thanks* to Darren.

As an afterthought he steps back up the stairs and says quietly, out of the Mrs. Raymond's earshot, "My auntie used her breathing. Said it helped her. She said it was like meditating. Do you know how to meditate?"

"Yeah. Thanks."

And so I'm left alone with victim number one. I look at the photos again, looking into Sally-Anne's eyes, just as the killer had. Now I know why his eyes were drawn to her throat. As he strangled her, the pendant captivated him. He was so enamoured of it that he took it and probably used it to relive the murder and sexual release hundreds of times…until a few days ago, when he decided he would leave it at Sam's, presumably to mark his territory and increase the thrill. After all, I wouldn't have noticed it except it was the symbol I'd seen on Jean's thigh in my dream. It was a safe taunt as far as he was concerned. By itself the necklace would have gone unnoticed. In fact, I wouldn't be surprised if he went back to Sam's to retrieve it. I'm sure he never expected to have to part with it forever. He must be mad as hell. I wonder if the guys are still keeping an eye on her apartment. I must ring and check… I take a deep breath and try to refocus. I'm in this room to see if I get another vision, not to think about what's happening in D.C.

I sit down on the end of Sally-Anne's bed and take deep, slow breaths, trying to induce something. With each breath, I clear my mind of all lingering thoughts, trying to think of nothing. Not the case, not Sam, not the killer. Just nothingness. But I'm not greeted with an image of Sally-Anne or her murderer. This time I'm with Sam, in that dark place he has her.

She's tied to a gurney, with several gashes across her body. Some ooze red, while others have formed a scab. She's perfectly still and, for a moment I fear the worst. Then I see her naked breasts move up as her lungs fill with oxygen. On her left arm is a pressure bandage, but it's covered in blood. That's one of the deep wounds he makes. I look around the room, trying to see something that will give away the location. But everything's blurry. I try to move closer to Sam and I'm surprised that it's as if my body's there too. I can walk. I go over to her and try to stroke her hair. I see my hand but it goes through her, as if I'm a ghost. Sam flinches.

"Sam. It's me, Sophie," I try to say, but my voice sounds strange and garbled.

Sam opens her eyes and I see so much fear in them that I have to look away.

I look back at her. "I'm going to find you, Sam. I'm going to find you," I say, but again the words are garbled. Then her eyes show relief and for an instant comfort. So much so that I wonder if she's seen me, or somehow knows I'm there with her. She wears a gag in her mouth, but she strains against it and tries to make sounds. The sounds are indecipherable, but I can't help wondering if she is saying my name. Can she sense my presence? I reach my hand out once again, but this time my hand turns into a man's hand and the fear comes back into Sam's eyes. It's him. I'm him.

"What's that, my love?" I say and pull down her gag. "Sophie?"

"No, it's not Sophie." I laugh. But then a cold shiver runs down my spine and I look around. It doesn't feel as though we're alone in the room.

I push the sensation away.

"Let's see how you're doing. Would you like something for the pain?"

Samantha nods her head and opens her mouth in what, I feel, is a somewhat suggestive manner. I smile. She is a loving girlfriend. It'll be a shame to get rid of her, especially now that she knows who I am and loves me. But my plan must go on.

I take two Tylenol out of the cabinet and pop them in her sensuous mouth. She murmurs something through the tablets.

"What, my darling?"

Again, she murmurs something. I bend down closely to hear her submissive voice. So different than the voice I'm used to hearing from Sam Wright. I bend my head down to hers, but she raises hers quickly and violently, head-butting me.

"Bitch!" I scream, and slap her hard. I grab my knife from behind me and slice one of her superficial wounds so it's deeper. She screams but I slam her gag down on her mouth again.

"Don't you ever, ever try anything like that again!"

I kick my instruments across the room. That little bitch. I want to kill her now. I want to punish her for what she's done.

But it's not time.

I manage to control my temper…for the moment.
I prefer my killing to be planned, controlled.

I control my anger, it does not control me.

CHAPTER 15

Carter's still in the doorway talking to the Raymonds, but I stand out front near the car and call O'Donnell. I brief him on the meeting with the Raymonds.

"So we definitely have the necklace," he says.

"It's our guy. He carved the crude tattoos on those Michigan girls to relive Sally-Anne's murder."

"Mmm." He pauses. "What's Carter like?"

"Good. He's being very helpful."

"Anderson, watch yourself."

That's the second time he's said that.

"Any particular reason?" I ask.

"I'm personally investigating everyone who's worked the cases, including Detective Carter and his old partner, Bob Watson."

"I'm meeting Watson in a few minutes." I look up at Darren and he smiles. "So they're suspects?" I know Carter or Watson can't be the killer because my vision just told me our perp is in D.C. with Sam, but I can't share this with O'Donnell.

"With the law-enforcement background from the profile, it's something we have to look at. I've spoken to Rivers." He pauses. "I'm even investigating some of the task force members."

"Really?" I say, but I'm not surprised. It had to be done.

"You and Couples are clear, because of your sex. Listen, keep this quiet. I'm only telling you in case you're in danger in Arizona."

"Okay. I'll check it out."

"No, don't go asking questions, just in case. I've got all the information coming through to me. It won't take long to check their movements over the past eleven years."

"Let me know."

"Will do. But just remember, our perp could be linked to Carter or Watson, someone they work with. Keep your wits about you."

"Always. Bye."

I hang up and look at Carter again. Could he have anything to do with the murderer? My instincts are saying no, but it might be unwise to rule him out totally.

Carter sees I'm finished on the phone and excuses himself. We ride a few blocks and pull up outside Bobby's Diner. To me, it's a stereotypical American diner. There's a white laminate counter that runs the length of the building with red vinyl bar stools dotted along its length. At the end of the counter is the kitchen. The rest of the diner consists of a dozen or so booths, each one a roomy fit for four but a squash for six.

Darren scans the room and his eyes fix on the third booth from the door. The man in the booth smiles at Darren, but when his eyes move to me the smile vanishes. Darren and I make our way over and Watson stands up. He's a stocky, slightly overweight man who looks as if he's lived life hard. His hair is thin and dark gray, and his face is etched with many wrinkles, perhaps a few more than is normal for his sixty-odd years. His nose seems to be permanently red—telling me that he is, or perhaps was, a bit of a drinker. Alcohol is a common vice in this business.

"Hey, Watson." Darren reaches out his hand.

Watson takes it and gives it two short pumps. "Bet you're missing me, Carter. Specially with that rookie you got."

Darren smiles. "She's doing fine." He steps aside. "Bob, this is Agent Anderson."

"Uh-huh. FBI."

"Yes, that's right."

"Take a seat." Watson motions to the other side of the booth.

He climbs back to his original seat and Darren and I move in on the opposite side. The bench seats are covered in red vinyl and the tables are white laminate, just like the bar. The menu stands up on the edge of the table, propped between salt, pepper and sugar on one side, and maple syrup on the other side.

"Marli's coming by later," Darren says to Watson.

"How's she doing?"

"Fine, I guess."

Watson fixes his hazel eyes on me. "So, Carter tells me Sally-Anne's pendant was left at the abduction site of the killer's latest victim."

Straight down to business. I like that.

"Yep. A definite link between the crime scenes."

"So, what do our friends at the FBI make of that?" he says.

"We're happy to have the link. It means we're heading in the right direction."

Watson nods and looks up behind us.

It's the waitress. "What can I get you folks?"

"I'll have a Bud," Watson says.

"Make it two," Darren says.

"Do you have Becks?" I ask.

"No, sorry, ma'am. No imports."

"I'll grab a Bud too, then."

"Anything to eat?"

"I'll have the Bobby's burger," Watson says.

I grab the menu and start scanning it. I couldn't face food on the plane, and for the first time since Sam was nabbed I feel a little hungry.

"The wings and the nachos are good," Darren says to me, then orders, himself. "I'll have wings, hot, and a salad."

I'm still scanning the menu. Nothing's really jumping out at me.

"I'll have the wings and a salad too," I say.

"Sure thing. Hot for you too, honey?"

My hunger suddenly disappears—she said "honey" and it reminds me of Sam.

"Hot?" she repeats. I'm wearing her patience thin.

"Yeah, hot."

She's cheery again. "Won't be long, folks."

Watson watches her retreat.

"Where were we?" he says after he's satisfied he's had enough of the waitress's butt.

"Some things never change, right, Bob?" Darren leans back into the seat and smiles. "The link. Heading in the right direction."

"Oh, yeah. That's right."

Watson seems to be with us again.

I make sure I have his eye contact. "We think the perp's in D.C. for the thrill. He wants to raise the stakes and do it under the FBI's nose. He left the pendant at the apartment of the last woman he abducted." I shift the sugar around with my right hand. It's hard referring to Sam in a detached manner, but maybe it's best that Watson doesn't know my relationship with the victim, especially given he's officially a suspect until further notice.

I continue. "Maybe he thinks he's untouchable, that no one would notice the necklace. Or maybe it's all part of the thrill for him. It's his way of taunting us."

"Catch me if you can?" Darren says.

"Yeah. But he doesn't really believe we can."

"He's graduated since Sally-Anne," Watson says.

His tone of voice reminds me that everyone at the table has a personal investment in this case. In this perp. It also makes me want to dismiss Watson as a suspect.

"You ever been to D.C.?"

"Sure," Watson says. "But it was twenty years ago."

I nod. He could be lying, or it could wipe him off our suspect list. Besides, he's here in front of me, not in D.C. What if my vision was inaccurate somehow? He knew I was coming, he could have hightailed it back to Arizona, but it's unlikely. And he certainly doesn't fit the age profile. But Darren does. Though I can't see Carter killing anyone, let alone a relative. Still, it'll be nice to get the official word.

I get back to the Raymond case. "So who was Sally-Anne meeting that day?"

"You think we'd be sitting here if we knew the answer to that?" Watson says.

"It's the million-dollar question. If we knew that, we'd have our guy," Darren adds.

"I find it hard to believe that Sally-Anne didn't tell anyone who she was meeting that day," I say.

"Well, believe it. 'Cause if she'd told anyone, we would have found it out," Watson replies.

The waitress comes back with our beers. We all take a swig—mine is a small mouthful, Darren's a couple of gulps and Watson drains nearly half the bottle.

"Okay, so why wouldn't she tell anyone? Including her best friend?" I ask.

Darren takes another mouthful. "Older man?"

"Possibly. Maybe older and a friend of the family." I pause to consider my own words. "Anyone you know through the family that was a suspect?" I ask Watson.

"I can't think of any of the Raymonds' friends who match the profile. Certainly none that have since moved to Michigan, then Chicago and then Washington. Besides, he couldn't have been that much older if you guys believe he studied in Michigan. Even as a grad he'd have been closer to Sally-Anne's age than to her parents'."

"True." I take another sip of beer and then twist the

bottle around on the table, making small wet circles on the white laminate. "But to a sixteen-year-old girl, even a twenty-year-old boyfriend might be something you feel you have to hide from your parents."

"So you're thinking early twenties—grad student or maybe someone who waited a few years to save for school?" Darren says.

"Could be," I say. I hadn't thought about the possibility that our perp took time off before college, but that would fit the profile.

We sit silently for a moment.

"You checking in again tonight?" Darren asks.

"Only if I find something. O'Donnell, the task force leader, wants me to phone him on his cell if anything comes up."

"You need something soon." Darren rubs his hand across his stubble.

"Time's running out."

Our meals arrive and Watson orders another beer.

"Darren, how come your reports don't mention that the second victim was your aunt, and that she was a psychic?"

"We can't write every detail in them reports, little lady," Watson says through a mouthful of fries.

Darren is a little more forthcoming. "At the time it seemed the right thing to do. We were worried the media would get hold of it, and that it might interfere with the case because I knew her. Plus, my aunt's husband didn't want anything to do with me or my family after what happened. Who could blame him? He begged us not to reveal that she'd been called in as a psychic. So we kept it quiet."

For a second time today I want to give Darren's arm a comforting squeeze but resist the urge.

"It's not your fault. How could you know the killer would track the case so carefully?"

"It was in the profile," he says, chastising himself.

I'm about to jump in again, when Watson saves me the effort. "The FBI profile came out after Rose's death. Well after." He shakes his head. They've obviously had this conversation several times. Guilt is such a hard thing to shake, even when it's irrational. I know that all too well.

Darren doesn't respond. Instead, he starts gnawing on a chicken wing.

I finish my mouthful and swallow. "So, let's go through your suspects and unusual interviews." Hopefully the killer was at least one of the suspects or one of the one hundred and twenty-plus people Darren and Watson interviewed during the course of the investigation.

We spend the next hour going through the murder in detail. From the person who found Sally-Anne's body to Jamie Wheelan, to her father—every male acquaintance of Sally-Anne's. No one sticks out to me. In fact, no one really seems to match the profile or the impressions I have of the killer. But we do keep coming back to Jamie Wheelan.

"The creep even admitted to seeing Sally-Anne that day, though he tried to cover it up at first," Watson says, now on his fifth beer.

"That's right." I say, remembering the case notes. "Claims he saw her at his place around midday. They talked, had sex and then she left around one in the afternoon."

"So he says," Watson says. I can see a paternal instinct coming through. Obviously when they started the investigation he saw a side of Sally-Anne he'd never seen before. She was certainly relatively sexually active for a sixteen-year-old.

"I always thought there was something fishy about Wheelan," Watson says. He stares behind Darren and I, and smiles at someone.

Darren turns around. "Marli's here."

I turn to look as Marli closes the door behind her. She's tall and slender and wears a tight black top that shows off her trim waist and pert breasts, and a shortish, classy, straight black skirt. Her long legs are tapered by slight heels. She looks like a woman who's used to getting her way. She saunters over to the table and smiles at us all, but her gaze lingers on Darren. They either had something going at one stage, or she wishes they had. I study Darren, trying to determine which, and I'm surprised by the ever-so-slight jealousy I feel. It's ridiculous.

He looks at her but doesn't respond to her blatant sexuality or the looks she gives him. I decide nothing ever happened between them.

"Hi, Darren," she says, smiling even wider to reveal perfectly straight teeth with some slight nicotine stains.

Darren returns the smile. "Hi."

"Hi, Bob," she says, like a child who's just called some older relative by their first name and is waiting to be told off.

Watson nods. "Marli."

"Marli, this is Agent Anderson from the FBI," Darren says.

"Hey." She holds out a jewelry-covered hand. I give her a firm handshake.

"Hi, Marli. Thanks for coming down to see us."

"No problem." She orders a beer from our waitress, who is clearing dinner plates from the table next to ours.

She sidles in next to Watson, sitting opposite Darren. She looks at Darren, then me. "So you want to know about Sally-Anne."

"Yes. I'm investigating her death in relation to some murders and one abduction in D.C."

"Yeah, I know. Darren told me."

"Good." I fix my eyes on her, ready to read her responses. "So, you have no idea who Sally-Anne was meeting that day?"

"Nope. She told me she liked a new guy and all, but was all secretive about it. Like he was a rock star or something. Said she'd tell me in a week or two. I could see she wasn't going to budge, so I left it."

"Did she normally keep secrets from you?"

"No. We were best friends. It was real unusual. She was weird about this guy, whoever he was."

"Do you think he was older? Or married?" I say.

Marli's beer arrives. She takes a long swig.

"Well, he wouldn't have been an old fuck, if that's what you're saying." She waits for a reaction but I don't give her one.

"She wouldn't have gone for that. But she did say something about Jamie being too immature for her. So I thought he may have been, you know, eighteen or twenty. A couple years older." She brings the beer bottle to her lips again and then stares at the bright red lipstick ring left on the neck.

"And you both used the spot by the river."

"Sure. It was romantic, and secluded." She leans in,

giving Darren an eyeful of cleavage. "Lots of us went down there. Sometimes Sally-Anne and I would even go down there together." She looks at me intently. "Like, as a group of four."

"Did you swap partners?" I ask, impassive.

"No. But we didn't mind doing it in front of each other." She looks at Darren.

I glance at him from the corner of my eye to see his response. He's not buying into her flirtation. He keeps eye contact with her and takes a mouthful of beer, finishing the bottle.

"Any of the guys you or Sally-Anne were with that you might suspect of murder?"

"Who knows what goes on in some people's heads." She pauses. "Nah, not really. They were pretty good guys."

"Jamie included?"

"Sure, Jamie. Him and Sally-Anne were together for about six months. He liked her a lot."

Jamie as the killer doesn't ring true to me. One death, Sally-Anne's, could have been through jealousy, but it wouldn't have explained the birth of a serial killer.

"Was she seeing anyone else during that six months?"

"Not that I know of. Not until they broke up. She still used to see Jamie from time to time, but she was seeing other people too."

"Was there anyone you knew who was sweet on Sally-Anne?"

"Heaps of guys. They all wanted to be with Sally-Anne."

"What about someone who hung around a little too much. Perhaps someone who's attention Sally-Anne didn't want?"

"Sure. All the geeks. You know what it's like," she says, looking me up and down, obviously deciding that I did know what it was like.

"No one specific though?"

"Not that I can remember. All this is in my original statement. Why don't you just read it?"

"I have read it. I'm hoping something else, something new will come up." Except for the necklace, Arizona is turning out to be a dead end.

"Can't think of anything." She pauses. "Sorry." And for an instant I see a flash of sadness. Of regret. She lost her best friend. I can relate to that. I think of Sam lying on a gurney somewhere. I don't want to lose her to this bastard too.

I twist my beer bottle around and start peeling off the label. "This was his first kill, he had to mess up something."

"He was either very smart or very lucky," Darren says.

Watson takes a swig of beer and slams the bottle down on the table. "Or both."

Marli is silent, sucking on her beer. We've moved out of the realm of questioning a witness and back into colleagues discussing a case. It isn't appropriate with Marli still sitting here.

"Is there anything, anything at all you can think of, Marli? Perhaps you've seen someone or something recently that made you think of Sally-Anne," I say.

"I'm sorry. I've been through this hundreds and hundreds of times in my head. There's nothing I didn't tell these guys in the first place." She stares at her beer bottle. "I wish I could help, I really do. I wish something

I knew would help find Sally-Anne's murderer." The "bad girl" has almost totally disappeared.

"That's okay, Marli. I'm sorry to bring all this up again. If you think of anything, give me a call, okay?" I hand her my card.

She knows the interview is over and I can tell she's relieved. She'd rather go back to the bad-girl image than talk about Sally-Anne—it's easier for her, less painful.

She nods, downs the rest of her beer and walks out, forgetting even to give Darren an extra smile.

"So, what about the other cases? Maybe there's something there. Something we've missed so far," I say.

"Well, the others were planned," Darren says. "The perp must have stalked the victims. His third victim, Mary Coles, was found dumped in the lake. It looked like she may have hitched a ride with him. She was a young waitress and often finished up work late, after the buses had stopped running. Sometimes she'd get a ride home from other staff, sometimes she'd walk, and sometimes she'd hitch. But no one saw her get into a car that night."

"He probably followed her while she was walking and made sure no one was in sight," I say. "Who'd she live with?"

Darren responds. "Her mother. It was just the two of them."

"Was there any sign of breaking and entering or that someone had been in the home?"

"She wasn't nabbed from home," Watson says.

"I know, but we think our guy has a way of getting in with a lock-picking set or lock-picking gun. He actually visits his victims' homes as part of the stalking process."

I feel the weight of the quilt from the dream last night and shiver. It felt so real. It's hard to believe it was only last night. It seems like weeks ago. "So any sign of entry at the victims' homes?"

"Not that I know of. But we didn't check, either," Watson says.

"Was anyone you spoke to a locksmith?" I ask. "Or become a locksmith later on?"

Both Carter and Watson are silent. After a couple of minutes Watson starts shuffling the papers Darren has brought.

"George Daly. His father was a locksmith," Watson says, fingering the transcript of that interview. He's enjoying being back on a case.

"Did he fit the profile?"

"In some areas, yes," Watson says. "But not in others."

"Do you know where he lives now?"

"No. He's not one of the ones I tracked," Watson says.

"Maybe you've got something for O'Donnell after all," Darren says, looking at the clock in the diner.

If George Daly was a student, or even lived in Michigan from 1997 to 2000… Hang on, Sam.

CHAPTER 16

Watson and Darren come back to my motel. I want O'Donnell to hear this firsthand and he might have questions for them.

I check in at the front desk, then hurry to my room. I dump my overnight bag on the spare bed and take out the Arizona files. I dial O'Donnell's cell phone. "Okay, go ahead, Anderson." O'Donnell sounds tired—I probably woke him. It is midnight in D.C. but, hey, he asked me to call. And even if he didn't I still would have. Sam's waiting for me, waiting for us to save her from that bastard. Holding off till morning could cost Sam her life. It isn't an option.

"I've got Detectives Watson and Carter here from Tucson Homicide. We may have a lead on the lock-picking angle. One of the men who was interviewed during the Sally-Anne Raymond case had a locksmith father."

"Really?" O'Donnell sounds wide awake now. "Any idea of his whereabouts?"

"No, I'm afraid not," Watson says.

"Tell me what you know," O'Donnell says.

We all huddle around the phone, with Watson sitting on one of the chairs and Darren standing. Watson leans back in his chair and nods at Darren. Darren starts. "We interviewed George Daly several times. He was never really a suspect because as far as we could make out he didn't even know Sally-Anne. We interviewed him because a couple of his friends hung out with a couple of her friends, and we thought maybe they'd crossed paths at some stage. But he denied having ever met her, and his friends corroborated this."

"How old was he at the time?"

Watson leans forward, closer to the phone. "He was twenty-two and working as a sales assistant in a men's clothing store."

"No idea if he went on to college?"

Darren paces a little while Watson takes the lead. "I just called an old friend of his. Turns out he was saving to study, but the friend can't remember what or where. His family moved out of town about a year after Sally-Anne's death and he lost contact with Daly."

"Okay. We'll track him down from this end. So it's George Daly, twenty-two in 1995. What's his father's name?"

"Um." Darren grabs the file and scans the pages. "Here it is. It's George too. His father is George John Daly and our guy is George Andrew Daly."

"Thanks, Detectives, that's a big help," O'Donnell says.

I pick up the phone, taking it off speaker. "You're off speakerphone now."

"I presume you didn't tell them about the FBI's stake in this case, Anderson," O'Donnell says.

"Of course not."

Watson stands up and walks over to the door. Darren follows suit and they talk in hushed tones. I can't make out what they're saying.

"Okay, good work. I'm going to get our guys working on the name right away. I'll also phone around and tell the rest of the team the news. I'm sure they'll all want to know."

"I'll see if I can get a flight out tonight."

"I'd rather you stay put until tomorrow. Let's see how this lead pans out."

"I'd be better back there. In D.C."

He sighs. "I want someone in Arizona, Anderson. You fit the bill."

I can tell there's no point arguing. "Okay," I say. But all I can think about is getting back to D.C. and Sam.

"Hopefully by tomorrow we'll have some hard evidence on George Daly. Then you can fly back."

I don't respond.

O'Donnell fills the silence. "Besides, the locksmith father could just be a coincidence."

God, I hope not. Time is running out. I know it's not a strong lead, yet, but it's all I've got. All Sam's got.

I change the subject. "Anything else your end? How'd it go with those checks?"

"Watson and Carter have both been stationed in Tucson, so they're clear. We haven't checked flights, but these weren't vacation killings."

"No, doesn't fit the killer's pattern or profile," I say.

"I'll keep most of the team on the students but I'll get someone on Daly right away. If we can place him in all cities or most cities, we'll bring him in for questioning. We'll look over the other case files with him in mind."

"Also, the perp might come back to get that necklace from Sam's place. Have you got someone watching it?"

"I think Couples kept a team on duty, but I'll check."

"Great," I say.

"The *Post* story will be in tomorrow's edition, but with any luck we won't need it."

"Things are looking up." I pause. "I'd better go."

"Okay, Anderson. I'll keep you informed…and don't worry. If Daly's our man, we'll get Sam."

"Thanks."

I flop into one of the armchairs and Darren and Watson come away from the door.

"I'm not convinced George is our guy. I remember interviewing him and he seemed kinda sweet to me," Darren says.

"So did Bundy," I fire back.

I have to believe the killer is within our grasp. If it's Daly, we'll get to Sam in time. I think back to the visions I've had about the D.C. Slasher—he's tall and muscular with brown hair.

"What does Daly look like?"

Watson scratches his stubble. "Tall and skinny."

Tall, yes. Skinny? Daly could have been working out. "What color hair?" I bite my lip.

Watson and Darren exchange looks.

"It was dark," Darren says.

"Yeah, black, I think," Watson adds.

They could be wrong. My visions could be wrong. lease let it be Daly.

Watson moves toward the door. "Well, I better get ome."

"Oh, ah, yeah, me too," Darren says and I notice the ay he's looking at me. He doesn't want to leave.

"Thanks, guys. I've got quite a bit of work to finish ff anyway," I say quickly, not wanting to be in an wkward position with Darren.

"So, do you need a lift to the other murder sites morrow?" Darren asks.

"Depends what happens with Daly tonight. I might be eading back to D.C."

Darren nods.

"If not, I will check out the other crime scenes," I say.

"I can swing by and pick you up, if you like."

"That'd be good. If it's not a problem with your ther cases."

"Look, I'm the retired one, why don't I take you?" Vatson says, although somewhat begrudgingly.

I shrug.

"It's settled then," Watson says. "Nine okay?"

"Are you sure? I don't want to be any trouble. I mean, ve got all the files and I can rent a car."

"It'll give me something to do."

"Thanks. Nine sounds good. I'll call you by eight if I'm eading back to D.C."

Watson nods in response, scribbles down his cell umber, then leaves.

"Well, um, I guess I'll catch up with you before yo go," Darren says, lingering at the door. He smile "Good night."

"Good night."

He keeps smiling and walks out the door.

I sigh. I'm not really sure why I'm so attracted t Darren. I don't know him, not like I know Marco, bu there's some connection there. I think of Sam. I know exactly what she'd do if she were here—she'd get up an do a perfect, gutsy rendition of "It's Raining Men." Hope fully I'll be cheering her up with this story in a coupl of days. But for now I can't afford to think about Josh o Darren. It's Sam who needs my attention.

God, I wish she were here. I let slow, silent tears flow down my cheeks. Finally I pull myself together. Tears aren going to help Sam.

I empty the contents of the files onto the desk. I hop we're closing in on the killer. That Daly's our man. But can't ignore the fact that some things don't ring true wit Daly. Besides, I can't rest until Sam's in front of me and give her a big hug.

There's also something about the knife wounds o Jean's leg that still bothers me. Why did I see the Triqu tra symbol on her leg if it's not there? And if it's th murderer's signature, why isn't it on all the victims?

I start with the blowup of her thigh, and the kni wounds on the other D.C. victims. Again I search care fully for the tattoo on all the bodies. Nothing. Next I loo at the other crime-scene photos that came in from Arizona, Michigan, Florida and Chicago. I start off wit the Michigan photos. The first two Michigan victims hav

ot crude tattoos of Sally-Anne's pendant, just like O'Don-
ell said. Obviously it was carved into their flesh by the
killer. The third and fourth Michigan victims both have
nife wounds that replicate half of the symbol, almost as
f the killer was interrupted. That leaves the last two
Michigan girls, the one in Florida, two Chicago victims
nd the three in D.C. I wonder…

I draw the symbol from the pendant, much bigger
han the photo we've got. Then I look at the thighs of
ach of the eight, apparently unbranded victims, turning
he photos around to see all angles.

"Son of a bitch!" I stand up.

Each of the knife markings on the victims makes up
art of the symbol. Each victim has got such a small
art of the symbol carved into her that it's barely dis-
ernible. I sit down and look again, making sure it's
ot a coincidence. To double-check I cut up the
hotos, taking out only the section of the symbol. On
he bed I piece the bits of the eight different photos
ogether and in front of me is about three-quarters of
he pendant.

"Son of a bitch," I repeat. It's his signature all right.

My phone rings. I grab it from the front pocket of my
riefcase. "Agent Anderson."

"Hi, Soph. It's Josh. How are you?"

"Josh, you won't believe this." I pace around the room.
The killer's stab wounds partially form that Celtic
ymbol from Sally-Anne's pendant!"

"What?"

"Have you got the files there?"

"Hang on a sec." I hear him moving to another part of

his house. He keeps talking. "Hey, congrats on Georg
Daly. A suspect at last."

"I just hope he's the one."

"Okay, I've got the files," Josh says.

I move back to my bed, staring at the collage of photos
"Get out the photos of the victims' thighs and the phot
of the pendant we found at Sam's. Victims five and six i
Michigan have got the bottom left-hand portion of th
symbol. Now, if you turn the photos of the Chicago an
Florida victims upside down, you'll see they fit togethe
to form the top section of the symbol. Jean from D.C. ha
got the very center of the symbol, where the three piece
intersect."

"Uh-huh."

"Now turn the photos of Teresa and Susan ninet
degrees to the right and you'll see they've got part of th
bottom right-hand section of the symbol."

"God, you're right. No one noticed this."

"Neither did I until just now. They're such sma
sections. It's all coming together." I go over to the ba
fridge and get out an orange juice. "Hey, O'Donnell sai
you were happy with the *Post* article."

"Yeah, it's come up well."

I imagine seeing Sam again. God, I can't wait, but th
thought of what's happened to her disgusts and anger
me.

"Poor Sam. I can't bear to imagine the state she'll be in.

"Let's get her home safe, Sophie, before you sta
worrying about her mental health."

"Yeah." I pause and sit down on the bed. "So what a
you guys doing on George Daly?"

"Tax records, college records, payroll and credit cards. t shouldn't take us long to get the evidence together if t's there. And we'll have a current address soon. I'll call you with any news."

"Do you think it will be tonight?"

"I'd say so. We're all on call and staying close. I don't think we'll be getting any sleep."

"Call me. No matter what time. I wish I was there."

"I wish you were here too," he says slowly.

"Thanks," I say, picking up his double meaning and feeling slightly guilty that I'm also attracted to Darren. "You working at the moment?"

"Yeah, looking over the college lists. We're getting a database together to run an electronic cross-reference. We're almost there."

"What about the FBI applicants and police lists?" I lie down on the bed but leave my legs hanging over the edge. My feet just touch the floor.

"Flynn, Jones and Krip are working on those."

"I hope O'Donnell's got enough people."

"Daly's really only a computer search for the moment. Hopefully there aren't too many George Dalys. With any luck we'll have an address within the hour."

"Maybe I should get on a flight now."

"Would you get a flight out at this time of night?"

"No, probably not. O'Donnell wants me to stay put anyway."

"Don't worry, Soph. We can handle it at this end. You've done the hard work and got the name, let us do the rest. Plus, we've got definite links between all the victims now. The pendant thing plus the body position-

ing should stand up in court. So we only have to get a
case against this guy for one of the murders."

"Yeah, I thought about that today, when I was with the
Raymonds. I hadn't given it much thought before that."

"Naturally. You're worried about Sam."

"God, I hope she's okay." I sit up again. She might
never be okay. How can anyone really deal with being
abducted, raped and tortured by a serial killer?

"We'll help her through this, Soph. And so will the
FBI. Amanda Rosen is good."

"Yeah, she's damn good," I say.

"She'll be there for Sam. We all will be."

I lie back on the bed again. There's a pause and I
wonder what Josh is thinking. I'd love to have him next
to me right now.

"Listen, I'm going to try to get some sleep before the
call comes in," Josh says.

"Sure. Don't forget…"

"I know. Call you."

"Thanks, Josh."

We say our good-nights and hang up. I feel useless
now, hanging around in Tucson when Sam's somewhere
in D.C. and the bust is about to go down. I spend the next
hour looking through the case files on the motel bed,
before falling asleep.

I wake up with a start when the phone rings.

"Hello," I say, groggy and shaken by another nightmare I can't remember.

"It's me. Josh. We've got something on Daly."

"Yes?"

"He studied in Michigan."

I sit up and swing my feet off the bed and onto the floor. "That's fantastic news. From 1997 to 2000?"

"The dates are a year off. He was there from 1998 to 2001. It's still possible though."

"So we've got him in Arizona and Michigan. That's two."

"Three. We've got a current address on him and it's here in D.C. We're going to bring him in for questioning."

"What if Sam's hidden on the premises? Have you got a search warrant?"

A pause. "No."

"Shit!"

"We need more for a warrant."

"But what about Sam?"

"If Daly knows anything, I'll get it out of him." There's a steeliness in Marco's voice that surprises me. But I can't imagine he'll break any rules with Daly, even for Sam.

I sigh. "Okay."

"I'll call you just before I go in. I can keep the line open so you can hear what's going on."

"Thanks, Josh. I couldn't bear to sit here and not know."

"Yeah, I figured as much. I'll call you back."

I wait impatiently, unsure what to do with myself. I get up and pace the room, glaring at my watch every few seconds. Hang on, Sam.

I decide to try to see what's happening to Sam, like I did earlier today. I sit on the edge of my bed and push the thoughts away. I take deep breaths and with each breath try to relax. But it's no use; I'm too wound up to clear my mind. I keep thinking about George Daly, and about Sam lying on a gurney somewhere.

Finally, after twenty minutes of pacing, looking at crime-scene photos and drinking water, my phone rings.

"Josh?"

"Hi. I'm at the door. I'll leave my cell phone in my pocket."

"Okay."

I hear Josh knocking on a door. He knocks again. At this time of the night/morning, Daly's bound to be asleep. I hear a muffled man's voice but I can't make out what's being said.

"It's Special Agent Marco, FBI, and Detective Flynn from the D.C. police."

The door opens.

"Yes?"

"Are you George Daly?"

"Yes." The voice is uncertain.

"We'd like to talk to you about some murders. Can we come in?" Flynn speaks for the first time.

"Sure...sure." The voice is still uncertain, now perhaps intermingled with curiosity. God, I hate this. I hate not being there. I stop pacing and crouch down, almost in a fetal position.

Daly's voice again. "Is everything all right? Who's been murdered?"

Now I can hear fear. But is it fear that someone he knows has been killed or fear that he's been found out?

"You here alone, Mr. Daly?"

"Yes."

"We'd like to talk to you about the D.C. Slasher case. You grew up in Arizona?"

"Yes, that's right."

"Did you know Sally-Anne Raymond?"

"No, but I remember her murder. What's all this got to do with me?"

"And you studied in Michigan?" Josh asks, not answering Daly's question.

"Yes." Very hesitant now.

"Did you know Candice Lane, Georgina Craig, Beth Walters, Jenny Brightman, Susannah Armstrong or Kelly Lee?" Marco reels off the Michigan victims.

"No. Look, where the hell's this going?"

"We'd like to question you in relation to these murders, and others."

"What!" His voice is loud. "Murder? But...but...I didn't know those girls."

"We just want to ask you a few questions. We believe you may be able to help us with our investigation."

"Um...um...don't I need a lawyer or something?"

"They're just routine questions, but by all means call a lawyer if you like. If you think you need one." Marco's pushing Daly into a corner. If he calls a lawyer, it may indicate guilt and something to hide.

Silence.

"Let's go, Mr. Daly."

"I'll just..." He pauses again. "I'll just get dressed."

"Sure. Mind if we look around a bit while we're waiting?" Josh's voice is now friendly, open.

A pause. "I guess not. I don't have anything to hide."

He's either innocent or very confident that Josh and Flynn won't find anything. He's letting them look around without a search warrant.

A crackle comes through the phone. "Sophie?"

"Yeah, I'm here. What do you think?"

"Hate to say it, but he's not acting particularly suspiciously. Surprised more than anything else."

"Mmm."

"I'll look around, just in case. Flynn is keeping an eye on Daly."

I listen to Josh move through the house. After several minutes he speaks. "The house is clear. No sign of Sam."

"You checked the basement?"

"It's clear. We knew there was a chance he took his girls somewhere other than his house," Josh says quietly. "It might still be Daly."

"I know. I know." I sink on the bed and rest my head in my free hand. "If she's got some of those deeper wounds like the other victims—"

"We're going to question him now. We will find out."

"Sam may bleed out if we don't find her."

"I know. Look, Soph, we haven't confirmed him for all states yet. We have to face the fact that he might not be our guy."

"Yeah, or he might be the murdering SOB who's got Sam."

No response from Josh.

"I'll fly back in the morning. Help you guys question him."

"We may need you to place him at the other Arizona crime scenes."

I clench my fists, frustrated, powerless. I puff air forcefully out of my mouth. "I'll give you a call in a few hours and see how the questioning's going."

"Okay. Let's see how it plays out. And don't worry, I'll call you as soon as we get anything from him."

I hang up, wired. We got him. We got him. We just have to find out where he's keeping Sam. I have to believe that. I walk across to the bar fridge and take out a chocolate bar. I stare out the window, chewing. Oh God, they have to find Sam.

I decide to go over the Daly interviews from Sally-Anne's case. Maybe there's something there. Some slip I didn't see the first time. I grab the reports and lie down on the bed to read. However, it's only a few minutes before I'm fighting back sleep. But I don't want to sleep, I want to find evidence against Daly.

Finally I submit…I need to get at least a couple of hours' sleep if I want to function tomorrow. My alarm is set for 5:30 a.m. That's only three hours away. I let myself drift off and I dream, again.

I'm standing at a door, but I don't know where I am. There are people everywhere. Uniformed people. I cross over a crime-scene tape and walk in, dazed. I see a mirror with writing on it.

A figure comes out at me from nowhere. I run. I can't run fast enough. My legs are like jelly.

The phone's ringing and I'm covered in sweat. Small parts of my dream come back to me, but it's all in pieces, like a jigsaw puzzle. I remember blood, something about a mirror, and running.

"Hello?" I say, looking at the clock. It's 5:25 a.m.

"Sophie," says a strange, tight voice.

"Yes?" I say, shaking.

There's a pause.

"We've found Sam." Another pause. "She's dead." The voice is Josh's.

"What?" I whisper. "What?" I scream. "But you've got Daly. You've got the killer. This can't be. She's not dead."

"Sophie, it wasn't Daly. He's got alibis."

"It's got to be him."

"Sam's body was dumped when we were questioning Daly. It's not him."

"No! No."

I can't help myself from picturing Sam's naked, dead body. She was never meant to die like that. Not Sam.

"I'm sorry, Sophie. I'm so sorry." His voice is croaky. Tired and upset.

"Don't, Josh. Please don't."

"Come back, Sophie. Get the first flight out."

I hang up and finally release my emotions. The tears aren't silent anymore.

CHAPTER 17

Amanda leans forward in her chair. "Sophie, I'm so sorry."

"Yeah." My arms hang limply and rest on my legs. This can't really be happening.

She rests her hands on her knees, leaning farther forward. "I think we all thought we'd get him before he killed her."

"I should have done more."

"What could you have done?"

"I don't know. I've missed something."

"What did you find out in Arizona?"

I tell her about Sally-Anne, about the pendant and about the marks on all the girls, including the knife wounds that have been cut to partially form the Triquetra.

"So you've definitely linked them. That's a big step, Sophie."

"Doesn't matter to Sam." I lean on one armrest.

"No, but it's helped the case. The next victim."

"But not Sam."

"No, not Sam. But you can't help everyone, Sophie. You can't always win."

"I should have. I should have helped Sam."

"You did."

"How?" I say.

"You've got evidence that means when we find this guy, you'll be able to put him away."

"How has that helped Sam?" I hold her gaze, knowing how cold my pale blue eyes can be.

"At least you'll find and convict her killer. That's what Sam would have wanted."

Amanda's right, but it doesn't console me. "I want to go to the scene."

Josh picked me up from the airport and told me Rivers's orders—straight to see Amanda. I haven't even seen Sam yet.

"There might be something at the scene. Some clue. This is different from the other murders. He took her back to her apartment. She was found inside. I know that apartment. I know Sam."

She pauses. "There are things at the crime scene, Sophie. Things that are meant to taunt you."

"Like his letter to Sam?"

"Yes. But this time it's you." She monitors my reaction.

"Another letter?"

"Not exactly."

"It doesn't matter anyway." I keep my voice controlled. Even. "I'm going to kill him."

"You've got every right to be angry, but—"

"I don't need your permission!" I scream, letting my anger overflow.

"Sophie, I'm here to help you." She pauses, waiting for my response.

I sigh. "I'm sorry." I clasp my hands together. "If you want to help me, let me go to the crime scene."

She pauses. "Okay. But I'd like to go with you. To help you deal with it."

"Let's go." I stand up, eager to get there.

"Hold on." She picks up her phone and I know she's talking to Rivers. "She may be able to shed some light...she saw the necklace..."

Rivers mustn't want me there.

"I'll make sure she's all right." Amanda hangs up. "Okay. The others are all there. We'll join them," she says.

We arrive at Sam's apartment. On the street there are about five uniformed cops and a gathering of onlookers. I walk up the pathway and cameras snap my picture. The press take photos of everyone and work out who's important later. In the corridor on Sam's floor are more cops and several FBI agents. It feels familiar. Did I dream this? I walk to her apartment door and move inside. Everything seems to be in slow motion. Josh walks toward me. He holds me again, but this time it's a quicker hug, not like the long one we shared at the airport. But I'm not really here. I'm watching my body from somewhere else. Somewhere safe.

Sandra Couples approaches me. "I'm so sorry, Sophie. I'm so sorry." She takes my hand and looks into my eyes. "My guys left the place for fifteen minutes to check out a house alarm down the street." It's a confession.

"It's all right, Sandra. He would have taken her somewhere else if he couldn't get in here. Or he would have killed your people."

Sandra opens her mouth but no words come out. Rivers comes from Sam's bedroom. He looks pale and his skin doesn't have its usual smoothness.

"Sophie. You okay?"

I nod.

Rivers awkwardly puts his arm around me. "I'm still not sure it's such a good idea you being here."

"I had to come. He might have left something again."

He says nothing—he knows I'm right.

I'm drawn down the hallway to Sam's bedroom. I pass several forensics experts, all collecting evidence.

"Is she still here?" I ask.

"No. The coroner's taken her back to start the autopsy."

I flinch.

I walk toward Sam's bedroom, preparing myself for the scene. Amanda, Josh and Rivers accompany me, but Couples hangs back. I see the rest of the task force in the bedroom and we all nod at each other, uncomfortable. We all failed Sam.

More forensics people circle the crime scene, including Marty. Everyone walks around in a stupor. It's not like a normal crime scene. It's *not* a normal crime scene. This time we all knew the victim. Most people in this room would have worked with Sam at one time or another.

I can see from the markings on Sam's bed exactly how she was positioned. I shudder, thinking of what her final few days must have been like.

Next I look at the mirror. *I'm coming Sophie.*

I stare at the handwritten message. I don't feel fear, I feel anger. He's not going to get to me. I won't give him that power.

"Have we got anything?" I say, straight down to business.

"Coroner puts the time of death between two and five this morning. The body was moved postmortem. Lividity is a little different this time. We think she may have been in a van for longer than the others.

"He must have been waiting to see if the cops left the apartment block."

"She was dumped between five and five-fifteen this morning," O'Donnell says. He flips his notebook shut. "We hope to know more after the autopsy."

"DNA? Prints? The writing?" I ask, motioning toward the mirror.

"Marty's team is just finishing up," Josh says. I follow Josh's gaze and turn around.

"Hi, Marty."

He gives me a small smile. I can see the concern in his eyes.

"Well?" I say.

"We've taken photos and samples back to the lab, we'll have to wait for the tests. But so far it looks like the writing is in nail polish. The color seems to match one of Sam's," he says, holding up an evidence bag with a Revlon nail polish in it. I recognize it—a dark plum.

"Any prints?"

"We've lifted a few, but we won't know whose for a few hours."

"Fibers?"

"I'm sorry, Sophie. Nothing yet."

"Oh God."

He hesitates, about to say something, but then changes his mind.

"Do whatever you can, won't you?" I say, holding on to his arm.

"We'll do our best."

Marty leaves and Josh is by my side. "If there's anything here, he'll find it," he says.

I nod.

O'Donnell comes to the center of the room. "Okay, let's have another half an hour, then the task force should go back to the D.C. Field Office and keep working on our other leads."

We all agree and wander around—some aimlessly and others purposefully.

"Anderson, I need to talk to you." Rivers takes me aside and Amanda follows. We move into the corridor outside Sam's apartment, to a quiet section.

"You up to this, Anderson?"

"Yes, sir."

He looks at Amanda, then back at me. Please no, don't let him do it.

"You're off the case. You know that, don't you?" Rivers says.

"No, you can't. I have to stay on this case. I have to," I say, grabbing his elbow tightly with one hand and showing my desperation. I quickly let go.

"There's no discussion." He takes his glasses off. "I should have realized Wright was a target. And I'm sure as hell not going to make that mistake again."

"I'll be fine."

"You got to be kidding me, Anderson. Look at that damn mirror!" he says, gesturing into Sam's apartment.

I've got to be the bait. "You're right. I'm a target. So use me. I can be the bait."

Rivers looks at me and leans against the wall. He takes a deep breath and shakes his head.

I move closer to him. "We can catch him this way. He'll come after me and we'll get him."

Rivers looks at Amanda. "Do you think she's up to it?"

I resent being spoken about as though I'm not even here, but now's not the time to dwell on that. "This is the only way to stop him," I add. I have to convince him. I must find the killer. I owe it to Sam.

Amanda stares at me for a moment before replying. "If you decide to go ahead, I'll want a one-hour appointment every day. And she needs to feel safe."

"I'd put two agents on her around the clock," Rivers says, but I can see he still hasn't made a final decision.

I push him. "So I can stay on the case?"

"I never said that."

"Oh, come on, sir. You know he's more likely to keep targeting me if I'm working his case." I pause. "Besides, with agents on me, what does it matter what I do? I'll be protected."

Rivers studies my face. After about ten incredibly long seconds, he pushes off the wall and takes one step toward me. "You're on. Don't leave this apartment until your protection arrives. Got it?" He jabs his finger at me.

"Yes, sir."

And with that he's gone, flipping his cell phone open and dialing as he walks back into Sam's.

"Sophie, I've got to get back. You need to come and see me later today and we'll finish our session. Three o'clock, my office." Amanda doesn't give me a chance to respond.

Just over fifty minutes later we're back at the D.C. Field Office. My protective agents are parked out front, and the task force is in the project room. The whiteboard's still got the map of D.C. pinned to it, and now Sam's apartment is also marked.

"Anderson, I updated the team members on your discoveries in Arizona yesterday. Anything else to tell us?"

"Did you fill them in about the knife wounds?" I ask Josh.

"Shit. No. With everything that's happened in the past eight hours I totally forgot."

"What'd you find?" O'Donnell asks.

"Late last night I was looking at the photos from the murders." I stand up and take the photos over to the whiteboard. Getting back into the case is a welcome distraction. I draw an enlarged diagram of the Triquetra. "If you look at the knife wounds on the victims' thighs, they're all part of this diagram." I take them through each victim and what part of the symbol the killer engraved into her thigh.

"Sam's leg was cut pretty bad too," Couples says.

"Yeah, I noticed that. I'm trying to picture it," Josh says. He pauses. "It must be part of the bottom, right-hand section. That's all that's left."

I shake my head. "That's already covered. It must be the very bottom section."

Josh nods. "The symbol's almost complete."

"So, he's making the symbol, bit by bit this time. Why?" Flynn says.

Josh gives his pen a double click. "Who knows? Maybe he knew it was only a matter of time before VICAP linked all his murders and he didn't want to make it too obvious for us. Something obvious like that on all the victims would have meant an earlier VICAP match."

"How are you guys going with your lists?" I ask, sitting back down.

O'Donnell answers. "We've got full enrollment names from the twenty-two colleges with science or medical programs. Our list was finalized last night and the computer geeks have been doing their work, running the list against payroll records and locations where each student took their SATs. The computer's spitting out names alphabetically, and we're getting them from the boys in groups of ten." He squeezes the bridge of his nose. He looks tired. We all do. "We've also got a list of all the FBI and CIA applicants from Arizona, Michigan, Chicago and D.C. We're crossing that against studying in Michigan, plus the SATs and the payroll stuff. Again, I've told the guys to give the names to us in groups of ten so we can get started ASAP. And we're doing a search for any cops who've transferred across from Michigan to Chicago and then to D.C."

"How many names have we got so far?" I ask.

"Two hundred."

I can't hide my disappointment. "Shit! How far have we got to go?"

"We're two-thirds the way through both lists. It'll only be a couple of hours before we get the final lists," he says, pausing and scribbling down the alphabet. "When it comes through, I'll take surnames A to C, Couples, you take D through F, Anderson, you take G to I, Flynn, J to L, Jones, M to P, Marco, Q to T, and Krip, you get the easy one, U to X."

"Any update on the lock-picking angle?" I ask, looking at Jones.

"On the master-key front, none of the locksmiths have a common employee, so it would be pretty impossible for our perp to have entered using a master key." He stares down at his notepad. "I also managed to get as many names as I could from Arizona lock manufacturers. Some have kept the records and some haven't. We're cross-checking the names against our college, FBI, CIA and law-enforcement lists to date, but nothing's matched so far."

"What about Michigan?"

"I've made a few calls to the manufacturers, but haven't got through to them all yet."

Krip leans forward. "As far as we know, Sam's the only person he's ever nabbed from inside an apartment, and maybe Jean. The rest were in parking lots, maybe at the front door, but no struggles inside."

I can sense that no one feels this is a strong lead except me.

"I don't know about the trash can lead, Sophie. We don't have any proof he's getting into their apartments," Flynn says.

I stand up and lean on the table. "Guys, he gets in. I'm telling you. And I don't see Sam leaving that window open."

"Anderson, why don't you take over the lock-picking angle. Maybe also check if any lock-picking sets or guns have been reported stolen," O'Donnell says. I'm not sure that he's taking me, or this lead, seriously.

He moves on. "I've been checking out the cops who worked the cases. Nothing's come up yet, but there's still a few to chase down."

I wonder what he's found out about the task force.

The meeting winds up and I get a small desk and phone to start my research. Josh and Couples stay in the meeting room, O'Donnell goes back to his office and Krip goes back to his desk. Flynn and Jones share a small desk opposite mine.

My cell phone rings and I answer it.

"Hi, Sophie, it's Darren. Darren Carter."

"Hi, Darren."

"Look, Bob told me about your friend. I'm real sorry."

"Thanks, Darren. I should have told you myself, but I barely remembered to call Watson to tell him not to pick me up."

"That's okay. I understand. Listen, I'm in D.C."

"What?"

"I've taken a couple of vacation days. I thought maybe there was something I could do to help you guys. I'll chase down leads or talk to you more about the Arizona murders. Anything at all."

Is it desire for revenge or closure that's brought him to D.C.? I walk away from Flynn and Jones and into a quieter corner. "To be honest, I don't know if they'll want an outsider on this case."

"Totally informal, of course. I don't need to know any federal secrets. But I think I could help."

"Where are you now?"

"D.C. airport."

"Grab a cab to 601 Fourth Street Northwest. It's the

D.C. Field Office. In the meantime, I'll talk to the task force leader. Call me when you're out front."

At O'Donnell's office I tell him about Detective Carter.

"Look, you know we can't get this approved," O'Donnell says.

"It doesn't need to be official. It's just a helping hand."

He takes his glasses off and stares out the window. "What you do in your free time is up to you. You've got a friend flying in from Arizona, I say you meet him and talk to him. Unofficially."

I get the message.

"Can I tell him about Sam. Who she is?" I say, not able to talk about Sam in the past tense.

"You know the official line on that one." Again he pauses. "But it's your call."

"Thanks." I walk toward the doorway and then turn back. "Anything suspicious on the task force members?"

"Not yet. I'm checking everyone's movements though."

I nod and leave his office. Would he tell me if he'd found something? Hard to say. He might be under orders to keep everything under wraps.

Thirty minutes later Darren phones again.

I meet him in front of the building. The agents assigned to me keep a close eye on Darren, and I wave at them to signal he's okay. I sign Darren in and we go upstairs and I take him around to meet the task force members, including O'Donnell.

He shakes Darren's hand. "I understand you've got a few days off."

"That's right. A holiday in our nation's capital."

O'Donnell smiles, happy Carter's getting the drift. He

shuffles some papers on his desk and pulls out a two-page list. He hands it to me.

"Anderson, this is the list of Arizona police officers or applicants, and FBI and CIA applicants from Arizona." He looks back at Carter, then at me. "See if any names ring a bell."

"Will do," I say.

Once we're out of the office I hand the list over to Darren. He folds it up and puts it in his jacket pocket.

Lastly, I take Darren in to Josh and Couples in the project room. They both look up as I enter. Couples is on the phone and nods, but Josh, who was obviously about to make a call, puts the handset down. I'm about to introduce Darren when Couples finishes.

"This is Sandra Couples, D.C. police, and Josh Marco, FBI. This is Detective Darren Carter from Tucson Homicide. He worked on the Arizona murders. Detective Carter is on a couple of days' leave and wanted to see how we're progressing with the case."

Sandra nods and shakes his hand. Josh copies Sandra's response and adds, "Nice to meet you."

Josh and Darren look at each other strangely. Do I sense a tension between the pair?

I smile. "Don't mind us. I'm just going to fill Darren in on our current status."

Sandra picks up the phone and starts dialing.

I move to the whiteboard and take Darren through the map and the different abduction and dump sites.

"The pattern's different with your friend."

"Yes. We're not sure why yet."

Josh comes up behind us. "Taking Sam back to her

apartment was more personal than the way he left the other victims."

"Yes. Yes, it was," Darren says somewhat distractedly.

I hand Darren the file to date on Sam, but I can't bear to look at it myself. He flicks through it, and Josh and I sit next to each other to expand the profile. After about ten minutes Darren hands me the file.

"I've just got to look into something."

"To do with the case?"

"Maybe. Maybe. It's something I remembered about Sally-Anne."

CHAPTER 18

After my afternoon appointment with Amanda I go straight to the ladies' room. A quick glance shows me no one else is in the four-cubicle bathroom. I lean on the sink and study my reflection.

"God, you look like shit," I say out loud. My eyes are red and puffy from crying. My skin looks pasty and there are large dark circles under my blue eyes. I try to cover it all up with another layer of makeup. The puffiness will go down in the car as long as I don't think about Sam. I flip my phone open and power it up. One message. It's from Josh, but I'll call him back later, when I'm more together.

I make my way through the corridors, head down. I don't want to run into anyone in my current state. I know they'd understand, after all, Sam's…

I can't bring myself to acknowledge it. I only want to think about her alive.

I get into the car and turn the radio on, loud. I surf

until I find the most upbeat song, then I sing, louder than the radio. I need to keep myself distracted. I can't cry, not now. I refocus my tears into thoughts of revenge.

I walk into Café Alcasto. It's one of my favorite places for pasta and coffee. The coffee machine sits up front and is one of the coolest-looking pieces of machinery I've ever seen. But it's not simply for looks—the coffee is amazing.

My two bodyguards are close behind me. They're in the door before I've even made my way over to Darren. It's weird being followed. Really weird.

Papers are fanned out on Darren's table, but he's not reading. Instead, he stares out the window. He doesn't see me until I pull out the chair opposite him. He looks wired, distracted. It could just be the coffee. They make it strong.

"Hi, Darren."

He smiles, a strange smile. The way his eyes follow me as I sit down shows me that he's glad to see me, but the smile is forced.

"How's it going with the Arizona lists?" I ask.

"No names are ringing bells." He looks down at the pages in front of him. "Not from the list."

I lean forward. "What's up?"

"Sophie, there's something I have to tell you."

Oh God, I hope this doesn't have anything to do with the attraction between us. Not now.

"Yes?"

"There's another reason I came up here."

Here we go… I take a breath in, ready to ask him to stop there, but he holds his hand up. I hear him out.

"It's about Josh."

"What about Josh?" This is getting complicated.

"I don't know how to say this." He pauses again. "But Josh was a suspect for Sally-Anne."

"What?" I stand up forcefully and the two agents rise quickly. I wave them back and sit down again. "But how could that be? His name wasn't even on your interview list."

"Josh lived in Tucson for about a year and a half. Between 1995 and 1996."

"No, there must be some mistake."

"I'm sorry, Sophie."

"But he wasn't on your suspect list."

"That was Watson. Josh's father was a well-known local politician and a friend of the Raymonds, and of Bob. He wanted Josh to go into politics and asked that his name never go on the records. I didn't like it, but Bob agreed and told me to keep my mouth shut. It was my first case in Homicide. I did what I was told."

"But you eliminated him as a suspect?"

"Watson did. But I was never totally convinced."

This is unbelievable.

"So that's why you two were so odd when I introduced you earlier today."

"When we were in Tucson you mentioned a Josh. That was the first time I'd given much thought to Josh Marco in eleven years. I had to come up and do some checking of my own. See if it was the same guy." He looks down at the table. "I had to warn you."

I try to absorb what Darren's just said, but my mind battles against it, unwilling to think Josh, the man I'm sleeping with, is a killer.

"Have you told anyone else?"

"Not yet. I wanted you to be the first to know."

I nod and manage a small smile.

He looks down. "Me not telling anyone isn't a totally selfless act." He looks me in the eye again. "There could be repercussions. For me."

Darren's right, altering police records is a big deal and someone would have to pay. "But it was your first case in Homicide."

"So? There was only me and Watson."

With Watson, the natural contender, retired and out of the picture, the heat will fall on Darren. "Let's wait a bit, then, before we tell the others. There's no point ruining your career over this if we clear Josh."

Darren looks relieved.

"Have you spoken to Josh?" I ask.

"No. Again, I wanted to tell you before I confronted him."

"Josh left me a message about an hour ago. Maybe he wanted to tell me about Sally-Anne himself."

"Probably. He must have guessed I'd tell you."

I punch Josh's number into my phone. I want to give him the opportunity to tell me about his involvement in Arizona. I stand up and hover a few feet away from Darren.

"Hi, Josh. It's me. You rang?"

"Hi." He pauses. "I just wanted to see how you were doing."

"I'm okay. I'm with Darren."

"Oh."

I keep quiet, giving him the chance to come clean. Nothing. "Listen, I better go. We're running through the cases." I'm disappointed.

A beat of silence. "Okay."

"Nothing else?" I give him one last opening.

"No. I'll see you later."

I hang up and sit down next to Darren.

"Well?"

"Nothing."

I run through it all in my head. The killer can't be Josh. But the pieces begin to fall into place.

I look up at Darren. "Josh studied in Michigan."

"Michigan? During the murders?"

"Yes. He says that's what made him go into law enforcement, why he applied to the FBI."

"Maybe we *should* tell someone now. I mean, he even fits your goddamn profile." Darren leans backward and glances out the window. "Law-enforcement background, knowledge of crime scenes, smart…" He trails off.

"Except for the medical background," I say.

"One thing?"

And I think about it. I mean really think about it. Is it possible? How can it be possible? I mean, I am, or was, falling for him. "This can't be."

I think about O'Donnell. What's he found on Josh so far? He must be looking into him.

"Well, let's try to eliminate him," Darren says. "So, we've got him in Arizona and Michigan around the times of the murders. What about Chicago?"

"Oh God." I cover my mouth with my hand.

"I take it he worked in Chicago."

"He was at the Chicago Field Office before he transferred to D.C., but I don't know the dates."

"Do you know when he started at Quantico?"

"About a year ago."

"How does that go with your dates for the D.C. murders?"

"We've just placed him in all murder cities except Florida, and roughly at the same time as the killings." I put my head in my hands. "Shit."

"Did he work on any of the cases?"

"He couldn't have." I shake my head. "He would have told us." I pause—he didn't tell us about Sally-Anne. "No, he mustn't have. It would be in the case files."

"You sure?"

"Yes, I would have noticed."

"Okay, so he was in the cities but not working the cases."

"He's got a damn good knowledge of crime scenes too. It would explain the perfect crime scenes. No DNA, no footprints, no tire marks." Part of me is actually starting to believe Josh could be a suspect.

"Perfect enough to be a pro."

"Exactly. But it just can't be. Not Josh," I say.

Darren clears his throat and stares at the papers in front of him. "I take it you and Josh are more than friends."

I can feel how upset this makes Darren and I want to comfort him. I reach out and put my hand on top of his, but withdraw it quickly.

There's silence for a few seconds.

"How long for?" he asks.

"That's not really any of your business." I keep my voice open, not defensive.

He stares at me. God, he's so sweet.

"Things have been heading in that direction recently," I say.

"Since you've been working this case?"

I pause. "Yes…"

"Convenient. Maybe he's trying to keep you off his trail."

"No, that's madness. He couldn't. He just couldn't. And certainly not Sam." But Sam was different. The crime scene was different. More personal. Maybe…

I voice my opinion. "Sam was different from the others because he took her back to her apartment. We were wondering if this time he knew her. Really knew her."

"We?"

I laugh at the irony. "Josh and I. We reviewed the profile after you left the field office."

Darren is silent.

I rub my hand across my forehead and down the side of my face. "But if he's the killer, why would he point us in the right direction?"

"You tell me, you're the profiler."

It would tie in with a high-risk offender. I put my head in my hands again and pull my hair off my face with my fingers. "My taste in men can't be this crap."

He laughs a little. "It might not be. It could all be coincidence."

But this doesn't reassure me.

"Anything else?" Darren asks.

There must be something we're missing…

"He couldn't have dumped Sam's body. He was questioning George Daly," I say.

"Okay. Now we're getting somewhere. Are you sure he was with Daly the whole time?"

"Pretty sure. But I can check the interview transcript."

"Okay. Is there anything else suspicious? What about your premonitions?"

"Josh does fit the build of the killer I've seen. Six-one, broad."

"That'd fit a lot of guys. But it's still interesting. Anything else?"

I think of something, but can hardly bring myself to say it.

"Yes?" Darren prompts.

It can't be, can it?

I take a deep breath in, delaying verbalizing it. "Josh is left-handed and the knife wounds indicate a left-hander. The note was written by a left-hander."

Darren nods.

"It's a lot of coincidences," I say.

"Yes. It's the locations that we need to confirm. And see if he really did interview George Daly all morning yesterday."

"I think I better talk to O'Donnell too." I pause. "I'm sorry."

"Don't be. This is more important than protecting my career. A helluva lot more important. But it's also a pretty heavy accusation. It'll probably get back to Josh. Are you ready for that?"

Darren's right. "Let's check out the dates before I say anything to O'Donnell. See if they match. I'll check out Josh's movements during Daly's questioning too."

I read the article... How ridiculous. Who's playing whom?

Fourth Slasher victim gives police lead

The fourth Slasher victim, an off-duty call girl, was found late last night. Police believe the killer didn't realize the woman was a prostitute when he picked her up.

This latest murder comes on the tail of the FBI profile of the killer. According to the FBI, police are looking for a white male in his early to late thirties. He is a blue-collar worker or possibly a security guard.

Blue-collar, my ass. But it doesn't matter. I've got their attention now.

It's broad daylight, a risk I wouldn't normally take, but my patience is running out. Sophie's almost ready to be mine.

At her apartment block I randomly press apartment numbers. Someone buzzes me in. The security door releases and I walk up the three small steps into the main foyer. She's on the third floor, apartment 310. I take the stairs, head down. No one can see my face. At her door I look around. The coast is clear. My lock-picking gun gently hums and within a few seconds I'm in. I don't have as long as I'd like, but I can't resist being inside her apartment once more.

I look around. It's immaculate. I must have her.

I survey each room, spending the longest in the bedroom. I look through her chest of drawers, her closet, her makeup and her jewelry. I smell her clothes, letting myself become accustomed to her scent. I saw her in a beige, low-cut blouse. I hunt for this item and find it in the dirty-clothes basket. I take it up to my nose and inhale deeply…

She smells beautiful. I can't wait until she's really mine. I keep the blouse to my nose and turn around to look at her bed. I'd like to lie down, smell this blouse and picture her naked…but I don't have time. I put the blouse back in the basket and move to the kitchen. It's spotless.

I open her fridge: cottage cheese, yogurt, milk, eggs, crisp vegetables, chili sauce, a few different curry pastes and a bowl of leftovers—chicken curry. I check all the cartons and jars. They're all fine, nothing past its use-by date. People really have no idea how many germs are out there, especially in dairy. But maybe she knows. I have to look after my girls. Keep them healthy for me.

The leftovers? They could be swarming with listeria and other bacteria. But it's too noticeable, too obvious. I don't want her to guess I've been here.

I leave, frustrated. I haven't made my mark. I'll come back another time.

CHAPTER 19

"Where are we at with our lists, people?" O'Donnell says at our 6:00 p.m. meeting. "I know we only got them a few hours ago, but I want to see some progress."

Flynn clears his throat. "I've tracked down eleven out of my twenty-three and eliminated ten out of that eleven."

"Eliminated how?"

"Alibis, too different from the profile, or right-handers."

"Okay. Good work. What about the remaining one?"

"I'm going to question him tonight."

"Good. You'll take Jones?"

"Yes."

"We'll have to keep it to two-person questioning for the moment. We don't have the resources for anything more." O'Donnell waves his finger at us. "But I don't want anyone questioning a suspect by themselves."

We all nod.

"Couples, where are you at?"

"I'm halfway through my list of eighteen names."

"Any contenders or eliminations?" O'Donnell asks.

"All eliminated."

"Jones?"

"Same as Couples. The left-hander thing is really narrowing the list down."

With only thirteen to twenty percent of the population left-handers, it's a godsend when the physical evidence lets you eliminate over eighty percent of the population. That's eighty percent of your suspect pool gone in one fell swoop.

"How are you finding out if they're left-handers?" I ask.

"Calling on behalf of the Society of Left-handers," O'Donnell says. Obviously this strategy was worked out when I was back at Quantico with Amanda.

"Nice."

O'Donnell stands up and paces. "Still, we need visual confirmation at this stage. If our guy's on to us, he may be wary. We've whittled the list down to one hundred and twenty in total. Let's get picky. Once you're through the list, go back to the ones that only got eliminated on the strength of the right-hander lead. I want you to actually see them using their right hand before we cross them off the list altogether. Krip?"

Krip leans forward ever so slightly. "I'm about halfway through. One contender. I'll pay him a visit tonight."

"Okay, take Couples as backup. Jones?"

"I'm almost through my list. One contender too…oh, and Marco."

I study O'Donnell's face. Nothing. Either he's got his poker face on or he doesn't suspect Josh.

"I was wondering if I'd come up," Josh says. "Given I studied at Michigan an' all."

"You lived in Arizona and Chicago?" Flynn asks.

"Yep. I lived most places growing up. My old man's a politician. And then I moved around with the air force and the Bureau."

I look at the other faces in the room. It's hard to tell if they suspect Josh. They must be wondering, at least—how many coincidences is one too many? Or maybe I'm being crazy. I mean, he has admitted to being in the states in question, surely he wouldn't be so relaxed about it if it were him. Thrill killer or not, our guy's smarter than that, isn't he?

I study him closely, looking for a telltale sign like sweat, blinking or fidgeting. But he's clean. He smiles my way but I look away.

O'Donnell takes his glasses off. "Marco, how's your list looking?"

"Getting smaller. I eliminated quite a few on the left-hander thing and I've got two possibilities that I'll pay a visit tonight or tomorrow morning. I'll take Anderson with me." He smiles at me again and I shift awkwardly in my chair before flashing an insincere smile his way.

"Fine. Fine. By the way, people, I believe most of you know that Anderson's got a tail on her at the moment."

Everyone nods.

"We've got a spare room at my place," Flynn says. "The wife won't mind."

"Thanks, but no. I'm hoping I'll be a piece of tempting bait for our perp."

"Be safe," O'Donnell says.

"I'll be fine. I'm sure no one will get past Laurel and Hardy." I'll actually have three law-enforcement professionals looking out for me because I've also invited Darren to stay on my sofa bed—but I don't bother telling the others that.

Flynn laughs. "Yeah, I saw them sitting out front. They really do look like Laurel and Hardy."

O'Donnell doesn't laugh. "It's Montana and Sargent, both good agents." He gives Flynn a look, then shoots his blue eyes my way again. They soften slightly. "But it will be someone different by the time you get out. Shift change."

"Of course," I say.

"How did you go with the lock-picking lead, anyway, Anderson?" O'Donnell asks.

"I spent most of the afternoon going through the case files, and I think he started using the lock-pick in Michigan."

"Why?" asks O'Donnell, still skeptical.

"The victims in Arizona were all abducted outdoors and a reasonable distance from their homes. It wasn't until Michigan that some of the victims were abducted closer to home. Like in parking lots, or at the door to their homes. In two of the Michigan murders all the lights were on, and at one place there was even food in the oven. The victims weren't planning on leaving."

"Okay. Run with this hard. He's definitely getting in."

Krip looks at me somewhat apologetically. No one really believed me before, and Krip was one of the public disbelievers.

"I'd say they may have even been abducted from inside their places."

"But no sign of a struggle?" O'Donnell says.

"No. They may have left in a hurry if he spun a story about a loved one."

O'Donnell scratches his face. "Okay, keep working on those lists. Anderson, I want you to question Marco's suspects with him. Let's see if we can't get enough to make an arrest." He looks down at his notes. "Oh, by the way, I'm halfway through my list. All eliminated so far. We've got computers and forensics until midnight tonight, if you need 'em."

"Anything on the mirror?"

"The report's coming back to me tonight."

Everyone starts packing up.

"You worried about the message?" Josh asks quietly.

"A little."

"I'm worried too. More than a little," he says.

I smile, trying to be normal. But it's no good. I have to put my mind at rest about Josh.

"So, tell me about the questioning of George Daly."

"Not much to tell. O'Donnell did most of it."

"But you were there, right?"

"For some of it. We questioned him for a few hours. Checking out his story."

"So what parts were you there for?" I bite my lip.

"About two hours. We took shifts so we could all get some sleep."

"So you slept at the station?"

He looks at me oddly. "Some of us did, but I went home. It's just around the corner. What's this about, Sophie?"

The room has emptied, except for Couples. Then she leaves. I'm alone with Josh. I back away from him and stuff the rest of the files into my briefcase.

"What's wrong, Sophie?"

"Nothing. Nothing's wrong."

"You don't regret what happened, do you?" He takes both of my hands in his.

He thinks it's about sex?

"What?" I pull my hands away from his. "How can you ask me that now?"

"I'm sorry. Sophie, I'm worried about you." He moves closer.

I back away again. "I'm fine."

"Look, let's ring Marty about the mirror. See if he's got prints or anything. I know that message is freaking you out."

It's not the message. It's Josh. But I am anxious to find out anything I can about the evidence at Sam's place.

Josh flips his binder shut and slips it into his briefcase. "It won't take long. And then we can go and interview my suspects."

He switches to speakerphone and is about to start dialing, when my cell phone rings.

I pick it up. "Agent Anderson."

"Hi, Sophie. It's Amanda"

I hold my hand up to Josh, asking him to wait, and then walk off to one side.

"Hi, Amanda."

"How are you doing?"

"You know. Fine. I guess."

"It will get easier, Sophie. You just have to give it time."

Josh leans against the window, one leg bent with the sole of his foot on the window. He's pretending not to listen.

"I know. I know. I'm trying not to think about Sam, and the case is keeping me occupied." But now that Amanda's brought it up, the pain comes back. A lump sticks in my throat—my emotions aren't doing what I'm telling them to.

"You were pretty upset in our session today and I wanted to see if you needed to talk some more."

"I'm fine."

Silence.

"Honest." I'm not surprised she doesn't believe me. For the first part of the session we talked about Sam. I could deal with that…sort of. But then she brought up John and my tough exterior crumbled. Within minutes I was in tears, confessing the sense of responsibility I feel over their deaths. But I couldn't tell her why. I couldn't tell her about the psychic stuff.

Once the tears had started, I couldn't stop them and by the end of the session I was a mess.

"Well, I'll see for myself tomorrow."

"Yep," I say, dreading my next appointment.

"Any breakthroughs from the task force?"

"Not really. It's a process of elimination. We've got quite a good list to work from."

I look up at Josh again. He smiles and I force myself to return the smile.

"Listen, Sophie, you're going to get through this. You'll find the guy and I'll help you deal with the loss of Sam."

I don't think I'll ever be able to deal with it. But I can't say that.

"Thanks, Amanda."

"And there are agents on you, right?"

"Yes. Two of them."

"Okay. Well, I'll see you tomorrow morning."

"Yep, thanks. Good night," I say and hang up.

Josh pushes himself off the window. "Amanda Rosen?"

"Yeah. She was just checking up on me."

He nods. "Sophie?"

"Yes."

"You know I'm here for you too." He pauses and I look around, hoping someone will show up so I can avoid this conversation.

"I don't want to crowd you when you're dealing with so much, but…" He pauses again. "Well, I'm here for you. That's all."

"Thanks, Josh," I say with as much sincerity as I can muster.

I'm glad we're in a work environment, otherwise Josh would be trying to hug me now.

"Let's try Marty," I say.

Josh starts to dial.

"Do you think Marty will still be there?" I ask.

"Yeah. He said he'd be staying back, with everything that's happening."

Marty answers the phone after several rings.

"Marty, it's Josh. I've got you on speakerphone. Sophie's here."

"Hi, guys." A beat of silence. "How are you holding up, Sophie?"

"I'm okay." A standard response. Of course it's not true, but everyone knows that.

"Thought we'd see if you've got anything on Sam's mirror," Josh says.

"The mirror."

Papers shuffle in the background.

"We've found prints, but only Sam's and the cleaning lady's," he says. "The substance used for the writing is a blend of nail polish and blood."

He gives us time for it to sink in.

"Blood?"

"Charming, isn't it. Concentration's at nine percent."

"Whose blood?" I ask.

"DNA match just came back." He pauses. "It's Sam's blood."

"How did he mix it?" Josh says.

"He put blood into the nail-polish bottle. We examined the remainder," he says. "And it's been applied with the normal applicator."

"So, we've got nothing... Yet again."

"I'm sorry, Sophie. It doesn't look promising. The guy's been careful. Real careful."

"And the writing?"

"The handwriting analyst has positively matched it to the note Sam got last week."

"That's no surprise," I say.

"I'm finishing up my report for O'Donnell now."

"Yeah, he said it was coming through tonight."

We're silent, heads bowed for a moment.

"Thanks, Marty," Josh says. "Speak to you later." He hangs up the phone.

I grab my briefcase, disheartened.

"I've got two names. Shall we go and interview them?" Josh says.

"Okay."

"Are you sure you're up to it?"

"I'm fine," I say. "Let's take Darren."

"Darren?"

"Detective Carter."

Josh winces. Jealousy or fear of being found out?

"He might be useful from the Arizona point of view," I say.

But that's not the real reason. The real reason is that I don't want to be alone with Josh, even with two agents watching me.

"I don't think that's a good idea," Josh says.

"Why not?"

"I don't know. I'm just not crazy about the guy." He shifts uneasily from foot to foot. Josh is worried that his involvement in Arizona will come out. So he should be. A moment of courage takes over—he had his chance to tell me.

"I know all about you and Arizona," I say.

Josh looks at me. What's he thinking? Is he trying to come up with an excuse?

Finally he responds.

"I wondered if Carter would tell you. I was going to tell you myself. That's why I called."

"And you still didn't tell me!" I pause. "Why, Josh? Why would you keep that from me?"

"Because it was nothing. I was one of over a hundred people they interviewed. I was never a real suspect."

"That's not how Darren tells it."

Josh takes a sharp breath in and his eyes narrow slightly. "And I wonder why he'd say that to you, Sophie." His tone is sharp.

"What do you mean?"

"You know what I mean. Darren Carter has an ulterior motive. You!"

"You're accusing him of lying?"

"He's painting the picture to suit his needs."

"Are you sure that's what this is about?"

"I didn't care that the police questioned me. I had nothing to hide."

"Really?"

"Sophie, what are you saying?"

"You're left-handed, Josh."

"You can't be serious. You think…" He pauses and his fists clench. "You think I did this?" He backs away from me and shakes his head. "You think I killed Sam? How could you think that, even for a moment?"

I look at his hurt face and it's a good question… How could I think it? But then I answer the question myself… Because all the evidence points to it.

But I don't say that. "I don't know, Josh. I don't know what to think."

Couples walks back into the room, a cup of coffee and a sandwich in her hand. "Sorry, am I interrupting something?" She's embarrassed.

"No. I was just leaving." Josh grabs his things. "Make sure you're not by yourself tonight, Sophie," he says, then leans in closer to me so Sandra won't hear him. "Even if you have to be with *him*." He storms out of the room.

It was either one hell of a good performance or I've just thrown away any chance of ever having a relationship with Josh.

CHAPTER 20

I look out my window at the car parked on my street—half the new shift of agents assigned to me. I wave and he holds his hand up in a small salute. The other agent is loitering somewhere in the corridor outside my apartment.

I stare out the window and replay the conversation with O'Donnell. I went to him as soon as Josh left the field office. I had to.

"Have you got a minute?"

"Sure, Anderson. Come in."

"Some information has come to me. Information I need to tell you."

"Yes?" He's hesitant. He knows it's something big from my tone of voice.

"It's about Agent Marco."

"Yes?"

"Are you investigating him for this?"

"I'm investigating all task force members, like I told you." He keeps his cards close to his chest.

"I discovered something this afternoon. Some pertinent information." I stall, hardly able to believe I'm about to enter Josh as an official suspect.

"Well, go on, Anderson."

I take a deep breath. "Josh Marco was questioned about Sally-Anne Raymond."

O'Donnell raises his eyebrows. "Questioned? I don't remember seeing his name in any of the files."

"Marco's name was deleted from the list as a personal favor to his father."

"Governor Marco." O'Donnell doesn't seem surprised.

"Yes."

He sits down. "Marco's the only one in the task force I haven't been able to eliminate." He takes off his glasses. "I just don't see it."

"I know what you mean. But he fits the profile, he was in all the states and he's a left-hander."

"I noticed that. The evidence is overwhelming."

"What are you going to do?"

A moment of silence. "One way or another, Marco's got to come off this case."

I nod.

A few seconds later O'Donnell stands up. "Thanks Anderson. I'll take care of this." And I was dismissed.

I wonder what Josh's response was. First I accuse him and then the Bureau?

A faint whiff of something burning brings my focus back to the kitchen. I stir the pasta sauce on the stove, taste it and add some more cracked pepper. This will b

ιe first decent meal I've had since the diner in Arizona.
Darren wasn't here, I would have gone without again.

My security phone buzzes. I pick it up but don't
other talking. I know it's Darren, he called me fifteen
ιinutes ago on his way back to my apartment to see if I
referred red or white wine. I buzz him in and unlock
ιy apartment door.

"I got Merlot. Hope that's okay," Darren says as he
alks in.

"Sounds good." I love Merlot. Sam loved Merlot.

"Did you check the dates for Josh?"

"I didn't have to. He's on one of our goddamn lists. I
onfronted him earlier this evening and he's either a
ɔod actor, or innocent," I say. "I told O'Donnell too."

"What did he say?"

"He was already investigating Josh, anyway. After I told
ιm about Sally-Anne, he decided to pull Josh off the case."

"So he's definitely off?"

"I presume so. O'Donnell was going to deal with it
ɔnight." I put my head down, ashamed. Even though part
ɛ me does suspect Josh, I feel as though I've betrayed him,
ɛtrayed my lover and betrayed a work colleague. I also
ιte to think of the repercussions if I'm wrong. It's bad
ιough that O'Donnell has been investigating everyone.

Darren puts the bottle down and stands real close. He
rokes my hair. I start to cry and he pulls me closer to
m. I pull away—if anyone holds me now I'll never stop
ying. I need to keep myself together. The tears are
placed by anger. I want to kill the pervert. For Sam.

I stand over the stove and stir the pasta again. "I
ɔuld do with a drink."

"Good idea." Darren opens the wine.

Five minutes later we're sitting down.

"Do you really think it's Josh?" I say.

"I don't know." Darren pauses. "Sophie, let's not talk about the case. For the next twenty or thirty minutes, let's just enjoy the food, wine and company."

I hesitate. Will I be able to not think about it?

"It'll do you good. You need some time off," Darren says. "Deal?"

"Okay." I'll try at least. Maybe I do need some time off. Sam's no longer waiting for me to save her.

"So you're from Melbourne, right?"

I finish a small mouthful of pasta. The food feels strange in my mouth and I'm already full and nauseous after only a few bites.

"Yeah. I grew up in Shepparton, rural Victoria, then we moved into the city when I was ten." We'd moved soon after John's body was found. The old house in Shepparton held too many memories, too many reminders. "What about you? Born and bred in Tucson?" I ask, trying to force myself to have a normal conversation and not think about the case, Josh or my brother.

"Yep. My folks were both from Phoenix but moved to Tucson just before I was born."

"Why'd they move?"

"Dad's company wanted him to open up the Tucson office."

I nod. "They still live in Tucson?"

"Yeah, I see them most weeks."

I force a smile, thinking of my parents and home.

"You miss Australia."

"Yeah, I do."

"Friends? Family?" He pauses. "Someone special?"

"Yeah, I miss my friends and my mom and dad."

He looks at me. I have avoided the last part of his question, but he seems determined.

"There was someone, but we broke up. You?"

"Nah. You know what it's like, married to the job as they say."

"Yeah." I push the spaghetti from side to side.

"You're not eating any more?"

"I don't feel like it," I say.

"Hey, remember our deal."

I force a smile. "Nothing about the case until we've finished our meal."

Darren nods and takes a sip of wine.

"It just seems wrong...sitting here, eating and drinking while he's out there."

He gives up too. "You're right. You're right." He pushes his food away. "I'm not hungry either." He stands up and clears the plates.

"I'm sorry, Darren."

"No, don't be. Like I said, you're right. Who knows, maybe we'll find something."

He comes back and we empty the files onto my dining-room table, grouping them in piles by state. I also take out a map of D.C. and lay it out on one end of the table. I mark the abduction and dump sites and stick passport-size photos of Jean, Teresa and Susan around the edge of the map. I can't bring myself to put Sam's photo on there too. Not yet.

"Any pattern?" Darren peers over my shoulder.

"Not that I can see."

He moves closer and studies the map, drawing lines between all four abduction sites and then between all four dump sites. "If there is a pattern we might need more victims before we can see it."

He's right. You never hope for another victim, but sometimes it's the only thing that gets the perp.

Darren backs away from the table. "Have you tried inducing a premonition?"

"No. And I haven't had any since Sam was found." I hadn't bothered even trying since Sam was found. What was the point?

"Why don't you give it a shot."

"Okay." I sit in the armchair.

"Comfortable?"

"Yes."

"Remember, it's like meditation."

I close my eyes and slow down my breathing. I concentrate on each inhalation and exhalation, blocking out everything else. But my mind keeps wandering to Josh. Could he really be the killer? I'm about to give up when suddenly I see a woman running through the woods. She's terrified, looking behind her as she runs. I try to focus on her face and make out her features.

The vision vanishes. I open my eyes and gasp for air. Darren kneels down in front of me. "What did you see?"

"A woman. She was being chased in the woods."

"The killer's next victim?"

I wrinkle my forehead in response to the onset of a headache. "Perhaps." But the message on the mirror indicated I was next.

"Teresa was found in the woods, wasn't she?"

"Cedarville Forest. It wasn't Teresa though."

"Did you see anything else? What did she look like?"

"All I could see was the woman." I shudder, remembering the fear on her face. "She had short blond hair, with a slight wave in it. She looked petite, but it could have just been the size of the trees around her."

"Go on."

I shrug. "That's it." I rub my forehead with my index finger and thumb.

"You're tired. It makes a difference."

"Really?"

"My aunt was a pro, but if she was tired or sick her visions were always unreliable and sometimes nonexistent." He stands up. "Come on, let's stick to the standard detective work."

I follow him over to the table and take him through the D.C. murders again, hoping he'll see something that we haven't been able to—fresh eyes. But we draw a blank. We go back to Michigan, the perp's busiest years in terms of murders. Six murders in Michigan, five college girls and the shoe-store employee. We push the other files aside and spread the Michigan photos out on my table. We use vertical lines to separate each murder but have to overlap the photos to fit everything.

I finger the first column of photos. "First-year college student." Her body was found in a dumpster on campus. She'd been cut, like the rest, but also took a beating around the head and face. I trace my finger along the bruises. "She must have said something that got him angry. Too angry to use the knife on her." It was out of character for our guy.

"But what?" Darren says.

"Some sort of derogatory comment would be my guess. Probably of a sexual nature. Or maybe she recognized him and she got a beating for her smarts."

Darren flips through the coroner's report. "She died of this cut here." He points to a vertical cut on her throat. "And from the blood in the Dumpster, she was still alive when she was dumped."

"Yeah, I saw that. Weird. He usually likes to finish it with his victims. I think he was ashamed that he beat her and wanted to get her out of his sight as soon as possible."

"But he doesn't mind slicing and dicing."

"He sees the knife as controlled, refined. But beating with his bare hands when he was now a college man, educated…it was beneath him. It would be enough to throw him."

Darren shakes his head. "Nut job."

I look at the line of photos. "They found a carpet fiber on her body but could never match it. It's about the only time he left evidence too."

I move my gaze to the next column. Michigan victim two. Another freshman.

"She's pretty," Darren says.

"Yeah. She was. Also found on campus. He liked being close by when the discoveries were made. It enhanced the thrill."

"So do you think he lived on campus?"

"On campus, or nearby." I grab the coroner's report and read through it again.

Darren skips forward to Michigan victim number three and reads the coroner's report.

I flip over the last page of the report for victim number two, and then put it down.

"Anything?" Darren asks.

"Not really. Same old story."

"Me too."

I stand up and lean on the back of my chair. "The guy's a ghost." I put my head down.

Darren stands up and hovers behind me. His hands touch the back of my shoulders and he starts massaging my shoulders and neck. It feels good. The combination of stress and hunching over desks and tables is taking its toll.

"Good?"

"Yep."

"You're very tense."

"I wonder why."

He laughs. And for a second even I laugh. His thumbs move rhythmically on either side of my vertebrae. He's a good masseur. I lean back into him slightly. His lips brush my neck. I could easily succumb to this. Maybe it would take my mind off things, but it doesn't feel right. Not with everything that's happened with Sam, and not when my feelings for Josh are so confused.

I step forward. "Victim number four. Michigan."

Darren's hands release their grip. He hovers behind me and I sense his indecision. He wants to keep touching me, but after a few seconds he sits back down at the table.

"Victim number four," he says somewhat reluctantly.

We finally give up at about 4:00 a.m. We wearily set up the sofa bed and then Darren lies on top of the sheets and stretches out—it's way too small for him.

"Sorry," I say.

"It'll be fine."

We say our good-nights and I wander down to my bedroom. I take Jones's lock-picking information with me in case I can't sleep. I walk past the linen press and pause.... Shall I check the apartment? Darren's here. The agents are out front. The perp can't be here. I keep walking and give my teeth a quick brush. I avoid looking at my face, knowing it's the worse for wear.

Lying in bed, I lift the pages up high, in front of my face, but my eyes are too weary to stay open. I put the information on my bedside table and turn on my side. I need sleep.

Two hours later I wake up, bolt upright. I rack my brain, hoping I've had a meaningful dream. But I can't remember anything. I get up, move into the living room and shake Darren awake. Then I jump straight in the shower. Today will be the day. Today we'll nail the bastard. I stay positive.

Once out of the shower I dress quickly and throw a groggy Darren a towel. "Shower's yours." He catches the towel, smiles and walks into the bathroom. He looks pretty good in his boxers and T-shirt, his ruffled hair falling into his blue eyes.

"What do you normally eat for breakfast?" I call.

"Anything. Cereal, toast, whatever."

I hear the shower start.

"What's on the agenda today?" he yells.

I can hear him easily, but he won't hear me over the shower, so I go over to the bathroom door.

"I'm hoping to hear back from Michigan about locksmiths this morning and I've got to chase down the online lock-picking resellers," I say. "And then I'll help the others with their lists."

"Count me in."

"Thanks, Darren." It's great to have someone here. Someone I can trust. Particularly with what's going on with Josh.

"No problem."

The shower stops. That was quick. I go back to the kitchen and fill two bowls with cereal. I haven't made my usual fruit salad in days.

Darren emerges with a towel wrapped around his waist. I avert my eyes and pour milk over my cereal. Darren rummages through his sports bag and picks out some fresh clothes. He moves back into the bathroom. A couple of minutes later he returns to the living room, wearing blue jeans and a long-sleeve red turtleneck. He sits down at the table and pours milk over his cereal.

"Today's the day," I say in between mouthfuls.

"Today," Darren agrees.

The phone rings. I get up and reach for the portable. "Hello."

"Sophie. It's Josh. I've got a good lead. Do you want to question him with me?" His voice is cold, a monotone.

"Um…I thought…" I leave the sentence hanging.

"You thought I was off the case."

I pause, guilty. "Yes."

"I am, Sophie. In fact, I'm officially suspended. But I'll be damned if I'm going to let the real killer get away with it. Especially when you might be in danger."

"But—"

"I'm not a murderer, Sophie. You must know that."

I don't respond. I still don't know what to think and who to believe.

"I'm going to 25 Greene Street, Edgewood. Bring Carter if you don't want to be alone with me." He hangs up.

"Who was it?" Carter takes the last few mouthfuls of his cereal.

"Josh."

"What did he want?"

"He's on his way to question someone now."

"I thought he was off the case."

I shrug. "He is. But he says he's innocent and that he's going to catch the real murderer."

Darren seems unconvinced.

I cross my arms. "If it's true, we can't let him interview someone by himself. He won't even have his gun—O'Donnell would have taken it." I pause. "I should go."

"It could be a trap," Darren says. "I'll come with you."

"Okay," I say, not looking forward to Josh's reaction when the two of us show up together.

Thirty minutes later we pull into Greene Street. Josh is leaning on his car. He is wearing a long overcoat and leather gloves. It's a cold morning.

I get out of the car and avoid his gaze. I'm ashamed I've brought Darren with me. Ashamed I don't trust Josh. And now I only want to escape. I don't want to be in a room with either of them, questioning a suspect and pretending everything's fine. That none of this affects me.

My protection pulls up behind us but they stay in their car. Montana and Sargent are back on shift.

"This is insane," Josh says, eyeballing Darren.

"Keeping Sophie safe is what's important."

"She's a hell of a lot safer with me."

"We don't know that, do we?"

"Guys, I'm standing right here." But nothing I say is going to make a difference. Not now. There's too much testosterone pumping.

"You've only known her for a few days. How can she be safer with you?"

"Listen, buddy, I'm not the one in all states at the times of the murders."

"How do we even know that? We know nothing about you. What you've done over the past eleven years."

"Stop it! Both of you stop it!"

Josh turns to me. "You don't know anything about this guy."

I look away, then back to Josh. "O'Donnell's checked him out. He's clean."

Josh is quiet, as is Darren.

Finally Josh speaks. "Let's go." He starts walking then turns back. "The real murderer could be standing on the other side of that door." Josh points toward number twenty-five.

"Or I could be looking at him now."

Is Darren crazy? He's pushing Josh to the limit.

Josh stops and stiffens. For a moment I think he's going to take a swing at Darren.

"I'm out of here." I walk away.

Darren grabs my arm. "Wait, Sophie. You shouldn't be alone."

Josh looks at me, defeated. He wants to be the one

holding my arm, telling me I shouldn't be alone. He turns away and starts for the door.

I pull my arm away from Darren. "I'll be fine. I've got Laurel and Hardy, remember?" I motion toward the Bureau car. "I'll meet you back at the D.C. Field Office. I've got to go to my place anyway. I left the lock-picking information on my bedside table."

"I'll come with you."

"It's fine. I've got these guys watching me, and Josh needs backup," I say. "Go."

"But…"

"No buts. Josh just rang the doorbell. He's going in now." I run back toward the car.

Darren stands near the fence of number twenty-five, still unsure. Then the front door opens and Darren moves toward the house. He's a cop. I knew he wouldn't let Josh interrogate a potentially dangerous suspect by himself. There are still too many unanswered questions.

CHAPTER 21

I pull up outside my building, with Montana and Sargent behind me.

Sargent leans his head out the window. "Want one of us to come up?"

"Nah. I won't be long."

"I'll come up," he says, unbuckling his seat belt.

"I've just got to grab a few papers. I'll be five minutes, tops."

Sargent settles back in, then thinks better of it.

"Not by yourself."

I can't help but resent my babysitters. I haven't had time alone in days.

He shrugs. "I need the exercise." He gets out of his car and pats his sizable stomach. How does he pass his yearly physical?

I manage a laugh.

I walk into the building foyer and start up the stairs, slowly. Sargent follows close behind. I know I should strike up a polite conversation, but I don't have the energy. Physical and emotional exhaustion are catching up with me. Even the three flights of stairs wear me out, as does the thought of having to see Darren or Josh; or worse, both of them at the same time. It's gotten so complicated. I don't know what I feel for either of them, and I still can't put my mind at rest about Josh. It all seems too coincidental.

I walk into the apartment and leave the door open for Sargent.

I get distracted on my way to the bedroom and lean over the dining-room table, taking another look at the map. It still bothers me.

Sargent stands at the door, but I notice he's unclipped his gun holster. He's ready for action, if need be.

I shift each photo to where the victim was found. Still nothing. I reluctantly add Sam's photo. I maneuver photos around, checking out different angles. And that's when I notice it. I rummage through the main D.C. photos on the other end of the table, and consult the relevant crime-scene reports to determine the positioning of the bodies in relation to the locations. I replicate the way the victims' heads were facing on the map, using the passport-size photos. They're all facing toward the same direction, as though they're looking at something. This can't be a coincidence. I trace the eye lines to find the point of intersection. Maybe this is his special place. He wants the victims, his ex-girlfriends, to keep watching him. I need to check it out.

I grab the map. "Come on. We've got a lead to track down."

I jump in the car with Montana and Sargent, sitting in the back with the map. As far as I can tell, the women are all looking at one particular area. I navigate, taking us into D.C. and through the busy streets.

I lean over and show Sargent the map. "Tell me about this area," I say, pointing to the map.

"Not much there. It's a poor area. Lots of housing projects, a couple of abandoned warehouses and St. Anne's Hospital."

"A hospital?" I remember my impression that the women were tied to gurneys.

Sargent continues. "It's abandoned now."

It would be a perfect hiding spot. "Let's go there."

In terms of evidence the killer's been careful at the abduction and dump sites, but would he have been that careful in his lair? In his private place? The hospital may contain evidence, evidence that will also eliminate or confirm Josh as a suspect. And now is the best time to look; with Sam recently killed and the perp targeting me, the building will be empty.

We arrive at the front of the redbrick building about twenty minutes later. The whole area is surrounded by a six-foot fence, with Do Not Enter signs hanging on the fence every few feet. The three of us climb over. I drop to the ground, bending my knees to soften the impact.

"What are we looking for?" Sargent asks.

"Evidence. This may be where the D.C. Slasher took his victims. I'm hoping he left something behind for us."

I draw my gun, as do Montana and Sargent. The hospital

is five stories high. Most of the windows are broken and there's no roof. The building is covered in graffiti.

"How long has this place been closed?" I ask.

"Years. It was supposed to be fixed up. Then they were going to tear it down and build a new hospital, but it never happened," Montana explains.

I move to the nearest window and knock out the remaining glass with my gun. I climb up onto the window-sill and drop down into the room. Glass crunches underneath my shoes as I land. Sargent and Montana are hot on my heels. Once we're all through, we move into the nearest corridor.

"Let's split up," I say.

Sargent shakes his head. "One of us needs to stick with you."

Montana motions toward the end of the corridor, where it ends with a T-intersection. "I'll take the left, you guys take the right."

We make our way to the end, checking the five rooms off the main corridor, and then we split up.

Sargent and I move through the old emergency department. The hospital looks like a war zone, with broken glass, chipping paint, graffiti and even some of the old fittings still here, broken and strewn across the floor. But no evidence of murder. Soon we reach what looks like the children's ward. An old, faded painting of a clown is pinned to a board.

"Did you hear that?"

Sargent stops and listens.

The unmistakable sound of voices, but they're too far away to make out. Then silence.

"Must be Montana," Sargent says. "Maybe he's found something." Sargent flips his cell phone open and punches in a number. We can hear the phone ringing down the corridor we came from. But Montana doesn't answer his phone.

"Shit!" Sargent and I start running back the way we came. Within a few minutes we're standing over the still figure of Agent Montana. Blood is spreading underneath him. I bend down to check his pulse. It's there, but weak.

"He's alive," I say. "We need backup. There's more than evidence here."

Sargent nods and flips his cell phone open again. But as he's about to dial, I hear a slight thud. I know that sound. It's a gun with a silencer. Sargent's eyes widen. As I stand up, he folds. He must have been shot in the back.

I look up but can't see the shooter. I dive for cover, launching myself across the corridor toward the nearest room. But I'm too slow. I hear the thud again and then a sharp piercing pain in my side. I look down at my rib cage, confused, then black out.

I wake up, disorientated and groggy. I remember being shot, then realizing it was a tranquilizer. I was hit by a tranquilizer. I open my eyes, hoping to find nurses around me, but instead I'm tied to something. Tied to his gurney. I'm naked.

Panic engulfs me. My biggest fear realized. I think about all the bodies I've seen, all the women who've been in this situation.

I tug on my ropes. They're tight, very tight. I can't move my limbs more than half an inch in any direction.

It's cold and only a small bar heater takes the chill off the room. I take another look around. The room's still a little hazy, but gradually things start to take shape. It's dark, but I can make out shapes and some colors around me. The floors are covered in white tiles that spread halfway up the wall, like a bathroom or kitchen. But some of the tiles are broken. One corner of the room is filled with building materials. A piece of plywood with nails sticking out, a broken chair and electrical wires, coiled. I'm still at St. Anne's. The gurney is ice cold and I look down at it—stainless steel. Next to my head is a tray of surgical instruments. That fucking bastard.

There are no windows and only one door. Part of the door is covered in hessian; there must have been glass there at some stage.

The swinging door opens and a man in a balaclava comes in.

"Hello, darling. You're awake."

"Josh?"

A hollow laugh rings out. "You think Josh is man enough for this? He's pathetic." He hangs his head close to mine and smiles through his balaclava. "Oh, and by the way, he won't be mounting any rescue mission, if that's what you're thinking. I've made sure of that."

"What have you done to him?"

He shakes his head. "Poor Josh. No girl, no badge, no gun. But it gets worse."

Josh's ID would have been taken away with his gun when he was suspended. "What have you done to him?" I repeat.

The balaclava moves with the killer's grin. "It's terrible

when an FBI agent goes bad, isn't it?" He shakes his head. "First it was Sally-Anne in Arizona, then those other poor women. Michigan, Chicago, D.C. and even his coworker. Sorry, two coworkers."

"You bastard." I struggle against my restraints. "The Bureau will realize you're framing Josh."

"You think? Even after they find your body and Josh's DNA at the scene of the crime."

"Josh will find out who you are!"

"How? He's cut off from the FBI, a disgraced agent. No one wants to help him. They just need someone to pin Sam's death on."

"You fucking bastard. You've been framing him all this time."

He laughs. "He had everything. I had nothing."

I start to cry.

He looks at me and what I can see of his face changes. He smiles a more genuine, sympathetic smile. He reaches out and strokes my hair.

"There, there, darling. It's just the two of us now. I've got the one thing Josh wants the most. You. I've never seen him look at a woman the way he looks at you."

"Who are you? Who are you, you freak!"

He pulls his head back and stands upright. "Temper, temper." His eyes follow the length of my body, from my toes to my head.

His eyes are cold, dead.

He stares at my stomach. "I loved it when Detective Carter came to D.C. Josh was so jealous. It was about time he suffered." He puts a hand on either side of my waist and leans over me. "What a loser."

He stands back up again, moves to the end of the gurney and places his hand on my foot. I cringe at his touch and move my foot.

"Never, never do that again!" he screams. "You like it when I touch you!"

He puts his hand back on my foot and I play along, resisting the urge to shrink from his repulsive touch. There's no point anyway. I can't get away. Not yet. His fingers move up and he runs them along my leg up to my hip. I close my eyes and pretend I'm somewhere else. He does a small circle on my hip before continuing his journey. His hand passes over my waist and finally comes to rest on my head.

"I thought you were different, special. You must be if Josh wants you so bad." His stroke becomes harder and he pulls his fingers through my hair. I wince in pain and my eyes water.

He's oblivious. "But you're no different from the rest." He pulls my hair harder and then reaches for the tray of instruments.

"You're a slut!" He pauses, casting his eyes over the choice of knives. "Josh *and* Carter?"

I brace myself.

The cold point of a knife touches the top of my inner thigh. Then he pushes and the coldness turns into burning pain. I scream. The knife keeps digging into my flesh and I feel blood trickle down my leg. He withdraws the blade.

I think fast. "I don't clot. I've got a blood disorder."

"Really? We'll see about that." He returns the knife to one end of the cut and pushes down, lengthening the incision.

I scream. The pain is almost unbearable. I concentrate on not passing out. The knife is sexual for him—penetration—and I'd rather the knife than any part of him.

I watch his hand…his hand. "You're not left-handed," I say.

"Very good. Aren't you a clever girl." He pulls the two sides of the wound apart and I scream in pain once again. Now blood surges down the side of my leg. Everything goes a little hazy. I'm about to pass out.

"Your blood looks normal to me, Sophie. Nice try, though." He puts the bloody knife back on the tray. He stands silently, looking at the wall for a few seconds, then he turns back to me. "Don't ever lie to me again!"

What am I going to do? Think. Think.

He tears off a piece of paper towel and picks up the knife. He slowly wipes the knife clean, all the while focusing on the blade. "It doesn't have to be like this. I want to be kind to you, even though you don't deserve it." He throws the paper towel into the bin and places the knife back on the tray. He positions it so it's exactly centered. "Carter was a mistake is all."

The faint feeling eases. "Nothing happened with Carter, I swear." I hope to diffuse his anger.

"Really?" He leans in to my face again.

"I promise. Absolutely nothing." I fight the pain.

He moves over to the cabinet and grabs a bandage. He applies the tourniquet. Good, it'll stop the bleeding.

"Nothing happened with Carter," I repeat.

He grunts and leaves the room.

There's got to be a way out. There has to be. I'm not going to die. Not at the hands of this son of a bitch. I move my restraints, testing the give again. There's not much. Not enough to slip my hands through. Next I try my legs again. I can still only move my legs and arms about half an inch in any direction. Okay, what about the task force? This guy must be on our list. They'll question him soon enough. And maybe someone else will work out the significance of the body positioning and where all the victims are looking toward. Surely Darren will notice the map's missing from the dining-room table.

I start to cry. "No," I whisper, defeat taking over. Sam's dead. And I'm next. I bite my lip. I can't cry. He kills them when they break. I push the tears away. I don't know what to do. There must be a way out. I can't accept that this is how I'm going to die. I can't. The tears start again, but I fight them back. I think about my parents. I want to be at home, sitting in front of the fire with Mom and Dad. I don't want to die.

I steady my breath. I need to focus. My restraints…I need to keep working on the rope. I start with my hands. I need my hands free. I wriggle and twist my wrists around. I pull against the rope. I keep this up for about ten minutes and then stop. The rope burns have become almost unbearable. I need to rest. I need to get my strength back and think of a way out. But my escape plans will have to wait…the grogginess finally takes over and I pass out.

I wake up with a start, disorientated. Then I realize where I am. I've got no idea how much time has passed. An hour? A day? The door creaks open.

"Oh, thank God." I lift my head up. "You found me." I knew the Bureau would be on to this guy and find me. It was just a matter of how long it would take them. Thank God they found me in time.

Marty reaches over me, going for my arm ropes. But his reach falls short and his hand rests on my face.

"I never lost you."

It can't be.

"No. No," I say. Not Marty. I close my eyes, not wanting to look at his face. I'm still in the killer's hands.

But it all makes sense. The perfect crime scenes, the knowledge of the cases. His relationship with Josh. And if he ever left DNA or other trace evidence at a crime scene, he'd be able to get rid of it after the fact, during the investigation. I think about Sam's profile. The age and race are right, the occupation, marital status, his current living situation, education level…I mentally cross the items off, one by one.

"You're surprised."

"Yes. Yes, I am." I hide my anger, only letting him see my shock.

"Surprised at how clever I am."

"No. I always knew you were clever." I play to his ego.

He smiles. "I sent them all off in the wrong direction."

"But you're not left-handed," I say, still trying to put the pieces together.

"No." He grins. "I'm ambidextrous. The original report said that the killer was probably ambidextrous. But I made a few amendments when I collated the information. The evidence had to point to Josh."

I think back to the report Marty left in my tray. At the time I thought how kind it was of him to collate the reports and hand them directly to me.

And his handwriting was on the Post-it note. I didn't even think to look at that. To really look at it. If I had, perhaps I would have noticed that the handwriting was similar to the note left for Sam.

He strokes my hair, tender. "Enough. We could admire my handiwork for hours. But I want to know how your day was."

He must be joking. But I play along. My options are limited.

"I missed you." I try to sound sincere. I hide the hate.

I hope these are the words he wants to hear. Is he aware that I'm going along with his role-play, or does he actually think this is a normal relationship?

He comes toward me and kisses me passionately. I respond, trying not to show my revulsion. He rests his right hand on my breast.

"None of that. Later," I say, like I'd sometimes say to Matt when he was in the mood and I wasn't.

"Why?"

"Because I want our first time to be special, Marty."

He nods. "I've loved you from the first moment I saw you."

But of course it's not true. He "loves" me because I'm something of Josh's that he can possess.

"The other women meant nothing to me. Nothing to Josh either." He strokes my hair.

I hide a wince, thinking of Sam and the others. Nothing. They died for nothing? "Josh knew them all?" I ask.

"Not all. But they were all his type. Our type. Apart from Sam, he only knew Sally-Anne."

I can't hide my surprise. Josh was actually seeing Sally-

Anne? Romantically? If he was involved with an underage girl his father definitely would have wanted to keep that quiet.

"Ah...no. Of course, he didn't tell you, did he?"

"No."

"I was hoping Josh would incriminate himself by keeping quiet. So egotistical that he didn't think anyone could possibly believe he was the killer. His DNA will seal the deal."

I ignore him. I've still got questions. "So how did you lure Sally-Anne?"

He breathes deeply, excited. "I phoned her and pretended to be Josh. I organized a little meeting. But she wanted Josh, not me."

"So you punished her?"

"I had to. The little slut was giving it out to everyone else, why not me? I was certainly more worthy than Josh."

"So you knew Josh?"

"Yes. But that was when I was Matthew Lande. Josh thought I was nothing. A nobody. Josh was just like my brothers."

"Older?"

He smiles. "Yes. Sam's profile was right. That's what you want to know, isn't it? That's why you're asking all the questions."

I don't respond.

"Josh." He spits the name, then chuckles. "He didn't even recognize me in Michigan. And not even when we worked together in D.C. See how stupid he is?"

I have to play along. "Yes. I'm glad I'm with you and not Josh." I'm not sure if the lie is convincing.

He rests his head on my breast and I move my chin down in an intimate gesture. I move my right hand.

He jerks his head up. "What are you doing?"

"I only wanted to touch you."

He looks at me suspiciously then gently undoes my right hand. My heart beats faster and I hope he can't hear it. I think about escape, but I can't do anything. Not with only one arm free. No, this is a trust game and, like it or not, I'm in for the long haul. I run my hand along his arm and gently pull him back down to my chest. I play with his hair and caress his neck as though he really is my lover.

But soon my touches excite him sexually.

"Don't spoil it," I say.

He moves away. "You're right. We've waited this long, we should wait until we know each other better."

"Yes, let's make it special." I hold his hand.

"I'll make us some dinner." He disappears out the door.

My hand's free. My hand's free!

But the door opens again and he ties my hand back up. I don't show my disappointment. If I can get that hand free again, I should be able to undo my ropes. I wonder if any of the other girls managed to get their hand untied. Maybe they did but still couldn't get out, or maybe he'll never untie me again. I push these thoughts away; I must try to stay positive.

My leg still throbs, but I can feel the tightness of a scab. The wound is healing. I lift my head up and stare at the door. I imagine myself walking out.

He returns later. I don't know how much later, because all sense of time seems to be gone. He carries two bowls of pasta and two candles. He lights the candles and puts them both on the instrument tray next to my head. I pretend not to notice the ghastly assortment of knives. He undoes my hand again and pulls it up to his face. He uses my hand to caress his face.

I smile. "How about some wine?"

"Of course. Wine." He leaves the room. Can I be this lucky? I look at the instruments. They're lined up precisely and I stare at one of the sharp implements, trying to decide whether to grab it or not. He'll notice if one is missing. I hear footsteps outside the door and lie back down quickly.

The door opens. "I got us a Merlot," he says.

The glasses clink together as he puts them down. He opens the wine and the liquid gurgles into the glass. I reach my hand out to take the glass.

"No," he says. "I'm going to feed you."

I lay my hand by my side and open my mouth.

"That's a girl," he says and a spoonful of pasta slides into my mouth. I chew.

"Good?" he asks.

I finish my mouthful. "Delicious."

"Better than Josh's beef bourguignon?"

"Definitely." But it's a lie.

"I knew you'd love me more than Josh. I just knew it."

I don't respond. I chew the next mouthful. His hand slides under my hair and he raises my head enough for me to take a sip of wine. The cool glass touches my lips and I gulp greedily, wanting alcohol to numb myself.

"Take it easy," he says.

"It's a beautiful wine."

He lowers my head back to the table and sips some wine. He takes several mouthfuls of food himself.

"Open wide," he says. The fork is on my lips. I open my mouth and eat. But I don't want any more. I feel sick. Sick to my stomach that he is feeding me. That I'm going along with it. I start my internal dialogue: It's all right. You're doing the right thing. This will get you out. Somehow.

"It's very filling," I say.

"You need the nourishment."

What for? To lie here and be raped? I push the tears away.

He presses the fork on my closed lips. I take another mouthful. "Thank you," I force myself to say.

He feeds himself.

"Can I have some more wine?" I ask. Again, when the glass touches my lips I take several large gulps. "Beautiful." I take another few mouthfuls of food, until I've had as much as I physically can. "I'm full."

"But you've only eaten half of it."

"You know me and my appetite." I hope the familiarity will stop him from pushing the matter.

"Yes. Yes, you eat like a little sparrow."

I watch as he finishes his meal and his glass of wine. What will he do to me when he finishes?

He takes my hand and ties it up again. I get ready to go somewhere else mentally. To be someone else. It's the only way I'll be able to cope. But instead of climbing on top of me, he leaves.

I did it. I stopped him from raping me. For now.

CHAPTER 22

Once more I awaken to the door opening. Marty's in a hurry…that means he's going to work, so it must be morning. Something's in his hand, but I can't see what. I hear a clatter of metal and see what he's got. I feel the coldness of the bedpan against my hip. It disgusts me, but I lift my hips off the metal gurney. He slides the bedpan in underneath me.

I empty my bladder slowly so it dribbles into the bedpan. "I'm finished."

He dabs me with toilet paper and pulls the bedpan from underneath. He leaves the room but is back within a few seconds. He pulls my head up.

"Orange juice," he says.

I take a few gulps but it goes down the wrong way and I cough.

"What's wrong?"

"It just went down the wrong way," I say between splutters.

He feeds me toast with jam, but I've barely finished each mouthful before he's cramming the piece of toast into my mouth again.

"Too fast," I say.

"I'm late. They're waiting on a fingerprint analysis of your apartment." He smirks.

God, they all still think he's one of the good guys.

"Josh is particularly anxious for those results. I'm his one and only link to the Bureau now. Poor thing."

"How is he?" I try not to show how much I care about Josh—that could set Marty off.

"He's pathetic. He's nothing without the FBI trimmings. A powerless, weak man. He sits in the living room with photos from the cases spread out around him. Somehow he managed to keep the files. He begs me to help him, to help clear his name." He laughs. "But like I said, the best is yet to come."

I turn my head away from the food. "I've had enough."

He pushes the toast against my lips. "One more," he says, as though I'm a child.

I take another bite.

He leaves the room and I heave a sigh of relief. He's gone. But he returns.

He touches my stomach lightly. I stiffen.

His hand lazily runs across my body. There's no hint that he's in a hurry now. He runs his fingers over the bandaged cut. It still throbs. He moves to my groin and twirls my pubic hair. I don't make a sound.

He brings his face up to mine. I look into his eyes and

hide my revulsion. His breath is on my face and he kisses me. I don't fight, but I don't respond fully either. I don't know how to play it. Can I stop him again from raping me? Maybe it's better to get it over with.

He pulls his lips and hand away.

"Shit, I'm late." And then he's gone.

I wait five minutes and then let myself cry. I cry and scream, even though I know no one can hear me. God knows what he's done with Montana and Sargent.

I've got to get out of here. If I can just get off this gurney.

Okay. Think, Sophie. Think. I shiver with the cold. The room is cold and the metal gurney feels like ice against my back. I wiggle my toes and hands. I need my strength and I don't want my foot or leg to go to sleep.

I think about what I know about him. What I can use. I form a list in my head.

He's meticulous, a health and neat freak.

He's smart.

He's been jealous of Josh for years and feels he's in competition with him.

He thinks he's in love with me.

He thinks I can love him.

He wants to make it special with me.

He's clearly delusional.

He's strong.

I lie on the table and go through these points in my head over and over. I need to push his buttons and escape. What if I went to the toilet, right on the gurney? That would be too messy for him. Surely he'd have to move me. But that could make him angry too. It might make him hurt me or tie my ropes tighter. Or it might mean I never get my arm free again. No, there's another way, and I have to figure it out by tonight.

I know his routine. He'll make us dinner again and untie my arm. How can I get him to untie both my arms? I need them both, and preferably a leg too. My legs are stronger than my arms. I wonder if I'm going to have to let him rape me to get my leg free. Could I cope with rape if I knew it might save my life?

I'm not sure how much time has passed when the door opens. I give both my hands and feet another wiggle to make sure they're not asleep. My heart beats faster. It's time.

Marty runs his hands along the soles of my feet and up my legs as he walks toward my head. He checks my ropes carefully.

"How was your day?" I ask, hoping to distract him from my bindings.

"Busy. Very busy." He runs his hand around my breast.

I've got nowhere to go. I can't even shrink any farther into the gurney.

"How is the task force taking my disappearance?"

He smiles. "Rivers is pissed. Josh is the prime suspect. Everything's pretty much perfect." He runs his hand through my hair. "I can't wait to see Josh's face when he's accused of murder. Of killing so many women." He pauses. "Are you hungry?"

"Yes." My voice is soft. I just want him to stop touching me.

He leaves the room.

I pull on the ropes—maybe they loosened a little when he was checking them. No, they're still tight. I wiggle my fingers, toes and move my arms and legs as much as I can. I have to be ready. The pit of my stomach feels strange—the adrenaline is kicking in and I'm thankful for the extra energy. I go through my plan, making sure I've thought of everything.

He comes back and I can smell the food. The smell both sickens me and hungers me.

"Tonight's the night," he says.

I pause. It better go my way, not his. "Yes, it is."

He unties one of my arms and I reach up toward his face and run my hand along his jaw. He kisses my hand. Then he moves back to the bench and starts dishing out dinner.

"What is it?" I ask.

"Prawn in black-bean sauce, darling." He comes back with a bowl and fork. "Open up."

I open my lips and take a mouthful.

"I forgot the wine," he says. He opens a bottle and pours two glasses. He lifts my head and I prop myself up with my free arm. I take a tiny sip.

"It's good. Have you tried it?" I want him to drink as much as possible. If I can get him a little bit tipsy, his reflexes down, it may just push the scales in my favor. I think about Susan Young. Her toxicology came back with 0.01 blood alcohol—he shared wine with her too. I shudder.

I take another mouthful of prawn and force it down. Under normal circumstances I would say it was great Chinese food. But not now.

He gives me more wine. I take the tiniest sip possible. "Have some yourself too," I say.

He gulps the wine.

Soon. It will be time soon.

The fork moves toward me and I open up.

"Mmm," I say, but I fight the urge to be sick.

"It's perfect, isn't it," he says.

He feeds himself.

The next mouthful. This is it. I close my eyes.

The fork pushes on my lips. I take the prawn and chew. Then I swallow. I cough, one short, silenced cough. Then I pant, as though no air can get to my lungs. I thrash about a bit and bring my free hand up to my throat.

"Sophie!" He hits my diaphragm hard. "Sophie!"

The punch winds me slightly but I pretend I still can't breathe. He comes behind me and tries the Heimlich maneuver. But he doesn't have the angle with me lying down.

"Shit!" he screams.

He unties my other arm and sits me forward on the table. Again, he tries the maneuver and this time my bottom left rib cracks. The sound resonates throughout my body. I cry out in pain, but silence it quickly. I wouldn't be able to make that sound if I were really choking. I pull on his arms, like a desperate plea, then collapse back onto the gurney. I hear him move around to the foot of the trolley.

Yes, yes, please. If he doesn't untie my legs I'll try to overcome him, but I don't like my chances. He unties one leg, then the next, and then he gathers me up in a bear hug from behind and tries the maneuver again, this time tipping me off the gurney and into a vertical position first. The pain on my rib is excruciating and I can't stop myself from crying out this time. I spit a piece of food that I'd kept under my tongue across the room and I hear him breathe a sigh of relief. Bastard. He's planning to kill me yet he's desperate to keep me alive. He wants control of the situation. Control over my death.

This is my chance. I grab the bottle of wine just as he grabs my hair. I turn against his pull, even though it feels as though I'm being scalped alive, and bring the bottle down hard over his head. Red wine runs down his face and into his eyes. He's stunned but not unconscious. He loosens his grip on my hair.

Now I have to get away.

Before he can get his bearings back, I kick him in the groin, hard. He doubles over in pain and releases my hair fully. Then I run. Out the door, to the right and down the corridor. With each step glass cuts into my feet, but I keep running, barely able to feel the pain. Once I'm a few steps away, it's pitch-black. I keep running.

I have no idea where in the hospital I am. The corridors and doors seem to go on forever and I run blindly, turning at each junction, always hoping I'm not running into a dead end. My legs are weak and uncoordinated. I'll never be able to outrun him. But I have to try.

I come to a corner window and glance down. It looks like I'm on the third floor. I consider leaping out the window, but there's no one around and I'd be badly injured in the fall. Too injured to escape by myself. I keep running.

There are footsteps behind me and I scream. I have to get away. If Marty catches me now he'll kill me for sure. I'm no longer his placid girlfriend, the object of Josh's desire.

I see stairs and hurtle my naked body up them. My eyes have adjusted somewhat and I can make out vague shapes.

Run, run, you've got to run. I come to a door and open it. I'm up a level. I launch myself out the door. The footsteps are close behind me. Which way?

I move to the left and stumble over something metal and hard. I'm sprawled over the floor and I look back—it was a fire extinguisher.

The handle moves on the door to the stairwell. I scramble along the floor, crawling first and then breaking into an upright run. I need to get around the corner so he doesn't know which way I've gone.

But it's too late, I can hear footsteps behind me again. I take a few steps forward then double back, walking on tiptoe into the nearest room. My feet are bleeding and I don't want an obvious trail.

The room looks like an old ward. A dilapidated wardrobe stands in one corner, one door fallen off. I stagger toward it and climb in. This could be dangerous. If he comes in I'm trapped, but at the moment he's on my tail and I need to get him off it. It's a gamble I have to take.

Underneath the ward door I see light. Marty must have a flashlight. Another advantage he has over me. I didn't cover my bloody trail very well. I didn't know he had a light. My heart beats faster. I think of all the photos of the victims. I bite my lip. I don't want to end up like them. The light passes. He's not coming in. I wait a couple minutes, but I don't want to wait too long, because no doubt he'll double back and check the blood trail. I slip out the side of the wardrobe and creep toward the ward door. I open the door. It creaks ever so slightly and I hope he hasn't heard it. No light. Good.

I run quietly back toward the staircase, careful not to

trip over the fire extinguisher this time. I travel quickly down the stairs—I need to get out of the building. I run down another level. Am I at the ground yet?

I come down the last flight of stairs and hurtle my way out of the stairway. I'm nearly out. But instead of a free path, I slam into somebody. I start crying. How could he have gotten down here? I turn to run in the other direction, but he grabs me from behind with his hand over my mouth. I try to break free.

"Sophie, it's me. You're safe," a voice says.

I can hardly focus through the tears in my eyes.

"Josh?" I say. "Josh," I say again as my eyes focus on him. I hug him desperately. "It's Marty, Josh. It's Marty." My voice is quite loud.

"Shh. I know." Josh takes off the parka he is wearing and puts it over my shoulders. That's right, I'm naked. I slip my arms into the sleeves and do up the zipper.

"Carter figured it out."

"Darren?" I follow Josh's lead and whisper.

"He's here too. Looking for you."

Last time I saw Darren and Josh together, they weren't exactly cooperating. "Darren realized the killer wasn't you?"

"Not exactly. He saw the map was missing from your place, so he knew the map held the key. But he still thought I was guilty. He came over to confront me and picked up a map of D.C. on the way. I insisted we work on the map together. Eventually we saw the head positioning. We were on our way over here when Carter recognized Marty in the photos in the living room. But Carter knows him as Matthew Lande."

"Marty's real name," I say.

"Yes. I went to school with him, but I don't even remember the guy."

"Well, he remembers you. He's obsessed with you."

"Fuck. I still can't believe all this was him."

"I know. It's been you for years. He's been setting you up."

Josh shakes his head. "He did a good job."

I gulp. I'd believed it. I change the topic. "Montana and Sargent. I don't know where they are…if they're okay."

"We'll worry about that later."

"Are any of the others here?"

"Not yet. It's just me and Carter. But we've called it in. Backup's on its way."

Our conversation is silenced by the sound of a shot.

We both look at each other. Shit. Who's been shot—Marty or Darren?

"I need a gun," I say.

Josh reaches into his ankle holster and gives me a small, nonregulation thirty-eight.

"Take this."

"What about you?" I think of Josh's Bureau issue, locked away in an office somewhere.

He smiles. "I keep a couple of spares." He moves his arm and I look down, noticing the gun he holds in his left hand. "Wait outside." He motions toward a set of double doors behind him. "You'll be safe there."

I look at the doors and the temptation is strong. Very strong. But then I think about Sam and what Marty did to her and all those other women. What he wanted to do to me.

"No." I turn back up the stairs I'd come down. All I can think about is revenge. I run up the stairs, spurred on by adrenaline and anger.

"Sophie?" Josh calls, but it's too late. I'm already moving. He catches up to me and we proceed up the stairs slowly. Josh passes me and moves in front, covering up the stairs, while I cover down the staircase, just in case he somehow got below us into the basement.

We move out onto the level I'd come from.

"Shit," Josh says. I look down.

In front of us is the slumped figure of Darren.

Josh bends down and feels his neck for a pulse, all the while keeping his eyes down one end of the corridor while I watch the other.

"He's alive," he says. "You stay with him."

"No, Josh. I'm coming with you," I whisper. I'm not willing to let Josh face Marty alone. Besides, I need to see the bastard die with my own eyes.

Josh nods, perhaps even now preferring me to be with him rather than Darren. "Which way did you come from?" he asks.

"That way...I think."

We're in a corridor that runs at least fifty feet, with identical corridors in either direction running off it. It all looks the same and now I'm confused.

"When I heard footsteps behind me I panicked." I pause, trying to remember. "I'm sorry, I don't know." I feel stupid. I'm trained to take notice and remember things like this. People's faces, the layout of a room. But I guess my survival instinct took over when I ran.

Josh nods and we're silent once more. He motions

to the left and we move in that direction, him looking ahead, me covering behind, walking back to back. After a few steps Josh nudges me. I turn around. We're at the first open corridor. Josh mouths, "One, two, three," and we both charge around the corner, guns first. Nothing. No one.

Which way do we go?

"Marty, it's all over. The FBI and D.C. police are on their way," Josh yells.

Silence for a minute, then: "Good. They'll find you and Sophie dead. A murder-suicide." The voice comes from our left. We go back to the corridor we were in and keep moving down.

"I don't think so, Marty. It's over." Josh keeps talking.

"Over for you. You never were that bright, were you?"

"Not like you, right?"

"Exactly. But you got all the glory. Popular at school, with the women. And then you waltzed into the police."

We come to another corridor. Which way? "So you were trying to set the record straight."

"You bet."

Josh points to the sound of the voice and we move to our left.

"I finally made the FBI three years ago," Marty says. "So then it was just a matter of destroying your world."

"Well, you've failed. And Sophie's still mine, not yours."

He's trying to rile Marty. That could be dangerous, very dangerous.

"Careful," I whisper, but not quietly enough.

"I see you've found each other." Marty's anger is obvious.

It's hard to pinpoint the voice because of the long corridors and the echo that accompanies every word, but we're heading in the right direction.

"Marty, give yourself up and no one will get hurt," Josh says.

It's a promise Josh is willing to make, but I am not.

"You think you're so good, the lot of you," Marty says.

"Who?" I ask. If we keep him talking we can close in on his voice.

"Agents."

Josh says quietly to me: "Marty applied as a field agent three times, then finally got in with forensics."

"It's forensics who are the important ones," I say.

"You think I'm going to fall for your flattery again, bitch."

"This way," I mouth at Josh, pointing to a corridor.

"It's true, Marty. That's why we couldn't get you, isn't it? Forensics."

He doesn't answer, but we keep moving down the corridor, checking out each door we pass. We're moving slowly and quietly, listening intently for any noise. A footfall. A door opening or closing.

We come to the end of our corridor, to a T-intersection. Josh turns back to me, deciding which way to go.

Suddenly Marty comes charging around the corner, firing. Josh hears the steps and dives to the right, into a doorway. I dive forward and fire.

Four shots go into Marty's chest, one after another. He falls. I land on the floor hard, but roll out of it and stand back up. I grimace with the pain from my rib. I race over to Marty and kick the gun out of his hand. I study him for any sign of life and then kneel down and check his pulse. He's dead. The bastard's dead.

I automatically go to reholster my weapon, and then look down at myself in Josh's oversize parka. I haven't got underwear on, let alone a holster.

"He's dead," I say to Josh, and then realize he's not moving. "Josh!" I slide across the floor on my knees to the spot where he is lying.

I see a bullet entry point in his jacket, and pray to God he's got a bulletproof vest on under it. I start to tear off his jacket. He opens his eyes and smiles. He coughs. He's winded, that's all. No blood.

"Thank God you're okay."

He sits up. "I'm fine." He undoes his bulletproof vest and examines the point of contact on his skin. It's bright red and he'll have an almighty bruise, but the jacket stopped the bullet.

We look at each other, silent. So much has happened. Maybe he'll never speak to me again. How could I blame him—I thought he was a killer.

Finally he breaks the awkward moment. "You hurt?"

"Just a cracked rib." I pause. "And a couple of cuts."

Then I hear the sirens.

CHAPTER 23

I sit in the debriefing room, still sore. I've got a heat pack on my ribs, which is helping to numb the pain—that and the painkillers. My thigh's got fifteen stitches and I even had to get a couple of stitches in my left foot. The rest of the cuts on my feet are covered and my soles are lightly bandaged. Walking is difficult and slow. No help from adrenaline now.

The task force and everyone from the Behavioral Analysis Unit, including Pike, are present. Rivers leads the meeting, a piece of paper in his hand.

"Marty Connor Tyrone," he says. "One of our own." He shakes his head. "Born in Tucson, Arizona, in 1974, Matthew Connor Lande. Went to Catalina High School, graduating in 1991." Rivers looks at Josh.

"The year below me."

"Yes, that's when his obsession with Marco started."

Josh nods and Rivers continues. "Applied for Arizona Police Force straight out of school and was rejected. Applied for the FBI in 1995, also rejected. A month later he killed Sally-Anne Raymond. He changed his name in 1996 before studying forensic science at Michigan University. Applied for FBI field training another two times, in 1998 and 1999. Worked with the Chicago Coroner's Office at the end of 2000. And of course, we've got him on flights to Florida for a vacation in 2000."

"But we must have had his real name on record," Krip says.

"We did, but we never cross-checked aliases against the college lists," O'Donnell says.

We would have searched for name changes and aliases if all our leads turned up blank, but it would have been a week or two down the road.

"Now we know why the crime scenes were so clean," Pike says.

Josh double-clicks his pen. "Even if he slipped up in Chicago or here, he could have tampered with the evidence. He was always protected."

"He changed the handwriting report and that kept us focused on the left-hander angle," I say.

"Part of his attempt to set up Marco," Rivers says.

I sigh, tired. "I gave a sample of Marty's writing to Questioned Documents. It matched the note to Sam."

A few nods. It was a given anyway, but we still had to be sure.

"How'd he get it so clean in Arizona though? Before he even started studying?" Flynn asks.

"Oh, he'd been studying all right, self-studying," Josh says.

I picture the tree underneath which Sally-Anne died. "The rain helped with Sally-Anne." I pause. "He was lucky that day."

"Did he actually know Sally-Anne?" Flynn asks.

"From afar. He'd seen her with Marco a few times," I say.

"Was he on the Arizona suspect list?" Couples asks, looking at me.

"Yeah, but under Matthew Lande."

There's silence for a few moments, then Josh slams his pen down on the table. "Right under my nose."

I want to reassure Josh. Not that it will make up for the trust we've lost, but I can't help wanting to reach out to him. "That was the point for him. It was all part of the thrill. It was why he came to D.C. Why he applied for FBI forensics. And no doubt why he wanted to share with you. He wanted to *be* you."

Josh pushes his chair back and shakes his head. "*Single White Female* eat your heart out."

"How does he compare to the profile?" Jones asks.

"Perfectly," I say. "He even had much older brothers."

Josh is silent.

"Any domestic violence?" I ask.

"The father was on the police radar for years, but when Marty…I mean Matthew…was sixteen it all stopped. The father sobered up."

I cup my hand around my cracked rib. "But the example had already been set. It's okay to hurt the woman you love."

"I guess so," Rivers says. "I spoke to Mrs. Lande. I

couldn't get much out of her, but we'll be following up his background very carefully."

I nod. No doubt we'll dig up the early indicators of a serial killer—bed-wetting, animal torture and the like.

"When did he meet you?" Flynn asks me.

"The Henley case."

I've been over every interaction I've ever had with Marty at least a hundred times. I'd seen him both at work and at Josh's, but each encounter was short. I had no idea he saw me as yet another thing that Josh had and he didn't.

"And you worked out the body positioning, Anderson?" Pike says.

"Yeah. I realized all the victims' heads were looking roughly toward the same spot." I pause, thinking about Sargent and Montana. We found them both dead, shoved in a janitor's room.

"I can't believe we missed the head positioning," Jones says.

O'Donnell rests his arms on the table. "We were looking for a pattern in the locations, not the victims' head positioning."

I should have picked it up earlier. Maybe then Sam would be sitting in this meeting. I still can't believe she's really gone.

"How's Carter doing?" Pike asks.

Pike's voice gets my attention and I slowly move my gaze from the window to Pike.

"He lost a lot of blood, but he'll live. They're going to release him in a few days. He'll be off work for a couple of weeks though," O'Donnell answers.

"Some vacation," Krip says.

"Vacation?" There's a hint of disapproval in Rivers's voice, but he leaves it.

"It was a good holiday. He caught his man," Josh says.

O'Donnell takes his glasses off. "True."

There's silence again.

"Right, well. We may as well wrap it up," Rivers says. "Thanks to the task force for coming in and for all your work. And the rest of you, back to work." Rivers looks up at Josh and me. "Except for you two. I want to see you in my office."

The room empties without any fuss or hint of victory. There's not really much to celebrate. We caught our guy, but we lost so much on the way.

We follow Rivers to his office. I hobble, the cuts on the soles of my feet still very sore.

Rivers sits down and motions to two chairs at his desk. Josh and I also sit.

"I want you two to take a few days off."

Josh takes a breath in. "But—"

"Not buts, Marco. Marty has been targeting you for years and he was framing you."

"But you didn't believe that, did you?"

Poor Josh. It must be hard to know that others suspected you of being a serial killer. Work colleagues, your girl…

"You were never a suspect in my mind," Rivers says. "But we had to investigate you properly and do the right thing."

Is he being diplomatic or truthful?

"Anyway, I'm fine," Marco says.

Rivers shakes his head. "You took a bullet."

"I had a vest on."

"I know. But you'll be sore for a few days, and time off will do you good."

Josh doesn't respond.

"And as for you," Rivers says, looking at me, "if I had my way you'd still be in the hospital."

"For a broken rib and a few cuts?"

"You need time out, Sophie. And you'll need to spend a lot of time with Dr. Rosen." He looks at Josh. "Both of you will."

Josh speaks up again. "What? For a bullet?"

"You'd have to see Rosen for a bullet, it's procedure. But it's more than a simple bullet and you know it, Marco."

As much as I hate to admit it, Rivers is right, for both Josh and I. I've been trying not to think about what happened in that room. I was lucky, lucky that he didn't rape me. Lucky that I escaped. But I know I'll have nightmares about it every night. And Josh? He feels guilty about all of this, especially Sam. I know he does. After all, the murders were about Josh.

I look up at Rivers and nod. Even Josh keeps quiet.

Rivers clears his throat. "There's also the matter of procedure. Shots fired and one person killed. There'll be an investigation."

"What?"

"It's routine, you know that. You had to shoot him, of course. And personally, I think you did the world a favor. But—"

"It has to be investigated," I say.

"Yeah. And…" He pauses. "I'm going to need your gun."

That's the last thing I want to give anyone. I know that Marty's dead. I saw him die. I killed him. But I still expect to see him waiting for me around every corner. The gun is my comfort. But it's policy when an agent shoots someone—no matter what the circumstance. I take my gun out of my holster and reach over to place it on Rivers's desk. I wince with pain from the cracked rib. As long as I keep my arm by my side, it doesn't hurt much, but reaching sends ripples of sharp pain straight into my rib cage.

"Okay, that's it. Take it easy," Rivers says.

We stand up.

"You'll both be getting a call from Dr. Rosen. You'll need to come in for appointments, even though you're off."

It's not such a bad idea.

We leave Rivers's office. In the corridor, Josh stops. I stop too.

"Do you want a ride home?" he asks.

"Um…"

"You're going to the hospital." He stares past me.

"Yeah, I was going to fill Darren in. Tell him about our debriefing."

Josh nods curtly.

"I won't be long though. Would you come with me?"

Josh hesitates. "Okay. I've got a few words I wouldn't mind saying to Darren Carter, anyway."

"Josh—"

"Don't worry, I'll be civil." He shoves his hands into his pockets.

Walking along the hospital corridor to Darren's room reminds me of St. Anne's. I remember running along the corridors, naked, with Marty right behind me. I thought

I was never going to escape. I can admit that now. I felt defeated. I'll never look at a hospital the same way again.

We arrive at Darren's ward and he pushes himself up in bed.

"Hi," he says, keeping his eyes on me.

"Hi," I say. Then there's an awkward silence.

"Apologies are in order," Darren says, looking at Josh.

"For thinking I was a serial killer? Damn straight an apology is in order."

Darren smiles. "I'm sorry," he says and holds out his hand.

Josh takes it.

"Thanks for helping us out on this one, Carter. Without you, we may not have found Sophie."

I hadn't thought about that before. It was Carter who recognized Marty from the photos. They interviewed him during Sally-Anne's investigation. It was also Carter who knew something was up with the map.

Darren shakes his head. "The two of us studied that map for a good couple of hours before we saw the head positioning."

"It took us a while." Josh transfers his weight from one foot to the other. "I'll wait outside."

"Thanks," I say.

I tell Darren all about Marty and everything we found out during the briefing. He listens intently, finding out about the man who shot him and killed his aunt all those years ago. Darren was lucky. The bullet pierced his right lung, but he's going to be okay. They weren't really prepared when they stormed into St. Anne's. Darren was unofficial, well and truly out of his jurisdiction, and Josh was suspended. Josh had some supplies at home—two guns and a vest—but Carter only had his gun and badge. They both took big risks to get me out.

He stares at me and smiles. "I'm glad you're okay." He grabs my hand.

"Thanks, Darren. Thanks for everything."

"So are you planning any trips to Tucson?"

I look down at his hand holding mine. "No. I'm afraid not." I withdraw my hand. I'm still attracted to Darren, but I need to sort out things with Josh.

Darren nods and rests his hand by his side. "Josh is lucky."

"I don't know if that's true. There are a lot of things I need to straighten out right now."

"I understand," Darren says.

But I don't think he does.

"And what are you going to do about your psychic abilities?"

"I need to learn to control them if they're going to be useful for profiling."

"You'll work it out. You need to practice, is all."

I nod. "I hope so. I think it can help others."

"I bet it can." He pauses and smiles. "I bet it can."

* * * * *

*Turn the page for a sneak preview of the second book in
this exciting series featuring Sophie Anderson.*

THE MURDERERS' CLUB
by P.D. Martin.

*On sale from MIRA Books
December 2007.*

"College kid?" I ask.

"Looks that way."

I nod, familiar enough with the territory. I've seen a few cases of a dead college coed. Usually it turns out to be misadventure but there are instances of murder. College students can be high-risk victims: friendly, accessible, sometimes walking around campus by themselves at night, high alcohol intake, and mostly experiencing their first taste of freedom. That's attractive bait for a killer. Bundy's a prime example—he often hunted at colleges.

From the outskirts of the college it's obvious something's not right, with a large crowd gathered about three hundred feet in front of us. We drive closer, until we're about one hundred feet from the group of people, and then Darren parks the car.

He unbuckles his seat belt. "Want to stay here?"

"Nah. You know me—can't resist a good meal or a dead body."

He manages a smile and we both get out of the car.

Darren flips open his phone and hits a speed-dial button. "Stone, it's Carter. I'm on fourth...uh-huh." Darren motions to me, quickening his pace, and I follow him. "Yup...see you in a minute." He snaps his phone shut and turns to me. "Come on. The body's near the stadium." With his badge out in front of him, he leads the way through the crowd. As we get closer I can see that expressions vary from curiosity to horror. Not many of them will have actually seen anything—the area would have been cordoned off pretty soon after the discovery— but the whispers would be enough, spreading and engulfing the onlookers like a runaway wave. For all they know, it could be their best friend or roomy lying lifeless on the ground.

We reach the police crime-scene tape, with a barrier of uniformed cops encircling the area, and the media right up front, with their cameras firing. One camera swings toward us and its reporter shoves the microphone in Darren's direction.

"Detective Carter, what are we looking at here?" Part of a crime reporter's job is to know the senior investigators on sight, so I'm not surprised that this one knows Darren.

Darren maintains his silence.

The nearest cop takes one look at Darren's badge and moves aside for him.

"Detective Carter..." yells the reporter in vain.

AmericanPsycho: Switch on NBC now. They're running a story about the University of Arizona.
NeverCaught: Cool.

BlackWidow: I don't care much about following the media reports on my vics.

NeverCaught: Are you ****ing crazy? That's half the fun. Okay, I've got it on. Gee, that reporter's hot.

AmericanPsycho: I love it when they look all serious like that.

NeverCaught: Yeah, they must practice that look in the mirror. Is that the lead cop?

AmericanPsycho: Yes. The reporter said he's from Tucson Homicide.

NeverCaught: Who's the blonde with him?

AmericanPsycho: Don't know. But I'll find out.

We walk across an open expanse of grass. About fifty feet ahead, the forensic activity is at its height, with several people hovering around some shrubs and others bent over. A woman in her late twenties is in the mix, and I assume she's Darren's partner, Jessica Stone. They've been partners for less than a year and I didn't meet her during the DC Slasher case.

The woman glances our way. "Sorry, Carter. Bolson's on another call-out."

"Bolson's always on another call." Darren looks at his partner. "Stone, Anderson." He looks at me. "Anderson, Stone." And so our formal introduction is complete.

Detective Jessica Stone is short but muscular, around five-three and about one hundred and ten pounds. She has auburn hair that she wears layered around her face, highlighting stunning green eyes. Her face is lightly freckled, mostly on her cheekbones, and her lips are full but her mouth is narrow.

Finally I cast my eyes to the body. The vic lies on his back, his arms tucked underneath him. On his hairless chest and extending down to the first two bulges of his six-pack is a bright-red love heart, about four inches square. It looks like it's been drawn with a marker or body paint.

I feel a slight dizziness and then it hits me, hard and fast like before.

A good-looking African-American man is lying on a bed, naked, handcuffed to the headboard. His body is slicked with sweat and he's smiling up at me.

As the vision fades I make a grab for something, but I wind up hitting the ground with a thud.

Darren's hand is quickly on my arm, helping me up. "You okay?"

I force my eyes open, force them to focus on Darren. "I'm fine." I look around and everyone's staring at me, not the dead guy. This is probably one of the most embarrassing things that can happen to a law-enforcement professional. Now it looks like the sight of a dead guy makes me weak at the knees. I'd almost prefer to tell them the truth than have them think I'm soft. But the truth isn't an option. The vision took me by surprise and I couldn't steady myself.

"Sorry, I must have tripped on something." I look back for the imaginary culprit and then shrug.

Everyone except Darren returns their attention to the body. He moves me away from the main group. "Did you...did you see something?"

"Yes." I bite my lip, puzzled, but Darren takes the confirmation that it was a vision in his stride.

"Was it him?" He looks at me, but motions his head to the body.

Even though I know it was the vic, I look down at him again. "Yes."

"What did you see?"

"He was handcuffed to a bed, covered in sweat." I recall the image. "I think he might have been having sex."

Darren makes a short humming noise.

"Let's go take a closer look," I say.

We move back to the main drag and sidle in next to Stone.

"The love heart is very ritualistic, very specific," I say. "Seen anything like this before?"

Darren shakes his head. "What have we got, Stone?"

She looks up and a longer strand of hair falls into her face, dancing in her eyes before she shoves it back and reclips a small barrette that captures the stray hairs. "Not much. Unidentified African-American male."

"Who found him?" Darren looks back at the perimeter.

"Jack Bode. He's one of the campus cops." Stone points out an older man sitting on a bench with his head in his hands.

Darren scribbles the information into a notebook. "Did he touch him?"

"No. He called it in and stayed with the body to make sure the scene was left intact."

"Good." Darren glances back at the crowd. "Any other witnesses?"

"Not yet."

"Cameras?"

Stone shakes her head. "The only camera that covers

this area was smashed a few days ago. The replacement's due to be put up tomorrow."

We look at the body again, watching as the medical examiner moves down to the victim's feet and secures clear plastic bags around each foot to preserve any evidence.

Darren puts Stone in charge of organizing a search team for the immediate area. At crime-scene locations investigators look for things like footprints, a murder weapon, trace evidence, or anything that seems out of place. Stone and most of the others move off, leaving only a few of us hanging around the body, like insects drawn to a light.

"Okay, let's move him," the ME says.

The ME's assistant lays down a large white sheet of plastic about ten feet to the left of the body—an area that would have already been extensively photographed and inspected for evidence. He moves back to the body, crouching at the feet.

"He's tall," the ME says, staring at the vic. "We might need a hand."

Two of the remaining uniforms join in and they lift the body upwards and step awkwardly to one side. Once the body is on the plastic, the photographer takes more shots.

Darren kneels down to get a closer look. "Let's turn him over."

They roll him onto his front. His arms are bound together at the back with a pair of handcuffs. The same cuffs from my vision?

The photographer takes several snaps of the victim's back and the ME's assistant bags the hands, just like the feet.

The ME examines the purplish marks on the body's

back and buttocks—lividity. When your heart stops pumping blood, gravity takes over and the blood settles. In this case, lividity indicates the vic died on his back or was moved to his back shortly after death. The victim's arms, however, do not show any sign of the red splotches. They were not the lowest point of the body after death.

The ME notices the arms too. "Looks like he was cuffed like this at least a few hours after death." He tries to move the body's arms. "Rigor's still in. We're probably looking at a time of death around eighteen to thirty-six hours ago."

I nod. Rigor mortis begins in the eyelids a few hours after death and spreads to the face and neck, then the limbs. After about thirty-six hours it starts to dissipate until the body is completely supple once more, about forty-eight to seventy-two hours after death. However, so many factors affect the onset and dissipation of rigor that it can be an unreliable measure of time of death.

"Cause of death?" Darren asks.

"The eyes show some signs of asphyxiation but we'll know more back at the morgue."

Darren nods, accepting that, until the autopsy is done, the body can't do much talking. He stands up and turns to me. "Sorry, Sophie."

I shrug. "These things happen."

"We will do some touristy stuff while you're here. Promise."

I laugh, knowing the job only too well. "Let's see how we go."

"Not much of a vacation for you so far."

I look up at the blue sky. "The warmer weather and change of scenery is a break."

Darren's eyes follow the ME and his assistant as they move past us with the body on a stretcher. "I wouldn't mind sitting in on the autopsy," he says.

"The love heart?" I picture the large heart in the middle of the vic's torso.

"Yup." Darren puts his notebook back in his pocket. "It bothers me."

"Me, too." Marking the victim's body is not something most killers would trouble themselves with, not unless it had personal significance to them. "It could just be a message to the vic." That's one alternative. The other is more ominous—serial killers like to mark their victims, too.

Darren sighs and kicks the ground with his foot. "Damn it! I was really looking forward to a few days off."

Silence. If it does turn out to be a serial killer, Darren will want to be involved. Like me, he's particularly drawn to serial cases, where you have a chance to stop the killer and save lives.

He changes the topic. "You feel okay now?"

"Fine. It was just a flash."

"So it's back. The psychic stuff." His blue eyes bore into me.

I'm uncomfortable under his gaze and look away. "One." I hold my forefinger up for emphasis and meet his eyes again. "I've had one vision." I chew on my lip, wondering *why now? Why this body?* "Any chance you could get me into that autopsy?"

"Doesn't sound very touristy to me," Darren teases.

"I need to find out why this victim is so special. Why I got the vision." I can be honest with Darren because there's no Bureau pressure and no repercussions.

Darren's the only person who knows about my visions. He saw me "experience" a young girl's murder during a particularly realistic vision. I still remember his words: My aunt had the gift and you've got it, too.

"No, no dreams."

"That a good thing?"

"The jury's out."

"I can understand that," Darren says.

A big part of me feels overwhelming relief that I'm not dreaming about murdered women, not experiencing the perverted feelings of pleasure in the mind of a killer. It freaked me out big-time, even though it helped me solve the Slasher case. And that's where the guilt comes in. It helped me save lives, so does that mean if I was dreaming and having waking visions now, I'd be saving victims from some other sick psycho?

KILLER FOCUS

THE SECOND BOOK IN
AN EXCITING NEW TRILOGY BY
FIONA BRAND

Courtesy of a new identity in the Witness Security Program
Taylor Jones was almost enjoying her quiet new life with
a nice, normal guy. Then her next-door neighbor turns
up dead, a stray bullet barely misses her and the former
FBI agent knows she's right in the crosshairs.

She discovers a chilling connection between the
South American cocaine trade, terrorism and, amazingly, a
secretive cabal that began with the fall of Nazi Germany...
and whose influence reaches all the way to the White House.

But even more frightening, she suspects her nice, normal
guy may be at the center of it all.

> "A rare and potent mixture of adventure,
> mystery and passion that shouldn't be missed."
> —*Romantic Times BOOKreviews*
> on *Touching Midnight*

MIRA®

*Available the first week of December 2007
wherever paperbacks are sold!*
www.MIRABooks.com

MFB2563

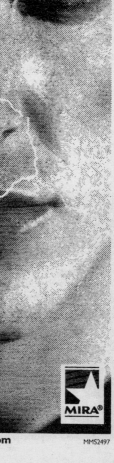

THE RIVETING DEBUT NOVEL BY
DEANNA RAYBOURN

"LET THE WICKED BE ASHAMED, AND LET THEM BE SILENT IN THE GRAVE."

These ominous words are the last threat that Sir Edward Grey receives from his killer. Before he can show them to Nicholas Brisbane, the private inquiry agent he has retained for his protection, he collapses and dies at his London home.

When Brisbane visits Sir Edward's widow, Julia, and suggests that her husband was murdered, Julia engages him to help her investigate. Pressing forward, Julia follows a trail of clues that lead her to even more unpleasant truths, and ever closer to a killer who waits expectantly for her arrival.

SILENT IN THE GRAVE

"A perfectly executed debut."
—*Publishers Weekly*, starred review

Available the first week of December 2007 wherever paperbacks are sold!

REQUEST YOUR
FREE BOOKS!

2 FREE NOVELS
FROM THE ROMANCE/SUSPENSE
COLLECTION PLUS 2 FREE GIFTS!

YES! Please send me 2 FREE novels from the Romance/Suspense Collection and my 2 FREE gifts. After receiving them, if I don't wish to receive any more books, I can return the shipping statement marked "cancel." If I don't cancel, I will receive 4 brand-new novels every month and be billed just $5.49 per book in the U.S., or $5.99 per book in Canada, plus 25¢ shipping and handling per book plus applicable taxes, if any*. That's a savings of at least 20% off the cover price! I understand that accepting the 2 free books and gifts places me under no obligation to buy anything. I can always return a shipment and cancel at any time. Even if I never buy another book from the Reader Service, the two free books and gifts are mine to keep forever.

185 MDN EF5Y   385 MDN EF6C

Name _____ (PLEASE PRINT) _____

Address _____ Apt. # _____

City _____ State/Prov. _____ Zip/Postal Code _____

Signature (if under 18, a parent or guardian must sign)

Mail to **The Reader Service:**
IN U.S.A.: P.O. Box 1867, Buffalo, NY 14240-1867
IN CANADA: P.O. Box 609, Fort Erie, Ontario L2A 5X3

Not valid to current subscribers to the Romance Collection,
the Suspense Collection or the Romance/Suspense Collection.

Want to try two free books from another line?
Call 1-800-873-8635 or visit www.morefreebooks.com.

* Terms and prices subject to change without notice. NY residents add applicable sales tax. Canadian residents will be charged applicable provincial taxes and GST. This offer is limited to one order per household. All orders subject to approval. Credit or debit balances in a customer's account(s) may be offset by any other outstanding balance owed by or to the customer. Please allow 4 to 6 weeks for delivery.

Your Privacy: Harlequin is committed to protecting your privacy. Our Privacy Policy is available online at www.eHarlequin.com or upon request from the Reader Service. From time to time we make our lists of customers available to reputable firms who may have a product or service of interest to you. If you would prefer we not share your name and address, please check here. ☐

New York Times bestselling author

CARLA NEGGERS

For the past seven years homicide detective Abigail Browning has been haunted by the fatal shooting of her husband, four days after their wedding. After receiving an anonymous tip, and determined to find the person who killed him, she returns to the foggy Maine island where it happened. As she begins to unravel the mystery with the help of search-and-rescue worker Owen Garrison, she learns that the layers of deceit and lies are even thicker than she could have imagined. Now it's up to Abigail and Owen to keep pushing for the truth—and stop a killer from striking again....

THE WIDOW

"No one does romantic suspense better!"—Janet Evanovich

Available the first week of December 2007 wherever paperbacks are sold!

A thrilling suspense novel, Trapped is every mother's nightmare and one monster's dream come true.

MIRA®

CHRIS JORDAN trapped

When sixteen-year-old Kelly Hartley disappears from her bedroom one night, the police believe that she ran off willingly with her boyfriend, Seth. Unaware that her daughter even had a boyfriend, her mother, Jane, soon discovers that Seth is no boy. He is an adult—a man who met Kelly on the Internet. Seems Jane's little girl has been hiding some dangerous secrets.

Like mother, like daughter.

Adamant that Kelly is not a runaway, Jane hires ex-FBI agent Randall Shane. But every step brings them closer to a cold-blooded predator lurking in the shadows...coiled around Jane's shameful secret...waiting to strike.

"Riveting suspense tale.... Jordan's full-throttle style makes this an emotionally rewarding thriller that moves like lightning."
–Publishers Weekly

Available the first week of November 2007 wherever paperbacks are sold!

www.MIRABooks.com

MCJ2471